P9-CJJ-847

NOVELS BY MERCEDES LACKEY
available from DAW Books:

THE HERALDS OF VALDEMAR
ARROWS OF THE QUEEN
ARROW'S FLIGHT
ARROW'S FALL

THE LAST HERALD-MAGE
MAGIC'S PAWN
MAGIC'S PROMISE
MAGIC'S PRICE

THE MAGE WINDS
WINDS OF FATE
WINDS OF CHANGE
WINDS OF FURY

THE MAGE STORMS
STORM WARNING
STORM RISING
STORM BREAKING

KEROWYN'S TALE
BY THE SWORD

VOWS AND HONOR
THE OATHBOUND
OATHBREAKERS
OATHBLOOD

BRIGHTLY BURNING

TAKE A THIEF*
KNIGHT'S GAMBIT*

DARKOVER NOVEL
(with Marion Zimmer Bradley)
REDISCOVERY

THE BLACK SWAN

THE SERPENT'S SHADOW
PHOENIX AND ASHES*
THE GATES OF SLEEP*

Written with Larry Dixon:

THE MAGE WARS
THE BLACK GRYPHON
THE WHITE GRYPHON
THE SILVER GRYPHON

OWLFLIGHT
OWLSIGHT
OWLKNIGHT

*forthcoming from DAW Books in hardcover

The
Serpent's
Shadow

MERCEDES LACKEY

The Serpent's Shadow

DAW BOOKS, INC.
DONALD A. WOLLHEIM, FOUNDER
375 Hudson Street, New York, NY 10014
ELIZABETH R. WOLLHEIM
SHEILA E. GILBERT
PUBLISHERS
http://www.dawbooks.com

Jacket art by Jody A. Lee

For color prints of Jody Lee's paintings, please contact:
The Cerridwen Enterprise
P.O. Box 10161
Kansas City, MO 64111
1-800-825-1281

DAW Books Collectors No. 1177

DAW Books are distributed by Penguin Putnam Inc.
Book designed by Stanley S. Drate/Folio Graphics Co. Inc.

This book is printed on acid-free paper ♾

First Printing, March 2001
1 2 3 4 5 6 7 8 9

DAW TRADEMARK REGISTERED
U.S. PAT. OFF. AND FOREIGN COUNTRIES
—MARCA REGISTRADA
HECHO EN U.S.A.

PRINTED IN THE U.S.A.

for Mike Gilbert
we'll miss you

1

LEADEN, self-important silence isolated the chief surgeon's office from the clamor of the hospital and the clangor of the street outside. A rain-dark day, a dim, chill room filled with cold, heavy, imposing mahogany office furniture and lined with ebony bookshelves containing dreary brown leather-bound volumes so perfectly arranged that it was not possible that any of them had ever been taken down and used—the room in which Maya found herself was designed to cow, confine, and intimidate. But Maya Witherspoon, though depressed by an atmosphere so alien to her native India, had spent most of her life perfecting the art of keeping a serene and unreadable expression on her face. All that practice stood her in good stead now.

Across from her, enthroned behind his mahogany desk of continental proportions, sat Doctor Octavian Clayton-Smythe, Chief Medical Officer of St. Mary's Hospital, Paddington, in the rattling heart of London. *One of Kipling's "little tin gods,"* she thought irreverently, clasping her ice-cold, black-gloved hands tightly on top of the handbag in her lap. *He would fit in quite perfectly in the Colonial Service. Stiffly propped up in his armor of utter respectability . . . so sure of his importance, so intent on forcing others to acknowledge it.*

Cocooned in the somber black woolen suit of the medical profession, as if he sat in mourning for all the patients he had managed to kill, he frowned down at the results of her various academic examinations—results that should leave no doubt in the mind of any sensible person that she was fitter to be granted the sacred title of "Doctor of Medicine and Surgery" than a good many of the young *men* who would have that very accolade bestowed on them in the course of this year of Our Lord, 1909. In point of fact, she already *had* that title—in her homeland of India. This, however, was not India; it was London, England, the heart of the British Empire and of civilization as the English knew it. And as such, there were two distinct handicaps to her ambition that Maya labored beneath at this moment. The first was her sex. Although female doctors were not unknown here, there were no more than three hundred in the British Isles, and most probably the actual number was less than that.

The second was that although Maya's father had been a perfectly respectable British doctor serving in the Army, stationed at Delhi, and although Maya herself had obtained her degree as a physician in the University of Delhi, her mother had *not* been a fellow exile. She had been a native, a Brahmin of high caste. And although in India it had been Surya who had wedded far beneath her state, the reverse was true here, and Maya, as a (to put it crudely) half-breed, bore the sign of her mother's non-English blood in her dusky complexion. All else could be disguised with education, clothing, careful diction, but not that. Maya's knee-length black hair had been knotted into a pompadour and covered with a proper hat and veil, her body wrapped in good British wool of proper tailoring, her accent trained away with years of careful, self-imposed lessons in speech. Yet none of that mattered very much to someone who was so fiercely determined to consider Maya as one of the barbaric and alien "They."

It was raining again outside the hospital; it seemed to Maya that it was *always* raining here. Cold wind blew the raindrops against the glass of the office windows, and Maya was glad of the warmth of her woolen suit coat—for she, too, was encased in the feminine version of the uniform of the office she aspired to, plus the added burden of corset, petticoats, and all the other wrappings deemed necessary to "decent" dressing. Doctor Clayton-Smythe had a gas fire laid on in his office, but he had not bothered to have it lit. Perhaps *he* didn't feel the cold; after all, it was spring by the British calendar, and the good doctor had plenty of good English fat to insulate him, seallike, from the cold.

He looks more like a walrus, though. I believe he probably bellows at his wife, and means as much by it as a walrus bellowing at his little cow.

Doctor Clayton-Smythe cleared his throat, immediately capturing her attention. "Your results are . . . remarkable," he said cautiously.

She nodded, part modest acknowledgment, part caution on her own part. In a way, she felt strangely calm; she had been nervous before this battle, but now that the enemy was engaged, her mind was cool, weighing every least inflection. *Not yet time to say anything, I think.*

Now the doctor looked up, at long last, meeting her eyes for the first time. He was a heavy man; the English staple diet of cream, cheese, beef and bread, vegetables boiled to tastelessness, heavy pastry, and more beef, had given him a florid complexion and jowls that were only imperfectly hidden behind old-fashioned gray mutton-chop whiskers and a heavy mustache, a salt-and-pepper color that matched his hair. *If he doesn't yet suffer from gout, he will,* she thought dispassionately, *and his heart will not long be able to maintain his increasing bulk.* Gray hair, neatly trimmed, and rather washed-out blue eyes behind gold-rimmed glasses completed the portrait of a highly successful physician and surgeon; the head of his hospital, and a man who could deny her, not only the right to practice here in his hospital but certification to practice medicine in the British Isles if he chose to exert his influence. However, Maya had chosen her adversary with care; if this man certified her, no one in the United Kingdom would ever deny her expertise.

"How old are you, if I may ask?" he continued.

"Five and twenty," she replied crisply. "And that may seem a trifle young to you to have become a physician and surgeon. But I had been studying medicine under the tutelage of my father since I was old enough to read, and achieved Doctor of Medicine at the University of Delhi at the age of twenty-two."

He nodded slowly. "And you were practicing alongside your father as well?"

"I *was* certified in India as a practicing physician," she reminded him, taking pains to keep her impatience and growing frustration out of her voice. "I was my father's partner in his practice. Wives and daughters of military personnel felt more comfortable consulting a female physician in matters of a personal and delicate nature. I aided him as a physician in my own right for a period of nearly four years."

"That was in India; you might find ladies feel differently about you here," he replied, the expected hint that her mixed blood would prove a handicap, and a more tactful hint than she had expected.

She smiled a small, cold smile, as cold as her feet in those wretched, tight little leather "walking" shoes she'd laced onto her feet. "The women of the poor take what they are offered; and for that matter, so do the men," she told him. "They can hardly afford to take their patronage elsewhere, since there *is* no alternative. I will—if certified—be undertaking work for certain Christian charities. The Fleet Charity Clinic, to be precise." There were also certain suffragist charities she would be working for as well, but it wasn't wise to mention those.

Charity work would scarcely allow her to earn much of a living, which was why most male physicians wouldn't even consider it. She would not tell him what else she had in mind to augment her income.

He brightened a little at that. *Probably because I won't be a threat to the practices of any of the young* male *physicians, who have wives with the proper attitudes to support,* she thought, amused in spite of her resentment. She suppressed the desire to sniff, as her nose tickled a little.

"Far be it from me to become an impediment to someone who wishes to devote herself to the welfare of the poor," he replied with ponderous piety, and removed a document from beneath the results of her examinations, signing it quickly. He passed it to her over the desk; she received it in those black-gloved hands—black, for she was still in mourning for her father, and though Society might forgive the occasional breach of strict mourning in a young *white* woman, it would never do so for her. The year of formal mourning was not yet up, and in the interest of economy, she had already decided to prolong it as long as she could. Mourning colors gave her a certain safety. Even a brute would not offer too much insult to a woman in mourning, even if she was a half-breed.

That paper was her medical certification, giving her the authority to practice medicine, and the right to practice surgery here in this hospital, admit patients, and treat them here.

"Congratulations, Doctor Witherspoon," he continued. "And may I repeat that the results of your examinations are remarkable, including those in surgery. I dare say your skills are equally outstanding."

"Thank you very much, Doctor," she replied with feigned meekness and gratitude; he swelled with self-importance, mistaking it for the genuine emotion. "I hope I will succeed in surpassing your expectations."

She rose. He did the same. She extended her right hand; he pressed it once in token of farewell, released it quickly, then immediately seated himself as she turned to leave. She was not important enough for him to remain standing until after she was gone, nor worthy of his time to be given a heartier handshake or more of his attention.

She closed the door of the office behind her, carefully and quietly, then smiled—this time with real warmth—at the doctor's receptionist and secretary, a young man with thin, blond hair, who had sincerely wished her good luck on her way in. She met his questioning blue eyes, and held up her signed certification in a gesture of triumph. The young man nodded vigorously, clasped both hands above his head in an athlete's gesture of victory, and gave a silent cheer. Maya's companion, a plump, animated woman three years her junior, who was seated in one of two chairs for visitors placed in this stuffy little reception room, was a trifle less circumspect.

"Oh, Maya! Well done!" Amelia Drew said aloud, leaping up from her chair to embrace her friend. Maya kissed her proffered cheek, waved cheerfully at the secretary, and guided Amelia out the door and into the hospital corridor before Amelia said anything that Doctor Clayton-Smythe might overhear and interpret as unflattering.

Nurses in nunlike uniforms hurried past, carrying trays and basins. Young men, medical students all, arrayed in their medical black, strode through the corridor like the would-be kings they all were.

Maya closed the reception-chamber door behind Amelia, and Amelia cast off any pretense of restraint, skipping like a schoolgirl. "You did it! You got the old crustacean to bend and give you your certification!"

"Not a crustacean, my dear. That was a fat, grumpy walrus on his very own sacred spot of beach." Maya's grimace betrayed her distaste. "It was a narrower thing than I care to think about." She stepped around an elderly charwoman scrubbing the floor on her hands and knees, bundled in so many layers of clothing her true shape could not be determined.

Amelia dodged a medical student on the run—probably late for a surgery. "But your marks were so good. And the letters from the other doctors at Royal Free Hospital—"

"I wasn't entirely certain of success, even with the highest of examination results," she replied, as they traversed the polished oak of the corridor, the starched frills of their petticoats rustling around their booted ankles. Amelia's costume, severe, and plain, was identical to Maya's but of dove-gray rather than stark black. Amelia was in the midst of her own medical education. Fortunately, both her parents were as supportive of her ambition as Maya's had been. Unfortunately, this gave young Amelia a distorted view of the prejudices of the majority of the male population of her land.

"I don't think I convinced him until I told him that I intended to practice among the poor." Maya smiled again, then laughed, thinking what shock the poor mummified man would have felt had she told him the entire truth.

"There's no harm in *intentions,* is there?" Amelia giggled. "And if there are those besides the poor who decide to ask for your services, well, that has nothing to do with your *intentions.*"

"True enough," Maya laughed. "But can you imagine what he would have said if he had known what I really planned to do?" Now that she was up and moving, warmth and life had returned to her feet, at least. And now that the ordeal was over and her victory laurels were firmly in her hands, she was feeling celebratory and just a little reckless.

Amelia was the only person outside Maya's household who knew what Maya intended, and even she blushed a brilliant scarlet as they moved side by side across the echoing foyer, heels clicking smartly on the tiles. "I daren't even guess," Amelia murmured, fanning her scarlet cheeks to cool them.

Just before they reached the doors giving out onto the street, Maya's fingers moved surreptitiously, and she murmured a few words that Amelia did not hear. She sensed a thin breath of energy wafting upward from the well of strength within her, and as they stepped out into the weather, the rain ceased for a moment.

"Well! There's more luck!" Amelia exclaimed as the clouds parted a little, letting a glimpse of blue peek through. She raised her hand imperiously, signaling their need for transportation. There was always a great coming and going of cabs here, both horse-drawn and motorized, and they procured a hansom without any difficulty whatsoever. Maya climbed in and gave her address to the driver through the little hatch above. It shut with a snap, and Amelia joined her.

It was, as she had specified with her tiny exercise of magic, a *clean* cab: no mud or worse on the floor, no cigar ash anywhere. And just as they settled themselves within the shelter of their conveyance and pulled their skirts well in, away from possible mud splashes, the rain began again. The cab moved off into a thin curtain of gray, the poor horse's ears signaling his dislike of the wet.

This was just as Maya had intended. It didn't do to *change* anything with magic, not if one wanted to remain undetected; one could only *arrange*. In this case, the break in the clouds that would have occurred a little later, and a few blocks away, happened above them and at the time they left the building, and closed again as soon as they were in shelter. And the cab was in good repair, the driver neither drunk nor mean spirited.

The precious certificate, now folded and safely inside Maya's handbag, rested beneath her hands on her lap. Amelia made small talk to which Maya responded with half of her attention. London, from within the partial enclosure of the hansom, was an assault on the senses of a very different sort than the heart of Delhi. In place of the scent—no, call it what it was, the *stench*—of hot, baked earth, dust, sweat, and dung, the smell of London enveloped them in damp, mold and mildew, wet wool, wet horse, smoke, stagnant water, the acrid tang of motor exhaust, a hint of sewage and horse droppings, and the river smell of the Thames. Harsher, deeper voices than the rapid twitter of her peoples' myriad tongues fell upon the ear. There was no bawl of livestock, only the clatter of wheels and hooves on cobblestones, neighing, the jingle of harness, and the alien noise of a motorcar or 'bus. And, of course, the atmosphere, so cheerless, so cold. . . .

But she had no other choice now; *this* was her home, and this strange island her refuge. If she was ever to find protection, it would be here. Her enemy was even more alien to this environment than she was.

She shook off her dark mood with an effort, turning all of her attention to her companion. Amelia was the most sensible, practical, and dauntless young woman that Maya had ever met. From the moment that they encountered each other at the London School of Medicine for Women, Maya had felt they had been friends or even sisters before, in some other lifetime. Naturally, she had not said anything of the sort to Amelia, who would only have been confused. The Church of England did not admit to the reincarnation of souls.

"Well, it will be your turn to beard the dragon in his den in another year or so," she told Amelia, who laughed.

"*I* am going to practice at the Royal Free Hospital," she replied. "They, at least, are open to women physicians. I'm not so ambitious as you."

"It wasn't ambition, it was necessity," Maya told her soberly. "What if Royal Free had balked? I would have nowhere to turn—"

"But why should they balk?" Amelia interrupted.

Maya gestured wordlessly to her own face, and Amelia flushed. "If I tried and failed to obtain certification at St. Mary's, then Royal Free would likely *have* certified me just out of spite," she continued cheerfully. "My father always taught me to try the hardest path first, you know, although if I had seen that man before I made that plan, I would have thought twice about the wisdom of it."

"I hadn't thought of that." Amelia pursed her lips. "Still, that won't do for me. St. Mary's might accept a woman physician, but they'll never accept a woman as a student. Not now, anyway. Perhaps in a few years."

"There is nothing wrong with Royal Free," Maya said firmly, "And a good many things that are right." She might have elaborated on the subject, but the cab had just turned down the shabby-genteel street that housed her home and surgery and was pulling up at the front door. Gupta, a shapeless bundle of waxed mackintosh and identifiable only by the white chalwars stuffed into his Wellingtons that peeked from under the hem of the mac, was setting the last screw into the inscribed brass plate beside her door—a plate that proclaimed this to be the surgery of Dr. M. Witherspoon.

"I suppose we won't see much of you anymore," Amelia said wistfully, as Maya dismounted from the hansom.

"Nonsense! You'll see me on Thursday at the latest, or have you forgotten our luncheon date?" Maya replied instantly. "Not to mention that you are welcome *here* at any hour of the day or night. Now, *you* go back to your studies, while I see what Gupta has found for me."

She circled around to the driver, perched up above the passenger compartment in the weather, and handed him a guinea—more than enough for her fare and Amelia's with a generous tip. "London School of Medicine for Women, please," she told him briskly. "My companion has a class at two."

"I'll 'ave 'er there well afore, ma'am," the cabby said, impressed by the guinea, if by nothing else. He chirruped to his horse, who trotted off without needing a slap of the reins or a touch of the whip. Amelia's gray-gloved hand waved farewell from the side of the cab, and Maya turned to Gupta.

"Was this bravado or anticipation, my friend?" she asked in Hindustani, touching the plaque.

"Neither, mem sahib," Gupta replied. "We knew, we all knew, you could not fail." His round, brown face held an expression of such earnest certainty that she wanted to laugh and cry at the same time.

"Well, let us go in out of this miserable weather. Come to me in the conservatory, and tell me what has happened to make you so sure of me." She waited while he put a last polish to the plate with a rag he stuffed back in his pocket, then moved past him into the little house she had bought to shelter her odd little "family."

It had taken most of her inheritance to buy it and fit it up, and had it been in better repair, or a better neighborhood, she could not have managed it. But *because* it was so shabby and had required the tearing out of walls, she had been able to install a great many comforts that better dwellings could not boast. The house was lit by electric light, which was much safer than gas. Hot water from a coal-fired boiler in the cellar circulated through the house via pipes and radiators, a luxury often used to keep conservatories and hothouses warm in winter on the Great Estates. More hot water was available for cleaning and bathing at all times, laid on in the bathrooms, without the need to heat water on the stove and carry it up in cans. At last she was warm enough so that she was able to throw off her coat as soon as she entered the front hall.

She had arranged for the hallway to be painted, rather than papered, in white. Furnished with pegs for coats, a bench for waiting patients, and a small table holding a brass dish from India for calling cards, she had hung prints of some of her father's favorite paintings on the walls. The impression was warmer than that of a hospital, but not "homelike"—wise, since this was the entrance to her surgery as well as to her home.

It was scarcely possible that she would have any patients calling yet, and she longed to shed her woolen suit with the coat and revert to more comfortable garb.

Not yet. Not yet. But I shall *be rid of these confounded shoes! Why is it that attractive shoes are a torture to wear?*

Hanging her coat on its peg in the hall, she passed the door to her examining room and surgery (formerly the parlor and smoking room) and climbed the stairs to the next floor. Here were the bedrooms, all alike, and the bathroom fitted up with the most modern of appointments. Her room was at the back of the house, away from street noise. The second bedroom, connected to hers, served as her parlor and sitting room.

Gupta had the third bedroom, and his son Gopal and his son's wife Sumi the fourth. Gopal and Sumi's four children shared the nursery on the floor above, where the servants' quarters had once been. Gupta had been her father's friend as well as his servant—but more importantly, he had been Surya's devoted guardian. There had been no question of whether or not the family would emigrate when Maya fled to England; she would have had to lock them all in prison to prevent them from coming with her.

Gupta had seen a great deal in his fifty-odd years, and she rather thought he was unshockable, which was just as well, considering what she was planning. She needed the help of a male to carry it out, and Gupta was the ideal man for the job.

The door to her bedroom stood invitingly open, and she hurried through it. With a sigh of relief, she sank down into a chair and unlaced her shoes. Exchanging them for soft leather slippers, she hesitated a moment, then shrugged.

Ridiculous. There is no reason to go out, and unlikely that anyone but a friend will call. I am getting out *of this rig!*

The rooms of this house were so tiny, compared with those in the bungalow in India. She had enough room to pass between the pieces of furniture, chair, bed, trunk, wardrobe, and table, but no more. Never, ever would she have needed the featherbed at home! Here, it, and the down-filled duvet and woolen blankets were absolute necessities, for not even the hot-water pipes could prevent the house from cooling at night.

In a trice, she slipped off the coat and skirt of her suit and hung them up on the outside of the mahogany wardrobe to be brushed later. The shirtwaist followed, then the corset cover, which she laid on the lace coverlet of the bed, and at last she could unhook the front busk of the corset and rid herself of the unwelcome constriction. At last she could *move!* She never laced her corsets anywhere near as tight as fashion dictated; she flattered herself to think that she didn't need to. Nevertheless, the garment restricted movement, if only because it was designed around what a lady would consider appropriate movement. Maya had chafed against those restrictions as a girl, and her feelings hadn't changed in the least now that she was an adult.

Fashion be hanged.

The corset joined the rest of her undergarments on the bed. Donning a far more comfortable flannel wrapper dress of a chocolate brown over her uncorseted petticoat, she went back out into the hall, then descended the stair at her end of the upstairs hall, passing the kitchen on her way to the conservatory. Gopal was in the throes of creativity in there, and she paused a moment to sniff the heavenly, familiar aromas appreciatively. Gopal had reacted to the presence of the modern iron stove set into the arch of the fireplace with tears of joy—though many of his countrymen preferred to cook over a tiny charcoal fire, Gopal was an artist and appreciated good tools. With so many thousands of British soldiers and civilians going out to Colonial Service and returning with a hunger for the foods they had grown accustomed to, it was a simple matter for Gopal to procure virtually any spice or foodstuff he required for them all to eat the way they had at home.

Home. Odd how the other Eurasians she had met would speak of Britain as Home—a "home" they had never seen—with as much longing as the expatriates. Home for Maya was and always would be India, the place where she had been born and where she had spent most of her life. How could you long for a place you had never even seen?

She stepped through the French doors into the warmth of her conservatory—which had required the lion's share of her inheritance to build—and was *almost* Home.

A little judicious use of magic had caused the flowering vines planted around the walls of the conservatory to grow at an accelerated pace, hiding the brickwork and the view of the houses on all sides. Passion flowers flung their great starburst blooms against the green of the vines. In bloom at all times and seasons, they filled the air with perfume, as did the jasmine, both day- and night-blooming. A fountain and generous pool added warm humidity and the music of falling water, the hot-water pipes around the perimeter a tropical heat. Here were the flowers she loved, and here, too, were her pets—

Not pets. Friends.

They rushed to greet her as soon as she set food on the gravel of her path—first the pair of mongooses, Sia and Singhe, romping toward her with their peculiar humpbacked gait. Rhadi, the ring-necked parrot, dove for her right shoulder, long tail trailing out behind him like a streamer, while the saker falcon Mala dropped down onto her left. Neither so much as scratched her skin, so soft footed were they, and though Mala was death incarnate to the sparrows, starlings, and pigeons, he would sooner starve than touch a feather of Rhadi's head. The peacock Rajah strode toward her with more dignity, his tail spread for her admiration. And last of all, Charan, her little monkey, sprang into her arms as soon as she held them out for him. Only the owl, named Nisha, whose round eyes seemed to stare straight into one's heart, did not stir from her slumber in the hollow of a dead oak tree that showed what a fine garden had once stood here. Maya had left it there for the benefit of her birds, who all found it a fine place to perch, and the vines twined around it just as happily as they climbed the brick of the walls, giving it a kind of new life.

"And have you been good?" she asked them all, as the mongooses romped around her ankles and the monkey put his arms around her neck, chattering softly into her ear. The falcon gave her a swift touch of his beak by way of a caress, and took off again to land in the tree.

The peacock shivered his tail feathers, and Rhadi said in his clear little voice, "Good! Good!" and laughed, following Mala up into the tree.

She laughed with him, and carried Charan to her favorite seat in the garden, a closely-woven rattan chair with a huge back that mimicked a peacock's tail. From here she could see only the green of her plants, the fountain and pool; she could forget for a while the cold world outside.

In a moment, Gopal brought mint tea, and placed the tray with two glasses on the rattan table beside her. Gupta arrived without a sound, as was his wont, materializing beside her and taking a second, smaller chair on the other side of the table, also facing the pool and fountain. He poured for both of them, and they each took a moment to savor the hot sweetness in companionable silence.

"We will prosper, mem sahib," Gupta said with satisfaction, putting his glass back down empty. "We will prosper. There is great progress today." He smiled. "I went, as you instructed, to the theater last night. I left your card with the man who attends to the stage door, and also with the stage manager, and the ballet master. I made mention that you were of liberal mind, and *not* one of those inclined to attempt reform on those who were merely making a living for themselves. It was he who asked for several more cards, on seeing it and hearing my words, and made me to believe that he would be giving them to some of the young ladies."

"Aha!" Maya responded. The cards she had given to Gupta, unlike her "official" business cards, had *not* been printed up, but had been calligraphed elegantly and by her own hand, because what they implied was risky, even scandalous.

Doctor Maya Witherspoon, Lady Physician. Female complaints. Absolute discretion, and her address. On the next lot, she would add, *Licensed to practice at St. Mary's, Paddington, and Royal Free Hospital.*

What the cards implied was that she would treat the women

who came to her for treatment of their "female complaints"—including inconvenient or unwedded pregnancy—without a lecture or a word slipped outside the office. And that she would give instructions and supplies to prevent inconvenient pregnancy, regardless of marital status.

"Ah, but I was wise and cunning, mem sahib," Gupta continued, his face wreathed in smiles. "I followed well-dressed gentlemen as they left the theater last night, and marked the houses they went to. This morning I looked the houses over, and chose the finest. There, too, did I leave your card, and pleased were the dwellers in those places to see it, though one did sigh that it was too bad you were a lady and they could not pay for your services with an exchange of trade."

"Gupta!" she exclaimed, and giggled, although her cheeks did heat up. "That was *very* well done! How clever of you!" She had not been able to work out a way to get her cards into the hands of the mistresses of the wealthy men of London. Now Gupta had managed that, and once one or two of the "Great Horizontals" came to her, they would see that the rest of their set knew her name.

"Yes," Gupta replied, not at all modest. "I know, mem sahib. I think you will have callers tomorrow, if not today." He cast his eye around the garden, which was growing darker as evening approached. "Will you have your tea here, mem sahib? I could light the lamps."

"Please," she said, as Charan nestled down into a corner of the chair. "And if friends call, bring them here instead of the parlor."

"And callers of another sort?" Gupta raised his eyebrows to signal what he meant.

"Use your own judgment," she told him. "You are a wise man, Gupta; I think you will know best whether to summon me to the office or bring the caller here."

Gopal soon brought her tea, a hybrid mix of the High Teas of India and of Britain. She shared the feast with her menagerie, other than Mala and Nisha, who ate only what they hunted, or the starlings and pigeons Gopal's eldest boy brought down with his catapult. Charan adored the clotted cream, as did Sia and Singhe; the latter swarmed up her skirt into her lap to lick their paws and faces clean as Rajah picked at the last tea-cake.

There is one good thing about this cold country, she thought, scratching the two little rowdies under their chins. *It is too cold for snakes.*

Or at least, it was at the moment.

She could only pray it would remain that way.

GOPAL had come and gone, taking the tea things with him, and Maya retreated to a hammock swung between two vine-covered posts in lieu of the tree trunks that would have suspended it back home. Surrounded by scented warmth, cradled in the gently swaying hammock, she closed her eyes and listened to the play of the water in her fountain, the soft chatter of the mongooses and the parrot. This time of the afternoon, full of shared treats, they all felt sleepy and were inclined to nap. Mala had been fed late this morning, and Nisha would be fed once dusk settled, so they, too, were content to doze. Charan curled up beside her, a little soft ball with his head pillowed against her cheek and both arms wrapped around her neck, and she had actually begun to doze when Gupta reappeared, waking her.

Charan awoke, too, and scampered up to an observation post in the dead tree. "Mem sahib, you have a caller," Gupta said, his expression one of intense satisfaction. He made a grand gesture toward the front of the house. "This will be a client, I do believe. I have taken her to the surgery office. She waits there for you."

Oh, heavens! She quickly tilted herself out of the hammock, glad that she had at least not taken her hair down, and that the sober brown dress disguised its comfort in its severity. Primly buttoned up to the neck, waistband tightened, and cuffs twitched straight, it would pass for professional attire. With a pat to her hair, she followed Gupta inside, and hurried to the surgery itself, for it would not do to have a potential client see her enter by the same door that the client herself had used. She passed through it, wrinkling her nose a trifle at the familiar scent of carbolic, entering the office from the surgery door rather than the hall door.

This was a comfortable room, meant to be the very opposite of the kind of office that Doctor Clayton-Smythe had. The wallpaper, a warm Morris print, softened the impression given by the rows of medical texts on the wall and the plain, uncompromising desk. The woman waiting there stood up slowly. The velvet coat lying beside her, the collar of jet beads at her throat, and the abundance of maroon lace making up the ornamentation of her deep red dress was nothing at all compared to the impact of her wide, limpid blue eyes and the shining mass of her golden hair. She could have been the wife of a peer, or a successful man of business—could have been, but was not. There was something indefinable about her dress and air—or perhaps it was only Maya's own ability to see deep past the surface of things. At any rate, there was no doubt in the young doctor's mind that this was one of the ladies with whom Gupta had left her card this morning.

Maya extended her hand across her desk, and it was taken tentatively by the other. "I am Doctor Witherspoon," Maya said, in a firm, but friendly tone. "Would you care to have a seat and tell me what brings you to my surgery, Miss—" she hesitated just a moment, then finished, "—Smith?" A raised eyebrow meant to convey a tacit understanding that there would be no real names used here evidently translated her meaning perfectly.

The woman released Maya's hand, and a smile curved those knowing lips, about which there was more than a suggestion that the ruddy color was not entirely due to the hand of nature. Certainly the pure, pale complexion had nothing at all to do with nature, and very much to do with the ingestion of tiny daily doses of arsenic or lead, a dangerous practice that many professional beauties resorted to, sometimes with fatal results. "Very good," she said, seating herself. "Miss Smith, indeed, will do as well as any other name."

Maya seated herself and folded her hands on the top of her desk. "Does anything bring you here besides curiosity, Miss Smith?"

"Your card." The woman slipped two fingers inside a beaded reticule and extracted the rectangle of heavy card stock. "I came to see—" She seemed for a moment at a loss for words.

"To see the horse, and perhaps try its paces?" Maya supplied, and again that winsome smile appeared. Calculated, perhaps, but this lady was a professional in every sense.

"Indeed. And I am not disappointed, although I expected to be. Too often those who advertise discretion are anything but discreet." Miss "Smith" placed the card back in her reticule. Maya made another addition to her mental assessment; though her caller might look little more than eighteen, she was much older—in spirit and experience if not in years. "As you might assume, although I am currently in good health with no—complaints—I am in need of a personal physician. As are several of my particular—circle. We conferred over tea, my friends of the theater and I, and I was chosen to approach you."

Aha. Candor. I, too, shall be candid. So this lady was from the theater—*not* in the chorus, probably not a dancer, or she might have mentioned it.

"In that case, if you will give me your medical history and any trifling troubles that might concern you, perhaps we can see if we shall suit each other." Maya took out a sheet of foolscap and dipped a pen in the inkwell, labeled it as "Miss Smith," and looked up attentively.

At the end of an hour, Maya had a reasonable history, along with some cautious advice for the "trifling troubles" the lady confessed to. The *best* advice she did not bother to give. There was no point in telling her new patient not to stay up until dawn, not to starve herself for days only to overindulge at a party or dinner engagement, and not to drink so much champagne.

I would like her to make some small changes in her diet. But not yet; I had better coat the bitter pill with sweetness. "Miss Smith, you need a rest, but I know you cannot afford to take one, at least, not until the theater season is at an end," she advised briskly. "Failing a little excursion to a sunnier clime, you should take fresh fruit at every meal. Especially citrus or hothouse fruits."

Miss Smith looked surprised, then calculating, and nodded. Maya had expected as much. The young woman had not gotten where she was now without being clever as well as beautiful, and it probably occurred to her that not only would the request for fruits instead of chocolates or wine cause her admirers just as much effort, and would be quite as expensive a way to show their interest, it would indicate a certain delicacy of body and mind on her part. That might, in turn, increase the attentions of those with better-lined pockets, who preferred that their mistresses be above the common touch.

"On the other hand, don't starve yourself on thin consommé and broth," Maya continued. "Small portions will do you more good than starving; leave off the sauces and butter, and vegetables will serve you better than breads. There is no harm at all in having very lean meat, but do avoid fat. Fat is very hard for a delicate appetite. Fish, on the other hand is excellent."

"Lobster?" Miss Smith ventured, hopefully. "Oysters?"

To accompany all that champagne? "All very well, but avoid rich sauces. They are often used to mask shellfish that are no longer wholesome, and can you afford a month of wretchedness for the sake of a lobster bisque?" Maya asked shrewdly. "A case of food poisoning would keep you off the stage for at least that long. Miss Smith, this is advice unsolicited, but it pays one to know precisely what transpires in one's kitchen. There are much worse things that could come from that domain than merely being cheated by the cook."

This time Miss Smith nodded knowingly. "My cook lives in terror of me," she replied with a *real* smile this time. "What of the shortness of breath?"

Don't lace your corsets so tightly and exercise, my dear.

"As you are in the theater, I venture to guess you might find a

Shakespearean coach who would give you fencing lessons; loosen your corsets or do without altogether for that hour, and put the same effort into it that he does. You might be surprised at how *flexible* fencing lessons can make one," Maya told her instantly. "You might also consider dancing lessons every day; good, brisk ones, perhaps with the ballet. The same lessons that make them so graceful will do the same for you—"

"Fencing lessons are quite fashionable, are they not?" the young woman said, after a moment staring off into space in thought. "The theater director might be pleased to find I'm taking them, and he's mentioned dancing class once or twice as well."

Ah. Music hall, operetta, or popular theater, I think. She is probably playing the "Ingenue" and the "Innocent Maid." And she wants to stay the Ingenue for as long as she can.

"Quite," Maya reassured her. "Now wait one moment; I will go and fetch a prescription I think will please you better than any pill or patent medicine to ensure a perfect complexion."

She rose and went to a very special cupboard which stood in the surgery office in place of one of the bookcases. From it, she brought out a carved sandalwood box, which she took to the desk, opening it to Miss Smith's curious gaze. It contained six carved stone jars.

"These are from India, are they not?" Miss Smith asked, newly aroused interest causing her intense blue eyes to shine in a way that must have been irresistible to any man. "Like . . ." she began, then flushed, and put her hand in its red-silk glove to her lips.

"Like me, you were about to say?" Maya laughed. "Miss Smith, I cannot conceal my parentage, so I do not trouble to try. But because of my parentage . . ." She lowered her voice, and Miss Smith leaned forward eagerly. "Because my mother was of great learning in the ancient ways of her people, I have knowledge that is not accessible to those of this land. My mother's people believe that female beauty is a thing to be cultivated and made to flourish, then preserved for as long as she lives. They do *not* believe that it is a sin to be lovely. I do not only supply physic internally, Miss Smith, I am prepared to supply it externally as well."

Great good heavens, I sound like a patent medicine man! But Miss Smith took in the words with parted lips and shining eyes, and Maya continued in the same vein. "Here are my special balms and lotions, meant to enhance and preserve against the threats of cruel weather and the hand of time. I have an apothecary at my disposal. He compounds them under my strict supervision."

She wrote down the name and address of the apothecary at the end of the street with whom she had set up her arrangement. She supplied the herbs, after a little preparation of her own, and he did the rest. There was more in those jars than just salves and balms; there was magic there, magic infused into the herbs with which they were made. It was not a magic that would ensnare a man's mind and passion for all time (although she *could,* but would not, do that as well). This was the gentle magic of the earth, green magic, Maya's own. It fed and nurtured, fed the generous instincts that were part of man *or* woman, creating a beauty that would not fade.

The young woman took out one of the jars, a gentle face cream compounded of aloe, rosewater, glycerin, and several healing herbs. She opened it gingerly and sniffed. Her face reflected her delight in the scent of roses that wafted up from the cream. "They are very effective, far more so than anything that you will have seen heretofore. See—here they are labeled, each for what it is for. You can leave off whatever you have been doing and use these preparations exclusively; I promise you will be very happy with the results. You may have these to try. When you are satisfied, you may have him make up more as you need them." *Getting her to stop taking those daily doses of arsenic will do a great deal to settle the rest of her problems.*

She closed the box and pushed it over to her visitor, who picked it up. Miss Smith's hands trembled only a little with eagerness. "These samples are included in your consultation fee," Maya continued. "Now, I think that we should suit well as patient and physician, but what say you?"

Miss Smith replied with a real smile. "I shall be returning—and so will my friends."

* * *

Once her visitor—her first patient—had gone, Maya cheerfully organized her notes under the name of Helen Smith—"Helen," for Helen of Troy. If Miss Smith's face failed to launch ships, it certainly had the power to create quite as much mischief as her namesake had. Subsequent patients would be filed under similarly fictional names, memorable only to Maya, so that if anyone should somehow gain access to her records, they would have no way of connecting real person to fictional identity. And the consultation fee of five whole shillings resided safely in Maya's strongbox; a woman of Miss Smith's profession might sometimes neglect her butcher's and dressmaker's bills, but dared not anger her physician, once she had found one who would not betray her.

A few more "Smiths," and not only would the household prosper, Maya could spare time and medicines for others who needed them, but had no means to pay for them.

And we can pay our own butcher's bills. Maya smiled, opened the heavy filing drawer in her desk, and filed Helen Smith's history away in an empty slot. It would be time for supper soon, and she was definitely looking forward to sharing it with her household, with this much good news to tell them.

Since her father's death, Maya no longer stood on ceremony with those others would call her servants. Yes, they performed tasks for her while she provided their incomes, food, and shelter, but without them, *she* would have been hard put to pursue the life she had chosen. Certainly, she could never have found English servants she could trust as she did her little family.

The single note of a gong vibrated through the house, telling her that supper was ready. She carefully turned out the electric light on her desk—a small miracle, one as marvelous as any magic of her own, to make light appear and vanish at the turn of a key! The sun had set while she played hostess to Miss Smith, and now the only light came from the corner gaslight out on the street. She shivered as she left the office, glancing out the window at the shiny, rain-drenched cobbles; it could have been ice that glazed them, and not water.

The noise and merriment in the small room just off the kitchen dispelled her shivers. The entire family, including the children, sat on the floor on cushions and carpets in the area that would have held a table for the servants in a proper English household. Maya took her place among them, and helped herself from the pots and plate of flatbread resting on a footed tray in the center of the group.

Why waste two rooms on *dining,* when there was small chance that she would ever play hostess to a meal for anyone outside her household? The former dining room was now an invalid's room, a place for a seriously ill patient to stay until she was well enough to be discharged and taken to her own home. And this servants' meal room was good enough for Maya; brightly lit, painted the same cream color of the walls of her old, beloved bungalow, redolent with saffron and spice, it was another small slice of the place she thought of as home.

The children, who had all gotten training in English from the time they were able to toddle, attended a local day school, and she listened with amusement as they chattered about their lessons and classmates in a mix of Hindustani and English. Their parents and grandfather listened to the babble with a tolerance no English parent (believing the rule that "children should be seen and not heard") would ever understand.

The four children made enough chatter for twice their number, but Maya enjoyed their artless confidences. Ravi, the eldest boy, was enough like his grandfather Gupta already that the elder man was in the habit of taking Ravi with him on his trips to the market and other harmless errands. Ravi was eleven; his brothers Amal and Jagan nine and five respectively, and their adorable, large-eyed sister Suli was seven and just beginning the schooling that Jagan had already started.

When the young ones finally ran out of chatter, Maya caught the eyes of their parents. "The lady who called will be my client, and will send her friends," she told them, and was rewarded with smiles and no little relief. "All will be well on that score."

"Ha!" Gupta said, looking wise. "It is well, mem sahib. Your father, blessed be his memory, would be pleased."

Privately Maya doubted that her father would have been *pleased* to learn that his daughter was the physician to music-hall singers and the kept mistresses of wealthy men, but she said nothing to Gupta on that score. Nigel Witherspoon, whether he was in the Christian Heaven that Maya had been brought up to believe in, or on Surya's karmic wheel of reincarnation, was no longer in a position to judge what Maya did. And Maya saw nothing sinful in what *she* was doing. *I am hardly in a position to judge them, after all, no matter what the vicar at the Fleet Clinic says. I will heal the sick and leave it to Christ to judge. And since* He *kept company with thieves and prostitutes, I doubt very much that He would so much as raise an eyebrow at what I am doing.*

She turned her attention back to the conversation. Gopal was planning a celebratory dinner and required her to make some choices. Not all the dishes were from India—in fact, the party would have a rather eclectic mix of Indian, British, and French dishes, for Gopal was trading lessons in Indian cuisine for those in Continental cooking with an expatriate Parisian cook he had come to be acquainted with. *For all I know,* she realized with amusement, *it might be the very own chef of a Member of Parliament!*

No British household would eat as they were doing tonight, with everything on the low table at once, and everyone helping himself; Maya hadn't actually had meals like this when her father was alive, at least not since she'd come out of the nursery. They'd always kept to proper manners, as absurd as that was with only three of them—later, two—at the long formal table, with servants attending and each course being removed as the next was brought in. But she'd begun dining with the others for comfort and company after he died, and kept on with it. Who was to see or care? Much better to have converted the dining room to a sick room; any seriously ill patient Maya wanted to keep an eye on would find she had excellent care here.

It *would* be a "she," of course. Maya doubted she'd get any male patients. This part of London was hardly the abode of the respectable middle class, but those who lived here were not so desperate that they couldn't make a choice in physicians. This wasn't the neighborhood of the poorest of the poor—not the Fleet, not Cheapside, and dear God, not Whitechapel. This was barely the East End. *On the other hand, you never know.* The working-class poor who lived here were also pragmatic; a man *might* bend his stiff neck to take the help of a woman doctor. . . .

Especially since I'm one of them, in a sense. But a man of this neighborhood would recover at home, tended by his own womenfolk. Only a woman needed to be *kept* here, lest she go back (or be driven back) to her wifely duties too soon.

The children finished their meal and ran up to the nursery. The other adults finished theirs and began to clean up. Maya took a cup of tea out with her to the conservatory, walking softly. All the other pets were asleep, but Nisha the owl was wide awake, and flew down, soundlessly, to perch on the back of a chair. A pigeon feather caught at the side of her beak told Maya that Nisha had already dined. Maya scratched her just under her beak and around her neck, a caress which the owl suffered for a moment before dipping her head and flying back up to her roost. Maya smiled; was there *anything* so soft as an owl's feathers?

It was time to make the nightly rounds. Not for the first time, Maya wished that her mother had taught her some of the secrets of her own native magic, and the enchantments and protections that she had learned in her temple, before she died.

"I cannot," she had said, her eyes dark with distress, whenever Maya begged. "Yours is the magic of your father's blood, not mine."

And she had never had the chance to explain what that meant.

Maya gazed up at the blank, black glass of the conservatory roof before she left her sanctum to circle the interior walls of the house. Even if the sky had not been overcast, it was unlikely that she would be able to see more than the very brightest of stars and the moon. How she missed the skies of home, where the stars hung like jeweled lamps in an ebony dome!

All the magic Maya knew had been learned by covertly spying on her mother as the former priestess spun protections for her family, or cobbled together from street magic gleaned from the few genuine *fakirs,* then compounded from a mixture of instinct, guess, and trial and error. She had woven a web of street-charm protections over this house and its occupants; every night she strengthened them, going over them three times to replace where the erosions of time and this city weakened them.

Three times she walked through each room of the first floor, in the dim light coming from the gaslights outside, or the light from the hall, bolstering her charms. There was no sign that anything had put those protections to the test, but would she be able to tell if anything had just probed at them rather than trying to destroy them?

I don't know. . . .

With a determined shake of her head, she thrust away the doubt. This was not the time to worry about her abilities; doubt made magic weak. That much, at least, she knew.

Besides, now that she had completed her protections, the charms she worked next were the ones she was sure of. Prosperity on the surgery and office and the front door, health on the kitchen, peace on the house itself. She smiled to herself as she heard the children above in the nursery mute their quarrel over a game into an amiable disagreement. Not that her charm stopped all quarrels; it was most effective right after it was first cast, and like the protections, it eroded a little with time and stress. But it did make life easier on everyone living here, making everyone a little more inclined to forgive and sweetening tempers.

Now her last, and easiest, work of the evening. She returned to the conservatory and spent a little time on each and every plant, strengthening it, encouraging it to grow at a rate much faster than "normal," and giving it the extra energy to do so. Once the trees, plants, and bushes were tall and strong enough to suit her, vigorous enough to cover the walls and give her the complete illusion of a tiny jungle, she would let them grow at their own pace. Until that time, she would use her own strength to build her sanctuary, the sanctuary she needed so desperately in this alien place.

It wearied her; it always did. When she was done, Nisha called her softly. She hooted at the owl comfortingly and blew out the candle-lamps as she left, so that the conservatory descended into the sweet, warm darkness her pets all loved.

She closed herself in her office to study, with the murmur of voices within the house and the sounds of wheels on cobblestones outside as a soothing counterpart to her reading. Her father had never scrimped on medical texts and journals, and neither would she. There was so much to learn! It seemed that not a week passed but that some new medical discovery was heralded. Some were nonsense, of course; she had an advantage over her colleagues in that she could *tell* if a treatment for an illness or injury was actually doing any good. X-ray photography was a boon, if one could keep the patient still enough—but electrical stimulation was stuff and nonsense. She could tell easily enough with her own special senses that the patient got no more benefit from it than from any other nostrum in which he *truly believed.* Belief was a powerful medicine, ofttimes more powerful than any pill or potion she could offer.

As for sanitary surgery, she already felt that simply boiling instruments before surgery was nowhere near enough. Although she had had no say in the matter when she operated or assisted under the supervision of one of Royal Free's senior surgeons, from now on she would have a nurse spritzing the patient and the hands of those operating on him with dilute carbolic acid during *her* surgeries. Dr. Lister was right, and he would save many, many lives with his ideas, if he could get other physicians to implement them.

Tonight she studied gas gangrene. It was not the sort of literature that anyone but a small percentage of people on this island would even consider for after-dinner reading, and only a minuscule number of those would think it suitable under any conditions for a woman. Maya didn't care; she wanted to see if there was any hint in the current papers that her carbolic-acid atomizer would prevent the spread of this fearful condition. By the time she finished for the evening, with the clock on the mantle over the unused fire striking eleven, she had come to the conclusion that it would *help,* but no more. If only there were thin, flexible gloves available, impermeable to those tiny creatures Louis Pasteur had discovered as the root cause of infection and disease! Then a surgeon could operate without fear that the dread *bacteria* would enter some tiny nick or cut on her hands!

But India rubber was too thick and became sticky when warm, lambskin and eelskin little better than bare hands, for they required seams and, once used, could not be used again. Washing, with soap and carbolic, before and after, thoroughly and exhaustively: that was the only preventative, and that a shallow one. But she could not let fear keep her from trying to save lives.

She rubbed her eyes and shut the cover of the latest issue of *The Lancet,* marveling that there were still so many men who dared to call themselves *doctors* who refused to believe that bacteria caused infection.

How could they not? In the face of all the evidence? She had never had a doubt, and never would have had, even without the evidence of her own very special senses that informed her of the work of those tiny, evil lives, glowing like sickly yellow coals, spreading through her patients' bodies like an ugly stain.

I can sense them, but there is so little that magic can do against them. Not even Surya had been able to prevail against the tiny lives that had devoured her own, and Surya's magic had been a tower, a monument, compared to the pitifully small and ragged prominence that was her daughter's. Magic could strengthen the body that fought disease, but it could not kill the disease, not when it was one that moved with the terrible swiftness of the cholera that had claimed Surya.

Maya clenched her jaw and swallowed hard; she squeezed her eyes tightly against the burning behind her lids, and fought the tears away.

"Enough," she said aloud, and pushed the chair away from the desk. Turning out the light, she went back out into the hall, closing the office door quietly behind her.

The house was quiet, except for the creakings and whispers of any house, new or old, as wood rubs against wood and whispers of draft creep under sills. Gupta and the rest must have gone to bed, which was where Maya would be shortly.

She turned out each light as she passed it to save the fragile bulb: the hallway downstairs, the light over the staircase, then the light just outside her door. Closing her door behind her, she leaned against it with her back to the wood for a moment and rubbed her eyes again. It was dark here, but she moved instinctively across the floor to the electric lamp beside her bed and turned the key to bring it to life.

This was a comfortable room. Quite small, it had probably been intended for a child, but Gopal and Sumi needed the much larger master bedroom, so despite their protests, Maya had insisted they take it. She had not been able to bring her furniture from home, but plenty of far wealthier folk who had gone to India and returned *had* brought furniture back with them, and there was a great deal of it in the flea markets at bargain prices after they tired of it. So here there were no lace curtains, no rose-garden carpets. The colors of home hung at the windows in vivid swags of red and yellow and orange muslin; the floor was covered with a worn silk rug figured like a Persian garden. The walls, painted white, played backdrop to a carved lacework of wooden panels with geometric embroidered tapestries, or hangings figured with the tree of life. The same carved wood supported her bed, made up the table beside it, and framed the cushions of a chair. Two sandalwood chests, one at the foot of her bed and the other at the window, and a wardrobe held her clothing; sandalwood boxes held her jewelry.

There wasn't much of that left; Surya had bequeathed her daughter a small fortune of gold and gems, but most of it had gone to bring them all to London, build this house, and keep them until now. Not that Maya begrudged the sale of any of it, but she had kept a few pieces that held special meaning for her.

She sat down on the side of her bed and opened a small sandalwood box on the bedside table next to the lamp, taking out the carved ivory ball that rested there. The filigreed ball was as big as her fist, and there was no piece of the lacework ivory that was wider than a quarter of an inch. Inside this ball was another, and another, and another. Twelve in all, they all moved freely inside one another. Maya turned it over and over in her hands, caressing the smooth ivory gently, remembering how her mother would hold the ball in front of her wondering eyes at bedtime, and tell her absurd tales about how it had been made—that ants had carved it, whittling it away from the inside out, or that a man had been shrunk to the size of a beetle so that he could create it.

I think she could have put Scheherazade to shame with her stories.

Her finger traced the arabesque of ivory, the tenderly curling vines, the tiny trumpet flowers, as each turn of the ball revealed another glimpse of more tendrils, more buds inside. The balls ticked quietly against each other as she turned the sphere over and over in her hands, not thinking, just remembering.

. . . her mother dancing in the garden, laughing, while Gupta played a tiny drum, her own stumbling, baby steps trying to imitate her; the jingle of the bells at her ankles, the flutter of the end of her sari. . . .

. . . her mother's low, whispered voice, as the lamp flickered; a murmur of fantastic tales as Maya's sleepy eyes followed a gigantic moth circling round and round the lamp. . . .

. . . a breath of patchouli and sandalwood, the featherlike caress of hennaed fingers. . . .

Slowly Maya felt the tension of the day drain out of her as the memories filled her. Surya had murmured mantras to guide her through the relaxations of yogaic magics; Maya had the mantra of memory to ease her path to sleep.

When at last her eyes felt heavy, and she had to stifle yawns, she put the ball back into its cotton nest, closed the box, and prepared for bed. Once into her nightgown and about to go to sleep, she opened the door to her room just a crack, so that Charan and the mongooses could roam about at will. Sia and Singhe would slip in and out of her bedroom at least five or six times during the night as they patrolled; so far all they had found was a few mice, and once, a rat, but they dispatched those just as readily as a snake. And she would probably find Charan curled up with her when she woke.

Tomorrow is my day at Fleet Clinic, she reminded herself, with a sense of anticipation. No more assisting, or nursing; she was a full physician now, and she might even have a surgical case! At the least, there would be a broken limb or two, perhaps a delivery, maybe a burn case—

Not too much enthusiasm, her conscience warned, as she got into bed and turned out the light. *You might enjoy practicing your art, but remember that this is going to be at the expense of someone else's misfortune, Doctor Witherspoon.*

You're right, she acknowledged the little voice with a twinge. *But—*

No buts, her conscience retorted, pleased with an easy victory.

As soon as her conscience turned its back on her, well satisfied with itself, she stuck out a metaphorical tongue at it like a naughty child and ran away to hide in sleep before it could catch her.

THE birds looked down on Maya and her guest with curiosity—all but Rajah, the peacock, who gazed at her with hopes of a biscuit from her plate. The mongooses were curled up around Maya's feet, hidden by the flounce of her skirt, and Charan sat primly in a third chair next to his mistress. This was the first time that anyone other than the "family" had been in the conservatory since the last of the workmen left, and all of the pets were intensely interested in the newcomer.

Maya handed a cup of tea across the tiny table to Amelia, who looked around her with a lively expression of interest. She had expressed approval of the office, envy of the surgery, and proclaimed that words failed her when it came to the conservatory. Since Maya's certification, Amelia had not only become *more* of a friend, Maya had gotten the distinct feeling that she was someone who could be trusted utterly. In fact, it seemed to her more and more often that Amelia was someone that Maya had known before. Surya, of course, would have said with that certainty that she *had* that Amelia and Maya had been sisters or bosom friends or even mother and daughter in some long-ago time. Maya wondered what Amelia's reaction would be to that. She no longer thought Amelia would be confused; her friend's mind was too broad, too quick to apprehend a new idea for her to be puzzled by the idea of reincarnation.

She'd probably just nod and accept it, even if she didn't entirely understand what I meant by it.

"This is a little Eden, and I cannot get over how polite your pets are!" Amelia exclaimed, handing Charan a plain biscuit in answer to his pitiful face and outstretched hand. Charan took it, bobbed his head once, and ran across the pavement to one of his favorite perches and began nibbling it at the edge, turning it around and around in his clever hands to preserve its shape. "I can see why you wanted this place. I wouldn't have thought I could find a spot so peaceful just off a busy street."

It's a good thing she doesn't know anything about tropical plants, though, or she would never have believed my blithe explanation of how fast they grow.

"I know children that aren't as well-behaved as your pets," Amelia continued with a smile. "Perhaps you ought to set yourself up as a deportment teacher as well as a doctor!"

"I suppose you could thank my mother for that, not me. They were hers originally," Maya told her, crumbling another biscuit for Rajah, who bowed his head graciously to accept the offering from her hand.

Amelia hesitated, then replied, cautiously, "You've never told me much about her. She must have been a remarkable woman. . . ."

Maya had already decided that this tea party would be a good time to open up further to her friend and see what came of it. She was tired of having no one to talk to except her household, most of whom really didn't understand half of what she told them. Granted, she wouldn't be able to tell Amelia about her magic—but it would be good to have a close friend near her own age and with most of the same interests.

So Maya laughed a little. "Remarkable? That's a rather *pale* word for my mother, considering that she defied her family, friends, and religion to marry my father, then continued to defy *his* people by being his very visible wife, rather than hiding away in his house and pretending she didn't exist."

"Oh, my—that must have put the fur up on the back of the old cats." Amelia put her hand up to her mouth, not quite hiding a smile, her cheeks turning very pink, but not from embarrassment. Amelia took an unhallowed glee in "tweaking the tails of the old cats." She was deeply involved in women's suffrage, and any time there was a prank played that showed up the antisuffragists for the fools they were, it was certain that Amelia had a hand in it. "Good for her! I just hope they didn't make her life a misery."

"Oh, the 'old cats' rule Colonial society with an iron rod in India," Maya sighed. "They managed to shut us out of the Club doings, the dances, and the rest of it. But love *will* break out, old cats notwithstanding, and there still aren't that many English women in the Raj. There are a good many native wives now, and by no means are they all the wives of Private Tommys. Mother wasn't alone, and neither was I; we had our own dances and club to go to and amusements—and *our* polo team beat *theirs* three times out of four."

Though most of the other women donned corsets and bustles, and tried to be more English than the exiles, talking about a home they'd never seen and weren't likely to, trying to pretend the world they left behind didn't exist. They'd even adopt English names, for heaven's sake!

"Ah," Amelia nodded wisely. "The Eurasians. I've read some little about them; I think they must be very brave people, when it all comes down to it. It's hard to defy society *and* manage to be happy at the same time. Are they all as handsome as you?"

Now it was Maya's turn to cover her lips, her cheeks flushing hotly. "Good heavens, Amelia, what a thing to say!"

"Well, are they?" The first thing that had attracted Maya to her friend was her artless candor, and it seemed that Amelia was determined to exercise that trait to the fullest today. Amelia waved her hand vaguely as she elaborated her question. "I mean, I've always heard it said that children of—I mean—when you have parents of two different races—and the male students at Royal Free—"

Amelia fumbled to a halt, finally realizing that she might have overstepped herself, but Maya laughed, fanning her cheeks to cool them, and over her head the parrot echoed her laugh. "I suppose, but it hardly matters," she said with great candor herself. "No gentleman who wishes to rise in the colonial ranks would ever marry a woman of mixed race, and as for the Eurasian men—well! *They* certainly need not apply to the mama of an English girl!"

Amelia flushed, but her eyes sparkled. "I've half a mind to go find out for myself, once I've been certified," she said with her chin raised defiantly. "Since no *proper* gentleman would ever marry a female doctor either! I want to be a doctor *and* a wife and mother, and I rather doubt I'm going to find that possible here. Perhaps someone whose parents have already flouted custom would find himself better able to do the same."

Maya sobered at once. "Your talent and training would be welcome in India," she said earnestly. "Half the English doctors of the male persuasion are so ham-handed they kill more female patients than they save, even here; *good* Western medicine is a rare thing there. You would be a godsend."

"And what about the gentlemen?" Amelia asked, dimpling.

Why, when she's animated, her whole face just comes to life! She'll never be pretty, but she's not going to turn into a dull lump of dough, either, as she gets older.

"I'm not sure what to say," Maya began hesitantly. "I can tell you that many quite eligible Eurasian gentlemen would pay you honorable court. For that matter, so would many eligible British officers and officials, though you might have to sift through quite a few toads to find the frog prince that will *allow* his wife to be herself." She paused, tapping one finger on her cheek, thinking, as Amelia cast her eyes upward at that last phrase.

Amelia persisted. "Anxious mommas have been sending spinster daughters out to India for decades to look for husbands, haven't they? And they do seem to find them there." She sighed and regarded her cup of tea pensively. "Today, at the Fleet, Doctor Stevens said that I have a real gift for handling babies and children and asked if I would mind being put on that duty on a permanent basis. I said yes, of course, that I'd enjoy that; and that it's a shame and a sin that no one has ever worked out medicine *for* children, that there's no specialty in children's medicine."

"And Doctor Stevens said—?"

Amelia laughed. "You know she would agree with me! Especially after that row she got into with Browning, and him trying to claim children don't feel pain! So we agreed, and it started me thinking that I'd like to have some of my own." A wistful expression crept over Amelia's face. "But—find a husband who'd accept that I'm a doctor with duties equal to his? Not in London. Not in all of England, *I* would think. Perhaps in Canada or America, but if I'm going to go abroad, I'd rather be among people who speak an English I can understand."

Maya stirred her tea. "I really don't know if you could find a suitor who would accept that you are a doctor as well as his wife. India makes some men more flexible in their views, but it makes others more rigid. And you might find yourself alternately appalled and enraged by the way that native women are treated, even by their own men."

"I'm alternately appalled and enraged by the way British women are treated by their own men," Amelia replied crisply. "*Could* I set up a private practice there? Is there enough need for one?"

"You'd have paying patients enough," Maya admitted, and took a sip of tea. "The Army surgeons are for the most part completely unsuited to treating women, and the military wives and daughters would be glad enough for a lady to confide in. There are high-caste women who *cannot* see a male physician by law and custom, though their lords and husbands are enlightened enough to value Western medicine, and those would pay you well indeed."

"Hmm. Pay we certainly don't find here, do we? Well, all but you, that is, and there aren't too many of us bold enough to take your course." Amelia tilted her head to the side. "Speaking of which, how is your practice?"

"I believe I'm seeing every dancer, actress, and singer within walking distance of this office," Maya told her, not troubling to conceal her amusement. "Not to mention that I'm starting to attend to the kept women and mistresses of—I presume—our lawyers, brokers, and merchants." She said it without a blush. Amelia giggled, but her cheeks were red. "It probably won't surprise you to know that I am introducing them all to the benefits of . . . hmm . . . limited births."

"Good," Amelia said with emphasis. "It will trickle down to their servants, and from there into the street. If I see one more woman at the Fleet with nothing more wrong with her than being worn to death with birth after birth—"

She snapped her mouth shut, but at Maya's nod of agreement, relaxed. "You should know that I share your opinion, dear," Maya said quietly. "Even though we've never discussed it before at length, I'm sure you've noticed that I make a point to educate my female patients at the Fleet—" She paused, and sighed. "The trouble is, of course, that *begetting* children costs nothing, but *preventing* them doesn't."

"Sadly true." Amelia echoed her sigh, then took another scone, with an air of changing the subject. "So why did *you* leave India? I can tell that you are homesick, more often than not, and what you've told me about needing lady doctors there goes for you as much as for me. And look at what you've done here! It's India in miniature, surely."

Maya bent to add more tea and sugar to her cup, and gave Charan a second biscuit. "Not quite. The native ladies won't see me, at least not the high-caste ones; I'm half-caste, and they are as prejudiced against my mixed blood as any bigot here."

"And being treated by our Colonial *ladies* as something a little below the invisible fellow who swings the *punkah*-fan rather than as a doctor would not be to my taste either," Amelia filled in, with a grimace of distaste, and Maya nodded, pleased at her quick understanding.

"It wasn't so bad when my parents were alive, but when I was alone, it got rather worse. My mother died in a cholera epidemic, despite all we could do for her, my father and I," she said slowly. *Was there something more to that than just a virulent disease?* she wondered, as Amelia expressed her sympathies. *Father never con-*

sidered that—but Father didn't believe in magic either. And when Mother wasn't there to protect us anymore. . . .

Surya had made enemies when she wedded a white man. There were as many Indians who felt she had committed the greatest and most heinous sin by marrying out of her race and caste as there were English who felt the same. More, actually—and at least one of them was a magician with powers equal to Surya's; a magician who wasn't averse to using those powers to take revenge on Surya, the man who had married her, and the daughter they had produced.

"My father didn't live long after she died," Maya continued, tight-lipped. "He was bitten by a snake. In our own bungalow."

Amelia's cup clattered in her saucer, and she hastily put it down on the tea trolley. Her eyes were wide, and she extended her hand to Maya in automatic sympathy. "Oh, Maya! Dear Lord—I cannot imagine—were you there? Was it a cobra?"

Maya shook her head. "He might have survived a cobra bite; this was a krait, a tiny little thing, no bigger than this." She held her hands out, about a foot apart. "They are far, far deadlier than the largest cobra. It was in his boot; he was dead in minutes. Some people said that Mother's death had affected him so badly that he forgot to take ordinary precautions—"

But I'm sure, sure, *that he would never have forgotten to shake out his boots. Never. And Sia and Singhe would never have missed a snake in the bungalow, unless some magic had been worked to keep them from scenting it.* Surya had tried to warn her daughter in her last hours, but by then she had been so delirious with fever that all she could manage was disjointed phrases. "Shivani," was the only name that Maya had recognized; Surya had been terrified of "the serpent's shadow," and that alone should have warned Maya to beware of snakes. But she had been prostrate with grief, and thinking not at all.

That had been no ordinary krait that killed her father, Maya was certain of it; that was when she had known she had to escape if she wanted to live. And despite her grief, her loss, she *did* want to live!

"Oh, Maya—I can see why you would want to leave. I am so sorry." Amelia reached for Maya's hands, and Maya reached to take hers, taking comfort from the younger woman's sympathy, even though she could not possibly understand the greater part of what had driven Maya here. "You *have* friends here, you know, and we'll try to keep you from being too lonely."

Maya held tightly to her friend's hands, glad beyond telling for the warmth of genuine friendship offered. "If you weren't my friend, Amelia, I would find this place desolate indeed," she said warmly, and was rewarded by Amelia's smile. "Thank you."

"Thank *you,* my dear," Amelia replied, and chuckled. "In all candor, I'm afraid you're sometimes going to think that my friendship is purely selfish. If you had never come here, I would never have been invited to a little paradise like this, and be treated to enough warmth that I can close my eyes and think I'm in a midsummer garden. Sometimes I think that spring will never come!"

"And I feel the same," Maya replied ruefully. "I cannot believe that spring is anything more than rain and leafless trees!"

"Oh, it's well worth the wait, thank goodness, or we English would go mad," Amelia laughed. "If you can get away for a weekend, I'll take you into the country once spring is properly here, and you'll see. We'll even take the train to Oxford, hire bicycles, try our hands in a punt, and go scandalize the male dons! What do you think?"

"I'll look forward to *that,*" Maya said, meaning every word, and from there the discussion diverted to Amelia's fellow medical students at the London School of Medicine for Women, then to the teachers. Amelia had a knack for mimicry that was the equal to a monkey or a parrot, and she had Maya in stitches before too long.

When she left, Maya was sorry to see her go, but Amelia needed to get back to her lodgings before dark, and Maya kept early evening office hours, since most of the women of her practice were never awake before noon.

Tonight she saw three women. One was a music-hall dancer, suffering from the usual foot and knee complaints, and terrified that she would lose her job if she couldn't perform. She had come straight from the theater, hoping against hope to have a cure before the curtain came up. Her friends had clubbed their pennies together for a cab because she couldn't walk the distance. She looked completely out of place in her short, frilled, scarlet dancing dress with a froth of cheap petticoats, bodice covered in cheap spangles and tinsel, her hair done up on her head and crowned with three faded ostrich plumes that had seen better days.

"It's that Frenchy can-can, Miss Doctor," the girl said, her face pasty beneath the makeup she wore, as Maya gently manipulated the swollen knee. Beneath the makeup she was also dowdy, to put it bluntly. Ordinary face, ordinary talent, but extraordinary legs. Her legs were what she'd been hired for; if they failed her—Maya didn't have to guess the rest. "It's thrown me knee out, it has, and me ankles hurt so—"

"I quite understand, dear," Maya soothed. "Now, you're making your muscles all tense, and that's making it hard for me to help. Can you sit back and relax for me?" She looked up at the pale round of a face with two red patches on the cheeks, and the eyes hidden in smudges of charcoal. "I think I can fix this for you, if you'll just relax."

"No knives, no operatin' then? You can fix it now?" There was hope there. "I saw a doctor at a clinic when it started gettin' sore, an' he said there oughta be an operation, so I left an' tried t' work it off."

The other doctor was probably looking for a poor little fool to experiment on, Maya thought bitterly. There *were* surgeons and doctors of that sort, perfectly willing to work at charity clinics just so they could find people who wouldn't complain if they were used to try out some new apparatus or theory.

"No, dear. Your knee just got a bit out of joint—not quite dislocated, but enough so you'd be in pain," Maya replied. A lie, of course; the ligaments were torn, but she could fix that. "Then your poor ankles weren't quite up to taking on the extra load, you see. The more it hurt, the more you threw yourself off balance, and that just made things worse. Like trying to put out a fire by throwing paraffin oil on it."

Satisfied with the explanation, the girl leaned back in the comfortable easy chair Maya had placed in the examination room, and Maya called on her magic.

This she could do, had been able to do from the time she could toddle, with no need of tutelage from Surya. Healing came as naturally to Maya as breathing. With her hands making slow, soothing massaging motions on the girl's knee, she reached down, down, deep into the native, living earth and rock beneath the pavements of the city, deep into the heart of her own little jungle, and up into the life force of the city itself. Where there was life, there was power, and that power could be channeled into healing. It poured generously into her, glowing emerald, sparkling topaz, golden brown and warm, bringing with it the taste of cinnamon and honey in the back of her mouth.

She gathered all of it into herself, the golds, yellows, and velvety browns of the earth-energy, the peridot and leaf-green and turquoise life-energy; she brought it in through her navel and transmuted it into the ever-verdant emerald green of healing, sending it out in a steady stream through her hands.

"Cor—that feels good, that does," the girl murmured, in a note of surprise. "Feels warm!"

"That's because I'm getting the blood to flow properly around your knee," Maya told her. "This is quite a new treatment—German, you know."

"Oh, *German,*" the child repeated, as if that explained everything. "Them Germans, they got all the tricks, don't they, then?"

Maya laughed, a low and rich chuckle. "So they think." She continued to pour healing into the knee, mending the tears invisibly, without scarring, and leaving enough residual energy that the ligaments could continue to strengthen themselves. The girl was going to need strong knees if she was going to dance the can-can. She moved down to the ankle, which fortunately suffered only from strain; she pulled out inflammation and pain, leaving ease in her wake. Simple magic, simply done, but satisfying. When she stood up, the girl got up carefully out of the chair, and her eyes widened as she tested her knee and found it strong and supple again, then rose on her toes and did an experimental kick over Maya's head. Maya had been expecting this, and didn't duck.

"Blimey! It's better!" she blurted, and flushed with pleasure.

"And mind you don't skimp on your exercises from now on, nor on your warm-ups," Maya replied, as the girl fumbled in her worn velvet reticule and pressed her five-shilling fee into Maya's hand. "That's what got you into this trouble, you said so yourself. Does a fiddler mistreat his fiddle? He keeps it warm and safe; he doesn't play it in the rain, nor ask too much of it until it's been limbered and ready. Those legs are your instrument, my girl. Treat them right, and they'll put bread in your mouth for a long, long time. Don't be tempted to show off your kicks until you've warmed up your muscles and stretched them out."

"Garn—" the girl shook her head. "Th' rest of 'em said you 'ad a way of puttin' things. Me mam allus said the legs was the last thing t' go. Dance th' can-can, an' they ain't lookin' none at yer face."

"Exactly. In fact, I've heard that the greatest star of the can-can in Paris is a hideous old washerwoman with a face like a flat-iron—but she has the best legs in all of France, and they throw money at her feet when she dances." Maya held the door of the examining room open for her, and the dancer frisked out with a laugh.

"Thank'ee, Miss Doctor!" the girl said gratefully, with a touch of the pertness that probably made her look prettier on stage than she really was. "If I walk at a good clip, I can make the theater in time for curtain *and* get me legs warmed up!"

"You're very welcome." Maya looked at the benches in the hall as the girl skipped out the door. There was one patient waiting, a woman who seemed a little shabbier than her usual run, and was coughing. The brown dress had once been fine velvet, but now was so rubbed that there was scarcely anything left of the pile anywhere, and it didn't look to have been cleaned or brushed in months. The girl had a new silk kerchief around her neck, her hair put up inexpertly beneath a bonnet that was liberally trimmed with motheaten feathers and stained rosettes of ribbon. She looked to be a little younger than the dancer who had just left; sixteen or seventeen, but older than her years.

Much older. Those eyes have seen more than anyone should see in a lifetime.

"Yes?" Maya said as the girl looked up, with a peculiar expression of mingled hope and fear of rejection on her face. "I take it that you are waiting to see me?"

"Oi carn't pay ye," the girl said flatly.

"You can, but not necessarily in money," Maya replied—and at the girl's look of alarm, she shook her head. "No, not like that, not what you're thinking. Come into the examining room and tell me what's wrong, and we'll see what we can do about it."

Slowly, reluctantly, the girl rose. Just as slowly, she sidled into the office, then into the examination room when Maya directed her to go onward. She looked about her with the wariness of a cornered animal, and was only a little less alarmed when Maya motioned to her to take a seat on the chair rather than the table.

She's not a whore—or not just *a whore. She's a pickpocket, I think,* Maya decided, sizing up her patient. She'd been expecting someone on the wrong side of the law to turn up sooner or later, but to have it be a female was beyond her hopes or expectations. This was going to present an excellent opportunity for a number of possibilities.

Maya remained standing. "The trouble is not your cough, I think," she said, crossing her arms over her chest and regarding the girl, who looked ready to bolt at any moment. "A good ruse to get past Gupta, but I believe you've come for another reason entirely."

The thief's eyes widened with surprise, then she shook her head. "Oi 'eard—ye know ways."

"Ways?" Maya thought she knew what the girl meant, but intended to find out for certain.

"Ways—not t' 'ave babies." The girl shuffled her feet and looked at the tips of her worn, cracked boots, then looked up at Maya defiantly. "Oi 'eard from someun' at th' Odeon."

Maya nodded. "I do. Some are more certain than others. Some

will cost you money, not for me, but for what you need to prevent a baby. So, that's what you want, then? Can you read?"

Again the girl nodded, almost defiantly. "Oi kin read, but wot's that got t' do wi' it?"

"Because I'm going to give you one of each of these." Maya went to the cupboard, and being careful to block what she was doing from the girl, opened a concealed panel and took out a pair of small, printed booklets from a stack of several like them. Possession of these booklets, which had been judged "obscene and pornographic" by men who should have been ashamed of themselves for making such a judgment, could have gotten her in a world of trouble. Distributing them, even more so.

Even though any man *can walk into his club with a copy of* The Lustful Turk *or* Fanny Hill *under his arm and no one would so much as blink an eye,* she thought resentfully. *And he can show his Japanese pillow book or illustrated* Kama Sutra *to select friends over brandy and cigars and be congratulated on his acquisition and refined tastes. But Anna Besant's* The Law of Population *and Dr. Allison's* Book for Married Women *are obscene, and cannot be permitted.*

Of course, as a lady, she wasn't supposed to know about those erotic books the men so enjoyed at their liberty at all, much less the titles of them. She *certainly* wasn't supposed to know about the two "bibles" of contraception. *Nor are their wives and sisters, and oh, the storm in the parlor if they ever learned how many copies are locked up in dressing-table drawers!*

"Here," she said, handing the girl the pamphlets; the patient looked at it dubiously, since the title of the first one, concerning itself with population, didn't seem to have anything to do with "not having babies."

"This will refresh your memory after you've left the office," Maya promised her. "There is so much information in these little books that no one could remember it all after one hearing. Now, this is basically what's in those pages."

She spent the next half hour giving the girl a detailed lecture on all of the varieties of conception prevention outlined in the famous "obscene" pamphlets, plus a couple more she herself knew about from India. At first, the girl seemed taken aback by her brutal frankness and uncompromising language, but she soon got over her shock. A time or two she shook her head as though objecting to what Maya told her—something Maya wasn't particularly surprised at, since some of the means she had described were probably out of the girl's hands or beyond her pocketbook. Unlikely that she would get the cooperation of her partner, for instance.

But when she finished, just as the clock struck ten, the girl looked satisfied, but still wary. "Wot's the proice?" she asked bluntly.

"There're two parts to the bargain. The first is to share what you've learned," Maya replied, just as bluntly. "Share it with the other girls working the streets, whether they're your friends or just the girlfriends of your man's friends. Share it with any other woman that will listen to you, washerwomen, seamstresses, factory girls—*anyone.* That, or tell them they can learn the same things here or at the Fleet Street Clinic, either from me, or from a lady named Amelia Drew."

"A' roight," the girl said. "Wot's the rest?"

"Pass the word that this place isn't to be robbed." Maya smiled thinly at the girl's start of surprise. "Don't think for a moment that I didn't know that was part of the reason you came here. Tell your friends that it's no use. My father was in the Army; I have a pistol. He taught me how to shoot it as soon as I could hold it. I've killed a tiger and dozens of cobras. It would be no challenge to shoot a thief. What's more, I'll make a point to shoot out the legs of any intruder, then call the police to deal with them."

The girl's eyes kept widening. This was clearly not what she had expected.

"If I don't happen to be here, I have two menservants with me here who used to be Gurkhas, and they have no compunction about slitting English throats." A lie on both counts, but one Indian looked like another to most Englishmen, and the Gurkhas had a fearsome reputation that reached even the illiterate and impoverished. Maya took a step nearer, towering over the girl. "In fact, I think they might enjoy it. Now, is that a fair bargain for what you've gotten tonight?"

She stuck out her hand. The girl looked at it dubiously, swallowed hard, then rubbed her own grubby palm over the equally grubby fabric of her dress and shook it solemnly. "Yes'm," she said slowly. "Cor, but yer a 'ard 'un!"

"I had to be; I still have to be," Maya replied, preferring that the girl use her own imagination to figure how Maya got to be so "hard."

"Reckon there's a chance Oi'll get some kicks an' curses from me man an' his mates, but fair's fair," the girl continued, then shivered. "There's stories about them 'Indoo 'eathen, an' once they settle, 'spect they'll see it moi way. How'd ye know Oi was on the ketchin' lay?"

"Silk kerchief," Maya said, and got a wince in return. "One more thing. This isn't a charity clinic, and I don't have to answer to anyone in a dog collar for what I do. I don't ask if people are *deserving* before I treat them."

The girl flashed her a conspiratorial look. " 'Appen some'un shows up on the step some noight?" she suggested coyly.

"Any woman, but only men who are sick, not drunk," Maya said adamantly. "If they're wounded, I'll see them only if it's something that won't involve the police. If I lose my licenses, I can't help anyone. It's *my* clinic, and I can make the rules here."

The girl took the words philosophically. " 'Appen we're nearer the Fleet, anyroad, an' they ain't too curious there," she replied, and stood up, the pamphlets vanishing somewhere inside her shawls. Maya noticed that her cough had vanished, too. It had probably been part of her habitual disguise, intended to garner sympathy while at the same time discouraging too close contact. "Thenkee," she said, as Maya opened the outer door for her. "Oi'll keep my side uv this."

Maya saw her out, then closed and locked the front door for the night, leaning her back against it as she exhaled a sigh. *Well! From Amelia to a cutpurse, I've had quite an assortment tonight.*

There might still be calls tonight, but those would be emergencies; at this point she was probably free for the evening. With an effort, she pushed her hands against the door and levered herself up. The garden would be the best place to settle her mind before she went on her nightly round before bed.

Charan might have been waiting for her to appear, and Sia and Singhe as well; they all ran to her, Charan springing up onto her shoulder and the mongooses winding around her ankles until she settled into her favorite chair. Sia and Singhe coiled around her feet, pinning her to the spot, while Charan dropped down off her shoulder into her lap, chittering up into her face.

"You don't say?" she responded indulgently, as if she were having a conversation with the little monkey. "Well, I'm glad you approve of my handling of the situation."

Charan shoved his head under her hand to be scratched. Obedient to his wishes, she obliged him. He was the most fastidious monkey she had ever seen; most of his tribe were filthy little wretches, but Charan was cleanly to a fault, bathing every day in the pool, and depositing his droppings in the same box of sand that the mongooses used. She had never seen so much as a single flea on any of them, which was nothing short of astonishing.

What were you to Mother? she wondered, not for the first time. *You were more than mere pets, that much I know, but what?* Charan looked up at her as if hearing her thoughts, and chittered softly.

She gathered him closely, like a child, and he nestled into her arms. Surya had had so many secrets, but surely she could have divulged this one.

Maya stared into the shadows, compulsively searching for a slim, slithering one, a shadow that slipped from shade to shade. *Blood of your blood, Mother. Why couldn't you have trusted me? I might have been able to protect Father, if only you had trusted me. . . .*

Two hot tears ran down her cheeks, and dropped into Charan's fur.

But perhaps not. Maybe everyone was right, that her father had been so distraught by her mother's death that he had been careless.

Maybe he wanted to die. That was something she hadn't wanted to consider, but it was an inescapable thought. And an uncomfortable one—not just that he had wanted to die, but that he had not loved her, his own daughter, enough to live.

Bitter, bitter—too bitter to contemplate for long. And *not* like the brave, stubborn man she had known all her life.

And I—I am just as stubborn as both of them put together. He left the family to me, as she left her pets, and I swear I will protect them both.

And with that determined thought, she set her chin, disentangled herself from mongooses and monkey, and went on her nightly rounds to bolster those protections that, she hoped, would keep them all safe.

THE Thames flowed sluggishly between the tides, making scarcely a sound against the jetties. Errant reflections from lanterns on the prows of scavenger boats out searching for treasure among the floating garbage showed that one quasilegal form of trade was active on the river tonight, and the curses of mud larks along the bank as they slipped and slid in noisome detritus left by the tide at least gave some sign of life near at hand. Peter Scott shivered and pulled his collar closer around his neck, then bound his muffler just a bit more snugly. Oily water lapped at the piers beneath the Thames-side dock beneath his boots, and a hint of damp in the air promised fog before morning. Peter Scott felt it in his knee, and looked forward to getting home to his cozy flat, his sea-coal fire, and the hot supper his landlady and housekeeper would have waiting for him.

Before he could do that, however, he still had to check the inventory of goods just arrived at the warehouse against the bill of lading. He could have left it to a clerk, but he hadn't gotten this far in his infant importation business by leaving critical things to a clerk, who had no personal stake in making certain everything was right and tight.

It was Egypt that was all the rage for decorations now, where it had been India when he'd first made his transition from ship's captain to tradesman. Egyptian gewgaws, thanks to old Petrie and Harold Carter; that was where the trade was, though Peter didn't import the real thing—*real* grave goods, or statues, or carvings, much less mummies.

No magician would, not if he wanted to stay sane. God help me, I can't even imagine what one of those blasted mummy-unwrapping parties must be like. Hate and resentment thick as a pea souper, and only the ancient gods know what curses are lurking in those wrappings along with the dust and the amulets. It's a wonder every guest at one of those cursed affairs doesn't get run over by a lorry, after.

But there were artists over there in Cairo and farther up the Nile that made a handsome living faking artifacts. Peter didn't sell what he bought as the genuine article; he sold it as *better* than genuine. His shop held some gorgeous work, he'd give those old fakers that much, and it sold and it sold, even if it didn't quite command the price of the real thing. Striking stuff. He was happy enough with it to have a few of the finer pieces displayed in the odd corners of his own flat.

His advertisements in the *Times* every Sunday brought in the scores of middle-class ladies anxious to ape their betters by having a bit of old Egypt in the parlor. "The masterpieces of artists who count the Pharaohs in their ancestry"—"Perfect in every detail, just as the mighty Ramses would have cherished"—"Each piece requiring months of painstaking labor, made of the finest materials, perfect in every detail"—it was the business of the salesman to sell the sizzle, not the steak, and Peter thought himself a dab hand at making the sizzle as good as the cut it came from.

Besides, these fellows probably do have the blood of the Pharaohs somewhere in their past, the pieces are exactly what the grave goods looked like when they were new, and if it didn't take my men months to produce 'em, at least they put their hearts into it. He had a grudging liking for the counterfeiters, and a genuine respect for the perfection of their copies.

Peter had gotten the help of a couple of good Egyptologists to help him track down some of the best of the counterfeiters, and hired the ones whose hearts were breaking because they had to deface or discolor their handiwork to make it look genuine. *They* were happy, *he* was happy, and what was more, the people who were buying his stuff were happier, on the whole, than those who bought what they thought was genuine.

Because the poor idiots buying what they think is the real thing can't ever be sure it is genuine, not when they're paying cheap prices for it. For that matter, they can't be sure when they've paid a small fortune for it. He had even, once or twice, had an ermine-wrapped social lion come slipping in on the sly, having gotten the chills from some of the real stuff, and not wanting it about the house. Borderline sensitive, they were, and he was all sympathy with 'em, poor things. *They* had to have something to stay current with fashion, but couldn't bear the presence of anything tomb-touched.

And I have the solution right there in my display room. They would choose one piece or several, and he would give them what they needed to make it look genuine. He'd make a couple of inconsequential chips in places, write up as nice a forged article of "genuine provenance" as ever you saw, charge the client the same price as for one of his fakes, and promise not to breathe a word to anyone about it. What harm was there in that? The lady's status-climbing spouse would be happy he had something to show to the lads in the curio cabinet, and *she* wouldn't be getting so many nightmares she'd be taking to the laudanum every night.

He was toying with the notion of having his men try their hands at making articles of modern use in the ancient fashion. Umbrella stands, perhaps? Writing-desk accessories? Articles for a lady's dressing table? That might be exactly the right direction to go in; a lady would never use an artifact on her dressing table when she never knew what it originally contained, but she could surround herself with alabaster hair receivers, faience cologne bottles, carved unguent jars and powder boxes from his works, happy in the knowledge that she was the first and only user, with no long-dead Egyptian princess coming to stare back at her with long, slanted eyes in her vanity mirror.

As he lifted vases and *ushabtis* from their packing crates, he marveled, as he always did, at the craftsmanship. These men took real pride in their work, and it showed. The alabaster of a replica oil lamp glowed in the light from his lantern, so thin was the stone of the lotus blossoms on their curving stems. And the tender expression on a goddess meant to protect one corner of a sarcophagus brought an answering smile to his lips; a sad smile, for he knew what the original had looked like, and who it had been for—and that all four of the sheltering goddesses had borne the lovely face of the dead Pharaoh's grief-stricken wife.

Oh, poor little Anksenamun, no more than a girl, and not only weighed down with grief but in fear for your own life. Wonder whatever became of you? Did you just fade away in mourning? Did you fly to safety somewhere? Or did you die at the hands of ambition and greed? Well, you died, soon or late, a thousand years and more ago. May your gods keep you and your Tut together forever.

Beautiful. And all of it free from the taint of the tomb, of the faint miasma of the rage of an impotent former owner. He often wondered how *anyone* could bear to have genuine artifacts anywhere near where they lived and slept.

I certainly couldn't. I'd wake up with terrors three times a night.

The scent of Egypt and warmth came up from the excelsior along with the artworks: dust and heat; incense mingled with dung; a hint of lotus. By the time he finished with his inventory, for once finding nothing missing, broken, used as a container to smuggle opium or hashish, or otherwise amiss, he was tired and the ache in his knee gnawed at the edges of his temper. He was glad enough to replace the last figure in its bed of excelsior and close the lid on the packing case. A cozy coal fire was sounding better by the moment.

Roast beef and 'taters, and good mushy peas. That's what will get me warmed inside and out. Bit of trifle, or pudding, or maybe treacle tart.

"Night, Cap'n," the night watchman saluted from his stool beside the door, as Peter left the warehouse. Peter hadn't been "Captain" Scott for a good six years and more, but the grizzled and weather-beaten night watchman had been one of his old hands, and habits died hard.

"Good night, Jeremiah," he replied, with a return salute. "Fog by morning."

"And hard luck to them on the water," Jeremiah said with sympathy. "Or off it. Keep an eye to your back on your way home. Fog's a blessin' t' them as is no better'n they should be, so mind ye take care."

"That I will," Peter assured him, and limped out onto the dock, listening to the water lick at the wooden pilings. But something in the sound of the water stopped him, just beyond the night watchman's line of sight. He listened again. Someone swam, gently and quietly, just beneath the pier. Just beneath *him,* following where he went, sending up a thin, telltale touch of magic to alert him, thin as fog, insubstantial, tasting of water weeds, a gleaming, furtive, and fugitive ribbon of palest green.

And he stifled a groan. *Not tonight. Not a messenger tonight. Oh, bloody hell.*

He walked to the edge of the dock, and looked down. A translucent, faintly glowing, narrow female face looked up at him from the water, surrounded by the tangle of her seaweed hair. The naiad scowled; they didn't like the filthy water of the Thames inside the London basin, and Peter didn't blame them. He wouldn't have taken a swim in that filthy stuff for a king's ransom.

"The Council summons, Water Master," the naiad told him, her voice the hiss of foam on the sand, the hollow gurgle of wavelets in the rocks. Then, her message discharged, she dove under the surface and vanished, heading for cleaner water as fast as she could swim.

Peter cursed under his breath. *"The Council summons," indeed.* He was the only member of the Council that was a middle-class, regular working man; the rest were moneyed. Some were "professional" fellows, doctors or lawyers or stockbrokers; some were titled or had other forms of inherited wealth. None of them were tradesmen. *They* didn't have to be up at dawn to mind the store. *They* wouldn't have to somehow find a bloody cabby at dockside, and *they* wouldn't have to find another way to go home in the cursed fog! Oh, granted, Scott could use a beckoning finger of magic to lure a cabby in, but it would still take doing, and waiting!

But do they ever "summon" me when it comes time for a nice dinner party, or a bit of an entertainment? he thought sourly. *Oh, no. I'm the most popular bloke on the Council when there's something to be done at a savage hour, though. Gawd Almighty, old Kipling's got it dead right. "Tommy this and Tommy that an' Tommy go away, but it's 'thenkee Mister Atkins' when the guns begin t' play."* He wasn't sure he had the quote dead right, but the sense of it certainly seemed to ring home tonight, in the cold and fog.

It crossed his mind, as it did every time he was called unexpectedly by the Council of Masters, to go directly home and tell them that their bloody Council could go straight to hell for all he cared. But the problem was that the Council was useful; without them, there would be open warfare between Elemental Masters and no doubt of it. And they did *good* work; the White Lodge had put down a couple of nasty bits of work, even if they couldn't do much about blatant idiots like Aleister-damn-his-eyes-Crowley. He couldn't quit, not in good conscience. Not while there was evil crawling around that no purging of the sewers was going to get rid of, and not while some arrogant, damned Elemental Masters thought the way to settle a quarrel was to ruin decent, normal folks' lives with floods, earthquakes, storms, and conflagrations.

So, still cursing under his breath, Peter Scott spun up his green-tinged summons, then limped off in search of a cabby brave enough to dare the docks after dark.

The meeting place was always the same; the Exeter Club, and if anyone happened to stumble in to see the poor old codgers dozing away in their chairs or pretending to read the *Times,* he'd assume it was just another backwater of retired Colonials. The codgers were a ruse, more than half of them the pensioned-off bachelor upper servants of the real members, kept in happy and comfortable retirement here to keep the work of their former masters as secret as anything you'd find at the Foreign Office. More so, actually. At the Foreign Office, you didn't have to worry about a salamander whipping down the nearest chimney to have a listen-in.

Peter limped up the stairs to be greeted by the night porter, who allowed his usual stony expression to slip just enough to display a hint of sympathy for the dodgy knee. Clive had one of his own, courtesy of the Boer War; they exchanged a wordless wince of mutual pain, and Clive took his coat, muffler, and hat. "They are in the Red Room, sir," the old soldier said, with a nod in the correct direction. "In view of the hour, I believe they've bespoken you some refreshment." *Of course, their idea of refreshment is usually purely alcoholic,* he thought with continued irritation. Still. It showed *some* consideration. He strode past the Club Room, even at this hour full of drowsing ancient men looking like Methuselah's grandpa, or slightly younger ones exchanging lies over pipes and port, and headed straight for the Red Room.

At least if it's the Red Room, it's not an all-out mage war, or some fool gone mad and trying to burn down London. If it had been something really, truly, serious, the Council would be in the War Room, not the Red Room, robed and begemmed to the teeth and staves or swords in hand.

The door opened just as he reached it, and to his relief, the fellow with his hand on the knob was Lord Peter Almsley, second son and—until his brother George came up to the paddock and produced a son—titular heir to the Almsley lands, estate, and strawberry leaves. Lord Peter stood on ceremony with no one, and was one of the few members of the Council and the Lodge that Peter Scott thought of as an actual friend.

"Get in here, Twin," Peter exclaimed—his own private joke, since they were both named Peter and both Water Masters. "You look fagged to death. I've ordered you up a rarebit; it's on a chafing dish and I've been guarding it with my life till you got here. Bunny keeps trying to bag some for himself." Lord Peter could not have looked less like Peter Scott; he had that thin, nervy, washed-out blondness and general air of idiot-about-town that Scott tended to associate with a bit too much inbreeding within the Royal Enclosure, but he was as sound as an oak inside, and tough whipcord came when it came down to cases. Scott had seen Lord Peter face down an ancient god without turning a hair, and knew for a fact there were at least nine ghosts haunting the old Almsley estate, all of whom Lord Peter had met and even conversed with. Lord Peter never said what the rest of his family (other than his grandmother) thought about the haunts, but he, at least, considered them to be personal friends.

With a hearty clap of his hand to Lord Peter's shoulder by way of thanks, Scott entered the Red Room—which was—red. Very, very red. Red brocade on the windows, red-silk wallpaper, red-leather chairs. It *must* have been decorated by a Fire Master, and it always made Peter want to throw buckets of blue or green paint over everything.

But the enticing aroma of hot cheese coming from the chafing dish on the sideboard was enough to make him overlook the decorating deficiencies for once. He ignored the rest of the Council and went straight for the bubbling rarebit, scooping up a plate, loading it liberally with toast from the rack beside the dish, and inundating the crisp triangles with cheese until there was danger of the plate overflowing. Only then did he take his place in the single empty seat around the table—and privately nominated Lord Peter for beatification when the man shoved a tall glass of stout silently toward him.

"Listen, Scott," began Dumbarton, one of the old lads who'd inherited a pile and made it bigger in the Exchange. "Apologies and all that—knew you were working—but there's something come up."

Peter made certain to demolish a satisfyingly hearty triangle of toast and cheese before replying. "Well, there always is, isn't there? What is it that the Council can't sort out over dinner without calling me in?"

Someone coughed. Owlswick, of course. Lord Owlswick, who never *left* the Club except for hunting season. "Well, ah—it's magic, Scott, don't you know. Earth Magic. New source of it, in the bottom of the garden, so to speak. And we're none of us . . . ah . . . Earth Masters."

Peter did not make the obvious retort that neither was he—nor that they *would* have more than half a dozen Earth Masters on the Council if they'd just give up their Old Boys nonsense and allow a few farm lads, a Scot or two, or, for God's own sake, a few of the *female* Earth Masters just west of London into their exclusive little enclave.

Old argument, and his silence said it all for him. It was Lord Peter who took pity on the rest and kept the ensuing silence from turning into an embarrassment. "The trouble is, old man, it's got bloody strong potential, but it's not *our* Earth Magic. Nothing remotely like our traditions. And we can't—well—trace it, locate it."

That got his attention, and he stopped with his fork halfway to his mouth. "You—what? You're having me on, right?"

Lord Peter shook his head. " 'Fraid not, old fellow. Wish I was. We get it narrowed down to a district, then—that's as far as we get. It's as if whoever is *doing* this has something going meant entirely to confuse and confusticate."

"And *that,*" rumbled old Lord Alderscroft, the head of the Council, at last, "is very interesting. Worrying. And we *damned* well want to know how it's done, especially if there's something more serious behind it."

Lord Alderscroft spoke in Council perhaps once a year, but when he did, even Peter lost his cynicism, sat up, and took notice. He was, perhaps, the most powerful Fire Master who had ever sat in the seat of the Master of the Council. Peter pushed away the last of his dinner, uneaten, and said respectfully, "What are my duties, sir?" He suspected that when Alderscroft spoke even the King stood humbly and waited for orders.

The great man moved forward, out of the shadows of his wingback chair, bringing his face into the light. It was the face of an old lion, old, but without one whit of his power diminished in any way; eyes that saw through to the soul, weighed it and measured the worth and strength of it, yet somehow made no judgment of it. His hair was longer than was fashionable; no one would ever have even *thought* of him with other than that half-tamed, gray-and-fawn mane around his face. Power under will, will under the law, tempered with compassion, endless tolerance and patience, and a clear and unflinching knowledge of the best and the worst in his fellow man. *That* was Lord Alderscroft, and Peter would have gone through fire and brimstone and hell itself if the old man asked him to. They *all* would have, including the ineffectual Owlswick.

"We know the general district, Scott; it's down near Fleet, and we've mapped out where the confusion-magic ends, so the source is likely to be somewhere within it." Alderscroft motioned to Lord Peter, who passed over a map with a ragged ovoid drawn on it. And Scott immediately saw the difficulty.

"You'd all stand out there like horses in a hat shop, wouldn't you?" he said, now with a touch of humor. "By heaven, I believe you couldn't go five feet in that area without losing everything but the lining of your pockets!"

"Now you see our difficulty," Alderscroft said, with a grave nod. "Can you go in there—and perhaps find the source of this—even give us some notion of who the person is, and why this mage has come to this city?"

"I can try," Peter acknowledged. "Water's closest to Earth anyway; likely I can get close when none of the rest of you can, at least not you Air and Fire Masters. The little water sprites like to hang about Earth Magic, especially in gardens, so long as the water's clean. I might get some luck."

"I'll send Gannet over to your warehouse and get things shipshape at your shop," Lord Peter promised, with a winning smile, that made him look considerably less like a prime silly ass and more like the intelligent fellow he was. "You remember Gannet, don't you?"

Scott managed a smile of his own. "Your pet burglar, I believe?"

"*Reformed* burglar, reborn in the Lord, baptized most faithfully in the Blood of the Lamb, I will have you know," Lord Peter corrected. "Just remember, with him in charge, *nothing's* going to go missing, not so much as a farthing from petty cash. Or—" The smile was still there, but there was a hint of grim chill that reminded

Scott just how dangerous Lord Peter really *was*. "He'll be answering about it to *me*. And trust me, he'd *much* rather have to answer to the Lord God Almighty than to me."

Gannet showed up promptly at seven, giving Peter time enough to give him some basic directions before the crew from the warehouse started arriving. Gannet did not look like an ex-burglar; he looked like a slightly shabby and terribly earnest old watchmaker—until you looked at his hands, with the fingertips sanded to make them that little bit more sensitive to the turn of a combination lock, the click of a lock pick. Still, he seemed sound enough, and by eight, Peter was out on the street, preferring to walk rather than take a cab or the Underground to where he was going. He needed to adjust his attitude and appearance, and the only way he could do that, would be to gradually acquire his local color, like a chameleon. The deeper he went, from upper middle class to middle, to lower, then to genteel poverty, then to poverty that was nothing like genteel, the more his appearance changed. Without adding or subtracting from his wardrobe, his cap acquired a tilt that furtively shaded his eyes, his grip on his walking stick changed to that of the grip on a weapon, his shoulders slouched, his path took him nearer the wall, nearer the shadows, and his eyes got a sideways slant that marked him as a wary, and possibly dangerous, man. And difficult though it was to conceal, he lost the limp entirely.

He who walks among jackals dares show no weakness.

Slowly, for he did not dare take his attention too far from the real world, he insinuated his senses into the unreal world, the one so few ever knew was all around them, even here in London, where the pavement covered the tender, nourishing earth, the water was awash in poison, the fire smoked hideously, and the air carried nearly as much poison as the water.

It was a long walk, but he was used to walking. A ship captain walked hundreds of miles on the deck of his ship; he probably walked three times the actual distance of every voyage. He walked now to keep that bad knee strong; and a shopkeeper walked nearly as much as a ship captain.

He followed his instincts into the theater district and out again.

Hmm. Interesting. As he passed from ungenteel poverty back into genteel and adjusted his appearance accordingly, he sensed his quarry, neared it, then arrived practically on top of it.

Very interesting. It pulsed just beside him, shields and other undefinable things, and over all a shifting, an urge to look somewhere else, that he had to fight to keep his attention concentrated. Power, certainly. But . . . it had a curiously cobbled-together feeling. As if it was the sheer strength of it alone that kept its spells from falling to mismatched bits.

Curiouser and curiouser. He bought a paper from a passing boy, leaned against an entryway fence, and pretended to read.

Definitely not ours. It should *be, but it isn't.* The spells had a foreign flavor, an unfamiliar spice or savor—as if he'd been served up with Thai tea, cold and laden with sweetened cream, instead of the hot, lemony Ceylon he'd been expecting. It *was* the Earth Magic native to this island Logres, but it was not being *used* in the same way.

What in the bloody hell?

A policeman on his beat eyed him dubiously for a moment; Peter met his gaze, straight on, eye to eye, then gave him a friendly nod, waited a moment, and folded his paper, once again on his way.

There was that other thing going on, too—that "I'm not here," the touch of "go hunt elsewhere," the gentle but insistent push to *go away and look somewhere else* that the others had described. Definitely there, all right, but not of much use as a defense unless you were trying to scry from a distance. Once on the spot, ridiculously easy to get past. All he needed to do was find the place where the push to *not look* was the hardest, and he'd find the source.

It took some sauntering—cheerful sauntering was good in this neighborhood, though once in a while if he touched his cap to a lady he got an unmistakable invitation in return that he didn't have the time (or the wish, for that matter) to follow up on. Bobbies on the beat had a well-fed and fairly relaxed air about them, which meant that whatever went on around here, as long as it wasn't in the public street, or occasioning a scream for help, they reckoned it wasn't any of their business to interfere.

That was good for him, since they assumed he was either looking for something but wasn't going to make trouble when he found it (oddly enough, the actual truth), or he was out of work, but not so long out of work that he was out of temper as well. He circled the neighborhood like a shark following the scent of blood in the water, moving in a tighter and tighter spiral, until at long last he came to his real goal.

And when he found it, his source, the place from which the skewed and strangely sculpted magic emanated, he stared at it with a gape on his face like a country cousin at the British Museum.

Doctor M. Witherspoon, said the discreet brass plaque beside the door. *Physician and surgeon.*

He shuttered his expression quickly, and wandered a slight distance away for a moment, taking out his paper to distract the eyes of passersby again, and sending out his *own* peculiar magic callings.

And got yet another gob-smacking shock.

Yes, there were happy little water sprites within that wall of protection. And no, they were *not* coming out, thank you. It was *nice* here, and they weren't going to leave—or provide him with any information—without being forced.

Peter Scott had never forced a Water Elemental to do anything it didn't want to in his entire career as a Master, and he wasn't about to jeopardize his standing with them by doing so now. There were, after all, more mundane ways of getting at some of the information locked inside that shell of magical protection.

He suddenly developed a much more pronounced version of his limp, and staggered, leaning on his walking stick, to the white-painted doorway. He stood there just a moment, then reached out and rang the bell.

It was answered, with great alacrity, by a stony-visaged, gray-haired man arrayed in pristine white chalwars and tunic, who looked him up and down with the same disconcerting thoroughness that Lord Alderscroft had used.

Peter hastily removed his cap. "Knee went all wonky," he said with great earnestness. "The doctor free?"

The Indian gentleman gave him a second head-to-toe examination, then nodded, though grudgingly. "You may wait," he said, as if conferring the Victoria Cross, and motioned Peter inside.

There was only one other patient waiting on the benches lining the hall, a young woman with a distinctly worried expression wearing a very cheap imitation of a fashionable gown (taffeta instead of satin, and trimmed in ribbon already fraying), who kept twisting her handkerchief in her hand as if to wring it dry. Peter studiously ignored her, keeping his eyes on the floorboards, as the Guardian of the Door kept watch over them both. They were very clean floorboards, that much he saw. There was a faint astringent scent in the air, but no odor of sickness.

A moment later, one of the doors into the hall opened, and a woman with a baby in her arms emerged. There were signs on her face that she *had* been weeping, and her eyes were still red, but her face was wreathed in smiles. "God bless 'ee, Miss Doctor!" she whispered; to *whom* these words were addressed, Peter was left in doubt, for between the bulk of the lady herself and the shadows of the doorway, he could only make out an imperfect form.

"Never hesitate to bring her in again, Delia," said a low, pleasant voice. "I've got plenty of stockings and other things needing mending, and I'd be just as happy to barter your skills for mine. Just take her home, put her to bed, and come back for the mending when you've got someone to watch her. Gupta will have it for you."

The patient—or perhaps, more correctly, the patient's mother, bowed her head in a brief nod of relief and agreement, then the shadowed figure caught sight of the first patient as "Delia" hurried out the door that Gupta (Peter presumed the man was the "Gupta" previously mentioned) held open for her with a more polite bow than he had offered to Peter.

The girl sprang up off of the bench as soon as Delia had cleared the way, and the shadow exclaimed, “Oh, Sally, not *again!*”

Whereupon Sally burst into tears and fled into the inner sanctum, leaving Peter wondering just what sort of “not again” could be going on here. His imagination supplied him with plenty—and the likeliest, given the girl’s tawdry, cheap taffeta dress, rouged cheeks, and kohled eyes, gave him a moment of queasiness.

Good God.

However, before his first impulse to flee had managed to manifest itself, Sally reappeared, all smiles again. Whatever had been transacted within that surgery, it had not taken as long as—well, what he had feared would have taken. “Yer a bleedin’ saint, ye are,” the girl said as fervently as the mother had. “I gotter get back—”

“Off with you, before that blackguard manager docks you for not being at rehearsal,” replied the doctor, making a shooing motion and coming fully into the light. “And don’t forget that if I’m not here, I’m generally at the Fleet, and you can come to me there.”

This was Peter’s day for shock, it seemed. It was not merely enough that the Dr. M. Witherspoon was female—nor that she attended to women no *lady* would be seen associating with—nor yet that her Door Dragon was Hindu.

No, there was no doubt whatsoever in Captain Peter Scott’s mind, he who had made the voyage to and from Calcutta any number of times, that Doctor M. Witherspoon was, if not fully Indian herself, certainly of half blood.

He rose to his feet, drawn by the sheer force of her personality. Stunningly attractive, despite the severe black twill skirt and suit coat, with its plain black blouse buttoned up to the chin and what *must* be a luxuriant fall of raven hair tightly wound into a chignon atop her head without the tiniest strand awry, she would have made him stare at her anyway. Skin the color of well-creamed coffee, enormous eyes so brown they were nearly black, and the faintest hint of sandalwood perfume coming from her, she made it impossible, for a critical moment, to remember what it was he was supposed to be here about.

Which was, of course, his undoing. For he stood with his weight distributed equally on *both* legs, and had risen without a hint of a groan or the help of his stick.

She pierced him with those eyes, like an insect to be studied, and he felt a flush creeping up from his collar.

"Well," she said at last, "you certainly aren't having any difficulty with that leg *now,* are you?"

He swallowed, with some trouble. "No," he replied, in a very meek voice. "At least, no more than usual."

"Then shall we come into my office and discuss why you *really* came to see me?" she asked, her voice as icy as the wind off the North Sea. "Or would you prefer to leave now—bearing in mind that my patients have a number of very large, very inhospitable friends of their own, who would *not* care to see me or my practice inconvenienced?" He ducked his head, squared his shoulders, and followed her direction—into the mysteries of her office.

He was not entirely certain that he was going to come out. At least, not in the same state—mental or physical, he was not sure—in which he had gone in.

5

PETER sat—carefully—on the single chair facing the Doctor's desk, in a room that appeared to serve as study, initial consultation room, and office. The Doctor studied him, her expression as serene as a bronze Buddha, and just as unreadable. He decided to show a bit more spine than he had for the past few moments, and studied her as well. Neither of them broke the silence; only the usual street sounds filtered in through the glass of the window facing the street—footsteps, hoofbeats, voices, and the occasional cough and chatter of a motorcar.

One day all our hansoms are going to be replaced by those wretched autos, Peter reflected, as a particularly noisy vehicle chugged by, drowning every other noise as it did. *And on that day—perhaps I'll move to the Isle of Man, or of Wight, or the Scillys—or some place equally remote. God, how I hate those things!*

As he continued to gaze unabashedly at the doctor's face, taking in the nuances of her features, he became more and more certain that his first guess about her parentage was correct.

Eurasian, no doubt. With the surname "Witherspoon" there wasn't much doubt which parent was the English one; the only question was—how on *earth* had this woman, of mixed blood, managed to become a doctor? The task was difficult enough for an

English girl! Who had sponsored her and given her the necessary education? The London School of Medicine for Women?

No, that surely wasn't possible; she looked too young. She must have begun her studies in her teens, and the London School wouldn't take a girl that young.

I don't think that I would care to stand between her and something she dearly wants. I would probably find her walking over the top of me to get it.

The office revealed very little of the doctor's personality, other than the fact that she—or her servants—were fanatically neat. Bookcases lined the wall behind her except for a space where a door broke the expanse, bookcases polished until they gleamed and filled with leather-bound volumes. Her desk, spartan and plain, held only pen, pencil, paper in a neat stack, an inkpot, and a blotter. There was one small framed print on the wall behind him, but he didn't dare turn around to look at it, not with those black eyes fixed on him. Printed wallpaper might be Morris; he wasn't sure; it was warm brown, yellow, and cream, exactly the colors he'd expect from an Earth Mage.

Nothing on the desk to help—no pictures, no trinkets. And nothing with writing on it. So she was the kind who put her patients' records out of sight before they even left the office. A careful woman; a *wise* woman, given what she'd implied about her last client.

Ah, but what he sensed, now that he was *within* the enclosure of her protective magics, made him long for fifteen minutes left alone in this—or, indeed, any—room in the house. It wasn't just the force of her personality that left him a little stunned, it was the strength of her magic. Strangest of all, was that *she wasn't using it.* She was certainly old enough to have learned as much as he about the arcane; certainly powerful enough—but the magic she had invested in the walls was held together mostly by the main strength of that power. If those spells had been put in place by an Elemental Apprentice, they'd have fallen apart before the mage turned around. She had taken a bit of this, a bit of that, and a heavy dose of willpower to create protections that were effective in their way, but with all the grace of a pig in a parlor, and all the symmetry of that poor bloke they called "The Elephant Man." This was patched-together, mismatched, unaesthetic, *ugly* magic, and not the elegant creation she should have been able to weave. This, he would bet his soul, was not a clumsy, inelegant, or inept woman. This was not by her choice; she'd done what she could with instruments flawed and warped.

But there was one little bit of nice work there—tangled in among the rest, like a shining silk thread running through a skein of ill-spun yarn, was a whisper of magery Peter would dearly love to learn to cast himself.

Turn your eyes aside, it whispered to those beyond the walls who looked with the inward eye and not the outward. *There is nothing here to interest you, there never was, and never will be. Seek elsewhere for your quarry; it is not here.*

Peter couldn't fathom it, and didn't know where to begin a conversation with this woman. As it happened, he didn't have to.

"Well, I would judge, Mr. Scott, that no one sent you here from one of the many well-intentioned religious organizations who are trying to 'save' young ladies like Sally without any plans for providing her with an alternate source of an income," the doctor said at last, leaning forward slightly and resting her weight on the arms laid across the top of her desk.

Peter didn't bother to ask her how she knew that; anyone with *her* potential would have intuition so accurate she might just as well be able to read minds.

Besides, it didn't take Conan Doyle's fictional detective to read a man's personality from his outward appearance.

And to put the cap on it, I didn't storm in waving a Bible either.

"My leg *is* dodgy," he offered, in hesitant truce. "Just not as bad as I made it out to be. Nobody's been able to do anything for it."

Now she leaned back, a slight frown crossing her face. "I wouldn't think they would be able to," she replied. "But you, sir, are *not* my usual sort of patient, and you would not have heard of me or my office from any of my usual clients. I would like to know why you appeared on *my* doorstep today."

Peter wasn't a Water Master for nothing—and now that he was *inside* the lady's boundaries, her unseen friends in her fountain had no qualms about tossing him just the bit of information he needed.

"Fleet Clinic," he said shortly—and knowing that his appearance, a bit down-at-heel though it was, put him a great deal more than a touch above those who stumbled into charity clinics, he added, "used to be a ship's captain on the India route. I ran into one of my old lads looking better than he had in ten years, and the old boy told me about how you fixed him up. Thought I'd look you up and see if you had any notions about the knee." Now he shrugged. "Reckoned it couldn't hurt to see, eh? Worst you can do is tell me what every other sawbones has."

As he'd hoped, the charity clinic where she worked was probably so overwhelmed with poor working men and women that she'd have seen dozens of sailors among her patients since she set up practice, and wouldn't remember any particular one. She lost her frown, and her expression became one of skepticism rather than suspicion.

"And you have no objection to being treated by a woman?" she asked.

He gave a short bark of a laugh. "I've got no objection to being treated by a Zulu witch doctor if he could do something with this knee," he retorted, with honesty that finally won her over. He was pleased to see a faint smile cross her lips, and the intelligent amusement he'd sensed lurking beneath her stern surface showing in her eyes.

"In that case, *Captain* Scott," she said, plucking her pen from the inkwell and holding it poised over the paper, "why don't we begin at the beginning? Just what happened to that knee to make it turn against you, and when?"

Maya used her note taking to conceal some observation of her possible patient of a very different sort—for there was something of Power about him, and that had surprised her so much that for a brief time she had been unable to do more than stare at him.

Another woman might have found him unremarkable in any way whatsoever. He certainly wasn't handsome, not by any stretch of the imagination. His dress was neat and clean, but no finer than that of any other man in her working-class neighborhood. Sailors *always* ended up with a commonality of features, given the beating their faces usually took from the elements, and Peter Scott was no different there. His face could easily have been sculpted from ancient, withered leather, and though the chin was firm and the brow was high, his mouth set in lines that suggested more smiles than frowns, there was little in the ruin of it to show if he had been handsome in his youth, or otherwise. Only a pair of remarkable green eyes, an emerald color with a hint of blue, peering at her from among a nest of wrinkles caused by much squinting against the sun and storm, served as any sort of distinguishing feature. He'd had the good manners to remove his cap, which he held easily in hands that were relaxed—but why did they remind her of the paws of an equally relaxed and well-fed tiger? His hair, some color between yellow and brown, had begun to sport a streak of gray here and there. Not a young man—but not an old one either.

Then there was the scent of magic. . . .

Magic! Here, in *London!* She would have been *less* shocked, had she hailed a cab only to find a camel and not a horse between the shafts.

What was he doing here? If he was a mage, surely he could do as much for his own ailments as she!

Is he looking—for me? That thought made her hand shake for a moment, so that she inadvertently blotted her notes. She exclaimed over her "clumsiness" and took the opportunity offered in repairing the damage to swiftly check her defenses.

They were intact. And although this man brought to mind the well-fed and sleepy-eyed panther—*yes; panther, and not a tiger*—she did not think she was in any danger. Not directly, at least, and not at this moment.

"Stand and walk for me," she ordered, both to study his movement, and give herself time to think. "How much pain does this afflict you with?"

"What a reasonable man would expect—not that my friends would ever accuse me of being reasonable," he replied, with a quick lift of his brow, inviting her to share the joke, and another glint of sapphire in the green of his eyes when he turned to look at her. "When the weather's fine, I get along all right; when it's foul, so's the knee and my temper both. And when it storms—"

For a moment, the briefest of moments, Maya saw the panther extend his claws and show a gleam of white teeth.

"—when it storms, then God help the man that crosses me."

Then the panther pulled in his talons, hid his fangs, and became the sleepy cat again. Peter Scott smiled, shrugged, and invited her to share his little "joke."

Except—it was no joke. And I do not think it was a rainstorm he was referring to.

"Please, take a seat again," Maya gestured. "I wouldn't care to be the one to put you or your knee to the test of that."

She tapped the feathered end of her quill against her cheek as she considered him. Dared she take him as a patient? Prudence shouted "No!" This man could be—*was*—dangerous. He'd shown that side, however briefly, and she had no doubt that he had done so deliberately, calculatedly. *He had Power.*

And it was that power that made him so tempting, so very, very tempting.

"You must learn the magics of your father's blood," Surya had said, so many times, when Maya had begged for the least, the littlest hint of instruction. *"It is that which flows through you, and not the magics of mine."* And now, here was a mage of her father's blood. . . .

Presented, oh so conveniently, so very opportunely—

A trap? Or a gift? How was she to tell the difference?

She had not asked for a sign, but one arrived on its own two feet to give her the answer she needed.

No part of the house was forbidden to Charan, although he seldom ventured anywhere but the conservatory, her bedroom, and occasionally, the kitchen. Yet, with no warning, no prompting, no hint whatsoever, the door—which must have been improperly closed, creaked slowly open. And there, clinging to it with his tiny hands, his great, solemn eyes fixed on the stranger, was Charan himself.

"By Jove!" Scott exclaimed, with as much pleasure as surprise. "A Hanuman langur!"

He was still seated, but leaned down so that he no longer loomed over Charan's head, and extended a hand. "Hello there, my fine fellow!" he said, in a coaxing tone that had none of the overly hearty tones of someone who is feigning interest in an animal or child. "I don't suppose you speak English, do you? My Hindu's a bit rusty. Would you care to come and make my acquaintance?"

Charan tilted his head to the side, then let go of the door and dropped to all fours, making his leisurely way to the stranger while Maya watched in mingled trepidation and astonishment. It *looked* as if Charan liked the newcomer—but Charan could be as duplicitous as any street brat, and was equally capable of pretending to like someone just so that he could get near enough to sink his fine set of fangs into the extended hand.

Peter Scott, if he knew enough to know what Charan was, surely knew that as well. But he didn't move, either to pull back, or to extend his hand further. And he didn't make any of the silly noises people often did to reassure the monkey. He didn't smile—wise, since the baring of teeth was a sign of incipient battle among those of Charan's ilk—but he did blink, slowly, and make a faint, clucking sound.

Charan sat down, just within reach. He contemplated the extended fingers, then raised his great, sad eyes to Scott's face and locked gazes with him.

Then with the greatest of casual ease, as if he had known Peter Scott all of his life, he put his tiny hand gravely into Peter's large one.

Peter gently closed his hand around Charan's. "I am pleased to meet you, sir," he said, and only then did he look up at Maya while Charan waited trustingly at Peter's feet. "Since he and I don't share a language, I don't suppose you could tell me what his name is, could you?"

"Charan," she replied, and before she could say more, Peter immediately returned his attention to the monkey.

"I am glad to meet you, Charan," he said, releasing the little paw. "My name is Peter. Would you care to join me? I'm afraid your protector has only provided a single seat, but you can use my good knee, if you wish."

Now Scott straightened up, and at that signal, as if he had understood every word—which, all things considered, he might very well have—Charan leaped up onto the correct knee, and balanced himself there quite as if he belonged.

"I haven't seen a Hanuman langur since my last trip out," Scott said softly, and ventured to scratch Charan's head. Charan closed his eyes and leaned into the scratching fingers, his face relaxed into a mask of bliss. "By heaven, he brings back memories! I know that a lot of the sahibs thought they were filthy little nuisances, but—well, I like them. I like their cheek, and their cleverness. So—" he faltered a moment, then looked squarely up into her eyes. "So few people take the trouble to bring a pet from abroad home with them; one sees the poor things wandering forlorn so often, in every land there is, not excepting this one. It speaks a great deal for you that *you* did not take that 'expedient' answer, Doctor, when you moved to our island."

She had noted that the longer he spoke, the less he sounded like a working man, and the more like a man of some education.

If this isn't a sign— "Antoine de Saint-Exupery," she said, a last test, and he nodded.

" 'Many have forgotten this truth, but you must not forget it,' " he quoted, with a kind of reverence most reserved for the words of the Bible, " 'You remain responsible, *forever,* for what you have tamed.' "

She let out her breath in a soft sigh. "I believe—perhaps—I can help you a little, Captain Scott. But it will take time and patience."

"Patience—so long as it isn't storming—I have plenty of, Doctor," he replied, looking down at Charan, who had decided that a man so adept at scratching must be equally adept at cuddling and had moved into the crook of his arm. "As for time—" He looked up, and a faint smile answered her shake of the head at Charan's boldness. "As for time, however much I have, it is *not* being spent well when I'm driven out of temper, is it?"

She had to laugh, for between Charan and this man's undeniable charm, she had been won over, entirely against her own judgment and will. "Very well, then, Captain Scott. If you will follow me into the examination room—and *yes,* Charan, he will carry you—" she added, as Charan opened one eye resentfully at the prospect of being forced from his comfortable "nest," "—I will make some more specific tests, and see just how much I can improve that temper of yours."

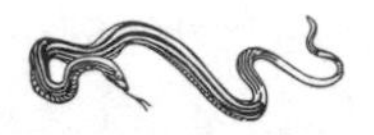

Peter Scott left Doctor Witherspoon's office knowing that however much he had managed to charm the doctor, she had entranced him that much again, and more. There being no further patients waiting, he had met the doctor's entire menagerie, been invited to what was clearly her true sanctum, a conservatory worthy of a horticulturist, and taken a cup of tea with her in her conservatory. Somehow, over the course of a mere two hours, he had become her friend. He sensed both that she did not boast too many friends, and that it was not a gift she was inclined to extend too readily.

He had in his pocket a packet of herbal powders, a small box of pills, and a prescription to be compounded at the apothecary at the end of the street. And he *thought*—although it was difficult to be certain—that during the course of the time when he had sat upon the examination table, pants leg rolled up absurdly to disclose a rather unattractive, hairy shank, when she had manipulated his knee, she had done something more to it than simply prodding and poking.

Earth Magic was healing magic, and even the untaught Earth Master could heal by sheer instinct. If she had sensed *his* power, she would not have been too eager to reveal her own. . . .

Untaught. She knows *that she's a mage, but she's untaught. That's the only answer.* But how, how, how had *that* come about? She had grown up in India, a land swarming with mages both real and charlatan. *How* had she missed finding a Master to take her as an Apprentice?

Then, as he paused in front of the apothecary, he could have struck himself for his stupidity. *Of course* no mage of India would take her as apprentice, or priestess, or anything else! Her mixed blood would have made her of no-caste; no less than the English, those of the high blood of India shunned the Eurasians. She was ranked with the street sweepers, the Untouchables; no Brahmin would ever teach her, no guru take her for his disciple, not even an old street babu accept her as his chela except on terms no woman of spirit or sense would agree to.

My God, my God, what a waste! He entered the dark and redolent apothecary shop and wordlessly handed his folded piece of paper over to the old, skullcapped man behind the counter. That, and the mezuzah at the door told him that the doctor looked after yet another outcast here.

"Bad knee, or is it elbow or shoulder?" the old Jew asked, perching a pair of gold-rimmed spectacles on the end of his nose to peruse the prescription.

"Knee," Scott replied. "Broke it in a storm at sea; went to the deck and hit it on a brass fitting."

"Ah. Never set right, then." The old man turned and began pulling ingredients from little drawers, muttering to himself as he worked—and sometimes adding a comment over his shoulder to Peter.

"This'll be what ye're to start on after ye finish what she give ye," he said once. And then, a little later, "No opium, no laudanum; she don't believe in that, no. I'll be giving ye two bottles and ye mind, ye look at the one, 'twill only have seven doses. And ye'll be gettin' no more from me without she gives ye a new 'scrip. That'll be for the bad nights, the stormy nights, when the pain takes ye. *One* of those, mind, for th' night. No more."

"Why?" Peter asked, surprised.

"Hemp," the old man said abruptly. "There's them as calls it hashish. 'Twill let ye sleep, but if ye misuse it, there'll be no more getting of it from *her* or *me*."

Well! Well indeed! There were doctors who handed out prescriptions containing opiates, laudanum, cocaine, and hemp as if they were no more dangerous than sugar pills. Peter had often considered a little hemp when the pain became too great, but he had feared it as well, for he did not know how much was enough, and how much would leave him with a craving he could not, as an Elemental Master and a member of the White Lodge, afford to have. Pain was preferable to a weakness that could all too easily be exploited. In fact, he doubted that he'd use those pills more often than once a month, and then only when he was not only within protections, but physically guarded.

"I understand your caution—and hers," he said, with a little nod of respect that seemed to amuse the old man.

A bit more work produced a pair of stoppered brown bottles, both holding pills, the second, as promised, holding no more than seven. Peter paid his bill and pocketed the bottles. Then, with another genial nod and a tinkle of the bell over the door, he left the shop.

There was no doubt in his mind, after a walk of a few blocks, that Doctor Witherspoon had improved his knee. It was just a trifle, and perhaps no one else would have noticed it, but an Elemental Master knew himself completely, inside and out, and *this* Elemental Master noticed a subtle improvement in his weakest physical point.

It wasn't so much that there was less pain—that could have been chalked up to the weather. It was that it no longer made that aggravating *click* it was wont to do, every third or fourth stride.

Now, pills and attention and the warmth of the doctor's hands, and even the determination of his own mind to sense an improvement could account for the loss of a little pain. The mind played an abundance of tricks, even on an experienced mage. But *nothing* in the power of persuasion was going to make that clicking go away.

He had a great deal to think about, and since he always thought better on his feet, he let them take him back through the varied neighborhoods until he reached one where cabs were thick upon the ground, and his gradually-assumed, confident, man-about-town air got him one without the least bit of difficulty.

He also climbed into the passenger compartment without difficulty; more evidence of the doctor's work. "Exeter Club," he ordered shortly as the cabman peered down through his hatch for orders, and sat back in a seat still smelling faintly of the cigar of its last occupant, to finish his thoughts.

She's hiding from something, or trying to. Something occult. What in heaven's name it could *be,* he had no clues. But if she had been hiding from something that wasn't arcane, she certainly wouldn't have the all-too-visible profession, the prosperous establishment in a slightly shabby street, or be spending part of her time doing charitable work at the Fleet Clinic, which had to be in one of the worst areas of London. Physical danger to her there would pass unnoticed in the general nastiness of the neighborhood.

It was clear, clear as the crystal sphere he kept in his own sanctum, that he didn't have nearly enough information about her to even make an educated guess as to what it was she was hiding from. But much as he found her a pleasant, highly intelligent, potential companion, and much as he would like to further their acquaintance, duty came before pleasure, and his duty was to first report to the Council and then to get back to his own shop. The lovely doctor could wait; he had a higher loyalty to the White Lodge and the Lodge Master that came before any considerations of a stranger. He also had a business to take care of, if he wished to continue eating and enjoying his current all-too-material lodgings.

The cab stopped directly in front of the club, which in the light of day was hardly distinguishable from the ordinary upper-class townhouses on either side of it. Enjoying the fact that he *could,* he took the stairs two at a time, earning himself a raised eyebrow from the daylight version of the Dragon of the Door.

"Good morning, Cedric. Been to see a new sawbones," he said by way of explanation. "She's done me a world of good. You ought to have a look in on her."

"I think not, sir," Cedric replied with his usual dignity. "I don't approve of these woman doctors. It's unnatural, sir."

Peter laughed, when he considered just *what* Cedric guarded from the intrusions of the outside world, and gave him a mocking little salute as he passed within.

The Council would not be meeting at this moment, of course, but Lord Alderscroft seldom left the premises. Rather than keeping a house in town, he kept a luxurious little set of his own rooms here, and as a consequence, needed only his own personal man, for all his other needs were attended to by the servants attached to the club. Peter sent his card up to Alderscroft's rooms with the cryptic message, "I've found what you were looking for," scribbled on the back, and it was a matter of moments before a boy came down with an invitation to dine with His Lordship in one of the private rooms.

The boy conducted him to what was less a "room" and more of a silk-papered alcove done in unobtrusive mellow blue, a pair of overstuffed leather chairs tucked in beneath a sturdy mahogany table. It earned the name of "private" because of a pair of blue-velvet curtains that *could* be drawn across the entrance to conceal the diners within, but so seldom were that there was a hint of dust along the top edges of the heavy velvet bands that tied them back to either side.

Alderscroft was already there but, from the presence of the waiter beside him, had not yet ordered. "Pork cutlet and new peas, Jerry," Peter said as he slid into the unoccupied seat. "Have to get back to the shop before that replacement Almsley conjured up for me frightens off all my customers."

Alderscroft chuckled, recognizing the joke for what it was, and said only, "Wellington and the rest, Jerry," before turning his attention to Peter. The waiter vanished with the discretion of all of the Club servants, leaving behind only a decanter and a pair of glasses. It was too early by Peter's standards for a whiskey, and Alderscroft never touched the stuff so far as Peter knew, but toying with quarter-filled glasses made their conversation look casual and ordinary, should anyone unexpected come past them. Alderscroft poured, and they both toyed, neither raising the glass to his lips.

"Your source . . . isn't what any of us expected," Peter said, in a quiet voice that only Alderscroft's ears would be able to pick up. "I'm not sure what to make of her."

"Her?" Alderscroft's mustache twitched.

"Her. Doctor Maya Witherspoon. Eurasian, and a physician and surgeon." Quickly, he passed over every scrap of information that he'd managed to glean, both openly and arcanely, from the moment he'd passed through the surgery's front door. Alderscroft didn't interrupt him a second time; he sat back in his chair, with his eyes fixed on Peter, until the narrative, what little there was of it, was over.

At that point, with the Club's usual impeccable timing, Jerry appeared with their luncheons. Neither of them said anything until after Jerry had finished arranging the plates to his satisfaction, and whisked the decanter and covers away.

"A pretty little puzzle," Alderscroft said at last. "One wonders what brought her here, when her—race—as well as her profession would have been more acceptable in her own homeland, or on the Continent."

"She's a British citizen; her father was an Army surgeon. She has every right to be here," Peter countered, covering his annoyance.

"As you say. Still. Why here? She'd go unremarked in France, or even in America." Alderscroft paused for a few deliberate bites of his luncheon, as Peter wolfed down his own food in a matter of moments. "And why now? And why, in the name of heaven, is she so *abominably* trained, as you claim she is?"

"I can't answer any of that, my lord," Peter replied, but did note with sharp irony the annoyance that Alderscroft had expressed over Maya's training—or lack thereof. Alderscroft might not *like* the idea of female mages, Adepts, or Elemental Masters, but he liked the idea of potential going to waste even less. "Perhaps her mother's people refused to train a half-breed, even a powerful one. There's no doubt that she knows something of what she is, but I very much doubt she knows the extent of her potential."

"I'd like to learn the trick of that hiding business she's worked out," Alderscroft grumbled under his breath. "Damnation! If she just wasn't a woman—"

"She's an Earth Master, or *will* be, and I suspect she's going to be one whether or not she gets formal training. You yourself were the one to tell me that the magic makes a Master or a madman, and given that she's forced her own way through medical training, I rather doubt she's so weak-willed as to go mad," Peter retorted, his tone acrid enough to cause Alderscroft to give him a sharpish glance. And since Alderscroft was treating him as an equal—for once—Peter decided to push the issue. "For God's sake, my lord, *bring her in.* Let one of us train her; she's the only Earth Master, or potential Earth Master, in the whole of London! Fire or Water could give her the basic grounding; it would be easy enough to pass her on to someone of her own Element when she's ready for full initiation—we could *use* her here—"

"She's *not our kind,* Scott," Lord Alderscroft interrupted. "Her magic isn't ours; the magic of East and West don't mix, never can, and never will! The Eastern mind can't understand the Western; live as long as I have, and you'll never doubt that for a moment!"

"But—" Peter started to object further, but saw from the stubborn expression on Lord Alderscroft's face that he would make no dent in the old boy's prejudices. "Well, she's doing no harm, and isn't likely to, magically, at least. As for her medical practice, I didn't bother to inquire, but since she's donating time to the Fleet Clinic, she apparently is fully enough acquainted with *Christian charity* to hold with the rest of the *Christian* virtues."

The heavy irony of his last sentence was—possibly—lost on Alderscroft. When the old man got that ponderously ruminative look on his face, one never knew how much he was taking in and thinking about.

"I will grant you all of that, Scott," he finally answered, as Peter chased a pea around his plate impatiently with his fork, with no intention whatsoever of eating it. "All right, then. We'll leave this lady doctor of yours to her charities and her patients. She won't be causing us any trouble, at least." Alderscroft finally put his focus back on Peter, and chuckled. "And you are impatient to get back to your business, I know. Well, thank you, Scott. Well done, as usual."

"My pleasure, sir," Peter replied, even though it had been nothing of the sort, and took his leave of the Head of the Lodge and Council before he could make any more remarks that would not—at the very least—be polite, nor politic.

But he as he waited for Cedric to hail a cab, then climbed into the conveyance, he found that he had fallen prey to a mood of resentment, and for once, it wasn't on his own behalf, but on a stranger's. Had she been fully white, had she been a man, Alderscroft would have had her brought into the fold and properly taught *immediately.* Had she even been of other than mixed blood, he'd have sent word to one of the Earth Masters who lived outside London—probably one of the ladies he *wouldn't* let into the Lodge, the Council, or the Club, but had no trouble in calling on for help. But no. No, with the double damnation of mixed blood and the incorrect sex, Maya Witherspoon must languish untaught, or struggle along on her own. And if, as Peter suspected, she was hiding from something. . . .

How long can someone self-taught hold out against any *enemy? It must have been someone in her homeland; why else flee all the way to Britain, and why choose the most populous city in Britain in which to hide? Here she can make alliances, obviously is making alliances, among the only people who have eyes and ears everywhere, and weapons to help protect her.* He thought about that thrown-away comment concerning "her patients' friends." There was no doubt that she'd earned a bodyguard of sorts among the half-honest and the fully criminal, and given Alderscroft's attitude, indeed, the attitude of nearly every "British gentleman" toward "her kind," well—he could only grant her mental congratulations.

But Alderscroft didn't say anything about me helping her, if I can, he suddenly realized, as the cab came to an abrupt halt in traffic. *I've no doubt he would have, if it had occurred to him that I'd dare, but he didn't. By God, he didn't, and I'll be damned if I let him have a hint that I'm going to!*

The sudden resolution erased his sour temper, and he almost

laughed out loud, which would have probably puzzled the cabby. *Oh, Peter, you dog, you were looking for an excuse to see more of the lady anyway, and you know it—*

Oh, yes, he knew himself too well to deny that. He'd walk half across London in a screaming storm just to take tea with her again.

Well, now he had a reason to see her, a good one, a solid one, a reason that any *real* gentleman would applaud, if said *real* gentleman could be persuaded to see past his own pigheaded prejudices.

Now all I have to do is find a way to broach the subject. All! Now he did laugh, at his own foolishness. *"Pardon me, Doctor, but I can't help noticing that you've been using a bit of magic, and I thought I'd offer—offer—"*

Offer what? Good lord, how am I to put this without offending her or *making her think I'm a madman and having that heathen warrior of hers throw me out on the street?*

Well, deciding how to put his "offer" to her ought to keep his brain spinning for the rest of the afternoon, at least. And perhaps by the time he'd managed that, he would also be able to figure out how to make it clear—in the most polite of fashions—that teaching her magic wasn't the only thing he had in mind in seeking her company.

Oh, what fools we mortals be! he thought, alighting at his own shop. *What fools, indeed.*

Nevertheless—he happened to have a new stock of incense just in, and a handsome statue of Ganesh, the elephant-headed Indian god reputed to be the remover of all obstacles. So—and only because the customers liked the hint of sandalwood in the air when they came to examine his wares—and only because there was a fine receptacle for such offerings at the foot of the statue—Lord Ganesh's serpentine trunk breathed in the airs of sacrifice that afternoon, while Peter helped ladies with more money than taste select "exotica" for their parlors.

After all . . . sometimes even unfamiliar magic worked, East and West *could* meet in harmony, and there was never any harm in asking someone for a bit of a favor.

6

MAYA paused for a moment beside the statue of elephant-headed Ganesh that stood beside the waterfall in her conservatory pool. The statue had been there from the time the pond and waterfall had been built, and blended into the rocks surrounding it so well that she hardly noticed the handsome little idol was there most of the time. There was a box of incense sticks and another of lucifer matches on a ledge nearby, out of reach of the damp—Gupta was particularly attached to Ganesh, and he often lit incense as an offering here. But this afternoon it was Maya who felt an unaccountable urge to make an offering.

Oh, well, God's commandment is "Thou shalt have no other gods BEFORE Me." That doesn't exclude getting a little help from a lesser power, now, does it? And since I don't happen to have a statue of Saint Jude around to patronize my hopeless cause, I believe the Remover of Obstacles will do.

With a chuckle at her own mendacity, she lit a lucifer and set flame to the tips of several incense sticks, placing them in the holder beside Gupta's previous offering. Just what obstacles she wanted removed from her path at the moment, she couldn't have stated clearly—just that she would very much like to see more of that charming Peter Scott. . . .

Just then, the parrot flew down to her shoulder, nibbled her ear, and murmured a clear, "I love you." It was in Hindu, of course, but she was reminded of the custom of the young men of India to teach their parrots seductive phrases before giving the birds to the maidens they were courting. That, in fact, was probably why her mother Surya, always fond of a clever joke, had sometimes called him "Kama"—a word and a god that encompassed every aspect of love.

"You may love me, my sweet, but it's cupboard love," she told him fondly. Nevertheless, she found one of the little sunflower seeds he craved in the recesses of her skirt pocket, and gave it to him. He took it, and flew off with a chortle.

Dusting off her hands, she squared her shoulders, and sternly told herself to forget daydreaming about sailors for the rest of the day. She had work to do; this was her afternoon at the Fleet, and, as always, the place would be a bedlam.

With an eye to more than the weather, she took her umbrella, a stout article that served double duty as a weapon, with its sharpened ferrule and sturdy ribs, twice as strong as any other she'd ever seen. Then, umbrella in her right hand and medical bag in her left, she began the walk to the Fleet Charity Clinic—for there were very few cabs that could ever be persuaded to go where the clinic lay.

At least, not during the daytime. Neither she nor Amelia had to pass through the hell that was their neighborhood at night, for they had a guardian angel in the form of Tom Larkin. Like so many of the working class, he had little to spare in the form of ready money to cope with an emergency—and like so many, he rightfully distrusted the doctors and the care he'd get at a hospital. Too often, those who entered the charity wards became the subject of either careless mishandling, callous disregard, or reckless experimentation. Sometimes, even all three.

So after fourteen agonizing hours of labor, when his wife was spent and exhausted and *still* no closer to giving birth than when labor had begun, he'd had to seek other help. At the urging of the Fleet-trained midwife and frantic with fear, he'd brought his wife to the Fleet, in his own cab. He'd all but killed his poor horse, getting her there.

Well that he had. By sheerest good luck, both Maya and Amelia were on duty. They'd had no choice but to perform the dangerous Caesarian operation.

Though why the Caesarian should be considered so dangerous, when ovectomies to "calm hysteria" were considered no great hazard, was beyond Maya's understanding. The death rate was nearly equal for either operation—well over half the patients died. Infection was the greatest killer, with blood loss running a close second.

But that was without Amelia's carbolic spray, or Maya's own—unique—talents.

Mother *and* child lived—and cab driver Tom Larkin had vowed that while he or his new son lived, breathed, and drove a cab, neither Amelia nor Maya would ever have to brave the dark to walk home at the end of a day at the Fleet. He turned up, every night at closing time, to see if either woman was there that day, taking them safely through every possible hazard and escorting them right to their own doorways.

Which was just as well, all things considered. Too many times, pre-Larkin, Maya had been forced to defend herself with her umbrella and Amelia with a string "miser's purse" that contained, not money, but a lump of lead. It wasn't so much the inhabitants of the neighborhood that were the problem, it was the "visitors," men drunk and looking for a whore, any whore, and knowing that the women of *these* streets could be had for less than a shilling. They tended to assume that any woman out on the street after dark was a whore, and that the only difference between a woman who rebuffed their offer and one who took it was the small matter of price.

"Mis'rble day, eh, Miz Maya?" The salute came from the pavement at her feet as she strode past, and she grinned down at the filthy face looking up at her.

"It would be less miserable if you hadn't a hangover, Bob," she replied, stepping over his sprawling legs, then making a skip to the side to avoid a puddle of liquid best left unidentified.

He only laughed. He was a day laborer, when he could find work, and when he couldn't, he drank up every cent he made or could borrow. He had no family, claimed he didn't want one, and as Maya knew only too well, was dying of tuberculosis. There was no cure for him, and he knew it, and so did she. Not even *her* healing talents could save him; she could prolong his life, but he didn't want her to. He had once, in a bout of drunken confession, told her that he hoped one day that his bottle of "blue ruin" would be out of a bad lot that would poison him and kill him quicker. That he wouldn't take his own life but courted an "accident" on a daily basis was a contradiction she never tried to resolve. Instead, on the rare occasions she could coax him into the Fleet, she did what she could to ease his pain and his breathing—and no more. It was her duty to fight death—but not when her patient pursued it, and had good reason to welcome its all-enfolding wings.

She dodged peddlers and pickpockets, pimps and prostitutes, human refuse and the refuse humans left behind, and was mostly greeted with the same ironic cheer that Bob had used with her. She was respected here, and if not beloved, was certainly welcome. She, unlike other charity doctors, made no demands that her patients "act like good Christians" or be one of the "worthy poor"—whatever that was supposed to mean. She dispensed medicine, sound advice, compassion, and some well-earned tongue-lashings in equal measure, and the people who came to her for help understood and respected that.

But as she neared the entrance to the clinic, shouts and shrieks of pain sent her from a brisk walk into a run; she picked up her skirts in both hands, the better to lengthen her stride, exposing ankles and even calves to the applause of a couple of drunken louts she didn't recognize. One was cuffed over the side of his head by a fellow with a barrowload of potatoes for sale as she sprinted past.

"Shoaw sum r'spect, ye buggerin' swine!" said the peddler as another shriek sent her into a full-out run. "That there's a doctor, not 'un'a yer tuppeny whoors!"

Yes, it was going to be a busy day at the Fleet. Perhaps she should not have asked Ganesh to remove unspecified obstacles, since it seemed that he had removed the ones between new patients and her!

Tom brought her home just after ten that night, limp as a rag, yet strangely elated. How could she *not* be elated? She had saved the hand of a man who would otherwise have lost it, she had delivered three healthy babies in rapid succession, one presented breech that she had somehow managed to turn in the womb before labor was too far along, and one set of twins. All the patients recovering in her ward were doing well. Although the work had come in the door steadily from the moment she arrived to when they closed their doors, for once nothing had gone horribly, or even mildly, wrong. It had been a day full of small triumphs, not disasters.

Tom descended from his perch up on the driver's box and handed her out with a sober propriety that would have had anyone who knew him and his usual truculent manner with a fare gaping in astonishment. "You look done in, Miss Maya," he said, as she smiled at him, grateful for the support of his hand tonight. "You go get some rest."

"I will, Tom, I promise," she said. *But not just now. . . .* There were too many things to do first, not the least of which was to check to see if there were any messages or letters for her. Her *other* clients, the ladies who paid her so very well, tended to make appointments for a given afternoon on the evening before. Unless, of course, there was an emergency, in which case she would find a frantic message waiting for her, or even a messenger waiting to guide her to the emergency.

There were no messages, but there was a letter, waiting on the tray beside the door. She frowned at it for a moment, not recognizing the handwriting. As she was about to open it, Gupta appeared at the end of the hall. He had such an odd expression on his face that she put the letter back down on the tray. It could wait.

"Gupta, is there something wrong?" she asked, hurrying toward him, her weariness forgotten.

"No, mem sahib—" He hesitated. "But I have great need to speak with you. There are things I must tell you; things it is time that you should hear." None of this made any sense to her. "Gupta, it *is* very late, and I am very tired—" she began.

But Gupta shook his head stubbornly. "I have seen a thing, and heard a thing, and there is much I must tell you. And tomorrow may be too late."

That, coupled with his expression, made her shake off her tiredness with an effort. "Then take me where you will, and I will listen," she replied.

She wasn't particularly surprised when he took her to the conservatory. Incense burned before the statue of Ganesh, and there were many candles burning among the plants. She settled into her usual chair; he sat cross-legged on the floor. She felt a little uncomfortable, looming above his head on her ersatz throne, but there was no way she could join him on a floor cushion, not in her confining Western clothing and corsets.

She waited for him to speak in his own time. There was no point in trying to hurry him, for he would not be hurried. He didn't force her to wait very long, however, just long enough for him to gather his thoughts and begin, as a storyteller would.

"There were, on a time, two sisters," he said gravely. "Both were beautiful, both were gifted with more than the common measure of the power to speak and act with the Unseen. The younger, who wept not at all at her birth and had eyes that hinted of hidden things, was named Shivani. The elder, who laughed at her birth and had dancing sparks of happiness in her eyes, they called Surya, the Fire."

"My mother?" Maya asked, with a feeling that something solid had dropped from beneath her, leaving her dangling in midair. She clutched the arms of her chair and breathed in the incense, a tightness in her chest. "My mother has a sister? But what happened to her?"

Why was I never told? Why did I never see her? How could she have deserted Mother if she was Mother's twin?

Gupta nodded. "As sisters should, they loved one another, despite such different natures. Your mother chose to study the powers of the day, her sister studied those of the night, as all expected, and still, despite that they now saw so little of one another, they were as sisters should be. But as time passed, Shivani withdrew into herself, kept her own counsel, and went ever more often to a certain temple and sect of the goddess Kali. At length, she treated Surya as she would a stranger, and your mother gathered about her these seven friends, to ease her loneliness."

Here Gupta waved his hand around the conservatory, where all seven of Maya's pets, some warring against their own need for slumber, sat watching her, wide-eyed.

"Still, there was no thought of enmity between them—until your mother met Sahib Witherspoon, your father." Gupta shook his gray head, with an ironic smile. "He had come to the temple where she served—came humbly, and not as the arrogant sahib of the all-wise English—to ask of the ways of our healing. He would learn, so he said. And he *did* learn; I was there, and I saw it all. He learned—and so did your mother. She taught healing, and she learned to love."

"So did he," Maya whispered softly, knowing how very much her father had loved her mother.

Gupta's nostrils flared. "Did I say he did not?" he demanded with annoyance. "But he was not my concern. *She* was my concern; I was her appointed guardian. I cared not what some English sahib felt or thought or did or did not do—not then—not then—"

He sighed deeply. "I was more than appointed guardian; I was your mother's friend. Never did she treat me as a servant, often did she confide to me her inmost thoughts. So she told me of her love, and of his. Then I feared for her, tried to dissuade her. Yet she would not be moved, and implored my help in convincing her father to allow a marriage." He shook his head. "Impossible, of course. There were hard words, then threats, then Surya was locked away. And it was my hand, my hand, that set her free, to fly to your father and make the marriage of his people." He smiled with great irony. "She did not go dowerless; she took what was hers by right, the gems and jewelry that formed her marriage portion, her seven friends, and her power. But it was for none of these that Sahib Witherspoon welcomed her into his arms and heart—I had seen that he would have her were she the lowest Untouchable. I, too, loved Surya as a daughter and a friend, and that was why it was my hand that turned the key in the lock that night."

Although much of this was new information, it was nothing she hadn't already guessed, and Gupta had yet to reveal what he had seen that led to this confession. "So her family cast her off," Maya prompted.

"As you know. What you do *not* know is that Shivani, her sister, was wild with anger. That Shivani, her sister, withdrew from her family into the heart of that temple of Kali. And that Shivani, her sister, vowed that neither the blood she shared with Surya, nor the power that Surya possessed, would remain in the barbarian hands of an unclean English sahib."

The way that he said this, the tone of his voice, made Maya's blood run cold. "What did she do?" Maya whispered, not certain she wished to know.

"First, she sent a man who had been as trusted by Surya as I in her father's household. She sent him with death in his heart and a blade in his hand." Gupta's eyes flashed in the darkness of his face, and he sat a little taller. "It was I who caught him in the garden, warned of his presence and his intention by Charan. It was I who spoke to him there in the shadows, as warrior to warrior and man to man, beneath the shelter of the drooping jasmine."

Maya closed her eyes for a moment; it was so easy to picture what had happened, there in her father's garden that near-fatal night. She knew the jasmine that Gupta spoke of; she pictured a shadowy figure concealed by the fragrant boughs, and Gupta (younger, of course) whispering urgently to the half-seen assassin, with Charan in the tree above, chittering angrily to himself.

"I spoke of the anger of the English should he slay the wife of an officer; of the good heart of Sahib Witherspoon, who healed all who came to him. I then spoke words that were less honest; of the fickle nature of women, the jealousy of a sister who had *not* won for herself a husband of any sort, of the foolishness of the female nature." Gupta shrugged as she raised an eyebrow at him. "I used the weapons that came into my hand, and I did not scruple that some were base. I fought for my lady's life that night, and I would have said any thing that won the day."

"And it is better to fight with words than knives," Maya replied. "You are wise as well as warrior, my friend. In a battle of words and wits, you would ever carry the day."

Gupta blushed. "I would not say I was wise, only cunning, perhaps, and perhaps the gods gave me the words to move my friend-foe's heart. So it was I convinced him to lie to Shivani, to bring her the heart of a doe, and not the heart of our gentle dove, your mother. This he did, then fled and took his service far into the north, lest she discover his deception."

"But how could she not know—" Maya began. Gupta cast her a withering glance.

"You, who weave protections about us every night, ask this? Your mother spent herself and her power in weaving a canopy of deception about herself, about the sahib, and about you. Her sister knew nothing, immured as she was in her temple, never coming forth either by day or night, weaving magics of her own, and plots to destroy the sahibs and all who fattened themselves at the English table."

Now Maya understood. The English who thought that they ruled India because India was not wise enough to rule herself were fools. There was enough resentment and anger at the arrogant foreigners to supply the fodder for a hundred outbreaks of rebellion a year, and it was surprising that there had actually been so few. So her mother's sister had allied herself with one of those factions . . . and not just any faction either, but with the *thugee* cult of Kali Durga.

"She dared not teach you the magics of your own people, although you begged to learn, for she could not have concealed your half-awakened power once it began to shine. She knew that you *must* come to learn one day, but she hoped that if you were to learn the magics of your father's people, her sister would not recognize that the magics were wielded by the hand of one of her own blood." Here Gupta smirked. "And when the Sahib Witherspoon went about with the Doctor his daughter, even if Shivani did hear of such a thing, her eyes were so blinded by hatred that she never would have thought the daughter to be other than wholly English, for she never would credit a Sahib with bringing a half-blood daughter into the sun, and never, never, would she credit him with giving her education and a high rank within the Sahibs' world."

"So—that was why we were safe for so long." Maya spoke slowly, her heart contracting with grief at her mother's long sacrifice. "Because *she* never went out if her sister would have heard of it, and her magic made it seem that we—just weren't there. I always knew we had an enemy, one who had great power—but I never knew it was one of her own blood."

Gupta's eyes clouded briefly. "Alas, that her magics were not enough to keep the wings of the plague-goddess from overshadowing her."

Maya's throat tightened, and she groped for her handkerchief, but her hand never reached it, for her heart froze within her at Gupta's next words.

"I have never been certain that was mere mischance," he said, with a hint of a growl of anger in his throat. "Kali Durga governs disease as well as the thugee. And the snake in the sahib's boot was no accident at all."

Of course, it couldn't have been, she thought, as Sia and Singhe flowed forward to twine around her ankles, as if seeking comfort and reassurance. She reached down to stroke them. "No. You're right, Gupta. No ordinary snake would have gotten past these little warriors. Never, ever, would they have let a serpent get so far as the bungalow door."

Sia whined in her throat; Maya cupped her hand comfortingly around the mongoose's cheek. "I have known for a very long time that we had an enemy with magic power, my oldest friend. I even guessed that this enemy caused my father's death. That was why I fled from home, and took you with me, for since you were willing to come, *I* would not leave you behind to face the wrath of one who had been thwarted. But I did not know that my enemy had so . . . familiar a face." She shivered. "*Why,* Gupta? My mother and father are dead. What possible quarrel can she have with me?"

"That you live is quarrel enough, to her and those who serve her," Gupta replied sourly. "And her anger and hatred would only be the greater, that Surya deceived her for so long. Your mother—and you—are everything she is not, *have* everything she has not. You earn respect; she has only fear. She is comely, but her bitter heart casts a blight over her beauty and her face—when last I set eyes on it—had the same icy beauty as a diamond. A man may admire a diamond, but he will not love it. And you have love. I do not think she is even *liked* by those she serves and those who serve her. Envy eats at her, waking and sleeping. Of this, I am certain." He pursed his lips. "And there is another thing," he added reluctantly. "It is only a thing that I have heard, once or twice, as a rumor. But it is said that if one who devotes her magic to the dark slays another mage, she will have that mage's power to add to her own. For that reason alone, she is likely to harm you."

Maya digested Gupta's words, feeling cold and very much alone. "And what have you seen and what have you heard, that you bring me these words now?" she asked him, at last.

His face took on the aspect of someone who is haunted, but is reluctant to speak of his fear. At last, he cleared his throat. "I have heard, when I have been abroad at night, the call that the thugee use, one to another. It was not near *here,*" he added hastily, "but they are within the city."

She didn't ask him how he knew what such a call sounded like. It was easy enough to guess that it would be the call of some night-walking bird or animal of India, and it was unlikely that anyone would be prowling the streets of London making such a sound, unless he was *from* her homeland, and he and those with him had a reason to keep their movements a secret.

"And you have seen?" she prompted.

"I have seen—in the bazaar where I go to buy our foodstuffs from home—the shadow of a serpent on a wall, where no serpent was, or should be." Fear stood unveiled in his eyes. "It was said that Shivani danced with the *rakshasha.* I believe the tale. The temple to which she took herself was not of good repute."

"That would," Maya murmured, half to herself, "explain the *krait.*"

Gupta nodded. The cobra was holy; given the number of prayers that went up daily in praise of Sahib Witherspoon and in gratitude for what he did among the sick, it would have been unlikely for the sorceress to dare to attempt to use the cobra as her unholy weapon. The krait, however, was another story entirely.

And if she had anything to do with the serpent demons, the rakshasha, any serpent she sent might not even be an ordinary snake. Maya looked into Gupta's eyes, and saw not only fear there, but trust and confidence. It was that which made her shake off the paralysis of her own sudden fears.

"You will no longer go to the bazaar, old friend," she said decisively. "You may be recognized; certainly you will be followed."

Gupta nodded, reluctantly. "My son—" he began.

She interrupted. "Nor will you send any of this household. I fear *anyone* from the homeland will be followed, to see where he goes. If my magics are succeeding, they will have no other way to find us but by looking for those from home. The longer we can elude them the better." She pondered her options. "The boy Jack, the eldest son of the woman who sews and mends for us to pay for her sick baby's care? He runs errands; he is quick to learn, and clever. You will *show* him what it is you need at the market, and send him for it. We can afford to pay him for such a service."

Gupta's face darkened. "But he will be cheated," he protested, unwilling to allow a mere English boy to venture into the treacherous waters of commerce with a fellow countryman of India.

Maya laughed, perhaps with a touch of hysteria, but Gupta's thriftiness was so ingrained that even in the shadow of terrible danger, he worried about being cheated! The absurdity of it countered some of her own fear. "I think not," she said, shaking her head. "I have seen this boy bargain like the sharpest old woman; it is more likely that he will leave the merchants feeling they have been bested! No, you tell him what is a fair price for a thing, and he will get that price, or better."

Gupta relaxed. "Then there is no need for any of this household to leave, except for the children to go to school."

"The children wear English clothing at school; they look no different than any other children," Maya pointed out. "There are the Vellechio boys, the Italians, who are darker than they. I do not think that the thugee will haunt every day school in the city on the chance that they *might* see a child of the homeland. So long as we hide among the English, it will be harder for them to find us."

"Except that you, who tend the sick at the Fleet—" again Gupta's face darkened.

"I will walk veiled by day, or take the omnibus as near as I may, and Tom brings me home by night," she said firmly. "There are none among the sick that I tend that would betray me, even should the thugee have the English to ask them."

Gupta sighed. "That is true. And there are many among your sick who will protect you, walking where I may not—and a thousand eyes and ears, should you ask for them."

She laughed at his exaggeration. "Not a thousand, Gupta, but enough. Especially among the children."

"And who looks at a child? Yet a child sees everything." Now Gupta smiled, at last. "I did well to confess to you, mem sahib. You, too, are a warrior, with a warrior's heart. You find weapons to your hand when you need them."

"And I will not scruple to use any and all of them," she replied firmly. "You may be sure that I will begin tonight, and go on tomorrow, sending the warning out amongst my 'eyes and ears.' "

Gupta bowed his head to her, an act of respect that touched her profoundly. "Then I will leave you to your work, mem sahib," he said, rising. "Shall I have my son bring food to you here, or in your office?"

"My office, please," she replied, though she made no move to rise as he left. She looked around at her circle of pets; all of them watched her closely. They acted as if they had been listening to the entire conversation, and anxiously awaited her reaction.

Pets. I'm not so sure now, that "pets" are all they are, she thought, noting the look of their eyes, the expressive postures of their bodies. The owl, Nisha, sat side by side with the falcon, their bodies so close that their wings touched. They seldom perched that closely together, but tonight it appeared, to her at least, as if they were telling her that they, too, were warriors in her service, and would stand sentry by night and day. The mongooses sat alertly on either side of her feet, and when she glanced down at them, they looked up. Their faces were easier to read; she had seen that look on them before. The hunt was up, and they would not let another enemy slip past them, having unaccountably failed once before. The neck hackles of Rajah the peacock bristled aggressively; she had seen *him* kill serpents in India, and his own talons could be formidable; she had the sense that he was not the decorative creature he had feigned to be.

Rhadi's eyes flashed; he flew to her shoulder as Charan leaped into her lap. "Love you!" the parrot exclaimed, as a declaration, and not an endearment. Then, astonishingly, "Watch for you! Fight for you! All! All! Shivani *bad!* We guard!"

Charan balled his little fists and nodded emphatically, even as Maya's mouth dropped open in shock. Reflexively, she looked at the others. As she met the eyes of each in turn, each one nodded, slowly and deliberately.

These—are not pets. Even as she thought that, she wondered just what they were. Or perhaps, what Surya had made them. . . .

They all clustered closely around until they touched her, the owl and the falcon swooping down to land on the arms of her chair, the peacock nestling in against her right leg, the mongooses jumping up into the chair to share her lap with Charan. Then Charan reached up, touched her cheek with his little black "hand" and turned her face so that she looked into his eyes.

And all that she could see were his eyes. She felt as if she were falling into them, but how could she be afraid? She had known him from her birth; he had shared her cradle, her playtime, her very food. He was her friend and companion. They trusted each other with a surety past words.

We are—briefly—more than we seem, little healer.

The words flowed into her mind. For this moment, astonishment, fear, any other thought or emotion that might interfere with this communication was held at bay, so that she could hear what they needed to say to her. A strength so great that it could easily crush her if it cared to cradled her instead, and dropped its words gently into her open heart.

This is not our land, and you are only half our child, but you are in our charge, the words went on. *We will fight for you and stand guard over you.* Charan's face took on a solemnity and wisdom mingled with a hint of great mischief; Nisha's feathers were as white as snow. Rajah spread his fan for her, the parrot's eyes flashed, and the two mongooses sat erect, small but proud warriors, their large eyes bright with intelligence. *But you, too, may come to a place where you must take up arms, and you* must *find an ally of the power of this place, or nothing we can do will help you prevail.* She *has grown stronger with every passing day, and grows stronger still. There is much evil in this city, and darkness feeds upon and strengthens darkness. Child, your foe will not rest until she drinks you dry and casts away the husk. She lusts for what you hold, and will pursue you no matter where you go to have it. Your magic cannot hide you forever, and when it fails, you must be ready.*

Charan dropped his hand from her cheek; suddenly she was herself again. She put her hand to her throat, feeling as if her collar choked her, cold with fear that bound her with rings of iron.

A touch from Charan's cheek on hers freed her from that terrible fear so quickly it *had* to have magic behind it. Her mind swirled with speculations, but one settled out and quickly became a certainty.

The many gods of India wore many faces and many guises, and not all of them were human.

Rhadi laughed, with a note in the laughter of triumph, and Charan nodded again. She all but collapsed against the back of her chair and stared at them.

"I need—a little time to absorb this," she said weakly.

"Yes," Rhadi said, and flew back up onto one of his perches, followed by the owl and the falcon. A little dazed, Maya was not so bedazzled that she did not notice that Nisha's feathers, which had been white, were slowly darkening to their usual brown and golden hues. *A white owl, a falcon, a peacock . . .* She tried to think; Charan surely was the voice of Hanuman—goodness, he was a *Hanuman langur,* how could she not have suspected? The others—

As often as Rhadi says "I love you," perhaps he does speak in the voice of Kama. Goodness—Kama, the god of all love—doesn't he even have a parrot as his chosen mount? A white *owl—that would be Laksmi; she's Vishnu's consort, and as fierce in fighting evil as he is. And when Rajah touched me, my fear was simply gone; the god Skanda slays terror, and I* know *he is represented by the fearless peacock. . . .*

Who or what the others could be eluded her for now; she had lived for so long among all the tales and beliefs of her homeland, and yet she could remember so little!

7

STILL trying to think her way past the shocks of the last hour, Maya made her way around the periphery of the house, reinforcing her magics, trailed by the mongooses and Charan. It seemed to her that tonight there was more power there, behind her own, perhaps coming from her little friends. The walls glowed brighter to her inner sight than they ever had before, and there was a strong taste of honey and sandalwood in her mouth as she worked. When she was finished, she went to her bedroom in a daze, and although she was bone-tired, she checked and rechecked her protections before she dared try to sleep.

But when she did sleep, it was a restless sleep, as mind and memory worked together to try to identify, out of the half-remembered tales of her childhood, the beings who walked in the guise of pets. Brahma, Vishnu, Shiva—Laksmi, Kama—surely not Ganesh—Skanda was obvious, and Hanuman, but the others—

The multi-limbed, multi-faced, multi-faceted deities of India whirled in a complicated dance of confusion in her dreams. Only Kali, with her protruding tongue and her necklace of skulls, held aloof; watching, waiting, singularly uncaring. *I am a healer, a physician!* she wanted to cry to them. *I am a Christian! I want no part of your quarrels, no part of your plans!* But it was like arguing with a thunderstorm; you could shout all you liked, but you were still going to get wet.

And possibly struck down by lightning, unless you were careful, careful, and kept meek and still.

But even if you keep meek and still, the storm can wash you away. . . .

It was late when her mind finally gave up the struggle and her restless tossing became the oblivion of true sleep. And when she woke, she was no wiser than she had been when she went to bed.

For some, the light of day might have dispelled the fears of last night, and the strange revelations would have dissolved like frost on a sunny window. How could a stolid Englishman, full of port and beef and the assurance of his own special superiority, ever have taken seriously a monkey that spoke, let alone some nebulous threat from a female votary of a god he didn't believe in, whose power could not even exist by the laws of creation as he knew them?

But that surety was not for her. In India, real magic blossomed in sunlight and moonlight alike. Wonders happened in the full of day, and she had seen too many of them to ever doubt that what had happened by night would not be as real in the daylight. *I am a physician, and English. But I am also Hindu, of Brahmin blood. I know that there are more things than can be observed in the lens of a microscope, weighed, and measured. I know that the world is not as we would have it, but as it is, and that is not always as an Englishman sees it.*

She made her preparations and dressed, preoccupied with the events of last night, so preoccupied that she didn't bother with more than the simplest of French braids for her hair. She drifted downstairs in a fugue, rather than a fog, of thought. It was clear *what* she needed to do—but how to do it?

But she had completely forgotten the letter left for her last night, until it turned up on the tea tray in the conservatory where she usually took her breakfast.

Once again, she turned it over in her hands, frowning slightly at the unfamiliar handwriting. The stationery was ordinary enough, and there was no seal, only a formless blob of sealing wax holding the flap shut.

She opened it, separating the wax from the paper, and pulled out the single folded sheet, covered with neat, evenly spaced lines of precise handwriting.

Dear Doctor Witherspoon, it began. *I believe that I have made and torn up a full dozen letters in attempting to couch what I would like to tell you in vague or indirect terms. Such an attempt is folly; I will be direct. When we met in your surgery today, we both recognized each other for what we were, and I do not believe that you will deny this. You and I are alike, for we are both magicians.*

That last sentence arrested her eyes, and she had to read it over three times before she truly understood it, in all its bald simplicity. She put one hand to the arm of her chair to steady herself, feeling as if the earth trembled, or at least, *should* have trembled. For a moment, the letter lay in her lap as she collected her wits.

Then she picked it back up and began again at that extraordinary sentence. *Yes; you and I recognized each other . . . for we are both magicians. Sorcerers, if you would rather. I am what is known as an Elemental Master; my mastery, such as it is, holds over the arcane creatures of water. I was trained and schooled, long and hard, to attain my Mastery, and there are others with whom I associate and sometimes work, Masters of other Elements, of creatures and magic that few Englishmen realize even exist side by side with their cozy bed sitters, their railways, and their cream teas.*

This brings me to my confession. I was sent by others of my kind to discover what it was that had made such unexpected stirrings in the occult world, stirrings that none of them recognized or could effectively trace. Because of what and who I am, because I can travel streets in London where they would be set upon in moments, they asked me to find the source of this strange and unfamiliar magic. For this, I apologize; I was sent as a spy to find you and there is no polite way to confess this. For my defense, I can only offer that the Unseen

World holds many perils, as I believe you know, and my fellows dare not let something they cannot recognize remain uninvestigated.

The bald, bold words reassured her, oddly enough. There was no doubt who the letter was from now. She did not even need to turn the page over to see the signature. And she agreed with him; in his position, she would have done the same.

Oh, yes. I would, indeed. If only I were able to sense the possible peril in the first place. . . . He had investigated, and finding her harmless, had honorably confessed the reason he had invaded her domain. What was more, had she been a man, he would probably have phrased his apology exactly the same way. She felt a tingle of pleasure, and her mouth curved in a slight smile. Here, at last, was a man and an Englishman willing to admit that her strength, wit, and intelligence were equal to his in all ways—and matter-of-factly made no effort to shield her from "unpleasantness," assuming that she would deal with unpleasantness in her own time and method.

Now, please forgive me if I presume, or if I have misjudged—but although I saw your defenses were strong, as strong as any that a Master could produce, I felt they were—there is no kind way to put this either—untutored.

Her cheeks heated, but she could not be honest with herself if she didn't agree with him. She *knew* her protections were clumsy, cobbled together.

If this is the case, I do not know why you have had no schooling, although I can hazard some guesses. Neither do I care why this is so, to be honest, for that *is none of my business unless you choose to make it so. I may be very wrong, and if I am, I can only humbly beg your forgiveness. If I am not wrong, I may have a solution for you. You have every right to ignore this—more right to tell me to go to Hades with my presumptions! If you choose to see me, you may also choose to tell me what you will of your past—or not. Your secrets may remain your secrets.*

If she chose to see him? Her eyes raced across the lines of neat script avidly, suddenly impatient to find the meat of the matter.

If you wish, I venture to offer my services, to tutor you in the basic schooling that all of the Elemental Masters receive. For the knowledge particular to your own Element—Earth, if I am not mistaken—I can and will pass you to one far more qualified than I when you have achieved the basics. But I can give you what you need to make sense of what may, at the moment, be of confusion to you. I offer this because if you have erected defenses, you must have enemies. In my own self-interest and that of my colleagues, I feel I must see to it that you can meet those enemies and defeat them, before they become a peril to the rest of us.

Her heart beat faster and she felt light-headed with relief. Was this not what she had prayed for? Was this not what her mother, what *Hanuman himself* had told her she must find?

If you are not utterly insulted by this letter, if you wish to accept my offer, you have but to reply to this address. I will come to your office at any day and hour you specify, or you may send to make an appointment at any other venue you choose. This is not an offer made out of pity or contempt, Doctor Witherspoon. You have not become what you are and achieved your current status without being an admirable and formidable person, *and as a woman, you must surely have faced longer odds and stiffer opposition in your endeavors than any mere male. This offer is made from one craftsman to another, who sees one who is struggling with inferior tools, and has the means to remedy that lack. Sincerely, Peter Scott*

A tugging at her skirt interrupted her before she got to the signature at the end of the letter. She looked down; there was Charan, his eyes fixed on hers, an inkwell and pen clutched carefully in one of his hands. Beside him were the mongooses, each with their sharp teeth piercing a corner of a piece of her monogrammed stationary, Sia with a flat sheet of notepaper, Singhe with an envelope, held high above the floor to avoid treading on it.

Torn between tears of relief and laughter, Maya gently took the writing instruments from them. There was no doubt how *they* thought she should reply.

Sia and Singhe had left neat little puncture marks in the corners of the stationery. She wondered what he would make of that, but put pen to paper, using the little table her breakfast had stood on as an impromptu desk. She wrote swiftly, without thinking, for she knew if she *thought* about what she must say, she would lose the courage to say it.

Dear Sir; I accept your generous offer. Please come to my surgery tonight, at eight o'clock, when the last of my patients will be seen to. There; short and to the point. She signed it, *Doctor M. Witherspoon,* and fanned the paper to dry the ink quickly. In moments, it was folded, tucked into the envelope and sealed with one of the gummed wafers she always kept in each envelope to avoid having to search for them. She didn't recognize the area of the address, but then again, she didn't know a great deal of London.

I've scarcely had time or opportunity to look about. I haven't even seen any of my theatrical patients at their jobs, and heaven knows they've offered me enough tickets, she thought wistfully as she searched in the hall closet for a hat with a veil. She donned the first that came to hand, pulling the concealing web down over her features. This was another Fleet day; she would have to hurry to get there in good time.

She stopped just long enough in her office for a stamp, making her decision to see Peter Scott irrevocable. *No one, having put a stamp to a letter, has ever been known to change his mind about sending it,* she thought wryly, gathering up her umbrella and her medical bag and going out the door. She was tempted to use a touch of magic to make the eyes of passersby avoid her, for she felt ridiculously conspicuous in the veil, but no one, not even people on her own street who knew her, seemed to take any notice of the change in her appearance. And now that she noticed, she was not the only lady to go veiled in the street. There was dust to consider, and the gaze of unwelcome strangers. The dust in particular was getting distinctly unhealthy. It hadn't rained in several days, the air warmed with the first hints of summer, and the "dust" was mostly dried and powdered horse dung. She would have to make certain to brush off at the door of the clinic, and insist that everyone tending patients wear clean boiled aprons and smocks.

There was a postbox on the corner; the letter went in, and she moved on. It was done, and she felt the letter leave her hand with a sense of having put something in motion that it was not in her power to stop. She sighed and quickened her pace. One thing was certain. If this was a typical day at the Fleet, she wouldn't have time to think about the meeting tonight, much less worry about it.

"Hello, old man—what *are* you brooding about? That's a perfectly delightful bit of lamb you've been frowning at for the past minute, and I'm sure it hasn't done anything to *you.*"

Peter Scott looked up from his luncheon with a start. Almsley stood just beside his table, looking at him with a particularly knowing expression. As usual, Lord Peter was impeccably attired in a neat morning suit of gray flannel, his cravat conservatively tied. He must have checked his hat with his coat at the entrance to the club, since he was bareheaded. Sunlight full of dust motes streamed in through the nearest window and glinted off his pale hair, giving him a kind of specious halo. Lord Peter Almsley was an excellent fellow, but no one would ever accuse him of being angelic.

Peter Scott had decided to eat at the club today, rather than one of the pubs or eateries local to his shop. He was out of the mood for bustle and noise, and there certainly wasn't any of *that* here. If anything, the atmosphere was positively drowsy. No one had spoken above a murmur since he sat down.

"Almsley, I didn't know you were in town!" he said, rather inanely, since it hadn't been more than two days since the meeting they had all attended. Lord Peter took that as an invitation to join him, and folded his thin limbs down onto the substantial mahogany chair across the round table, a table which was far too large for a single diner. A waiter appeared immediately, waiting attentively on Lord Peter's wishes. *Where* did they come from? Scott had never been able to catch one hovering, but the moment one wanted something, there was the waiter, at one's elbow. It was a trifle unnerving.

"Exactly what he's having, but I'll give it proper attention," Almsley said. The waiter nodded, and betook himself off, vanishing into that limbo in which the Exeter Club waiters existed when they were neither taking orders nor bringing food. "Now, what has that poor bit of meat done to make you so annoyed at it?" Almsley asked, taking a roll from among the folds of the linen napkin lining the breadbasket between them, breaking it apart with long fingers, and buttering it, somehow turning the simple act into a pantomime the equal of a Japanese tea ceremony, though with none of the solemnity.

Peter chuckled. "It's what I've done that worries me," he replied, rather glad to have someone to talk to. Once the letter had gone out, he'd been taken with mixed feelings. What if she replied? What if she *didn't?* "And I'm afraid that there's a distinct possibility that the other—members—will be more than merely annoyed at me if they find out." He explained what he had discovered about Doctor Witherspoon as succinctly as possible, although he had to catch himself once or twice when he realized he was dwelling on the lady's virtues a little more enthusiastically than the short acquaintance would warrant. Lord Peter's face remained an absolute blank the entire time, telling Scott little or nothing about what the other was thinking.

When he had finished Almsley examined his half-eaten roll with every sign of interest, but his pale blue eyes had that look in them that told Peter that his "twin" had absorbed and was now considering every word he said. He finished just as Almsley's luncheon arrived, but although the plate steamed invitingly when the waiter uncovered it and vanished again, Lord Peter made no move to take up his implements. Instead, he put both elbows on the table, steepled his fingers together, and stared intently at Peter Scott across them. The intelligent eyes took on a sharpness that few people ever saw in them.

"I think, Twin, that you had better not tell anyone about these plans of yours, at least not for a little while," Almsley said. "But I *also* think that this is the only possible thing you *could* do. In your place I'd have done exactly the same, and devil take the hindmost." His eyes gleamed with suppressed enthusiasm. "Even this moment, I'd make the offer to help her, if I wasn't a total stranger. I'd do it if *you* hadn't already, that is. She sounds completely fascinating, this paragon of yours."

"I think she'll be suspicious, and rightly," Scott said thoughtfully. "The trouble is, so far as what I've done is concerned, *and* the way the club is likely to think about it, you're far more likely to—to—"

"To get away with it!" Almsley laughed, loud enough to attract a curious glance or two before the other diners glanced away. Laughter seldom broke the sonorous murmuring of the club dining room. "I *will* help if you think you need an extra set of hands and talents. We can't just leave her the way she is; the magic *will* break out, one way or another, and it's just a jolly good thing that so far it's only broken out in healing and self-defense with her. My grandmother's told me stories—well, if I need to convince *her,* this doctor of yours, I'll trot them out, no need to bore you with them now."

Magic had skipped a generation in Lord Peter's family, and he was the only one of the four siblings in his own generation to have it. *I wonder if some of those stories are about Young Peter? He could very well have been an unholy terror as a child.* Scott kept his smiles to himself, but he was pretty sure that whatever else he'd been like, Peter Almsley had never been a timid or reticent child.

"I may hold you to that promise," Peter Scott replied. "You don't erect a defensive barrier unless there's something to defend against; you don't use magic that confuses other mages as to where you are unless you expect to find another mage looking for you."

"Agreed, to all of it," Lord Peter said, now moving to attack his meal. He sobered just a moment, then lightened again, as if he didn't want to voice his own unease. "Do get the trick of that last bit from her, if you can, won't you? I can think of any number of useful purposes a bit of 'don't look at me' could be put to. Better than being invisible, that."

Why Lord Peter's open approval should have made Peter feel as if a huge weight had been taken from him, he didn't know—until Almsley added, after allowing an expression of bliss to pass across his features following the first bite of his meal, "I'll back you in front of the Old Man himself, if that's needed. Absolutely. And I doubt he'll argue with *me.*"

"You will?" Perhaps he sounded a bit *too* surprised; Almsley chuckled.

"Oh, ye of little faith. Of course I will. We're not doddering about in Victorian parlors anymore. We have serious business to attend to and not enough hands to attend to it. Well, think of it! The more *people* there are in the world, the more *mages* there will be, of course! And the more mages there are, the more likely it is that some of 'em will go to the bad, or be born into it. The Old Man's obstinate refusal to bring in the ladies *or* the—ahem!—tradesmen—"

"Other than me, and that only because I was too strong to ignore—" Peter interrupted, with just a touch of bitterness. "—and even if I wasn't *one of you,* I was at least a ship's captain, which might slide in under the definition of 'gentleman.' "

"Pre-cisely." Lord Peter allowed another bite of the tender lamb to melt on his tongue, and Peter Scott followed his example, finally doing justice to the meal by according it the attention it deserved. "It's antiquated, it's ridiculous, and it's going to cost us one day. What if we need more manpower than we've got? That lot old Uncle Aleister's got hanging about him isn't worth much, but what if some day he corrupts a *real* Master? What if one of the ladies decides she's had enough of being patted on the head and patronized and tells us all to go to hell when we most need her? Have *you* ever had to try and placate an angry Earth Elemental?"

"Ah—no. The project's never come up on my watch." Scott replied carefully.

"I have." Lord Peter's wry expression held no pain, but from the shadows in his eyes, the experience had been no pleasure either. "And if you ever do, you'll be glad enough to have an Earth Master there. The ones that surface in the city are—not pleasant." Lord Peter shrugged. "For some reason, that Mastery tends to go to women and country folk. Neither of which are likely to be invited to the Council if the Old Man continues to have his way."

"See here, Twin—you're not talking palace revolution here, are you?" Peter asked, a spark of alarm lighting up within him. The last thing he wanted to do was to challenge the entire structure of the Council and Lodge! To his relief, Lord Peter laughed.

"Great heavens, no! Just that the Old Man needs to change with the times, and I think your clever doctor may be the one who makes him see that. She's certainly got the brains to best him in argument, and if she's as strong as you say—well, Earth can support Fire, but it can also smother it. I don't think he'd put it to the Challenge." He gestured with his fork. "Now—eat. I've got heredity to thank for my lean and hungry look; there's no excuse for you to go about looking as if you were starving for something."

It was on the tip of Peter's tongue to say that he *was* starving for something, but he was afraid that his "twin" would only make a joke of it. Lord Peter was, to all appearances, perfectly content with his ballet dancers and his sopranos, and to put it bluntly, he had the resources to indulge himself with them as much as he cared to. His rank and wealth allowed him to spend time in the company of many sorts of women, from the educated to the artists, the debutantes to the little dancers. If he wanted the company of an educated woman, or a clever one, he had any number of open invitations to the salons of the intelligentsia. If his need was more—well—carnal, he could afford a woman who made carnality into a delicate and sensual art.

With limited funds came limited choices. Peter Scott had no taste for dance-hall belles, or the women of the dockside bars, and the only other sorts of women he came into contact with were generally someone else's wives. Besides, most of the women he'd met in either venue had minds too shallow to drown a worm. Maya Witherspoon, however—

Enough of that. You're not only putting the cart before the horse, you haven't got cart or *horse yet.* The afternoon post hadn't come when he left the shop; there'd been nothing in the morning post. There was no telling what the doctor would think of his letter. She might not answer it at all.

No, she must! She's intelligent. Surely she's aware of how little she knows, how much more she could be with proper training. He recalled only too clearly the frustration he had felt when the magic began to wake in him, and his natural abilities far outstripped his knowledge. For someone like the doctor, accustomed to having the answers to every dilemma at her fingertips, it must be a torment. Almsley must have been starving; he finished long before Peter Scott did. There was no vulgar business with bills being presented in a private club like this one. A meal was tallied to the member's running account, which was presented at the end of the month. Lord Peter waved off a waiter who appeared to ask him if he wished a sweet, and stood up. "I've got business to attend to, old man—but send a note around when you've heard from the good doctor. I'm deuced curious now."

"I may not hear from her," Scott replied cautiously. "She may think I'm mad."

But his Lordship only chuckled. "Small chance of that," he said confidently. "Only think what you would do in her place, and you'll know I'm right there."

Lord Peter strode off, weaving his way expertly among the tables, leaving Scott to finish his meal in silence. He, too, waved the waiter away when he finally finished all he had an appetite for. The afternoon post should have arrived by now; he had to know if there was an answer in it.

He hurried back to the shop, unlocked it—and there on the mat was a letter, monogrammed in one corner with an M entwined with a W—and as if that wasn't enough to identify it for him, two little puncture marks crowned each end of the W.

He snatched it off the floor and ripped it open, in too much haste to neatly detach the wafer. Mere seconds later, he had her answer.

Initial elation was followed quickly by a certain disappointment. After his own long, heartfelt missive, to get only this bald, bare reply?

Then he shook himself into reasonableness. *What else can she say? She's a lady, she's reticent, she may even be shy; she isn't going to pour her heart out to a stranger, a strange* man. *She's opened herself up enough just by accepting my offer. And, good God, she wants the first meeting tonight! What more could I ask for?*

He looked around the empty shop then, and realized how very long it was going to be until eight o'clock that evening.

Maya alighted from the cab with more than her usual energy at this time of night. She hadn't bothered with the veil coming back; as poorly lit as the streets here were, why trouble herself? Besides, she was in the cab most of the time anyway.

"Thank you, Tom," she said with gratitude. She'd forgotten this was a Saturday, and the resultant number of drunks hanging about the Fleet was double the usual. She'd been glad to get past them and into the waiting cab.

"Moi pleasure, ma'am," Tom replied, with a grin. "The timin' is pretty good anyways, come Satterdays. I usually gets a fella t' take down nears t' the Fleet, an' by th' time I brings ye back here, it's about time fer th' theater crowd, an' you're handy t' that."

"Fair enough—and good luck to you for the rest of the night!" she called after him as he pulled away. She was about to enter the door of her surgery, when the unusual sound of *another* cab coming along arrested her before she could set her hand to the latch.

She wondered for a moment if it wasn't sheer coincidence—but then the cab stopped right at her door, and Peter Scott alighted, paid the driver and exchanged a few words with him, then turned toward her as the second cab moved off.

She smiled; she couldn't help herself. "Very punctual, Mister Scott," she said approvingly.

He touched his hat to her. "I try to be, Doctor Witherspoon."

Good. No "Miss Witherspoon," no "ma'am," and certainly no "Maya" or "Miss Maya." He's not presuming anything, except that I agree with his judgment and accept his offer of teaching. That pleased her; she'd had her fill and more of men who "presumed" far too much, given her mixed heritage. She unlocked the door. He opened it for her, a gentlemanly action, especially given that she was already burdened with her bag and umbrella.

Gupta, on hearing the cab and her key in the lock, materialized in the hallway, and looked surprised, even shocked, to see that she wasn't alone. "Mem sahib—" he began, and then stopped, for once caught without words.

"You remember Captain Scott from yesterday," she prompted. Gupta nodded, cautiously. "Captain Scott was *not* here for a knee ailment, as I'm sure you guessed. He is a man of magic; he came to see what was causing a—"

"—disturbance," Peter Scott supplied, when she groped for words; he did not seem at all surprised that she revealed her secret and his—if it even was one to those in her household—to her servant. "Doctor Witherspoon and I recognized each other for what we are. I am here to—" A slight hesitation, then that charming, faint smile crinkled the corners of his eyes "—to trade my lore for hers, seeing as we come from opposite sides of the world."

Oh, well said!

Gupta's face suddenly lit up, as if Peter Scott had given him his heart's desire. The transformation from suspicious old warrior and wary guardian to this was nothing short of startling. "You are to teach her! Blessed be Lord Ganesh, who has answered my prayers! Oh, mem sahib, this is good, this is *very* good!"

Peter Scott looked thunderstruck; Maya almost laughed at the comical expression on his face. *She* wasn't in the least surprised by Gupta's lightning conclusion, given the revelations she'd had from him last night and his quick mind. He'd known from the moment that Peter Scott entered the door that the knee was pretense; he'd also known that whatever reason there had been for the deception, Maya had penetrated it and dismissed it, because she had invited him into the garden. And the animals clearly approved of him—if Gupta didn't know *exactly* what they were (and she wouldn't necessarily wager that he didn't) he at least knew that they were something special, for they had been her mother's companions once her twin sister deserted her. Anyone *they* approved of could not be bad.

Thus—his quick appreciation of the reason for Captain Scott's appearance at this hour.

"Will you go to the garden? Or to—the other room?" he asked, as Peter Scott struggled to regain his composure.

"The garden for now, I think, Gupta. Please see that we are left alone," she replied, knowing that Gupta would carry out her wishes to the letter. After all, she didn't *need* his physical protection in the garden. *Nisha* was in the garden, and it was well after dark. She would be awake and watching, and eagle-owls had been known to kill (if not carry off) newborn kids and fawns. If Peter Scott dared to lay so much as an unwanted finger on her, he would shortly be displaying a bloody, furrowed scalp.

Gupta simply bowed and vanished. Maya herself led her guest back through the house into the conservatory. Once there, she delayed the moment of truth for a little by lighting several more candle-lanterns, while Scott settled himself into the same chair he had taken yesterday morning. She glanced up, and caught sight of Nisha's eyes gleaming down at her from the shadows above.

A moment more, however, and a swirl of mongooses enveloped Peter Scott's ankles, while Charan took imperious possession of his lap. A laugh escaped him, and he looked surprised that it had.

I don't think he laughs very much, she thought, as she took advantage of her little friends' purposeful confusion to take possession of her chair. *And I think that's a great pity.*

Only when she was seated did they grant him relief from their deliberately exuberant greetings. They both looked at each other for a long, silent moment. Maya decided to be the one to break the silence.

"I am glad that you wrote to me," she said, simply.

"I'm glad that you replied," he countered. "Very. Would it be too much to ask how it is that you—came to be what you are?"

"Not even half trained, you mean?" she responded ruefully. "What magic I learned, I learned on my own, from street magicians and fakirs. My mother could not teach me—oh, she had magic enough, more than enough, but she said that *my* magic was not the magic of *her* land, that it came to me through my father, and it was from my father's people that I must learn it."

"Ah." She watched the shadows of his thoughts flitting across his face. "Well, then," he finally said, with a certain cheer. "There won't be anything for you to unlearn."

She had to laugh at that. "One small blessing, and I suppose I must be grateful for every blessing in this sorry situation. So; please, start from the beginning. Explain to me; tell me about—" she thought quickly back to his letter "—explain to me about Elementals, and Masters, and all the rest."

"What, am I to be your storyteller now?" he asked, in what was clearly mock indignation, much to her delight. "Well, then, on your own head be it if you are bored—because I am very *bad* at telling stories!"

Actually, she thought, as she listened attentively to his explanations, he was a very *good* storyteller. Or to put it more truly, he was very good at making clear explanations of things she had felt, but could not articulate. She settled in to absorb all that she could, with all the intensity she had ever put into learning medicine.

There were no illusions about what she was about to learn, no matter how Peter Scott diverted her. This was more important than anything she had ever put her mind to, for if she did not master what she needed to know, and quickly . . .

. . . then she might never have the chance to learn anything ever again—other than the answer to the question of whether it was Christian Heaven, Hindu Wheel, or something else entirely that awaited after death.

SHADOWS moved in the corners of the room, but Kali Durga's priestess knew that there could be no one present here but herself. Her servants were afraid to come into the temple when the priestess was present, fearing, no doubt, that if a sacrifice was required and nothing appropriate was at hand, one of them would be taken. Silly creatures; Shivani would never sacrifice a servant, not unless the servant became intractable and disobedient, for where would she get a trained replacement? And no servant of Shivani's ever became disobedient. She never gave them the reason or the freedom to disobey. She never terrified them enough so that they felt pushed into an inescapable corner by their fears, and she never gave them enough leisure to contemplate any other life but this.

As for her followers, the thugees and the dacoits, they worshiped Shivani with a fervor second only to that which they very properly accorded the Goddess. She had told them never to enter while she was in meditation. Therefore, unless the temple was burning down around her ears, or the wretched English invaded it, they never would. It was quite that simple.

Incense smoke, heavy and sweet, with a faint hint in its odor that called up a memory of spilled blood, hung in uneven striations across the length of the room. The smoke diffused and dimmed the uncertain light of many candles ranged in pottery lanterns made to resemble carved stone. It overpowered the stink of boiled cabbage and sausages (a hideous, ancient smell of poverty and despair that permeated the entire building) and managed at last to sweep it away.

Shivani hated that smell. She hated everything about the English, it was true, but that *smell*—it was impossible to escape, a constant reminder of where she was. But she needed a place large enough to contain her, the temple, and her followers and servants, yet a place where she and hers would not attract undue attention. There *was* no Indian quarter; the immigrants from home here in London were either servants and had their own places in an English master's house, or the wealthy offspring of the Brahmin caste and were invariably male and attending Cambridge or Oxford. Although price had not played a factor in where Shivani settled her flock, the requirement for invisibility had. That meant there was only one place where she and Kali Durga's people could go; the East End, where immigrants of darker complexions than her, stranger languages than Urdu, and religions equally as alien to the English swarmed in their thousands. Shivani had commandeered a kind of warehouse with apartments attached, paying the asked-for price without bargaining, and the former owner had not asked questions. He had simply thrown out the current tenants at her request, clearing the way for her people.

But the stink of them remained, and the same smells penetrated the cleansed building at every meal.

At least the incense was able to chase it out of the temple. Blue wisps of the heavy smoke curled around the altar at the northern end of the room, garlanding the painted statue of Kali Durga, with Her blue tongue protruding, Her heavy, round breasts obscured by Her necklace and Her garlands, Her hands red, and not with henna or paint. The source of the smoke, charcoal braziers in each corner, kept the room at a properly elevated temperature, so that here in *Her* place, Shivani was warm enough without resorting to piles of wrappings.

Garlands of marigolds bedecked the statue, partly concealing the necklaces of skulls that were Kali Durga's only clothing above the waist. More of them draped over Her several arms, Her hands holding severed heads, daggers, or making sacred gestures. Kali Durga's altar, gilded and most gloriously carved, with demons of every description writhing about the skulls at each corner, was as magnificent as her statue, and just as newly created. Both, in fact, had been made in this very room, once the room had been cleansed and consecrated. Shivani knew that the wretched British sahibs, warned about the cult of thugee, were apt to poke their inquisitive noses into cargoes sent out of the country by natives rather than the trading companies of other sahibs. Unfortunately, the Colonial Police were perfectly capable of recognizing a statue of the Goddess of the cult when they saw it. So Shivani had emigrated with no statues, no altars, nothing to furnish a temple. She brought instead a skilled and devout woodcarver, an artist of the first rank, a maker of holy images with more talent in his littlest finger than most men could ever dream of commanding. Shivani truly believed that had his hands been amputated he could carve with his feet. Take them, and he would carve with a knife held in his teeth.

Only the altar and the statue needed to be made on the spot, for all the rest of the furnishings of a temple were to be had in the marketplaces of London. From the braziers to the incense burners, from the carved screens adorning the walls to the offering bowl at Kali's feet, everything in this room had been bought openly of dealers in exotic goods or in the myriad street markets. Often enough, Shivani's minions had purchased articles stolen from *other* temples to furnish Kali's place of worship. It gave her an ironic sense of satisfaction to beautify the temple of Kali Durga with holy things recleansed and redeemed from those who valued them not—except as trophies they did not understand.

One such piece was the throne that Shivani herself now occupied, set against the southern wall of the room, directly opposite the statue. From here she could sit and contemplate her Goddess and plan the next move in the chess game of power and death she was playing so far from her homeland.

It was a dangerous game, and one with high stakes. If she succeeded, she would bring the war to wrest India away from her conquerors right to the usurpers' very door—no, more than that. It would allow her to destroy the usurpers in their own, soft, safe beds. She would bring terror to the streets of London, which would in turn infect the rest of the country with its contagion. Her task was to make it clear to those *here* who made the decisions about the Empire that they were no longer safe, that they could no longer hide behind distance and the never-ending ranks of their soldiers. She must send that same unreasoning fear into the home of every ordinary shopkeeper and clerk as well. Only when the common man and sahib alike clamored that it was too expensive to hold India would the High and the Mighty consent to release it.

If she failed—

But she would not fail. Not she, not with all her cunning and knowledge. She *could* not fail.

Those carved screens fanned out to the rear of the statue in a semicircle; behind them, the walls and ceiling, for now, were swathed in silk. Beneath the silk, hidden until they were ready to be shown, were the mural-paintings that Rakesh was currently working on. These would not be unveiled until he had completed them, and even Shivani did not know what they would look like. Not that she was worried at all what they would show or even if they would be suitable, for Rakesh belonged to the Goddess, heart and soul, and as his statue and altar showed, he was the finest of all the artists of his own generation, finer than many of the previous generations.

The priestess smiled up into the eyes of her Goddess; for the first time since she had arrived in this wretched, cold country, Shivani was content. She sighed, and inhaled a deeper breath of the incense, reveling in the flat, sweet taste in the back of her throat that purged away the everlasting reek of garlic and cabbage. The compounding of the incense, one of her many tasks as Kali's servant, was accomplished from a recipe only Her priests and priestesses knew. Shivani made it herself, in a room in which she kept the myriad ingredients for her many, many purposes. The knife and the strangling scarf were not Kali's only weapons.

The shrine was not complete, but it was at last ready for ritual use. At this very moment, out there in the fog-wreathed streets, Shivani's minions were at work, harvesting lives for the Goddess. For now, those lives were petty ones, true, the sacrifices confined to those who probably would have come to a bad end before the year was out anyway. In places with strange names, like Cheapside and Whitechapel, life was of little worth, the coin quickly spent, and few of those who wandered the streets of a night had any who cared enough to look for former acquaintances when they vanished. No one of any real importance would notice these people missing, and no one in authority would bother to look for them even if they *were* missed. And why should they? Distasteful as it was, the creatures that Shivani's servants extinguished were nothings, nameless, the Untouchables of the sahibs' world. The power to be derived from these pitiful creatures was minimal, but each death sent strength and magic back to the shrine and to Shivani, and tiny sacrifices at this point were not to be despised.

Soon enough there would be more meaningful deaths, victims with longer lives ahead of them, perhaps even a hint of magic in their veins. *Those* would be more acceptable, and more useful to Shivani; fat, foolish, complacent English, harvested like their fat, foolish sheep. The thugee would be happier too, for there was no challenge in slipping the silk scarf about the neck of a drunken tramp sprawled in the street in a stupor, nor in tightening the cord about the neck of a worn-out, gin-steeped whore or a fallen fool dreaming over a pipe of the Black Smoke. Shivani didn't blame them for being disappointed at seeking such petty prey, but she needed more information before she could send them after richer game. They dared not chance discovery, not yet, so victims of a better class had to be selected with great care. There should be no relations to raise an alarm, no employers to seek for an errant employee. And most importantly, no police.

She already knew what class she would select for her first real blow of vengeance. Retired soldiers were what she needed, men who had once served in the Raj and so deserved death. Men, officers in particular, who were to be found frugally spending their pensions in little bed-sitters; those were the prey she wanted. Men who had never married or had lost their wives—men with no siblings, no parents. Later, of course, when her power was greater, she would take those she had rejected as too risky; she would take them, *and* their families, down to the least and littlest. Then the campaign of terror would begin. But for now, she must take her victims quietly, and that meant that the victims themselves must be nearly invisible.

She had another criterion as well; these, preferably, would be men who had shed Indian blood in the course of their careers, or equally well, had left deserted, weeping Indian girls behind them betraying them with promises of love and marriage. Or both. Revenge on men such as these would be pleasing to Kali Durga, and the power derived from their deaths would be pleasing to Her priestess. Shivani caressed the carved arms of her throne, knowing that it was only a matter of time before her intelligence gatherers brought her a list of such men.

They would die—oh, yes, they would die most satisfactorily, and then their bodies would slide soundlessly into the river, weighted down by bags of stones about their necks. *Perhaps,* weeks or months from now, what was left would rise sluggishly to the surface and be discovered, but Shivani thought that unlikely. There were too many hungry creatures in the Thames, and the waters ran swiftly to the ocean. Even with stones about the neck, the bodies swept on to feed the creatures of the sea.

This was, of course, by no means the limit of Shivani's plans for the immediate future. There were other possible victims as well, victims who could be lured *here* or would even come of their own free will. Once again, she would not take any who could be traced here, but there was an abundance of fools in this city, as demonstrated by the number of "mystic societies." Why was it that the English were such idiots about magic? No wise person meddled with magicians; the ignorant villager might seek out a guru to take off a curse or remove a demon, but he did so with great care, and did *not* run to discover the magician's power or claim it for himself. Not so the English, who prided themselves upon their bravery. One whiff of magic in the air, and the moths came swarming around, greedy, ineffectual aesthetes who longed for power but wanted it *given* them rather than putting in the effort to earn it. The chela of even the least offensive and meekest of gurus knew he must serve and serve diligently before the secrets would be unfolded to him; these arrogant ignoramuses demanded secrets they did not have the faintest hope of mastering.

It was unbelievable, how these arrogant, brainless peacocks came strutting to her, offering their throats for the knife if they but knew it! She had a guise in the world outside this basement room. There was a small apartment just above where Shivani held forth in the person of a dispenser of arcane knowledge of the shadow-shrouded sort. To her came the seekers who had no patience for study, who had rather they could achieve mastery over Fate and Men by overmastering demons and *that* by the quickest means possible. They thought themselves greatly daring, these chattering apes. They did not see the serpent gliding silently behind them.

Some would not be missed. Those, she would gather unto Kali, strengthen the Goddess with their blood, and thus increase her own strength.

One, she already had taken.

It had been a temptation she had not been able to resist, for the fool so courted his own death. Disowned by family, despised by those who knew him, even by his own fellows in the arts of darkness, he was overripe for the taking. Believing the tales she told him of his potential prowess and future bliss, he had drunk Shivani's potions, smoked her Black Smoke, and laid himself down on her altar without a qualm, so certain was he in his arrogance that she, a mere Hindu female, could never harm him. *She* was no more than the common vessel who brought him his just rewards, a bearer, a servant of a power far greater than she. He was Man, he was White, and he was destined to command Unseen Powers.

He was stupid, he was a fool, and his Powers answered him not when he commanded them. On her altar he died, the scarlet silk cord about his neck, tongue protruding, eyes bulging, face black-ened. Shivani herself had twisted the cord tight, taking the greatest of satisfaction in it.

Shivani dedicated his death to Kali Durga, but she drank his strength herself, imprisoning his spirit in a little, round mirror she had found in a street market. The stall keeper had not known what he had got, but few would have recognized the plate of black glass set in a carved wooden frame for what it was. She bought it for less than a shilling, and straightaway took it to her sanctuary.

The mystery of it delighted her; it was as if some unknown hand had made it and placed it in the market for her to find. A Black Mirror! Who in all this benighted country had the wit and the knowledge to create a Black Mirror? And mystery piled upon mystery—why had it never been used? For it was virgin, empty of the least hint of magic, when she discovered it.

One guess was that perhaps the Black Mirror was not used in this land as Shivani was wont to use it. That was the only answer *she* had for the puzzle.

Now the Mirror slept in the basket beside her throne, swathed in a shroud of black silk, waiting only until *she* was ready to make use of her newest servant.

She had made use of him already, in several smaller trials—ordering him to show her where her thugees were at work, or having him find the strongholds of other practitioners of magic, who could presumably see her as a rival or as a threat. She knew now where the strongest resided, and had added them to her long-term plans, but now it was time to put her servant to work on something nearer to home.

She sprinkled powder of a different kind on the charcoal in the brazier at her feet, breathed in the drug-laden air, and felt at last the moment of disorientation that she had been waiting for. She did not drift off, she merely felt as if she hovered just a little above her body.

That was all she wanted. Any more, and she would lose her grip on her awareness and drift free. That could be useful, but it was not what she wanted to do at this moment; she needed only to be relieved of the distractions of a physical form, not to escape altogether. Her hand reached, seemingly of its own volition, into the basket beside her, and brought out the little, round mirror of black glass.

She cradled it in her lap, staring into depths that did *not* reflect the lazy swirls of smoke, nor her own face, but held a restless, glowing, featureless shape that swam within the glass like a furtive fish among water weeds.

"Mirror-servant in my hand," she murmured languorously to it, "Answer thou to my command."

The glowing presence moved to the foreground, fogging the mirror with sickly light. *Release me!* the prisoner wailed soundlessly. *Let me go!*

"I thought you wanted to live forever?" she replied with a smile, aloud, although her servant understood her well enough if she only *thought* what she wanted to say at it. "You begged, you pleaded for magic and immortality, for the ability to understand the Unseen world, for the knowledge to move bodiless through this world and go into the realm of spirits. I gave you immortality, did I not? So long as a single grain of this glass remains intact, you are bound to it; surely you will live forever! I gave you all the rest as well!" Then she laughed, throatily. "You understand the Unseen as no other of your acquaintance, you go into the realm of the spirits, and though you move through the Unseen at my will, and not yours, *I* never told you that you would have freedom therein. But—still! You show your ingratitude, and how little you deserve any kind of freedom!"

You didn't tell me what you meant! the shape howled in protest. *You didn't tell me I'd* die! *You deceived me!*

"You deceived yourself," she retorted severely. "I told you, and promised you exactly the truth. That you put your own interpretation on that truth is hardly my fault. Now, enough of this nonsense. Obey me, else I will force you, and you have had a taste of what I can do to you. Show me the traitor to my people and my land!"

For a fleeting moment, before she lashed it with a spark of pain and punishment, so that the thing trapped within the glass cried out in anguish, the mirror showed her *own* face.

"No more of that!" she snapped, before regaining control and composure. "Show me the treacherous daughter of my traitoress sister! Show me the thing that claims the power that is mine by right of blood!"

But there was nothing forthcoming. Shivani frowned, and prodded the mirror-servant again with the sharp and punishing goad of her will. *I can't!* the servant wailed. *I cannot show you!*

"Cannot, or *will* not?" she asked, furious. "You *will* do what I command!"

Cannot! She is here, somewhere, she is near to you, within the bounds of the city but I cannot find her! There are signs of her everywhere, but not one leads to her!

Shivani cursed her pawn for being a fool, weak, and useless—but did not curse him as a liar. She could command the truth if she wished, but she already knew that her unwilling servant had told the truth in the first place. She had already tried every means at her disposal to find the girl, and had come to the same end as her servant. Surya's daughter was nowhere to be found, yet traces of her were everywhere. The only possible explanation for this was that she had somehow managed the magic that enabled holy men to walk amid crowds and yet remain unseen—or to be precise, completely ignored and isolated among them. That should *not* have been possible, with no one to teach her the secrets that Surya had learned in her own temple, but there was no denying the facts. The girl *knew,* was using her knowledge, and even a mirror-servant, who should have been able to eel his way past any common protections, could not find her.

Shivani ground her teeth and forbore to smash the mirror to pieces there and then. The mirror-servant was still useful, though clearly limited. She confined herself to punishing it with pain until nothing emerged from the depths of the black glass but incoherent whimpers.

Anger temporarily assuaged, she dropped the black mirror back into the cushioning swaths of black silk, and carelessly dropped a fold over the top of it. Let it rest and recover from its punishment. At least next time it would be more eager to placate and serve her.

Magic had failed her; no matter. Those who lived by magic often neglected to guard themselves in other ways. The girl could not possibly hide herself forever. Shivani grew stronger every day, and as she grew stronger, her small army of followers multiplied. At some point, she would have even English servants under her control. Granted, she would not trust them if they were *not* utterly under her power, but once she had them, she could loose them and let *them* do her hunting for her, in circles where her thugee could not go.

And that reminded her; she had an appointment.

With a grimace, she rose from her throne in a rustle of silk and a rasping of gold embroideries. It was time to dress; the idiot sahibs expected yards of white silk gauze and flowers, or black gauze and heavy gold jewelry, depending on whether she was feigning to be the dispenser of light or shadow. In either case, they would only have been confused by her embroidered red sari. They liked their symbols clear and simple to read.

She put herself into the hands of her waiting-woman, indicating with a nod of her head that she would be the mysterious "Lady of Night" for this meeting and not the innocent "Lady of the Moon." When she emerged from the secret passage that connected the apartments she used for the cult and the tiny flat she used for her English assignations, she was swathed in a cloud of darkness that merely hinted at the trim body beneath, and veiled with black silk as well. She found it easier to be in the same room as the English when she wore a veil; they were mesmerized by the thing, unable to read her eyes, and she didn't feel as if she was forced to breathe their tainted exhalations.

This was as much a staged setting as the temple, but here she was the focus of the room. A deep-pile, figured carpet laid over a padding of more carpets so worn as to be worthless created a floor that didn't even squeak when she walked over it. In this room, all the walls were swathed in dark maroon fabric that was gathered together at the midpoint of the ceiling, like a tent. From that point depended a pierced-metal lantern fitted with colored glass panels. This was the sole source of light in the room, and the colored light, red and blue, served to confuse more than it revealed. At the back, she had made use of a little alcove, pulling aside the fabric and creating a canopy above it. Creating a platform within the alcove and piling it with pillows gave her a kind of dais on which she sat. Petitioners standing before her were at her eye level. If they chose to sit, they had to do so on one of the several flat cushions placed in front of her, and so would be much below her. On either side of the platform were incense holders.

Shivani arranged herself in full lotus position on her platform, and gestured to the servant who had followed her to light the incense burners on either side of it. The drugs she had inhaled earlier had worn off, leaving her mind clear, making everything sharp-edged. She made a pattern in the air, whispered a few words as the smoke from the braziers rose about her. There was more hashish mixed in with the strong incense; not enough to bother *her,* bolstered as she now was against its effects by the subtle spell, but enough to fuddle her visitors.

She used every weapon she could get against the English sahibs, especially when she had one in her view that could prove more than merely useful.

Such a one was this, who stepped into the room with all the arrogant confidence of one who felt he had the right to anything that met his eye.

This man was not the sort—outwardly—to be expected in this place. His type was of the sort that figured in advertisements and tales of "manly men." Tall, with hair of short-cropped, new-minted gold, the body of a warrior of sorts, with ruddy cheeks, a small mustache, and a perfectly pressed suit, he was the very epitome of everything Shivani hated.

He was used to his steps sounding firmly on the floor, and was slightly nonplussed when they made not a whisper on the soft carpets. He was accustomed to having someone meeting him when he entered a room. It took him aback to be forced to scan a darkened chamber for the person he had come to see, and then have the disadvantage that *she* could see *him* clearly, but he could not see very much of her. He didn't even notice the drug taking hold of him, making him a little more clumsy (and self-conscious) when he stood before her and had to decide between the indignity of facing her on his feet, like a child about to be chastised, or sitting uncomfortably on the ground.

He finally chose the ground, and she was much amused, watching him folding his long legs as he tried to find something like a position he could hold for any length of time.

All this time, she had not said a word to him. Only when he was seated did she acknowledge his presence.

"Speak," she said. Nothing more. No questions, no greetings, only the barest of beginnings. And an order—not a request, nor the expected query of "how may I serve you?" He was here as the petitioner; it was *she* who would be served, and she would drive that home to him with even the tiniest of gestures.

Nothing loath—and aided, no doubt, by the drugs in his brain, he carried on for some time. He began with his importance (largely existing only in his own eyes, although the one claim to status he had, he did not mention), his occult prowess (minimal), his knowledge (surface), and ended in a demand that she add to his enlightenment (as she had expected).

But this man was not *quite* such a fool as others of his sort had been, and Shivani gave him a different answer than she had the rest. He had seen through to the heart of the group headed by one called "Crawly" (or something like it), and had found it rotten. He had gone to the woman Blat-sky and discovered that the only things *she* had to offer were stolen and discarded bits of true wisdom, overlaid with a tinsel-dross of half-truth, flattery, and lies to make it pretty and palatable. He *did* have enough native talent in the occult to see that she had real power. So instead of giving him half-truth herself, and implying she could grant him things she had no intention of granting, she gave him a less embroidered version than the one she had caught her mirror-servant with.

But first, she laughed scornfully.

"So, the novice seeks to be Archbishop before he has even made his first vows!" she taunted him in flawless English, which probably startled him the more. "Either you are a fool, or you take me for one. So which is it, O Lord of the World? Are *you* the fool, or do you think you can deceive one who can see into your empty head and heart?" She tilted her head mockingly, and waited for his answer.

He gritted his teeth, but did not get up and walk out, nor snap back an immediate insult.

"So, you have *some* self-control, at least," she said when he made no reply. "That is better than your erstwhile friends who follow the Dawn." He started, and stared at her, the whites showing momentarily about his eyes. "Oh yes, I know of them, and of *you,* and all you have said and done with them; why should this surprise you?" she continued. "I have what they only pretend to, *as* you know. Well. You have ordered me about, and you have seen what that brings you. Now what will you do?"

What he did was the unusual but not entirely unexpected step of humbling himself. He bowed his proud head to her, although the stiffness in his neck was due entirely to pride and not to muscle strain.

"I apologize for my poor manners," he said at last, after taking himself in hand and subduing his temper and his arrogance.

"That is an improvement." She nodded, indicating that he should go on.

"I—" He gritted his teeth again; she heard them grinding. "I beg that you should accept me as a disciple."

"And what will you offer me for the privilege?" she asked, again surprising him. "What, why should you be astonished? What I have is of value. Every Master is entitled to a fee for taking an Apprentice; the difference between me and those you have sought out in the past is that I am honest about requiring that fee, and I have far more to teach you than they have. You have so far given me no indication that you have any intention of making an exchange of value for value."

His indignation was evident in every movement of his body—but he reached into his pocket for his wallet before she stopped him with an abrupt gesture of rejection.

"Money? I think *not,* Englishman," she said sharply. "What need have I of the dross of your money? My Goddess grants anything I need; I need not contaminate myself with your leavings to supply my wants." She waved her hand around her chamber. "Look about you! I have no hordes of idiot English hangers-on, and you see how I live. That I choose to dwell *here* and not in some 'fashionable district' is a matter of my convenience and privacy, and not because I cannot *afford* to live there. You must offer me something better than your abominable English pounds and pence."

Clearly he had never found anyone who so forcefully rejected his money before. Shivani wasn't at all surprised at that; the Blat woman's begging habits were a matter of mirth among her dacoits, one or two of whom had penetrated the ranks of her servants before they learned just how empty her promises were. And the Crawly-man regularly milked the largesse of his disciples, though with a little more finesse.

Now the petitioner's mood shifted from indignation to puzzlement. "Then what do you want?" he asked, so thoroughly discomfited that he had become, had he but known it, as malleable as she could have wished. She leaned forward; he mirrored her action, his ruddy cheeks pale with strain. He wanted what she had, more than wanted it. Under the influence of her manner and the drugs, he craved it. He would not yet do *anything* to get it, but that would come.

"Nothing small," she replied in a low voice. "Only what is proper. For the reward of becoming my disciple, I demand no less than your service, your devotion, and your obedience in all things."

Over the course of the next hour, they bargained, but it was hopeless on his side of the bargain from the moment that he had asked what she wanted. In the end, she had him. He didn't know she had him, body and soul, but she did. He went away with orders to carry out; only when he had fulfilled them would she teach him anything.

For now his orders were simple things, and so far as he knew, harmless. He was merely to procure a list of addresses from the pension rolls of an importation company—one which imported opium as well as tea, and dealt in jewels which were not always honestly gotten—in which he was a not-so-petty official. When he brought it back to her, she would have a list of men who had worked in one of the many companies that traded in Indian misery, in this case, headquartered in Calcutta. From this, she could choose potential victims.

He protested over her instructions, and blustered, but they both knew it was merely for form's sake. *He* had not enough imagination to construe what she wanted with the list, and even if he had known, he probably would not have believed she had the means to carry out her plans. He went away knowing that there is always a price for anything that is genuine. That was the first step in what *might* become an extensive education, if he returned.

She summoned her handmaiden to escort the man to the street. The girl came with one of the dacoits, which was wise of her, in case the English decided to take out his humiliation on his escort. The dacoit was the one who took the man away; the handmaiden remained with her mistress.

"Come," Shivani said, and returned to her private rooms to take off her ridiculous guise and assume a more comfortable set of garments.

There was, of course, the chance that the man would get his wits about him and not make a second visit; that was the chance she always had to take. You did not capture an ape with shouting and chasing after it. You caught it by careful planning, tempting it in with things it could not resist, and seducing it with pleasures it was loath to do without. Only when the pleasures had become necessities did you close the door of the trap.

If he did not return, there would be others like him. This one was useful in that he had already tried and tested other groups in this place who purported to have some dealings with the Unseen—and he had access to those "lists." It would be much easier to choose those who should die first, if she had those lists.

Of course, if all went according to her plans, eventually there would not be an English soul on this island that was not dead or a slave to the shrine of Kali Durga (or both)—but until that bright day dawned—it would be convenient, so *very* convenient—to have the lists.

PETER Scott had never been a teacher before, but Maya Witherspoon was such an eager learner that any defects in his teaching were inconsequential. "The main thing is that all of these names and conventions we use are only that, and no more: conventions," Peter pointed out, doing his best to keep from being distracted by the doctor's intense gaze and proximity. The way she concentrated on him reminded him strongly of the owl on the branch just overhead. She didn't look away for a second, and her gaze, while not threatening, was not in the least *mild.* He'd seen that look before—most notably on Almsley's face—and it meant that nothing was going to distract that person from whatever his or her goal was.

He struggled for a moment with an analogy, and finally the conservatory in which they sat gave him one. "Magic is—oh—like sunlight; it's everywhere, even moonlight is reflected sunlight, after all. We just deal with it inside of a structure *we* understand—and in the case of the Elemental Masters, the structure is mostly Greek, some Egyptian, and a bit of all the old pagans that ever roamed Europe."

Did she smile? It was hard to tell if there had been a faint smile on her lips, or if the subtly shifting lamplight had put the fleeting expression there. "We are a bit like that in India, too," she murmured. “A little borrowed from this, a minor god of the crossroads added there—the hand of Buddha, the touch of Mohammed—and who knows? Perhaps even the words of Christian teachers who came even before Constantine ruled. We are great borrowers.”

Her voice soothed his nerves, for they were certainly playing him up in her presence, and he went on, encouraged. “The thing is, that over time—centuries!—that structure’s taken on a life of its own, just as yours has, I suppose. Magic’s also like metal; heat it and pour it into a mold, or sculpt it like wax, and it’s going to keep that shape. So *here,* in the West, we have Water, Earth, Fire, and Air Magic, and the corresponding Elemental Creatures to serve our uses—that’s the structure, the mold that we pour the magic into to give it shape, and what we use to shape the magic to our own ends.”

“I wish I had the benefit of a structure,” she said wistfully, for a moment just speaking her thoughts aloud. “I have never learned the structure of the magic of home. I have been groping in the darkness, like the blind men with their elephant. I have bits, but no grasp of the whole.” Maya did not pause long for any self-pity, but drove back to the subject at hand. “But why do you have *this* shape and no other? How is it that you actually have creatures of the Elements to command?” she asked.

Here he was on solid ground, and felt comfortable providing an explanation. “It’s my theory that we can blame the Greeks, since they were the first old fellows to have much of a written tradition. It’s easier to preserve a way of thinking if it’s written down, you see. It’s easier to *have* a structure and build on it if you’ve got it written and less subject to change.”

“I *do* see,” Maya said, nodding, oblivious to the soft strands of hair that had escaped from her chignon and curled charmingly around her face. Peter tried to remain oblivious too, but with less success.

“*I* think that’s the entire reason for why our magic works this way,” Peter continued. “I think we’ve got the Elementals because we’ve believed in ’em for so long, but there are those who say the Elementals came first.”

"There is probably no way to tell now," Maya replied, tapping one finger thoughtfully on the arm of her chair. "And except for a scholar, who cares only for hunting down the roots of things, I cannot see that it matters." She shrugged. "It *is.* So I must and will work with it. If my patient has a wound, it is my duty to treat and heal it, not wonder about how he got it."

"It matters to the insatiably curious," Peter amended, thinking with amusement of Almsley. "I can think of a couple of my colleagues who'll want to stir about in your recollections and try and pick out the differences between Western magic and Eastern."

She made a dismissive gesture. "They will have to wait until we—I—have more leisure. You say that *I* have the magic of Earth? How did you know? And what, then, is yours?"

"I knew because of affinities," he responded. "That is—how *my* magic responded to yours. I'm Water; Water nourishes Earth, or washes it away, and I saw that in the colors, in the *sense* of your magic. You do know that magic has colors?"

"Oh, yes!" she responded. "My mother's was like mine, all warm golds and yellow-browns; it tastes of cinnamon and saffron, and feels like velvet warmed in front of a fire."

She tastes and feels her magic? Good Lord—she's stronger in it than I thought!

"Well, mine's greens and turquoise, and it tastes of exactly what you'd expect—*water.* Every kind of water there is, depending on where I am and what I'm doing," he told her. "It feels like water, too—in every way that water can be felt, especially things like currents. If I'd been Fire, I'd see and feel things about Fire that are just as subtle. I'd also have recognized that you were Earth, and have known—just in the way that you can recognize the familiar accent of someone from India speaking English when you hear it—that Earth can support Fire, or smother it. Now, Earth and Air have no affinity at all, and if I'd been Air, I would have felt that as well—a lack of anything connecting us. Earth and Air are the complete opposites; so are Fire and Water."

"I should think more so—with Fire and Water," Maya said, weighing her words. "Wouldn't they be enemies?"

She picked up that quickly enough. "Ye-es, sometimes. Mind you, any mage who's gone over to the Black Lodges can be the enemy of any mage of the White. But, well, it's prudent on the part of a Fire Master to be circumspect with a Master of Water. In a duel of equals, should it come to that, Water almost always has the advantage." *Which might account for the way that Alderscroft treats me.* "By the same logic, though, Air and Fire are natural allies, and work very well together."

"And so are Earth and Water." She tilted her head to one side, and added dryly, "How fortunate for me."

"So are Earth and Earth!" he said hastily. "The *only* reason I haven't turned you over to an Earth Master for training is that there aren't any in London. They don't like cities, as a rule. I don't think you've got the time to trot out to Surrey two or three times a week or more—that's where the nearest one I know of is—and I couldn't get Mrs. Phyllis into London with a team of horses dragging her here. Peter Almsley's got another in his family—a cousin—but that's even farther out, and Cousin Reuben won't ever leave his gardens *or* his flock. He's a vicar, you see."

"I can't say that I blame him," Maya replied, with a hint of a wistful note. "No, I can't leave my patients any more than he can leave his charges. Not at the moment, anyway. If I'm to go haring off into the countryside, I'll have to find another physician to take some of my days at the Fleet, and that won't be easy. Not a full physician, anyway, not even another female physician; they all have their own concerns." Once again, she was thinking aloud, and he was secretly pleased that she had sufficient trust in him to relax enough to do so. "I *might* be able to get those who want surgery practice, though, so they can be certified . . . if I offer to pay them for other work on condition they act as surgeons for gratis." Making her own calculations, she didn't need any opinions from him, and Peter held his tongue. "It can wait, though—you said as much. *You* can teach me for now, without my trying to find substitutes."

He nodded. "It's the affinities—Water can serve as an initial teacher to Earth easily enough, just as Fire can to Air. And vice versa, of course."

"Of course," she echoed, her eyes reflecting that her mind was already elsewhere. "Is that why you became a man of the sea? That you were already a Water Master?"

Oh, he liked the quick way she picked up on things! "I wasn't a *Master* at the time, but yes." He nodded. "I went straight off to the first ship that *felt* right, and applied as a cabin boy when I was eleven. Would it surprise you to learn that the captain of *that* ship was a Water Master?"

She looked amused. "Not very, no."

He made a gesture with his upturned hand. "There you have it. If we have the choice, mages tend to pick occupations that reflect their magic, *and* if they aren't singled out by a Master of their own element, they go looking for one. Earth—well, you get some trades that are obvious, farmers, herdsmen, herbalists, gamekeepers, gardeners—but there are also a fair lot of midwives, animal handlers, and trainers, and although you're the first physician I know of, there're clergymen, a lawyer or two, and the odd squire here and there. Water's almost always a sailor or fisherman, a riverman, a canal worker, but I know of a couple of artistic types, another lawyer and an architect and several fellows who work in the city and never have anything to do with sailing. And Lord Peter, of course; he's some sort of diplomat. Fire—metalsmiths, glassworkers, firefighters, but also soldiers, the odd lad in government service. Air, though, they tend to be the scholars, the artists, or the entertainers. *Lots* of creative types in Air."

"But not always."

"But not always," he agreed. "Lord Peter Almsley's Water and, as I mentioned, diplomat—I think. They're always sending him off to the continent chasing this or that, anyway. He's really creative in his own sphere; he's certainly entertaining, and he's as persuasive a speaker as any great actor. It isn't his Element that gave him his purpose and job, it's his glib tongue. It's not just the magic, you see, it's what situation in life you were born to, and your natural talents, which don't necessarily march in time with your magic. And anyway, you never *start* with learning Elemental Magic."

Her eyes grew puzzled. "Why not?"

"Because you either have to coax or coerce the Elementals to work for you, and that takes practice and working in the raw basics first. Not all Elementals are—nice." He thought for a moment about some of the habits of his own affinity. "Some are vicious. If they heard your call, they might come to it, just so they could hurt you. If you weren't strong enough to defend yourself, they *would.* Hurt you, that is."

Maya's lips formed a surprised "O" although she made no sound.

He decided at that point that both of them had enough of abstracts for the moment. "Just so you know. Forewarned and all that. Are you ready to try some of those basics?"

"I think so. Can we work here?" Her last words were hesitant, and he suspected that she had preserved a chamber here in the house where she worked her spells. He also suspected that it was an annex of her own bedchamber, and she hesitated to bring a man and a stranger so near to it. *I* am *a stranger,* he reminded himself. *No matter that it seems less that way with every minute that passes. I'm lucky she lets me in here alone with her at all.*

"We can," he said, and was rewarded with a genuine smile of relief. "Of course we can. Especially since the first of your lessons will be in constructing protections between your household and whatever is—" he waved his hand in the general direction of the street, "—out there. The difference between what you've been doing until now and what I'll show you is that we'll be building those protections on a foundation based in your own Element."

Oh, Peter, that *made you sound like a right pompous ass!* He winced. She didn't notice, though; or at least, she was too polite to show that she had.

He rose; she did the same. "Would you feel more comfortable with some concrete symbols of what we're doing, or not?" he asked diffidently. "I mean, would it help you if I actually drew chalk diagrams on the floor, or outlines, or whatever?"

"I think," she said, with a flavoring of irony, "that we needn't frighten the others with chalked diagrams. As a doctor, I have to imagine what is going on inside my patients, to lay them bare in my mind so that I can treat them."

He flushed with acute embarrassment, and tried to cover it by getting to his feet. "Right—ah—well, if you were a real beginner, I'd have told you how to cleanse the area that you're going to protect, but as it happens, it's already cleansed. If it wasn't, *they* wouldn't be here."

He pointed to the fountain where, attracted by a Master of their own element inside their domain, two undines drifted in the lower pool, forms visible as an occasional undulation of wave-into-arm or a transparent face briefly showing on the surface. Maya looked, and then looked again, staring.

"I never saw *them* before!" she exclaimed.

"They wouldn't show themselves, not to you, without me being there; you aren't their Element, and you aren't a Master yet," Peter replied, hoping that she didn't think his automatic smile was patronizing. "The point is that they're here, which means that the Earth through which they had to go to get into your fountain is clean. By that, I don't mean that it's sterile or anything like that; I mean that there's none of the usual city poisons in the water and earth here—you can't help the ones in the Air—and no poisonous energies here either."

"But how—" she began.

"They probably got in here the last time it rained, following the runoff, or perhaps there's a connection to an underground water supply on your property. There are lots of old wells and springs that have been forgotten." Peter shrugged. "The point is that this kind of Elemental can't move through anything that's unclean."

"But how did it become clean?" she asked, frowning. "I did nothing—"

Peter could only shrug again. *I wish she'd stop asking questions I don't know the answer to. I really don't want to look like a right dunce in front of her.* "I don't know," he admitted. "But there are parts of the city that manage to stay clean no matter what. A lot of them are old shrines or even the sites of old churches that got built over. What's been cleansed stays cleansed, unless someone comes along and deliberately deconsecrates it. Gods have a way of hanging onto what's theirs, and of making where they live into a place where they can be—oh, I don't know—I suppose the word is *comfortable.* And only a Dark god is comfortable in a place that's contaminated."

Maya opened her mouth, and Peter waited expectantly. Then she shut it again, abruptly. "Never mind," she said. "Never mind." He was faintly disappointed; he would have liked to hear her think out loud again, but plowed on regardless with the lesson.

"Well, you need to actually establish the boundaries of your clean area first," he said, waving his hand at the wall around the greenhouse. "You said you can see Earth Magic—go ahead and see where it ends."

She turned toward the back wall of the conservatory, dropped her gaze to the foot of the wall, and frowned. Then, slowly, understanding drifted over her features.

"If you hadn't told me, I'd never have looked for it," she said carefully, her eyes alight with satisfaction. "But there *is,* there *is* a boundary space right at that wall, and it isn't the one I made! It's where the earth in my garden stops, and something else that isn't as—nice—starts." Now it was her turn to grope after words.

"That edge is what you're going to use, and not just a 'fence' of power either," he told her. "Now that you see where I want you to put it, I want you to drain the power out of the existing barrier. Go on—" he urged, as she hesitated doubtfully. "I'll have a shield of my own in place before you can drain yours away." And he quickly made good on his word, putting up a shield to surround the entire house, cleverly using (or at least *he* thought he was being clever) the electrical wiring and the pipes to carry his protections. Things like copper wire and copper pipes carried magical currents as readily as they carried water or electricity. Since he'd discovered *that,* Peter'd had a much easier time of casting shields.

Ah, but *she* must have discovered the same thing, for he sensed the flow of energies *out* even as his own poured in. Unmaking was always quicker and easier than making, if the thing you were tackling happened to be your own.

"Now we'll go about this the correct way," he told her, as the Earth power around the perimeter faded from his perception. He picked up a stone and placed it right at her feet. "We'll be using that in a moment, but for now, look beyond the surface and read the energies under your garden. See how strong they are?"

She nodded slowly.

"Don't just look at them. *Touch* them. Then when you've touched them, let them flow into you from the soles of your feet." He gave her an encouraging smile. "You can do it; you already have, a little. You can't help it."

"If I relax . . ." she muttered, then took several slow, deep breaths. Meanwhile, *he* watched her like a cat at a mouse hole, waiting for the mouse to poke a whisker out. And after two false starts, he watched as the warm yellow-gold of Earth energy crept upward and engulfed her, leaving her haloed in light.

She laughed with delight and surprise. "My word! It's like—like gulping down an entire bottle of champagne!" she exulted. He chuckled, recalling the first time that Water energies had flowed into him. It *had* been very like being drunk—the giddiness, the increased pulse rate—and yet he'd remained perfectly sober.

"Now concentrate on that rock," he continued. Immediately, the little pebble glowed with an inner life, glowed with the power she had taken from the earth. *He* would have used a clear glass of water—glass being a kind of liquid, and so akin to water—if he needed a focus, which he really didn't anymore. "Think of it as the world in miniature, and weave a *single* protection around it. Like this—"

He quickly shielded the rock with his own, Watery energies. These were the most basic, but basic did not mean "lesser." "Watch closely," he warned, and slowly expanded the shields in all directions, exactly like blowing up a soap bubble. But unlike a soap bubble, this one remained just as tough and strong as it got bigger, for he kept pouring energy into it as it expanded. And when it met the shields he already *had* on the place, they merged immediately into a seamless whole.

"Now it's your turn," he told her. She bit her lip, and started as he had.

By Jove! She's a fast learner! It only took a single false start, and her own shields began to expand from the point where they'd begun. The movement was painfully slow at first; she couldn't expand and increase the energy going into the shield at the same time. No matter, that would come in time.

When her shields touched his, they did *not* merge. Instead, they layered, hers overlaying his. She looked nonplussed when that happened; she had probably thought that they would become a single entity.

"Is that right?" she asked, with a sharp look at him. "Are they supposed to do that?"

"Put earth and water in a jar and shake them together; no matter how hard you shake, the earth separates from the water once you stop agitating the jar," he replied. "And that is how you build proper shields. *Layer* them, don't try to braid them until you have more skill and practice. Bring them up on a central point, then expand them to meet your perimeter. Again?"

"Absolutely!" Now she seemed eager for the task; as Peter watched her establish her initial shield, he recognized it as the 'I'm not here' camouflage, and paid close attention to how she spun it up. When she expanded it—more smoothly this time, but by no means as quickly as he had—he was pleased to see it layer into the previous set. It was stronger now than it had been. That was part of being better integrated, but was also due to having more energy behind it.

"Feeling tired yet?" he asked her, once the shield was up and established. He knew she wouldn't be, because she wasn't using her own power, but it was time to call her attention to that fact.

"Why—no!" She was astonished by her own answer, and looked down at her hands with a quizzical expression, as if looking for the reason there.

"That's because you used the energies of your Element, and not your own personal power," he replied. "*Now* you don't need to depend on yourself to work magic; you have a source of energy outside yourself. So think about that for a moment. What is that going to mean to you, and not just here and now, but outside these four walls?"

"That— Can I use this for healing as well?" she asked instantly. "Oh, of course I can! There's no reason why I couldn't, is there, and every reason why I should?"

Oh, well done! he applauded. "Exactly. Just make sure that you set up shields and cleanse the area first. This is another thing to remember, that other magicians and magical beings will see the flow of power and come to find out what's going on, and some of them are not what you'd like to have hanging about you. But you can't do that right now, all right? At this moment, right now, you need to practice all the different kinds of shields and protections you were *trying* to build weeks ago. When we've got something like what you were trying to produce, I will show you how to link the shields into the Earth energy so that the shields will maintain themselves, and that will be enough for one day."

She blinked, and was lost within herself for a moment. "Ah. I *am* using my own power to control the Earth Magic, am I not?" she asked.

"Exactly so." *Brilliant! I'll have to ask Almsley, but I don't think I've ever heard of anyone picking up on the Art so quickly!* He smiled. "Now, are you ready to learn about the kinds of shields that *I* know of?"

The hour that Maya had allotted to herself for this lesson simply flew past, and she decided to go a little short of sleep rather than cut the lesson short. When Peter Scott finally left, she was tired, but not with the bone-deep weariness that she often felt after establishing her guardian borders, and *now* she wouldn't have to go over and over her protections every night. Now they would take care of themselves—unless someone tried to break them. Then she would have to make repairs, of course.

But not out of my own storehouse. She made the rounds of the oil-lamps and candles in the garden, making certain that they were all extinguished.

She had sensed the presence of strange life hiding within the bounds of her sanctuary—nothing inimical, in fact, she got a feeling of comfort and warmth from them, even though they wouldn't show themselves. There was definitely something alive here, and she wondered, given the little she knew, what it could be. Little forest gods? It could be. The garden in the conservatory had taken on the sense of being a vaster space than it truly was.

Perhaps I'll stumble across a faun lurking behind the vines some time soon.

She felt as excited as she had after her first successful surgery, as enthralled by the sense of power, of the things she could do with her own two hands.

"It is a start, and a good one, little chela."

A familiar voice, but not human.

She looked up and saw Nisha's glowing eyes gazing down at her. The owl had turned as white as bleached linen. The huge yellow eyes held her, as mesmerized as if she were a little mouse and Nisha contemplating her as a light snack.

It is not wise to tempt the gods, even (or especially?) if they are not yours, she thought, with a sudden chill.

"It is a start," she agreed, as her heart gave an unpleasant jump. "I hope it is the right path."

"It is, and because it is, your enemy will strew it with difficulties," Nisha replied somberly. *"Be wary, for they will not always come in a form you will recognize. Your enemy can do you much harm without needing to know where you are."*

The owl blinked once, then swiveled her head away, looking up and out into the darkness beyond the glazed roof. Freed from those eyes, Maya could move; she stepped back a pace and took a deep breath.

Nisha swiveled her head and caught her again. *"She is here. Her creatures already crowd the night, and she gathers in those who walk in the sun as well as the shadows. Be wary."*

And with that, it seemed Nisha had no more to say—or rather, the being that used Nisha had said all that she wished. The spectral white of her feathers darkened, and she looked back up into the night. Maya found she had been holding her breath, and let out the air she had been holding in a long, shaken sigh.

The faint sound of something at her feet made her look down with a nervous jerk, but it was only Charan, and he showed no sign of wanting to add to Nisha's warning. He pulled at her skirt and chirruped at her. She leaned down and gathered him up in her arms, feeling a little chilled.

It is more than time I got some sleep. Although her knees trembled for a moment and felt as if they might not hold her, she steadied herself with a hand to the tree trunk, then left the conservatory for the hall and the staircase.

She used the railing as support and climbed the stairs to her room. She had rounds of some of her patients in the hospital to make in the morning, and would need all her wits about her, with or without the interference of her unwelcome relations.

In the morning, she had managed to put Nisha's words into the back of her mind. There was no point in dwelling on the warning, not when she had so much else to concern herself with. The patients she needed to attend today were *not* in Royal Free, but in St. Mary's, and the atmosphere in St. Mary's was distinctly cooler toward her and her few fellow female physicians than it was in the smaller hospital. She earned the right to install her own patients here by helping with the work in the charity wards, and every difficult charity case she took, as she saw it, was one more chip out of the edifice of Masculine Superiority.

Nevertheless, she was grateful that she had invited Amelia along and that Amelia's classes permitted her to attend. The surprised glances, the knowing smirks they occasionally got as they worked their way down the wards were not so bad—but the glares of outright resentment and hostility were difficult to face down. It was good to have someone here who was prepared to render glare for glare.

It was hard work made harder by the fact that the other physicians gave her no help, and even pulled nurses away from helping her without so much as a "by your leave," but Maya's patients here needed her, and she would not leave them to the tender mercies of the less competent. These were working-class patients, mostly laborers, who had come to grief in work-related accidents. The moment they became injured, they ceased to earn their income, and the longer they remained out of work, the longer their families had to scrape by on nothing, or on the pittance that wives and those children old enough to work could bring in. *She* did what few other doctors would trouble themselves about; she brought cases to the attention of the parish and other charities, vouched for the men that they were genuinely injured and not attempting to collect money on false pretenses, and helped to steer them through the tangles of suspicion and doubt until they reached the other side with a little relief money to feed their families. She also did not wield the amputation saw with the vigor that other surgeons did. For a working man, that was more important than being helped to charity, for if appendages were amputated, he would find it hard to earn a living again, and if entire limbs were lopped off by someone who seemed to think humans as much in need of pruning as trees, it would be next to impossible to find employment.

Maya bent over one of these, Bill Joad, a tough, ugly man whose suspiciously glittering eyes had softened as soon as he saw her coming toward him down the ward.

"Well, Bill, I think another few days will be all you'll need," she said, removing the dressings and examining the hand he held out to her. "Bill, this is Amelia. She's a student friend of mine that I want to show injuries like yours. I think she'll be better than I am, one day."

Amelia blushed. With his right hand imprisoned by Maya's grip, Bill couldn't touch his finger to his temple in salute, but he did offer a ghost of a smile. "I hain't gonna say it's a pleasure, Miss, 'cause it hain't—but I reckon if Doctor Maya 'as ye in tow, ye'll be comin' on pretty well."

Amelia bent over the swollen fingers with interest, noting the neat sutures along the sides. "What happened here, Bill?" she asked. "I don't think I've ever seen anything like this before."

"Eh, not likely ye would," he replied. "Caught me 'and in summat new. 'Sthis machine, like a bloody great mangle." His expression turned sour. "Coulda stopped it hearlier and saved me 'and, but foreman wouldn't let 'em 'till 'e figured it was gonna jam 'is works if 'e let it go. Gonna see more o' these, I reckon. Hain't no room between them machines, an' no way of keepin' clear of 'em if ye put a foot wrong. 'Slike that ev'rwhere now."

"And no guards on the machines to keep you from getting caught foul and dragged into the works if you fall against one," Maya added, her expression as sour as Bill Joad's. "I don't know what they're making there—"

"Trimmin's," Bill broke in. "Fancy trimmin's for dresses an' bonnets an' all. Laces an' ribbons, Rooshes, an' bows an'—oh, the wife'd know what-all, *I* don't. Machine that got me's fer cuttin' an smoothin' the ribbon, then winding 'er all up on spool."

"Makes me ashamed to put trimming on my dress!" Amelia burst out indignantly. Maya gave her a look of gratitude, but Bill shook his head.

"Not puttin' on trimmins 'ud just put us out o' work," he replied. "Tha's not the way. Dunno what is, but tha's not." He did give Amelia one of his rare looks of gratitude, though. "Th' butchers 'ere 'ud have took off me 'and, but I 'membered that me missus seen Doctor Maya at Fleet an' sez she wuz a corker, so I ast fer 'er. Man can't work 'thout a 'and."

"It wasn't exactly a crushing injury, although it did break some of the bones of the fingers," Maya went on, pointing out where she'd splinted the fingers with a care to the slashes she'd sutured. "It was the knives that cut the fabric into ribbons that did most of the damage; I sewed them up, but then made open, removable splints so I could keep an eye on the slashes—"

"And a very neat job of sewing, but better served in mending shirts and gowns for your betters," said a loud voice behind them. Maya put Bill's hand down carefully, then turned, slowly and deliberately, to face the speaker. She looked him up and down with calculated insolence.

A medical student—probably a surgeon in training, since they were the most arrogant of the lot—dressed as nattily as any West Ender on an outing, in his gray suit, waistcoat with a thick gold watch chain draped across the front, and impeccable linen.

"Thank you for the . . . compliment," she replied, keeping her voice smooth and level, although Amelia seethed with resentment. "I don't believe I caught your name; I thought it was considered appropriate for students to introduce themselves to surgeons before joining their rounds."

"Perhaps. I shouldn't think I'd be demanding that sort of ceremony if I were in your place," the man replied, a sneer disfiguring an otherwise handsome face. "A half-breed mongrel bitch like *you* should consider herself lucky to be allowed inside these walls, much less permitted to practice as a doctor here."

The words struck Maya like blows, and before she could recover from them, he turned on his heel and stalked away toward the entrance to the ward, between the rows of beds.

Anger made her flush hotly and tremble as she tried to hold it in; for a moment, she had no thought other than for her anger. Her palm itched to slap him; no, more than that, she wanted to run after him, jerk him around, and *hit* him.

Commotion next to her distracted her; she turned back to see Amelia holding Bill Joad down. "Lemme up!" he begged her, as she sat on his chest to keep him in his bed. "By gawd, *I'll* fix 'is face so's 'e sneers out 'tother side of 'is mouth! Jes lemme up! No fancy-boy says *that* about th' doctor! I'll show 'im 'oo 'e's gotta beware of!"

That cooled her off, as if someone had dropped her into an icy pond, and she joined Amelia in remonstrating with the factory worker.

"Bill, you can't do any such thing," she replied, shaking his shoulders a little. "He'll not only have you thrown out of the hospital, he *might* have you declared insane and chuck you into Bedlam, and then where would you be? You *know* no one ever leaves Bedlam!"

That threat was enough to quiet him, for Bill Joad had not survived this long without being well aware what the "toffs" could and could not do to a poor working man. He subsided, although his stormy expression left her with no doubt that if the man came within his reach again, Bill Joad would extract some form of revenge.

Maya released him and signed to Amelia to get off him before someone noticed. She leaned down and spoke to him, urgently, but quietly, words meant only for his ears. "Don't do anything right now," she urged. "Don't do anything he can pin to *you.* It was only words, and words mean *nothing.* Not to you, and not to me."

Bill snorted, and made a wry mouth. "Pull 'tother one. I seen yer face."

"I'm here right now because I'm *better* than he is—whoever he is—and he knows it," she told him fiercely. "Think about it! Why did you ask for me, insist on someone sending for me, instead of letting whoever was here at the time work on you?"

" 'Cause *ev'ryone* knows—" Bill Joad was not stupid; as the import of his own words dawned on him, his expression turned from angry and sullen to shrewd. " 'Cause ev'ryone at th' Fleet, an' ev'ryone what knows *about* th' Fleet knows 'bout you. 'Get Doctor Maya,' they sez. 'She'll save aught there's t'save.' "

"And?" she prompted.

"Won't be long 'fore them as got more'n we do finds out." He nodded.

"Got it in one, Bill," she replied. "Right now, all I have are cases like yours, but how long will it be before people with a great deal of money begin to notice how well my patients do? He's jealous," she continued, taking cold comfort in the fact. "Neither of us can afford to have someone like *that* for an enemy, Bill. Not now, anyway, and if important people *do* start to notice me, the important *patients* I take away from him will be revenge enough."

Bill's brow furrowed as he frowned. "Still. It hain't *right,* Miss Maya. 'E's got no call t' say things loik that, an' some'un had oughta teach 'im better manners."

"Don't let it be you—or at least, don't let him find out it's you behind it," she said sternly. "There's no justice for the poor man. Money buys justice, and I have no doubt there's a great deal of money in that man's pockets to buy the finest judge on the bench."

"Should be," said someone from the next bed with a bitter laugh, a man in an unusually clean and well-mended white nightshirt with a bandage over half of his face. "His uncle's the head of this hospital. I should know; I worked for him as his secretary before one of his damned dogs tried to tear my face off."

Maya traded startled looks with Bill, turned to stare back down the ward, along the way where the arrogant young man had gone, then turned back toward the stranger.

"If that's the case, what are you doing here?" she asked carefully.

Another bitter laugh. "Because the dog attacked me on the master's orders," came the astonishing reply.

10

"WOULD you care to elaborate on that . . . remarkable story?" Maya asked carefully, aware that this could all too easily be a trap for her. It seemed too much of a coincidence—and after the warning of last night, she was very wary of coincidence. And yet, if her enemy didn't know who or where she was, how could so specific a trap be laid?

It doesn't have to be her. *It could be a trap laid to discredit me as a physician.*

"You don't believe me," the injured man said flatly. "You think I'm mad. That's what he's told everyone, that my 'nerves failed me' and the dog attacked me because it thought I was going to harm its master." Beneath the bandage that swathed most of his head, his pale face was only a shade darker than the linen surrounding it, and his single visible eye was a mournful burned-out coal dropped into a snowbank.

Maya glanced at Bill Joad, who only shrugged. Evidently he had no notion who this man was, or if his story was true or not. The man *was* new here; Bill's former neighbor had been another of Maya's patients whom she had discharged yesterday. She was actually surprised that there hadn't been another body in that bed before the sheets had a chance to cool. Despite the fact that people were afraid to go to hospitals—because people died there, far more often than they were cured—there were never enough beds.

"He's *not* a doctor, by the way," the stranger continued, his single eye staring off into the distance, as if he didn't want to meet Maya's gaze and see doubt and disbelief there. "Mostly he pretends to work in the city, at the behest of his father. He's got positions in the main offices of two companies that trade in the East, one in China and one in India, and by day, when he isn't at his club, he's usually pretending to work. Really, though, all he does is saunter late into one of his two offices, read the paper, sign a few letters, dawdle to his club, and go home again, proclaiming how difficult his job is and how the firms couldn't get on without him."

Bill laughed without humor. "Puppy!" he snorted in contempt. "Meantimes, th' loiks uv us is breakin' their 'ands an' 'eads an' 'ealth from dark t' dark. Tha's enough t' make ye disbelieve in God, so 'tis! For sure, there's a Divil."

The stranger nodded. "Oddly enough, he'd *like* to be a doctor—he claims—and I know he tried to study to be one, but he hadn't the stomach for it. Or the brains," the man added, by way of an afterthought. "He got sent down from Oxford in disgrace after failing utterly at everything but cricket and football."

"Interesting." Maya was trying to remain noncommittal, but it was difficult to remain that way in the presence of such abysmal bitterness. *How does he know? Why is he telling us all of this?* "You know his history well, then."

"I think that might be why he hired me, so that he could humiliate Oxford in my person," the man said distantly, as if he wished with all his heart that he could pretend his misfortunes had happened to someone else. "I knew him by sight and reputation before he offered me a position; we were in the same College—Trinity. He knew I was as poor as a churchmouse when I finished my degree, and I thought—well, never mind what I thought." He uttered a sound that might have been a laugh, but might equally well have been a sob. "It hardly matters. How I'm to get another position looking like Frankenstein's monster and with the reputation of a madman—"

He broke off there, as if he had said too much. Maya waited for him to continue, but he had run out of words, and the noise of the ward filled the place his speech would have taken. It was never silent in the wards; the constant background noise of moans, weeping, coughing, and buzz of talk echoed all throughout the enormous room. The walls of sound surrounded those who were having quiet speech, and gave their conversations a strange feeling of privacy.

Amelia clearly did not share Maya's doubts about this fellow. She held herself back from converse with him with great difficulty, and there was sympathy warring with anger in her eyes on his behalf.

Careful, Amelia. This might be no more than a story to get our attention and our sympathy. There are plenty of people here who would like to see us overreach ourselves and get into trouble.

"Who *is* your physician, if he is not?" Maya asked, when Bill wriggled his eyebrows at her, urging her silently to keep up the conversation.

"Anyone. No one," he said listlessly. "I've been seen by half a dozen people since I was brought in. There was an Irishman that stitched me up. He's looked in on me, but so have a flock of jackdaws posing as medical students. I've been on a cot in a corridor and was just moved here when the bed went empty, I suppose; I don't remember much before this morning. That's when they stopped giving me anything for the pain. When I woke up, I was here."

This was altogether very strange, and Maya didn't quite know what to make of the situation. One thing she *could* do, though, was to have a look at the man. "Could you go get me some fresh dressings, Amelia?" she asked in an undertone. "It doesn't look as if he's been attended to today."

With a great deal of lively interest on her face, Amelia hurried off to the nurses' station.

"I take it that you wouldn't object to me having a look at you, then?" she asked.

He waved a hand at her. With his initial burst of accusation over with, all of the life and energy seemed to have drained out of him. "Go ahead. I can't see that it makes any difference one way or the other," he replied listlessly. "If you're a doctor, I suppose you have the stomach to look at wrecks like me."

With great care, she unwrapped the layers of gauze, and winced at what she found. He caught the wince, and a brief flash of despair passed over his face, before disappearing into malaise. "Not very pretty, is it?" he asked dully.

"I have seen worse," she replied truthfully. "There was a girl at the Fleet who'd had acid thrown in her face. . . ." It wasn't as bad as it could have been; it definitely was the result of an attack by some sort of canine, probably of the mastiff or pit bull breeds. It had essentially seized the flesh of the forehead and ripped downward, leaving the facial tissue hanging in strips; then it had made a second attempt and torn up the scalp. The wounds had been neatly stitched up, and there was no sign of infection, which was a mercy. She thought she recognized the suturing; the "Irishman" was probably Doctor O'Reilly, from Dublin, who tended to use blanket-sutures. She and the Irish physician shared a certain sympathy, since anyone from Ireland practicing in *this* hospital was considered no more than a short step above a female. "You've been well served," she continued, placing a finger just under his chin, and turning his face to examine the sutures. "Quite well, actually. There *will* be scars, but you aren't going to resemble anything from Mary Shelley's book. I should think you'd look more piratical than monstrous."

He didn't respond to her attempt at humor, but something flickered in the back of his eyes for a moment.

Some of his attitude must *be due to pain,* she decided. *if he's been left to suffer all day, his face and head must be in agony. That sort of pain would batter the bravest soul into a stupor.*

Just then, Amelia returned with fresh dressings and, unasked-for, the morphine pills. Maya took great care in rebandaging the man, then allowed him to see the bottle placed just out of his reach. His dull eye brightened with hope for a moment, but he did not beg for the relief she held in her hand. Had he done so once today, only to be denied?

"I would like to leave some medication with you, so you can have some relief now and sleep through the night," she said. "But I would also like to hear more than you've told me so far."

Now she had his interest. "What would you like to hear?" he asked, showing renewed life and liveliness. "I swear to you, I have not made any of this up."

She sat down on a chair at the side of his bed, and rested her elbow on the stand that held his washbasin and pitcher of water. Amelia took the chair on the other side of the bed, unasked, and Bill leaned over the better to hear. "Why don't you start at the beginning?" she suggested, pouring him a glass of water and handing him a pair of pills.

"My name is Paul Jenner," he said, when relief from pain had smoothed his features and given his gaze just the slightest unfocused quality. "My father is a country vicar. Nothing very distinguished, I'm afraid, but he was an Oxford man also, and it was his dream that I should go to his own College. He saved all he could so that I could have that chance. My ambition was not for the Church, which I think disappointed him a little. My thought was to get myself tied to the coattails of some rising man in politics, and perhaps do some good that way." He laughed a little. "I know that sounds very idealistic and naive, but I did think that I could work some good in the world, if I tried. Perhaps I should have followed in my father's footsteps after all."

"Positions of that sort are few and far between," Amelia noted, speaking up as if she could not help herself, and the bandage-shrouded face turned in her direction and nodded.

"So I found," young Jenner admitted. "And I confess I didn't know quite what to do at that point. I didn't have the friends to get into the Foreign Service, and I didn't have the money to get into business. I was about to fling myself into the stormy waters and look for a job as some well-born dunce's tutor, which would at least allow me to remain at Oxford, when along came my savior—I thought!"

"That would be the gentleman we were just discussing?" Maya asked.

Jenner laughed, with a note of anger in his voice. "Better to say the devil than my savior, and—no gentleman! But I didn't know that. All I knew was that Simon Parkening came looking for a secretary and found me. One thousand a year and all expenses, housed and fed at Parkening House! He said he wanted someone he knew and could trust, that some of what I would see and handle would be very confidential. It was princely, and how could I resist such an offer?"

"Obviously, you were not intended to," Maya observed. "And it sounds very much as if Master Parkening simply wished to get himself a secretary who would have the double ties of gratitude and school binding him. That should not have made you uneasy in itself. I am sure that there are many men who have gotten their personal secretaries with the same idea and motives."

"Nor did the work seem out of the ordinary—at first," Jenner responded. "It was normal enough, given that I performed the bulk of what work *he* was supposed to be doing. And that, so I am told, is hardly unusual among his set. But it wasn't long before he started to show a cruel streak, a meanness of spirit. He took a great deal of pleasure in ordering me to do some very menial tasks, and displayed a deal of dissatisfaction when I failed to display any emotion, or act affronted, but simply performed as he bid me. It was then that he took to demanding that I accompany him when he went out of an evening. . . ."

Difficult as it was to believe, the young man actually grew a shade paler, and he swallowed with great difficulty. "I will not burden you with the tale of his pleasures," Jenner said at last. "Suffice it that it was not enough that they were evil; they were blasphemous as well."

Amelia blushed, but Maya raised an eyebrow. *My word. Is this fellow a prude who has been bullied by his master, or is there something truly nasty going on here?* "Oh?" she replied. "Do have a care what you mean by that word. Not everyone would hold to the same definition of blasphemy as you."

A faint flush rose to his cheek. "Doctor, I do," he replied sturdily. "I mean by that his pleasures were uncleanly; the pagan and the priest alike would have been disgusted, even horrified. He consorted with that man Crowley, and if you know anything of his debaucheries, that name will tell you enough."

Maya nodded. "I know something of his reputation," she said, slowly becoming convinced that if this was a coincidence, it was *not* one engineered by her enemies. "There are things *I* have heard that have not appeared, or even been hinted at, in the papers."

"I know too much of it for my comfort," Amelia confessed in a small voice. "There was a girl I knew who somehow fell in with that set—" She shivered, and said nothing more.

And where was Amelia that she knows someone who managed to get entangled with Crowley's set? Maya thought with astonishment. There had even been rumors in India about the man—and certainly his so-called "novels" were enough to sicken and warn anyone with any sense away from him. *She* had learned more from one of her patients; what she had heard had given *her* a nightmare or two.

"Two nights ago I had enough, when I heard from him that he had found yet another haven of evil to investigate. I told him that I would not go. That was when he set his mastiffs on me." Jenner drew himself up and covered himself with the ragged remains of his dignity. "I will not pretend that I fought well. The dogs are hellishly strong and fierce. I will not pretend that I was not afraid, for I screamed for my very life. But that was my temporary salvation, for my cries attracted the servants, who pried the dogs off me and brought me here. I *think* he expected me to die, for I was left alone and tended properly until today. That was when Simon appeared here, claimed that I had attacked him, and let it be known that although he would—magnanimously!—not press charges against me, he would not be displeased if I died of my injuries."

"That tallies!" Bill exclaimed. "When th' orderlies brung 'im 'ere an' dumped 'im i' that bed, tha's what they said. 'No wastin' med'cins an' good care on a nutter, they said. An' that th' Big Man 'ad some machine or other 'e was gonna try out on 'im, seein' as 'e was crazy an' 'twouldn't matter."

"Interesting." Maya pondered the man and the story. *If it's a trap, it's one that's tangled beyond my unraveling. And if it's not, I cannot in good conscience leave this man here to be mauled and experimented upon.* "Amelia, I believe we should take a hand in this situation, don't you?"

"There's a bed at the Fleet gone empty," Amelia said eagerly. "Shall I have him discharged into your care?"

"Yes—no!" Maya corrected. "No, we don't want his employer to know where he went. No, this is what we'll do. I'll get some working-man's clothing for him and have O'Reilly come by and certify him as ready to leave. You wait here, and when O'Reilly signs him out of the ward, take him to a taxi and bring him to the Fleet. While you're taking him to the taxi, I'll get hold of his records and make them disappear." She chuckled. "Doctor O'Reilly and the head nurse won't go looking for him, because they signed him out, but when Mr. Parkening comes looking for him, he'll have vanished, and there will be no trace of him ever being here—except, perhaps, the clothing he was wearing when he was brought here."

"An' I won't know nothin'," Bill Joad said, with a grin. "Not that the loiks of *they* are gonna ask the loiks of *me*."

"Why are you doing this for me?" Paul Jenner asked, bewildered, looking from Maya's determined face to Amelia's eager one, to Bill's crafty smile and back to Maya.

I wish I could answer that! Maya thought—but at the same time, she *knew,* somehow, that this was the right, indeed the only, thing she could have done. "Because it is right," she said firmly. "Now, Amelia, let's get about this, before Mr. Parkening takes it into his head to return."

The clothing wasn't that difficult to obtain; she didn't even need to leave the hospital to get it. More poor men left this place dead than alive, and often in no need of the clothing they'd worn when they entered the hospital; if there were no relatives to claim the body, it was used for dissection and buried in potter's field. Generally, the clothing left behind was laundered, mended, and thriftily stored in case it was needed; after all, it cost the hospital nothing to store it. Most often, it went to clothe some poor fellow whose own garments had been cut off him during emergency treatment; dungarees and heavy canvas shirts were much alike, and it is doubtful that the few who received such largesse were aware they were wearing a dead man's clothing. Maya simply went to the storeroom, made certain there was no one about, then purloined a set of dungarees, a cap, and a rough shirt out of the piles waiting folded on a shelf.

She brought the clothing to Amelia and Paul, then she went in search of O'Reilly. It wasn't hard to find him; his head and beard of fiery red curls were visible across the dimmest ward.

"You're up to some deviltry, woman," the Irish doctor said, when she'd asked him to discharge Jenner with as scant an explanation as she thought she could get away with. "I know it; I see it in your eye."

"Let's say I'm attempting to *prevent* deviltry, shall we?" she replied, staring him straight in the face. "And the less you know, the less you have to lie about later."

O'Reilly stroked his abundant mustache and beard thoughtfully. "I've never heard anything but good about you from the nurses . . . and anything but *bad* about you from that worthless lot of puppies that trails about after Clayton-Smythe, hoping to snatch up his scraps. . . ." His thoughtful expression lightened into one holding a touch of mischief. "Aye, I'll do it, girl, if only to put one in the eye of that worthless nevvie of his. Oh, aye, I heard Parkening raving about the poor lad this morning—and a bigger pack of lies I can't imagine. The boy's no more mad than I am. There's something wrong there, but I'll wager a month's pay that it's not on Jenner's side."

"You won't be sorry," she breathed, hoping that she wouldn't be proved wrong about that. He laughed and patted her head as if she was a child, then turned to go—but just as quickly, turned back before she could hurry away.

"You'd like the man's records, wouldn't you?" he said casually, but with a twinkle of complicity in his eyes. "Just to look over, of course. I could bring them to you later. You can study them, and *of course* you'll put them back."

"That would be very—convenient," she managed, trying not to grin. "I'll be in the Poor Childrens' ward."

Not a quarter of an hour later, Doctor O'Reilly joined Maya in the childrens' ward, checking on three patients of his own there. He didn't actually say anything, just nodded in greeting as they passed each other—and handed her a slim sheaf of papers, which she stuffed into her medical bag. As soon as she finished with the last of her young patients, she made her unhurried way out to the street. Following her usual habit, she hailed a cab and directed the driver to the Fleet. On the way there, the seat got a little extra padding as she stuffed Paul Jenner's records down between the cushions. It had been a wet spring so far; *if* anyone ever found the papers, they'd be an illegible mess from dripping mackintoshes by the time they were located.

She got down at the Fleet, paid the driver, and hurried inside to find Amelia. She had expected to see Paul Jenner lying flat on his back in one of the Fleet's narrow cots, well-sedated, and safe. She found Paul Jenner safe and comfortable, right enough, but he was far from being flat on his back and well-sedated. To the contrary, he was quite alert and sitting up—and pouring out his heart and soul to Amelia, much to the intent interest of the other two patients nearby. One of them, a middle-aged woman Maya had successfully treated for a compound fracture of the leg, caught Maya's eye and put her finger to her lips. From the washerwoman's expression, it was quite clear to Maya that the experienced eye of a long-time matchmaker had detected more between Amelia and Paul Jenner than the interest of a doctor in a patient.

Maya nodded, smiling a little, and withdrew quietly before either of the two could notice her. There was plenty of work for her to catch up on in the rest of the clinic

The washerwoman's evaluation was confirmed for her an hour later, when the head nurse of the Fleet brought her a much-needed cup of tea after a round of sick and injured children had passed through her hands. "Who *is* that young man Amelia brought in?"

Sarah asked, eyes dancing with suppressed laughter. "He's a bit above us, isn't he?"

Maya sat down on the stool in the examination cubicle and cradled the mug in both hands. "Hmm—not in income, seeing as his employer tried to discharge him with a pack of dogs, then told everyone who would listen that he was mad," Maya temporized. "Amelia and I thought we'd get him out of harm's way—just in case. There's no way to trace him here, so I don't think you need to worry about him. We—and Doctor Reilly—made certain of that."

Sarah's expression went from amused to shocked. "Good heavens! But—well, you wouldn't have brought him here, miss, if you thought there was anything bad about him, would you?"

Strange—she works here, surrounded by some of the worst criminals and roughest characters in London, and yet she worries about this man? But Maya understood her concern. Even the worst wretch of the slums feared the mad, and even if Paul Jenner was as sane as Maya (and of course he was), a man who set a pack of dogs on another was ruthless enough to be very, very dangerous.

"It's all right, Sarah," Maya interrupted gently. "If there was any justice in the world, the shoe would be on the other foot, and Paul would be able to press legal charges against the wretch. He's a poor, good fellow that's been badly wronged by a very rich man, and we wanted to make sure no further harm came to him, that's all."

Sarah sighed and nodded. "And it's a bad world where a rich man can buy the harm of a poor one. There's no justice but in the hands of God," she said piously. "Well, Miss Amelia is *that* taken with the lad, I wouldn't want to see her feelings trifled with. Not—" she added hastily, at Maya's raised eyebrow, "—that he doesn't look and act every bit as taken with *her*. But you and I know that there are some men that are better actors than ever played on a stage when it comes to their dealings with women!"

"Not with half a grain of morphine in them," Maya chuckled, finishing her tea. "The old Romans had a saying that there was truth in wine—there's just as much truth in morphine, I think."

"Well, that's the case, sure enough," Sarah agreed, and laughed.

"Some of the things I've heard out of people's mouths when the drug's in them! Well, I just wanted to know what we were dealing with, miss, that's all. Now that I know, I won't worry."

Maya thought about warning Sarah specifically about Simon Parkening, then thought better of it. Sarah knew enough now to be wary of rich men asking questions, and a rich man (or a rich man's servants) prowling about *this* neighborhood would stand out like pampered white spaniels in a dustbin.

And serve them right if they come to grief as well, if they come sniffing about here, she thought. *I wouldn't mind seeing Simon Parkening bruised and bleeding and robbed of everything but his trousers.*

She got to her feet; since Amelia was taking such proprietary care of "the new lad," someone would have to do the same for the rest of the patients—and that "someone" was definitely Maya.

It would have been overstating the case to say that the disappearance of Paul Jenner from the ward caused an uproar. There were no orderlies searching the hospital, no policemen questioning the staff. When Maya returned the next day to check on Bill Joad, however, it was apparent that *someone* had been very upset about it, and had left signs of his agitation in the wards. The head nurse was sitting behind her desk with an expression of outraged innocence on her face, and stormclouds of temper on her brow that boded no good for anyone who crossed her today. Maya, however, had come armed, since she was expecting a tempest, and had brought some oil for the troubled waters in the form of a neat white pasteboard bakery box.

"Nurse Haredy," she said cheerfully, as the head nurse looked up, hearing her footstep. "You've been such a help with that old reprobate Bill Joad that I thought you were overdue for a treat for your tea by way of thanks." She dropped the box on the desk with a smile, knowing that the aroma of fresh-baked sugar-biscuits was unmistakable.

The sweet scent banished the stormclouds, and Nurse Haredy's expression softened. "Oh, Miss, there was no need of that," she replied, even as her hand cupped protectively around a corner of the box. "Bill Joad hasn't been any bother. Not like *some,*" she added darkly. "But, then—well, never mind. No matter what that limb of Satan thinks he can do around here, he's no doctor, and it's his uncle that runs this hospital."

"Or thinks he does, when we all know it's *you,* Nurse," Maya retorted with amusement, pretending to have no interest at all in "limbs of Satan." As Nurse Haredy chuckled reluctantly, she turned and made her way down the ward to Bill Joad's bed. As she had expected, there was already another man in the one that Paul Jenner had so lately occupied. The newcomer was blissfully snoring away. He had a splinted and bandaged leg, and looked like an Irish day laborer, and Maya suspected that his presence in that bed had a great deal to do with the actions of Doctor O'Reilly.

Bill was fairly bursting with impatience when she settled on the chair next to him, and if the nurse's expression had been stormy, *his* was of barely-contained hilarity. "Bloody *'ell* 'as broke out 'ere, Miss!" he chortled under his breath. "By God, you shoulda bin 'ere! First th' bleedin' bastard comes lookin' fer that Jenner feller, an' 'e finds Shamus there instead—goes to find out if Jenner's died or sumpin'—an' no papers! Storms up an' down the place, lookin'. No Jenner, no papers, no sign! Tries t' cut up th' old bat there, an' damn if *she* doesn't cut 'im up right an' proper, brings in O'Reilly t' back 'er up, an' *'e* brings in th' Big Man! Jesus, Mary, an' Joseph, you shoulda *seen* that! Th' Big Man don' like bein' dragged outa 'is cushy orfice for no puppy, an' I wisht y'd bin 'ere to 'ear 'im! 'Twoulda done yer sweet 'eart good! An 'Aredy lookin' like a righteous plaster saint, an' O'Reilly like th' cat in th' cream!"

Maya put her hand over her mouth to stifle her laughter. "I'm glad I wasn't, Bill. I doubt I could have kept a straight face, and then where would we be? I take it he was sent away with a flea in his ear?"

Bill wheezed with laughter. "More loik a burr up 'is bum!" he chortled. "An' th' on'y one in trouble is 'isself. Big Man tol' 'im t' get shut uv the 'orspital, and never show 'is face 'ere agin!"

Maya heaved a deep sigh of relief. Paul Jenner was safe, and no one had gotten into trouble over his escape. She gave Bill a perfunctory examination, more for the benefit of the head nurse than for his own well-being, and continued on her rounds.

But as she was halfway through them, another thought occurred to her; what if this Simon Parkening had other ways of tracing his former secretary—ways that didn't involve detectives and spies—

Or rather, one that involves spies that aren't of this world—

She checked the watch she kept hung around her neck. If she hurried, she could just make the morning mail. She scribbled a hasty note to Peter Scott, sealed it, and dropped it in the tray with the rest of the hospital missives. Feeling that caution was the order of the day, she didn't mention Paul Jenner either by name or by implication.

Something interesting has come up that I'd like to discuss with you, she had written. *Can we meet at the Reading Room in the British Museum after tea?*

Innocuous enough, and the Reading Room was a sufficiently neutral place to meet a casual male acquaintance in. Beneath the eyes of the librarians, with all of the weight of centuries of scholastic propriety behind them, no one would even consider so much as a mild flirtation. *I don't want him to have any—ideas,* she told herself. But to be absolutely honest, it was her own feelings that she didn't trust. She would be able to put the firm hands of control on the reins of her emotions in the staid surroundings of the British Museum.

An even briefer note than hers was waiting on her desk at home when she returned from her morning rounds, a short acceptance and an exact time. She tried not to be disappointed that it was so *very* short, and busied herself with afternoon patients.

At the appointed hour, she closed up her office and walked the few blocks to the point where she could catch a 'bus to the Museum—this time, one of the new motorized 'buses, which wheezed and clattered its way through the traffic, bouncing on the uneven cobblestones in a way quite unlike the horse-drawn 'buses. Maya didn't much like the things, not the way they smelled, nor the noise they made. *It doesn't matter, though,* she thought, gazing at the back of the passenger in front of her. *It's less expensive to keep one of these than to keep horses in the city. They're pushing out the horses; it's only a matter of time.*

The 'bus arrived at the museum and disgorged its passengers, Maya among them. She hurried up the steps with the rest, but passed by the enticing galleries, heading straight for the Reading Room.

She had been here before, but the sight never failed to awe and thrill her; where other children might have dreamed of toys, *she* had dreamed of the Reading Room and the implied treasures of the hundreds of thousands of books in it. Of course, as a child, her imagination had populated the walls with all of the most amazing story books in the world, but the reality, now that she had come to it as an adult, was just as dazzling. What wonders were here! The ceiling rose high above, like a cathedral in its proportions, and on all four walls were the books, the wonderful, wonderful *books,* ranged neatly on their shelves—some shelves open, others closed in with wooden doors. From floor to ceiling those shelves stood, taking the place of paintings or carvings of saints in this cathedral of knowledge. Beneath the books stood the catalogs and the carrels, the desks at which men studied (or pretended to) under the eyes of the librarians. The very air held an incense of *book,* a scent of old paper, parchment, vellum and ink, of leather and dust.

Maya entered and stood, just to one side of the door and out of the flow of traffic, and breathed in that beloved scent, her eyes closed. Here, if nowhere else in London, she felt completely at home. . . .

Then a hand closed on her elbow, and she stifled a yelp as her eyes flew open. A nearby librarian turned to level a glare at her.

"Much as I appreciate this place," Peter Scott breathed in her ear, "I don't think this is the best spot for a discussion. May I invite you to a late tea?"

Mutely, she nodded, and he let go of her. With a nod of his head, he indicated the way back out, and with a sigh of regret, she followed him back out, past the galleries, and into the clattering streets again.

11

PETER Scott did not venture to take her arm again, and Maya wasn't certain if she was pleased or disappointed by this. Such an action would have been improper in anyone but a relative or a suitor—

Yes, but just how "proper" is my position?

Young men in spectacles with rumpled suits, older men walking with careful dignity, and a loud American couple with their adolescent children passed them as they exited the building next to the left-hand lion. It was quite six o'clock, perhaps later; the museum remained open late on some nights, and this was one of them. Amateur scientists of all walks of life haunted the building in every possible hour that it was open, and many of them had livings to make. It was for the convenience of those who had to earn their bread that the museum kept later hours. Shops stayed open until eight or nine in the evening, men often worked that late in their offices, and dinner at six was something no one even considered except in the country. Londoners prided themselves on being cosmopolitan and modern; the gas and electric lights meant that no one was a slave to the sun going down anymore.

Which, for the working poor, only means longer and harder hours—but no one ever consults them. If a shop stayed open until eight, the poor little shopgirl didn't see her home until ten. If the museum stayed open until nine, the charwoman couldn't start her work until the last visitor left, which meant she worked all night. *Must it always be that great advances are always made at the expense of the poor?* Maya thought bleakly, then shook off her mood. She was doing what she could for others; the best she could do would be to continue doing that, and hope that her example would inspire more to do likewise. She had to be certain of that, or fall into despair.

She took a few deep breaths of relatively sweet air to raise her spirits. The museum stood in a neighborhood that was patrolled religiously by street sweepers, and until winter came, there would be no dense smoke from coal fires lingering in the air. Peter looked about for a moment, then turned back to her. "Would you mind terribly if I took you to my club for dinner?" he asked diffidently, as she stood on the sidewalk at the base of the lion statue and waited for him to indicate a direction. "I know I asked you to come here later than teatime, and I shouldn't like you to starve on my account."

"Your club?" she said with surprise. "I thought that men's clubs were havens *away* from the company of mere females." An older gentleman passing by overheard her response, and smiled briefly into her eyes before continuing on into the museum.

Peter chuckled. "They often are, but this one happens to have a room where one can bring lady guests for a meal without disturbing the meditations of the members—largely, I suspect, because the female relatives of our members have insisted on it."

"In that case—" She thought for a moment. She *had* told Gupta not to expect her for dinner, expecting to make a meal of whatever she found in the kitchen when she returned home. "I suppose it is a place where we won't be overheard? If so, I accept your kind invitation—if not, perhaps we ought to, oh, take a walk in Hyde Park instead?" She tilted her head to the side, quizzically. "I've no objection to a walk instead of a meal."

"Better to say that it's a place where it won't matter if we're overheard." With that mysterious statement, he hailed a passing cab—a hansom—and handed her into it.

With the cabby right overhead, they kept their conversation to commonplaces—he, inquiring if she intended to take a holiday anywhere this summer and commiserating when she admitted that neither her duties nor her schedule would permit it. "I'm afraid I'm in the situation where I cannot leave my business, and London in the summer can be stifling," he said with a grimace. "Especially in August. Usually the worst weather doesn't last long, but it can be very uncomfortable, even with doors and windows wide to catch whatever breeze there might be."

"You say this to someone who lived through summers in Delhi?" she laughed. "Pray complain about 'hot' weather to someone else! If the worst comes, I'll serve gin-and-tonics, then install a *punkah* fan in the conservatory and hire one of the neighborhood urchins to swing it!"

The cab stopped outside a staid old Georgian building of some pale-colored stone. Peter handed her out and paid the cabby, then offered his hand to help her up the steps to where a uniformed doorman waited. This worthy was a stiff-backed, stone-faced gentleman of military bearing, whose mustache fairly bristled disapproval as he looked at her.

"Good evening, Mr. Scott," he said unsmilingly, holding the door open immediately.

"And a good evening to you, Cedric," Peter Scott replied cheerfully. "Is Almsley in the club today?"

"I don't believe so, sir. Shall I tell him that you and your guest are here and would like to see him if he arrives?" Although the doorman's face held no expression at all, his eyes were narrowed in speculation.

"Please do." That was all Scott had time for before the door shut behind them. He didn't seem the least disturbed at the doorman's disapproval, though perhaps that was only because he had already known what the old fellow would think.

And what is he thinking, I wonder? That I'm fast for coming here unaccompanied by a relative? Or is it that he recognizes my mixed parentage?

She dismissed the thought and held her head high. No doorman was going to intimidate her. After all, she was a professional, a physician, and an adult, and had every right to go anywhere she pleased, *with* anyone she pleased. If it was her Indian heritage that the doorman disapproved of, well, that was his problem and not hers unless she chose to make it so. He could disapprove all he liked, since he was not in a position to bar her from entry.

They stood in a foyer that had probably been decorated in the first years of Victoria's reign or the last years of her father's, and hadn't been touched since. It featured the neoclassical motifs that had been popular then; the furniture was not burdened with draperies and flounces to hide its "limbs," although the colors were more in keeping with the Victorians' love of dark shades—the room had been papered in brocade of deep green, the Oriental carpet featured the same color, and the upholstery was a faded burgundy. There was a faint hint of old tobacco smoke in the air, and a great deal of dust. Peter Scott led Maya in through a door immediately to the right before she had much more time to look around.

This room had something of an air of disuse, but was furnished to more recent taste—the medievalism of the Pre-Raphaelite movement. The blue wallpaper, figured with peacocks and sinuous acanthus, supported a pair of Morris tapestries; the furnishings, upholstered in dark blue brocade, romantic in style and evocative of the great hall of an ancient castle, could only have come from the same workshop as the tapestries. The quaintly-figured carpet, also blue, had a pattern of twining green vines. There was even a painting over the fireplace that Maya was willing to swear was by Millais. A massive sideboard stood beneath the tapestries. There were couches beneath the two windows overlooking the street, two chairs with curvaceous side tables, one on either side of the fireplace, and four dinner tables with four chairs each, none of which were occupied. Peter made a motion to Maya to indicate that she could take her seat anywhere, and reached for a tapestry bell pull beside the doorway, giving it a firm yank.

By the time they were both seated—which was no time at all—a uniformed waiter had appeared at the door, bearing a tray that held two glasses, a bottle of whiskey, a siphon of soda, and a second bottle of something straw-colored.

"Would you or your guest like to see a menu, Mr. Scott?" the waiter asked, deftly pouring Peter a whisky and soda and setting it down in front of him. Maya held up her hand to prevent him from pouring her a glass of rattafia, since her nose identified the contents of the decanter as he unstoppered it.

"I should prefer a whisky and soda myself, please," she said firmly. "But I don't believe that I need a menu. If you have a roast or a curry, I shall have that, with steamed vegetables and rice."

The waiter raised an eyebrow; Peter's lips twitched, but something of a smile escaped him. The waiter poured her whiskey and soda, and murmured, with more respect, "It's lamb curry tonight, mum. Will that suit?"

"Admirably, thank you." She granted him a smile, and he vanished, leaving the door half open, and prudently leaving the bottle and soda siphon behind.

"I think you frightened him," Peter said, as she took her first sip and allowed the whiskey to burn its way down her throat. His eyes twinkled with suppressed amusement.

"What, because of this?" She raised her glass. "I rarely indulge, actually, but it has been a long day, and I am *not* going to be poured a glass of rataffia as if I was your maiden aunt!"

"Still, *whiskey?* And *before dinner?* I fear you have convinced him I've brought in a suffragette, and next you will be pulling out a cigar to smoke!" Peter was having a hard time concealing his mirth. "You will have quite shattered my reputation with the staff by the time dinner is over!"

She gazed at him penetratingly, then shrugged. "I *am* a suffragette, though I may not march in parades and carry banners. Or smoke cigars. I fear you may have mistaken me if you think differently. I am not the sort of woman of whom Marie Corelli would approve."

"I shouldn't care to be seen in the company of the sort of

woman of whom Marie Corelli would approve," said a strange voice at the door. A tall, thin, bare-headed blond with the face of a merry aesthete and a nervous manner leaned against the door-frame. Maya would have ventured to guess that he was quite ten years younger than Peter Scott, and perhaps more than that, but he saluted her companion with the further words, "Well, Twin, I understand you were looking for me?"

Peter sprang up, his expression one of open pleasure. "Almsley! Yes, I was! *This* is the young doctor I spoke to you about—Doctor Maya Witherspoon, may I introduce to you my friend Lord Peter Almsley?"

Lord Peter came forward, his hand extended; Maya swiveled in her chair and accepted it. She half expected him to kiss it in the Continental manner, but he just gave it a firm shake, with a mock suggestion of clicking his heels together.

"Might one ask what you meant by slighting Miss Corelli?" she asked, as he dropped into one of the armchairs. She had the impression of a high-strung greyhound pausing only long enough to see if it was truly wanted. "Not that I'm any great admirer of her work."

"Only that Miss Corelli has damned dull ideas of what women should do with their lives—which makes for damned dull women," Lord Peter said cheerfully. "Shall I join you, or would you twain prefer to condemn me to the outer hells of the member's dining room to eat my crust in woeful solitude?"

"Join us, by all means!" Peter Scott exclaimed, when Maya nodded her agreement. Maya had been disposed to like this man before she had ever met him. Scott had told her something of this young lordling, the most important fact of which was that he was another Water Master. Now that she'd seen him, she decided that he was worth knowing, and worth counting as a friend. And it occurred to her if she was going to have to lock horns in combat with Simon Parkening, it would be no bad thing to have someone with Lord Peter's money, title, and influence behind her.

Peter Scott rang for the waiter a second time; the man appeared, left a third whiskey glass, took Almsley's order, and vanished again.

"I assume it isn't pleasure that urges you to seek the company of my Twin, here," Almsley said, taking over the conversation with a natural arrogance that was both slightly irritating and very charming. "Not," he added, "that the company of a woman who was likely to incur the frowns of Marie Corelli isn't exactly what he needs in his life, but your expression leads me to think that this is not a mere social call."

Peter Scott actually blushed; Maya refused to allow this enchanting young rascal to get any kind of a rise in temper out of her. She had the notion that he was inclined to prick people at first in order to see what they were made of. "Actually, that is correct, it is not precisely a social call," she replied. "Though if it had not been for certain inferences on the part of my patient, I wouldn't have thought of consulting him—but I'm getting ahead of myself. Let me explain."

She began the short tale of Simon Parkening and Paul Jenner, pausing only when the waiter entered with their meals, and taking it up again as soon as he left. She made her story as detailed as possible, so that she only just finished as the meal did. The waiter came and cleaned away the remains, lighting the lamps and the gas fire, and set up liqueurs on the sideboard before he left. Peter poured himself a brandy and Maya accepted a liqueur in lieu of dessert, but Almsley retired to the sofa under the open window, lounging there with a cigarette, while Maya and Peter sat by the fire in the armchairs. By this time, the sun had set, and the street noises outside had subsided. Almsley's cigarette smoke drifted out the open window into the blue dusk.

"And so it occurred to me that there might be other ways of tracing Jenner to my clinic than the use of private agents," she concluded. "I don't know *how* one could employ magical creatures to spy, but I presume that a Master could do so. Furthermore, it occurred to me that there might be some danger to my patients, my clinic staff, and Mr. Jenner himself associated with those—other ways."

"Quite right," Peter Scott agreed, and looked to Almsley, who nodded.

"I don't much care for the acquaintances this Parkening fellow has made," Almsley said at last, after a thoughtful silence. "I admire Annie Besant when it comes to everything *but* her metaphysical notions. On that note, she and the Blavatsky crowd are harmless enough, for folk who are utterly deluded about their mystical powers. But when it comes to Uncle Aleister and his ilk, well, Jenner was right to get the wind up about some of them. And *you* are right to worry about Parkening tracing him to your clinic."

"What I don't like is that Parkening has been hanging about the hospital," Peter Scott interjected darkly. "Given what Jenner's said about him. Hmm? Gives him a far darker reason to linger than just his failed ambitions to be a doctor, or his uncle's position as Head."

"Oho! Good point, Twin," Almsley said, sitting bolt upright, his cigarette dangling forgotten from his fingers. "There's a lot of suffering around a hospital. No offense, Doctor, I know it's your job to relieve suffering, but—"

"No offense taken, Lord Peter," Maya replied, her brow furrowed with thought. "It hadn't occurred to me that the hospital could be a—a reservoir of—"

"Of the drink the Dark Powers savor most," Peter Scott said grimly. "If I were to hazard a guess, it would be that the hospital holds no charms for Parkening as a place of healing, but he finds it immensely useful as a source of power."

Maya nodded, but her mind had gone on to other possibilities. The movement of patients in and out of the hospital was not that strictly controlled; they'd had patients get up and walk out as soon as they were able before this. What if some of them hadn't gone off of their own accord?

No, surely not. He wouldn't dare kidnap sick and injured people to—to torture them! Would he? She wondered.

Parkening had dropped broad hints that he wouldn't be displeased if Jenner died, and those hints had been heeded and acted upon. How many *other* times had he hinted the same thing? And to what dark end had he done so?

"What do you say to a visit to your clinic, Doctor?" Almsley asked suddenly, interrupting her dire thoughts. "I'd like to have a word with this Jenner chap. He probably knows a great deal more than he's told you, and I'll be able to ask questions he'd be embarrassed to hear from your lips. And it might be *I* could use him when he's better. I wish I had somewhere to put him until he recovers—but frankly, I don't. Well, I could house him at the old barn in the country, but getting him there—"

"He's been moved enough as it is," Maya said firmly. "I had already considered taking him to my home, but he's safest at the clinic for now. A long train ride to your country estate is out of the question."

"*We* can hide him from those otherworldly eyes, though," Peter Scott offered. "And if Parkening has any sense, he'll steer clear of anything with *our* sign on it."

Maya didn't ask what he meant by that; Lord Peter nodded grimly at that point, and she decided that she didn't need to know. "If you don't mind—" she began.

"Mind? Not in the least. I'll have Clive get us a cab." Lord Peter shot up out of his chair like the greyhound he so closely resembled, and out of the door, returning a moment later.

"There. If you're ready, Doctor? Scott?" He chivvied them out a little like a sheepdog herding its charges, much to Maya's amusement. She had decided that she liked Peter Almsley very much, despite a slight touch of the unconscious arrogance that came with having money and rank bestowed on him at birth—and she pitied any woman who thought to wind him around her finger. He only played the fool; it was a mask, and a good one, but a mask nonetheless.

The three of them would never have fit in a hansom, but Clive (who evidently replaced Cedric in the evening, and looked far less grim), had gotten a motor taxi, with two broad bench seats. The men took one, and she sat facing them, in isolated splendor that felt a little ridiculous. The taxi chattered and chugged its way to the Fleet, attracting the attention of little urchins who ran alongside it, shouting. Nothing *this* modern had ever penetrated the neighborhood around the Fleet before, and it was a marvel to every small boy that beheld it.

The little boys followed it after it left them at the door of the Fleet. The driver did not care to linger in the neighborhood, and Maya was not particularly worried about getting home. Tom would take her back, then return for the two Peters.

The noise attracted all of the night staff—and Amelia—to the door of the clinic, however. It was Maya's turn to play sheepdog and herd everyone inside, before too much curiosity got the better of everyone.

"What are you still doing here?" she whispered to Amelia, as she closed the door behind them all. "I thought you would be home by now."

Amelia flushed and ducked her head. "I still had things to do," she confessed. "I couldn't go home with half my work undone."

Translation: "I left everything to do because I spent too much time talking to Paul Jenner," Maya thought, amused, but without a smile. "I hope you've caught up," was all she said.

"Oh, yes! I was just about to see if someone could find me a cab when you all arrived. What *is* all this about?" Amelia would have said more, but Lord Peter turned around at that very moment and accosted Maya.

"Doctor Witherspoon!" he said, with a charming smile. "Please introduce me to your staff—and give me a tour, if you would!"

Head Nurse Sarah Pleine smelled "wealthy donor," and her normally cheerful face was wreathed in smiles when Maya made the introductions. So did the rest of the night staff—Jeffry, the orphan who ran errands and slept in the garret, George, the man-of-all-work and porter, and Patience, Sarah's daughter and assistant. Maya let them think just that; who knew, it might even be true, for Lord Peter showed no impatience on his brief tour, and even asked a few pointed and pertinent questions about the operating costs of such a clinic.

"Some of our expenses are covered by a group donation—all the London newspapers put together a common fund, which is why this place is called the 'Fleet Clinic.' And once a year, they organize a subscription fund for us," Maya explained. "But that only takes care of some basic needs. I don't receive anything for my services, for instance, and neither does Amelia; the only paid staffers are our anesthetist, the nurses, and the porters."

"Still, it's better to have the papers as your founding sponsors, I would think," Lord Peter observed. "Isn't there less interference about who 'deserves' treatment this way? And I should think it highly unlikely that members of the press would find drinking and smoking as objectionable as some of our worthy clergy do." His wry smile made Maya and Amelia laugh.

"Oh, the myth of the Deserving Poor—" Maya replied. "As if we bothered to ask if a man screaming in pain was a regular church-goer and subscribed to the Temperance Union!" The more Lord Peter said, the more she liked him; it was such a relief to meet someone from the upper classes who really had a grasp of how things stood in the East End. *Where cheap gin numbs the pain of the joints of a man who has been working too long and too hard in the damp and cold—where "Sunday outfits" linger in the pawnshop until Saturday night, and if there is no money to redeem them, then there is no way to go to church—*

"Well, as a rule, I don't go subscribing to charities unless I know that they aren't wasting my donations on hymnbooks and tracts," Lord Peter told them, with a definite smile on his thin lips. He didn't say anything more, but when he reached into his breast pocket and brought out his notecase, then took Maya's unresisting hand and pressed several notes of large denomination into it, she stared at him in open-mouthed astonishment.

"But I didn't—" she managed, trying to grasp the fact that he had just given her the equivalent of a months' worth of operating expenses for the clinic.

"I know you didn't, which is why you can count on the Almsley fortunes augmenting yours from now on," Lord Peter said, with a chuckle. "Meanwhile, this should purchase you a few necessities. I shan't bother to suggest anything; you know your needs better than I."

Hastily, Maya transferred the handful of notes to Sarah, who took them off to be sequestered in the cashbox and added to the pathetic totals in the ledger. *Bandages—sticking-plaster—a set of good scalpels! A real bed for Jeffry! A spirit-lamp so Sarah can make tea at night—oh, and canisters of decent tea!*

"Now, shall we go have speech of your special patient?" Almsley continued, as if he hadn't done anything more costly than tipping a newsboy a farthing.

Well, perhaps for him, it wasn't, Maya reflected dazedly. If Lord Peter really *did* become a regular donor—there were so many things that she could do here—

She shook herself out of her daze; there was another reason why they were here, and it had nothing to do with the finances of the Fleet. "He's this way," she said, gesturing, as Amelia looked puzzled.

She was even more puzzled when they went straight through the clinic in the direction of Paul Jenner's bedside. He'd been installed in a kind of doorless closet at the end of the tiny sick ward—not out of any consideration for his privacy, but so that it wouldn't be immediately obvious to outsiders that he didn't fit in with the general run of Fleet patients. The closet was generally used for children, or for patients who needed relative isolation and quiet. But that very positioning gave them a chance to talk with him without disturbing—or being overheard by—the others here.

But the moment that Amelia realized where they must be going, she pushed herself forward. "Let me go first, so he isn't alarmed," she said, and without waiting for an answer, skipped past Peter Scott and on to the sick ward. Maya exchanged glances with Scott; his questioning, hers amused. Evidently it wasn't only unfinished work that had kept Amelia here tonight! *I wonder what's been going on in my absence?*

When the little group reached Paul Jenner's alcove, Amelia had lit the oil-lamp on the wall above his head. He was awake and sitting up, looking alert and wary. They couldn't hear what Amelia murmured to him, but Lord Peter came forward with his hand outstretched.

"You must be Paul Jenner. I'm Almsley of Magdalen," Lord

Peter said, an arcane incantation that meant nothing to Maya, but evidently spoke volumes to Paul Jenner, whose face (what could be seen of it) cleared immediately.

"Almsley of Magdalen! They still speak of your prowess at bat, sir, in hushed and reverent tones! Forgive me for not rising, my lord," Jenner began, but Almsley laughed, and sat down on the stool beside the bed.

"Not at all; now, I wish we didn't have to jump immediately into an unpleasant subject, but I've heard some things from Doctor Witherspoon that quite alarm me, and as it happens, I *may* be the fellow to do something about them. This is my good friend Peter Scott, and you can trust him as you would me. It seems that you and I and Scott here need to have a little discussion about a fellow Oxford man who has been a very naughty boy." Maya had no idea how they managed it, but in next to no time, Almsley and Peter Scott had Paul Jenner completely at his ease and talking frankly about his employer while Amelia and Maya simply stood in the background and listened.

Very frankly, as it turned out; what he'd told Maya was merely the visible tip of the iceberg. Within a very short period of time he'd revealed things that made the hair on the back of Maya's neck crawl.

She didn't know a very great deal about the dark side of magic, but some of what Jenner said made it very clear to her how closely he had come to things that were truly evil, and only his good sense and instincts had warned him away. *He* had no notion of how imperiled his very soul had been. From the looks that the two Peters exchanged, they didn't plan to enlighten him.

And why should they? It wouldn't help him now; there isn't anything he could do about it. But, oh, now I am so glad I went to Peter with this!

Amelia looked completely bewildered by some of it, but there were parts that even she understood. She went pale, and then greenish a time or two. The two healthy men, one standing, one sitting, bent over the injured one with faces that reflected nothing but concern and a certain urgency. They could have been his relatives or friends, just paying a visit to the sickroom; the heavily-shaded oil-lamp at Jenner's bed cast a circle of dim light that enclosed the three of them, with Maya and Amelia left in the shadows outside that magic space. Only the things they were calmly discussing—dark rituals involving blasphemy and pain in basement chambers, the spilling of blood on nameless altars, unsettling forms of Holy (or more aptly, Unholy) Communion, and things that Paul Jenner had only glimpsed or guessed at—were totally at odds with the otherwise pleasant scene.

Finally the two Peters seemed to have gleaned everything they could from Maya's patient, and Almsley sat up straighter. "Thank you, Jenner," Almsley said with a sigh. "Thank you very much for telling us all of this."

"Thank *you* for believing me," Jenner replied earnestly. "There aren't many who would."

"There aren't many who would understand the significance of what you had to tell us," Peter Scott said somberly.

Jenner looked from one Peter to the other, and his mouth tightened. "There's more to this, isn't there?" he asked. "You know something— No! I don't want to know what it is! It's enough that *somebody* does! Can you act on it?"

"We can," Peter Scott told him, as Almsley nodded in confirmation. Then Scott smiled, and added, "Think of us as a sort of police agency; rely on it, the information you've given us is going to have some results."

"And meanwhile, let me change the subject for a moment and ask if you're free to take a position outside of London as soon as you're well enough to move and work a little?" Almsley asked. "As it happens, I could use a private secretary of the sort who . . . now how shall I put this?"

"Of the sort *you* can trust to handle some rather odd correspondence, who won't be disturbed by it, or get the wind up about it," Scott supplied, and Almsley grinned broadly.

"Exactly! And one who won't lose his nerve if *I* happen to need some *very* odd jobs done." Almsley waggled a finger at Jenner. "Think of your experiences this way; *before* you'd had them, you'd have been useless to me, but now that you've seen some of the things that are 'not dreamt of in your philosophy' and know them for verifiable truth, you're invaluable to me! So, would you care for a position? Same conditions as your previous employer, but without the nastiness. *That* much I can assure you. Also that *I* am not a sadistic bully; I drive myself quite as hard as I drive my employees."

"Ah—" For a moment, Jenner was quite speechless, and it was Amelia who spoke up a bit sharply.

"Just where would this be, my lord?" she asked.

"The Almsley estate for now; Heartwood House. Between here and Oxford—just past Hatfield," Almsley replied, looking not at all surprised that it was Amelia who had posed the question. "Newport Pagnell, to be precise. A journey, but not a very long one, as rail journeys go; it wouldn't be a bad thing, I think, to get Master Jenner out of physical reach of Simon Parkening for a bit. In fact, when the time comes, if you would be willing to accompany him there as a sort of private physician and see him settled, I'd be obliged to you."

"Would you be wanting me to personally deal with some of the more outré matters that might involve you, my lord?" Jenner said at last, looking distinctly uneasy again. "Because—well, I'd really rather not. I'm not certain I've got the stomach for it."

"Nor do I blame you!" Almsley responded, as a trick of the light and the way he held his head made his hair shine, creating a kind of halo about it for a moment. "Jenner, I can't promise you that you wouldn't ever be called in to help *me* with such things, because that would be a lie. I'm not much good at foretelling the future, don't you know. I'd as soon tell you that sort of thing didn't happen, I really would, but it's a kind of nasty little war that Scott and I are engaged in, and war is no respecter of persons or promises."

Jenner nodded solemnly.

"So I shan't make a promise that I might have to break," Almsley continued, "But I can promise that if such a need would arise, I wouldn't spring it on you as a surprise, and you'd have at least one chance to tell me to take myself and my interests somewhere a great deal hotter than here!"

Jenner actually laughed weakly at that, much to Maya's relief. "In that case, Lord Peter, I would be honored to serve you," he said, holding out his hand, which Almsley shook firmly.

Maya let out the breath she had been holding in; two problems off her hands at once—three, if you counted Lord Peter's promise of support for the clinic. The whole atmosphere seemed to lighten, even though nothing had outwardly changed. Then Paul Jenner sagged a little, and Amelia moved into the circle of light cast by the shaded lamp.

"Lord Peter, Mr. Scott, if you are finished, P— my patient needs his rest," she said firmly. And neither Maya nor the other two missed how she'd almost called Jenner by his Christian name, nor how her fingers had reached for his, and his for hers, for just a moment.

"I quite agree," Lord Peter said, standing. "I'm sure we've fatigued him no end, and he could probably do with something to help him rest. We'll take our leave, Jenner—but I'll be checking on your progress, and the moment you're fit to take a rail journey, we'll get that organized and you can take up your position."

"Thank you again, Lord Peter," the injured man replied feelingly, before Amelia shooed them all out of the alcove. She busied herself with "her patient" as Maya beckoned them aside into the clinic's tiny office.

"Protections?" she whispered, in order not to wake sleeping patients or excite the curiosity of the night staff.

The two Peters nodded, oddly in unison, as if they *were* twins. "That was next," Peter Scott said. "Maya, could you help us with this? There isn't a great deal of water around here for us to draw on—would you be willing to supply us with the energy?"

She made a face; the Fleet was hardly a "cleansed" place, but she nodded anyway.

"It will be easier than you think," Scott said by way of encouragement, as Lord Peter straightened his back and braced his feet a little apart, closing his eyes as he did so, and tilting his head back a trifle. "You've been working here for some time, and you'll have actually done some cleansing without realizing it."

Maya closed her own eyes for a moment to orient herself, and "saw" that Peter Scott was right; in the immediate area of the Fleet Clinic the general "feeling" of the earth was nothing like as polluted as it was outside the walls. Encouraged, she plunged her spirit deep into the earth beneath the Fleet and pulled up strength from the enormous source she found there. Then, as if she poured what she found into a waiting vessel, she passed that energy to her two companions, who received it and transmuted it instantly.

It didn't take very long; the Peters worked with a unity she could only marvel at and envy, and in the time between one breath and the next, there was a shell of power standing between the Fleet and the rest of the world, a shining barrier of protection that swirled with opalescent color and light. When they no longer needed her, Maya relinquished her hold on the Earth Magic she'd called, and opened her eyes on the real world.

Almsley opened his eyes, grinned, then settled his collar and cuffs quite as if he did this sort of thing every day, as Peter Scott ran his fingers through his hair in a gesture that betrayed his nerves.

"That was a good day's work, I think," Almsley said cheerfully. "Now, is there any chance of a cab out here at this time of night, or must I see if my abilities to defend myself against footpads are up to the task?"

He looked so absurdly eager, as if he actually hoped for a chance to try his self-defense skills against the thieves and drunks outside, that Maya had to stifle a laugh behind her hands.

"Sorry to disappoint you, my lord," she replied, with mock regret that made his eyes gleam at her friendly insolence. "But I'll have to deny you that pleasure. I do believe I hear my friend's hansom pulling up outside."

"Ah, well, in that case I shall kidnap my twin and bid you adieu, then send him back for you and the other young lady. Come along,

Scott," he added imperiously. "We have a report to make to the Old Man."

What Old Man? she wondered, but didn't have a chance to ask. Peter only had a moment to press her hand and whisper, "May I come by tomorrow?" and accept her nod before Almsley whisked him off into the darkness.

12

SHIVANI sat comfortably in lotus position on her tiny cushioned "throne," as the Englishman she had recently annexed to her service stood before her. He shifted his weight from foot to foot uneasily, but made no move to seat himself before her, and thus put her head above his. He was *so* careful of his position, this sahib, and yet did he but know it, he might as well be in chains before her; he had forged them himself, of greed, desire, and ambition. This "Simon Parkening" could be very useful to her. She had learned much more about him since he had last brought her the list of names and addresses she had commanded. These had been culled from among the employees in the firms where he worked, and were all denoted men who had served in the Raj and thus were *her* enemies, and the enemies of her land. Those who would not be immediately missed had been marked out. Her thugee would seek them some dark night, and more enemies of India would fall, quietly, unregarded.

She had learned he could be even more useful to her. It transpired that his uncle was the head of a great hospital in London. This place could be the source of information on more enemies. Many retired soldiers and civil servants from the Colonies and Protectorates passed through the portals of his uncle's hospital for treatment of various tropical ailments they had contracted over the course of their careers. He was in a position to find out addresses and other details; he was also in a position to spirit some of them away and into Shivani's possession, were he inclined to cooperate.

Soon or late, he would cooperate.

"I trust that the Goddess has made all smooth for you with your uncle, as I promised?" she asked—knowing that of course She had. Or rather, Shivani had. The mere altering of a memory or two in the unguarded mind of a fat, foolish sahib was nothing, and never mind that he was supposedly an all-wise doctor. A spell, a word of power, a whisper on the wind, the clue of a strand of hair, and the Serpent slid into the old man's mind and swallowed a few memories of an unpleasant altercation over a vanished patient.

"Uncle doesn't recall a thing," Parkening replied, a gloating smile on his sensuous lips. "I'm back in his good graces again. I wish, though, you could get him to dismiss that damned Irishman; I'm *sure* he was the one that spirited Jenner out of there. He's too arrogant by half, that O'Reilly."

Shivani frowned behind the black cloud of her veil. She didn't like to admit that there were things she couldn't do, especially not to this barbarian. "If the Goddess had ample evidence of your commitment, something might be done," she temporized, her tone made sharper with an edge of accusation. "No!" she corrected waspishly as his hand moved slightly toward the wallet pocket in his jacket. "Not *money!* How often must I tell you that the Goddess requires coin of another color?"

"She'd have had it, if I'd been able to get my hands on Jenner," Parkening muttered, coloring angrily under her gaze.

Shivani only laughed at him; he was so easy to manipulate. "And what makes you think that a damaged sacrifice would have been acceptable to Her?" the priestess taunted. "You have access, means, and *money,* which latter you seem to believe can solve every dilemma. Your first gift was acceptable—but only acceptable. It proved your intent, but not your will. If you wish to move the Goddess to help you, you must show Her the level of your devotion. The man you intended to give to Her was no fit offering. He was damaged and he was of no interest to Her. Bring Her something *She* values, not some fool you wished to be revenged upon. Bring Her one who is—or was—Her enemy. That is the meat and drink She craves, not your leavings."

Parkening's high color faded, and his cheek paled. He fingered his lapel nervously. Shivani smiled. She knew that the way to keep this fool was to continue to challenge him to prove himself. While he focused on proving himself, he would not see the ropes binding him tighter and tighter. One day he would awaken and find it was no longer possible to escape, even into death. "I don't know—" he muttered.

"Then you are not fit to serve Her and be rewarded," Shivani replied contemptuously. "Every one of Her followers here has brought Her sacrifice after sacrifice with his own hands. If you truly desire Her blessings, you cannot do less." She made a dismissive motion with one tiny hand, on which gem-heavy rings sparkled in the dim light. Parkening gazed on that sparkle hungrily. He was well-off, but he craved riches, immense riches—among many other things.

As do all fools, jackdaws, and magpies who seek only pretty baubles to play with. Children! Shivani thought contemptuously.

"I'll see what I can do," he temporized.

"*Do,* or do not," she scoffed. "Make no half-promises you are too weak to keep and can renounce if you fail. The Goddess is not moved by promises, but by deeds. Make Her a gift, or seek elsewhere for what you desire."

This time she nodded to the dacoits who stood on either side of the door behind Parkening. They pulled the door open and waited impassively. There was no mistaking her intent. He was dismissed.

With ill grace, he bowed to her, turned on his heel, and left. The dacoits followed him, closing the door behind them, to make certain that he left the building.

Once they were gone, Shivani relaxed. She reclined in the cushions of her alcove, and carefully contemplated the person of Simon Parkening.

He was weak, but strong enough to be useful, and ruthless

enough so long as he himself was in no physical danger. He *had* brought the Goddess a sacrifice, in fact, one that Shivani was going to make use of in another hour or so, when the stars were right. He'd been clever enough to understand what it was that Kali Durga fed on. Last night he had gone out into the streets and obtained a girl, a child-whore, being careful to pay highly enough for her services that her "protector" focused on the money and not on the customer, and he saw that her panderer did not get a good look at his face nor inquire where he was going other than the cheap boarding house from which there were many exits. He'd brought the child here, unconscious from a light blow to the head. Kali Durga cared nothing for virginity, only for potential fecundity. In fact, the Goddess on occasion preferred a sacrifice that had been polluted. This child, her virginity plundered and potentially able to produce a dozen more enemies of the Goddess out of her body, was indeed a fitting sacrifice.

But this was only a sacrifice valuable enough to buy Parkening a small favor, and that favor had been granted. Parkening's servant had offended him. He set his dogs on the man, hoping to kill him, and fool as he was, had not made certain of the rest of his servants before he had given in to his impulse. They had rescued the man and had taken him to the very hospital where the uncle ruled. Parkening had again proved his lack of wit by not arranging the disposal of his servant immediately and personally. Instead, he had left it to others. By the time he realized that the servant was not going to favor him by dying and had moved to act, it was too late.

And there, yet again, he proved how foolish he was. At this point, Shivani would have washed her hands of the situation. The man could not possibly obtain another place in London, so if he lived, he would have to make his way elsewhere. The place he got would of necessity be obscure. He could do Parkening no harm. What point was there in pursuit, or in trying to punish those who had aided him?

None, of course, but Parkening was a creature of emotion and rash impulse rather than thought.

Shivani dismissed him from her mind. He was as yet only potentially of great use. She would not permit him to cost her any care.

There were, however, areas of potential trouble that she could not leave unwatched. As her own strength grew, she had become aware of certain strongholds of magic in this city. Some of those were of the sort Parkening had consorted with, commanded by those who walked the shadowed paths, and whose power, like Shivani's, was drawn from the wells of the suffering of others. But some—and these were stronger—were not.

Those who captained these strongholds took their strength from the elements of nature itself, and their magic was an alien thing to Shivani. She was wary of them in consequence; she could not reason out their aims or their attitudes. Yet—they were English. Thus, they were the Enemy. She must neutralize them if she could not yet rid herself of them altogether.

To that end, among others, tonight's sacrifice. She would use the power she gained to throw confusion among them. If she could not penetrate the shining walls of their strongholds, she could make it so that they were loath to venture beyond. She would strew their path with dissension, with reluctance, with doubt. There would be no direct attack upon them, only the subtle and ever-burgeoning poison of mistrust; no mighty blows to shatter defenses, only the acid of hesitation to eat at their foundations. For her purposes, that was as good as attacking them directly. She only needed for them to hold their own hands while they bickered among themselves for as long as it took her to become as firmly entrenched as they. Then if they could not agree to unite, she could defeat them singly.

The knives were ready, the restraints in place upon Kali Durga's altar. The little whore would be long in dying, for the Death of a Thousand Cuts was designed for this very purpose: to keep the victim alive as long as possible, and to make every living moment filled with unbearable pain from which there was no escape.

And Kali and Her votary would drink in the dark power of her agony, and thrive, and grow.

* * *

The girl breathed her last at dawn. Greatly pleased, if not sated, Shivani put her knives aside for the servants of the shrine to clean, and retired to her chamber.

She permitted her body servant to take her blood-drenched clothing, to wash the sticky residue of the night's work from her flesh, and to attire her in a loose, silk robe. The servant brought food and drink, sweet rice balls and fragrant tea, and she sat beside the table on which they were placed as if in a dream. While a dawn breeze played in at the window and incense perfumes disguised the alien scent with familiar fragrances, she reclined into her cushions, and listened to the music of wind chimes hanging wherever a breeze might find them. She ate and drank without noticing what was in the cup or on the plate, her mind busy with intricate plans that she spun out of all the myriad possible turnings ahead of her.

This was where her enemies always made their mistake. The moment that they achieved some triumph, they rested, thinking they could afford leisure. The moment of victory was *not* a time to rest, except so long as it took to spring into action again once one had one's bearings for a new direction.

In only one thing had she not made any progress. She was still no closer to discovering the whereabouts of her sister's child than she had been when she arrived in this city.

The girl had hidden herself well. She was nowhere that Shivani had expected to find her, not among the Hindu expatriates, not among the families of the men with whom her cursed father had served. If she was a physician, it was not in attendance to the people her father had tended among the enemy soldiers or the petty pushers of paper.

Therefore—since it was unlikely she had chosen some other way to make her livelihood—once again, Parkening might well be of service to her. There could not be two female physicians newly come from the Raj in London; even if the creature could disguise her half-Indian parentage, there were not that many *female* doctors about.

But she would have to be careful, very careful, in what she told Parkening. If he got the notion in his head that Shivani wanted the girl, he might try to take her himself, and hold her as a bargaining counter. That would give him power that Shivani was in nowise prepared to let him achieve.

No; go slow with this one. It were best to drop the most subtle of hints and see where the man's reactions led her.

Almost without thinking, Shivani dropped her hand into the basket at the side of her chair, and she felt the handle of the scrying mirror slip into her palm.

She smiled to herself with great amusement and pleasure. So, the slave of the mirror had tired of being wrapped in black silk, trapped in a limbo without sense, sound, or sight, and was willing to cooperate. She clasped her fingers around the handle and brought the mirror out.

The distorted features of the mirror-slave gazed back at her from the black glass. She breathed slowly and easily through her nostrils, marking what went on in the glass. The slave's face shifted as though seen through an imperfect pane, his features melted and twisted. He was having difficulty holding onto his sense of self.

Her smile broadened as she noted this; so much the better for her purposes. The less he was able to keep hold of himself, the less he would be able to fight her, and the more malleable he would be to her will.

"So, my faithful servant," she greeted him mockingly. "Have you found the one I seek?"

He opened his mouth in a soundless wail. She shook her head at him, and pursed her lips in cruel disapproval.

"Perhaps I should put you back in the basket—" she began, with a sadistic parody of doubt.

No! he begged. *No—please—I have been lost, so lost, I can scarcely find my way—* When she made no move to drop the mirror back among the folds of silk, the face brightened pathetically. *Put me in the sun!* he pleaded. *Put me where I can see the street. If I can find my way, perhaps I can find her.*

"A useful suggestion, at last!" she replied, and considered it. "Yes, I think I will, bodiless one. It will be an interesting experiment. But your task was to seek signs of her in the spirit realms—and have you nothing to tell me?"

There were some hints at first, he said in despair. *Traces of magic like yours, but crude, and when I thought I had found where they came from, they slipped out of my hands. It was like trying to catch a river—where they were strongest, they vanished faster. And now there is nothing like your power to be found at all.*

"No?" Could it be that the girl had died?

Unlikely. If such a thing had happened, Shivani would have known, would have felt it. There was the shared blood between them that had warned Shivani of the child's flight from India once the careful web of deception and protection that Surya had spun was gone. If the girl had met with an accident, Shivani would have sensed it.

No, the spirit insisted. *Nothing now. Only the towers of darkness and shadow that I dare not trouble, and those of light that I cannot look inside, and all of those, I know. The green of Water Masters, the blue of Air, the red of Fire, and the warm gold of Earth; there is nothing of the magic of your kind here anymore.*

Very interesting. She knew already that there were myriad auras of power playing about the strongholds of alien magic, but she had not known that the various colors denoted anything in particular. "Tell me more about these Masters and their colors!" she demanded sharply.

The mirror-servant was only too happy to tell her all he knew. From him she learned of the Elementals, their peculiar magics, and the Masters who commanded them. When he was done, she was altogether astonished, for the pattern of magic here in the West was so utterly unlike, and yet at its roots oddly similar to, the magic that she knew. She knew of the colors of magic, of course, including colors that did not appear in this Western tradition. There was the darker-than-red color that was often incorrectly termed "black" that corresponded to the blood-born power Kali Durga and her votary relied on—and the darker-than-violet color she had only seen used by great mystics of temples devoted to gods other than her own, great savants who were often referred to as *holy.*

Green, she associated with healing; red with passions and emotions. The golden-yellow that her mirror-slave identified as Earth Magic was that which she interpreted as both fecundity and death, just as Kali Durga was the goddess of both. Blue was the magic of intellect, and reserved for the most involved of spellcasting, the sort that required hours or days of calculation, intricate diagrams, and carefully cast horoscopes. But conversely, it was also the magic of forgetting. . . .

It was all so very fascinating that she quite lost track of her original intentions and continued to question her slave for some time, as the sounds of traffic and people from outside grew louder, and the sun rose farther above the horizon. Finally, she was caught unawares by the impulse to yawn hugely; it broke her concentration, and she realized how far advanced the hour had become. She was overdue for sleep, and well satisfied. Her slave was cooperating at last, her plans were well set in motion, and there was nothing much between her and her goals but hard work.

"You have done well, for once," she told the pathetic creature in the mirror. "And I shall grant your request." She stood, paused to stretch lazily, and took the mirror to the window, where she propped it up with two jars from her cosmetics table, facing down into the street. There was no chance it would fall, not with a pair of carved stone jars keeping it in place, and even if it did, it would fall back into the room, not down into the street.

She yawned again, closed the curtains against the light, and sought her bed in the sweet-scented gloom.

When she woke again, it was with a nagging sense of a task left uncompleted. She frowned into the darkness, as she realized *what* it was that had been left undone.

Her sister's child, of course; she had intended to work magic with her new-won power designed to drive her quarry out of hiding as well as garner yet more power to the altar of Kali Durga. The sacrifice last night had given her enough magic to conjure the Shadow Serpent, if the weather could be induced to cooperate.

The weather . . . that was the question. The Shadow Serpent depended upon mist and fog to give it form. In the summers of India, hot and dry, no such thing was possible, so the Shadow was not a creature she depended overly much on, preferring to trust to her followers to accomplish the same tasks it would have. What would the early mornings here bring? Shivani realized that she had no real idea, for *she* had never yet been awake at that hour—but her own servants would be able to tell her.

She swung her legs over the side of her bed, and clapped twice, quickly, summoning her body servant. When she was dressed and the curtains were opened wide to the night, the servant brought the mirror to her, carefully avoiding looking into its black surface. And when Shivani gazed into it, there was nothing to be seen.

Well! Perhaps the mirror-servant had spoken nothing less than the truth; by knowing where the mirror lay in the physical realm, he would know where to pursue her errands in the shadow realm that lay beneath the surface of the physical. She decided against summoning him; it might well be that he was on some profitable "scent," and she would leave him to it.

"Bring me Jayanti," she ordered her body servant, and the woman bowed low and scuttled away to fulfill the command. A moment later, the head of her dacoits appeared in the open doorway to her chamber. He bowed deeply, then went immediately to his hands and knees, and crawled into her presence.

"I would know what weathers there are in the hours between midnight and dawning in this land and city," she told him brusquely, seating herself in her favorite chair. "Most importantly, when is there like to be mist and fog?"

Without raising his eyes from the carpet, he told her. "When the day has been fair, but not over-warm, and there has been no rain for a day and a night, then the air is cool and clear from sunset to sunrise. When there has been rain, but the day has been cold, the night is like to be also, and there will oft be more rains before dawn, but no mist. Only when there has been rain and the day is warm and the air full of moisture, but the night itself is cool, will there be a fog between midnight and dawning. And that is perhaps three days out of ten."

"It is well," she told him, already tired of seeing only the back of his turban. "You may go."

He left, scuttling backward on hands and knees like a four-legged crab until he reached the doorway and vanished through it into the corridor beyond.

Shivani considered her options. She could wait until the fogs came, and hope that she had power enough to summon the Serpent then—or she could summon it now, knowing it would not appear until the conditions were right, and knowing that the power to create it would fade a little with every night that passed that it did not appear.

She might not have another sacrifice soon as perfect for the alignment of the stars as the last had been, and a little of that power would trickle away every day that she did not use it. On the other hand, once summoned, it would be no difficult thing to *replace* the power that drained from the Serpent in the time that it did not manifest.

Besides, she already had everything she needed to set the Serpent on some of those foes she could not touch with the thugee. Allowing the Serpent to take *them* would increase the Serpent's powers, without the need to do anything more on her part.

She realized that she had already made up her mind, and shrugged. Action was always better than delay to her mind. Better to act now than regret she had not done so when the time to act was long past.

She summoned her body servant again, and gave directions that she would be in the temple, and must not be disturbed for *any* cause. Then she left her apartment and descended the stairs to the basement, knowing that nothing and no one would be allowed to approach her until she rang a bell to summon a servant or left the temple herself.

The basement had been the obvious choice from the beginning for the temple room; Kali Durga's temples were often underground in India, the stone walls, floor, and laid-stone ceiling of the basement room provided adequate soundproofing, as last night's sacrifice had proven. The charcoal braziers used to warm the place kept any trace of damp at bay. Shivani rather liked the feeling of being enclosed in stone, although there were some among her followers who found the basement temple stifling. There were no windows or exterior entrances to betray the presence of the cellar, and no obvious way down into it from the ground floor. Shivani's clever builders had installed a cunningly hidden door in the back of a closet used to hold cleaning implements. A secret catch gave access to a spiral staircase descending to the antechamber, and the entrance to the temple itself was by means of a second secret door in the antechamber. Two hidden doors were always better than one. There was nothing to show that the antechamber—which held a number of rejected furnishings from Shivani's apartments and from the temple—was not the only reason for the staircase to exist. The secret door in the closet pivoted in the center, and brooms and mops were hung up on it; the secret door into the temple proper also pivoted, and some of the furnishings rested on a clever platform attached to it, so that there was no clue that there *was* a door there.

Once inside the temple, Shivani locked the door behind her, and went about lighting lamps and incense, until she was satisfied with the atmosphere. Then she retrieved a box from an alcove behind one of the fabric hangings at the rear of the temple, placed it beside a black iron brazier in which incense smoldered atop a bed of coals, and took her own place on a cushion behind it. The brazier stood between her and the statue of Kali Durga, and before she began her night's work, Shivani made a profound bow in homage to her Goddess. The statue stared impassively into the space above Shivani's head, the Goddess' ornaments glinting brightly from among the flower garlands.

There was no outward sign that there had ever been a sacrifice last night; all the residue of the occasion had been neatly cleaned away. Shivani had not asked what had become of the remains of the child-whore, and did not particularly care, so long as they did not come to light in a way or place that drew attention to her and her followers.

But to the inward eye, the temple was aroil with the dark energies that Shivani and her Goddess required, and Shivani licked her lips as she settled herself into a lotus position, for the very presence of those energies made her feel electrified and powerful, ready to accomplish almost anything.

She closed her eyes, set her hands palms down on her knees, and began to hum her spell, as the incense she required, compounded of fragrant herbs, blood of previous sacrifices, and snake dung, coiled around her.

She inhaled the pungent smoke deeply, building within her mind the shape of the Shadow Serpent, its huge, wedge-shaped head, its slowly flickering tongue, the cold yellow eyes, the loop upon loop of cool, scaled weight. The Shadow was not in the image of the cobra, but in that of the constrictor, for it did not kill by poison but, like the thugee, by strangulation. She summoned each tiny detail of the creature; how sinuous and silky smooth the muscular body felt as it slid over the arm or the leg, how the heavy head would lie in her lap as it waited for its directions. As she built the details within her mind, she began to spin the substance out of the air, the smoke, and the power that lay in sullen swaths within the temple.

A weight began to grow in her lap, as a cold place formed within her where her own energies were draining away. She accepted this; the Shadow was as much *her* shadow as it was a thing of magic. When she herself prowled the Outer and Inner Realms, it was often in this very shape. She was the mother of the Shadow, and like all mothers, it was her body that gave her "child" birth and sustenance.

As the weight in her lap increased, so did the subtle sense of pressure and support around her. She felt the energies assuming a new shape, coiling around her, taking on a form that was not—*quite*—material.

Still she continued to chant, keeping her mind firmly fixed upon the form she called and the words to give it life and being. Tension built within her as the words spiraled in tighter and tighter turns, the energies following them, tighter, faster, until, with a flick of her mind, as if she spun a cord, she bound and released them with a single, sharp syllable.

Then she opened her eyes and smiled down at the heavy, blunted triangle of shadow that lay in her lap, at the coil upon coil of misty scales that encircled her body.

This child of her spirit looked up at her from slitted eyes of smoke and fire, waiting.

Now she opened the box and took out a small, folded piece of paper from among the dozen or so lying therein. As the Shadow stirred and slowly moved its head from her lap, she dropped the paper into the brazier.

There were men that Shivani had specifically singled out from among her first list of those she would be revenged upon; men that she knew had served her land and people particularly ill. Some were petty administrators who took delight in abusing their power, some soldiers who had wrought private atrocities in small on the persons of their servants. She would not—yet—go after larger game, in no small part because she wanted the great sinners to *know* that she was coming, that vengeance was at hand—to know, and to fear, until fear left them small, shivering, and helpless. She wanted them to see what took them and know *why* it took them, to know that they were doomed long before doom actually descended.

She only required that these lesser fish die, and in dying, feed her, her child, and her Goddess.

So it would be the Shadow who took them.

These men were all surrounded by such protections as kept the thugee at bay—stout walls, many servants, police, and money. Oh, the thugee could easily slip inside those walls, past the servants and the police, strike, and escape, but the *money* ensured that these men would not die as the drunks and the dregs died, without notice. No, assuredly, a wealthy man strangled in his own household *would* be noticed, and there would be searching, and memories of other such deaths in India, and then the hunt would, inevitably, come here.

That would not do at all. Whether or not there was any evidence, men of India would be hailed into a British jail, and no doubt some of them would be hers. She could ill-afford to lose any servants, and those who had supported her intentions back home would swiftly cut her off if she came to the notice of the *sahibs* and the government.

This, though—

The Shadow slowly raised its massive head, supporting the weightless weight on a pillar of transparent scale and muscle as thick around as her body. The head hovered above the brazier, and the Shadow breathed in the smoke from the burning packet. If one of the thugee could get in and out of a rich man's house to kill him, one could as easily get in, and out again, bringing out a thing of little apparent value to a sightless Englishman. A bit of hair from a hairbrush, perhaps. From the faint stink as it burned, that was what this particular screw of paper held. The Shadow took the scent and the substance into itself; as the smoke became one with the Serpent, the scales of body and head took on a transient bluish cast for just a moment.

A true serpent had an acute sense of smell. This Shadow's senses were even keener, and it could track a single victim in a city of millions, once it had the scent.

When the last ghost of glowing paper ash evaporated in the breath she blew over the coals, she selected another packet, and dropped it in the brazier. Eight times she did this, and eight times the Shadow breathed in the scent and the smoke, and incorporated them into a memory that nothing would fade.

When the eighth packet was altogether gone, the Shadow lowered its head. It had taken in all it could hold for the moment. Later, when it was stronger, she could give it more victims at a single sitting, but for now, eight was all it could manage.

It knew its job; how not? It was spun of her spirit. It did not wait to be dismissed, but loosed the coils from about her body where it had clung for support even as it supported her. Without a backward glance, it slithered away toward the altar, moving far quicker than anything that large had a right to.

As it lost contact with her, and with the incense smoke, it began to fade. As its nose touched and passed through the door into the antechamber, it was scarcely a shimmer, a shape in the air.

Then it was gone.

Shivani sagged a little with fatigue, but her spirit rejoiced. The Shadow was strong, much stronger than she had thought it would be, for its first summoning in this strange, cold country. Eight victims! She had not expected it would be able to take so many!

Of course, she would have to call it to her each night that it did not feed, to give it of her own substance—and it would not be able to feed unless the fogs and mists came, for those would give it the body it needed, of water and air and smoke.

But the fogs *would* come, and then—

The Shadow would feed. And having fed, it could return to her, and *she* would send it out to find her sister's traitorous daughter.

13

MAYA bound her head with a strip of toweling to absorb the inevitable drops of perspiration from her forehead, then donned an enveloping apron that had been bleached in lye, then boiled. There was no proper sink for the surgeons to wash at in the female operating theater, only a basin and a pitcher of water, but she scrubbed her hands and arms as best she could anyway, using the harshest soap obtainable. The atomizer was full of carbolic acid to disinfect, and she would see to it that before this operation was over, it was empty.

"Maya," said Doctor O'Reilly, as he dried his scrubbed hands on a scrupulously clean towel, "thank you. This is not an easy case of mine that you've taken."

She turned to smile wanly at the Irishman, who, not being a surgeon, was acting as her anesthetist. O'Reilly's expression betrayed his strain despite the concealment of his red beard and mustache; he was only too correct that this was "not an easy case."

"After the way you helped with that little problem of mine, I could hardly refuse, now, could I? Besides, you know what anyone else would do with this girl."

"Take appendix, uterus, and child, without a second thought,"

O'Reilly said grimly. "And she a good Catholic girl, and this her first child! It would break her heart."

"If she lived through it," Maya replied, just as grimly. "Doctor, if I can save this girl without removing anything but what's diseased, you know I will."

The patient in question, who was one of O'Reilly's, a young Irish woman who had been brought in thinking she was miscarrying of her first child, was in fact in the throes of an attack of acute appendicitis. She *might* come through this attack without surgery to remove the diseased organ, but neither her doctor nor Maya thought it at all likely. When this had been made plain to her—and the fact that she must have surgery immediately—her first thought had been for her unborn child. She had begged Maya, clutching Maya's skirt with both hands, to save her baby.

She was with her priest now, for even now the removal of an appendix was a risky procedure. If it had burst—if it was perforated—and the infection had spread within the body cavity—well, there was very little chance that she would survive. Her seven-month pregnancy made things doubly complicated. Maya hoped that the priest was human enough to give her absolution before she must go under the knife; whatever such blessing meant or did not mean to the girl's immortal soul, it would surely make her calmer.

As O'Reilly had pointed out, any other surgeon would simply excise the uterus and its contents without a pause, simply to remove that complication. After all, the girl was a charity patient, a nobody, and if she complained, no one would care. It wasn't as if she was a woman of good birth who was expected to produce an heir for a family with money or social standing. She'd even be better off without the handicap of breeding a brat a year—

Or so the male Protestant physicians would say. And never mind how *she* would feel.

The Female Operating Theater, located in the attic of the Female Wing, was stiflingly hot now that it was late into July. Why they couldn't have used the regular operating theater—

Because the women cry and carry on so, it might disturb the male patients. As if the men don't cry and carry on just as much. Or—women are embarrassed to be prepared for surgery in the same room as the men. As if, at that point, they are thinking of anything but the surgery to come.

The excuses made no sense, for they were only that, excuses. But at least, being at the top of the building, there was not as much room for observers here—and the light was excellent, for the theater had been provided with two broad skylights.

Since it was Maya who operated here today, it was Maya who made the rules for this case. She had abolished the practice of leaving the bloodstained aprons on hooks to be used and reused until they were stiff. Aprons were bleached with lye and boiled, then wrapped in clean paper and stored here until use. After the conclusion of an operation, used aprons were taken away immediately to be boiled and bleached again. Water was never left in the pitcher; it was brought fresh before each surgery. Physician *and* assistants scrubbed hands and arms up to the elbow—in Maya's case, higher than that—and the carbolic atomizer was as much a fixture as the ether mask. Maya used only her own personal set of surgical implements, because she made sure to keep her own scalpels sharp and sterile, and didn't trust those left for the use of others.

And all those preparations would be in vain if that poor girl's appendix was not intact.

"Bring her in," Maya instructed, when her hands were just short of raw. O'Reilly and the nurse went to fetch the girl, and Maya saw to the laying out of her surgical instruments on the tray beside the wooden table.

O'Reilly carried the girl in his arms into the antechamber, wrapped in a clean sheet. She was in too much pain to walk, and in any case, Maya didn't want her to do anything that might stress that appendix. He put the patient down on the narrow table, giving her a reassuring smile before placing the prepared mask over her mouth and nose and pouring the anesthetic on it.

When she was asleep, they wheeled her into the operating theater and lifted her onto the immovable table. Maya adjusted the sheet she'd been wrapped in to expose as little as possible of anything other than the surgical site, then wiped the site itself clean with carbolic solution. Some physicians not only operated on patients while clothed in their street clothes, but on patients who were *also* still in their street clothes, and as unwashed as they had come in. This girl had been stripped and bathed by the nurses in the outer room, then wrapped in a sheet that, like the aprons, was boiled and bleached and kept wrapped in sterile paper until use. The plain, deal table had an inclined plane at one end to elevate the girl's head, and was covered with a piece of brown oilcloth. Once again, Maya's rules held sway here today; the oilcloth was new and had been wiped down with carbolic before being placed on the table.

As usual, the theater was full—there was a reason why it was called a "theater." The actual amount of floor space devoted to the operation was small in comparison with the tiers of stand-places rising for four rows, at an angle of sixty degrees, so that those standing in each tier could have an unobstructed view of the operation below. The students' entrance was at the top tier, and a metal rail on which to lean ran at the edge of each tier. It was the students' business to attend every operation he (or rarely, she) possibly could, so even Maya's operations were fully attended, and she was by no means a famous surgeon.

Today, however, there seemed to be more visitors than students. The usual hum of voices contained was louder, and there were finer coats in the audience than was normal.

But Maya didn't bother to examine her audience, not when there was far more pressing business at hand. The quicker she could operate, the less blood the girl would lose; next to infection, it was blood loss that carried off the largest number of patients after an otherwise successful procedure. But by the same token, she had to be as careful as she was quick. Being too hasty could mean she would slice through major vessels, or worse.

She adjusted the box full of sawdust under the table with her foot, nudging it to the place where she judged that the blood from the surgery was likeliest to begin dripping. Then, with a glance at O'Reilly and a nod to her dressers, Maya went to work.

She had planned this operation carefully in her mind as she and the patient were in preparation. The position and size of the uterus meant that nothing was straightforward. She took her scalpel and made her incision.

Almost immediately a cry arose from the tiers of "Heads! Heads!" since her own head and body obscured the small incision she had made. She ignored the cry, concentrating on making her cut so that she did not cut across any major vessels. Blood began to trickle down the girl's hip, onto the oilcloth, to drip into the pan of sawdust beneath the table.

Maya did not get the benefit of having as many dressers and attendants as she wanted; there was no one vying for the honor of holding her instruments or otherwise helping with the operation. There was no one to sponge the sweat from her forehead; hence the strip of toweling. She was not going to go through all the work of sterilizing patient and surface only to have it all ruined by sweat dropping into the open incision and contaminating the site.

She nodded at O'Reilly, who put the ether mask aside and sprayed carbolic over the incision and her hands. He would do this all through the operation, for as long as there was an open wound. The clamor of "Heads!" continued; she continued to ignore it.

"I can't believe it!" drawled a loud and obnoxiously familiar voice. "She's not taking the uterus!"

Maya kept herself from jerking around to stare at Simon Parkening in anger and disbelief only by a supreme act of will. That same will kept her hands steady as derisive shouts arose from other lungs. The voices were uniformly unfamiliar; so *that* was why the theater was so full! Parkening had packed it with his own cronies with the purpose of disturbing the operation!

"Steady, Doctor," came O'Reilly's low voice, as a bleat of "Stupid cow!" was aimed at her from the tiers above. "This is aimed at me, not at you."

"I will be damned," she replied through gritted teeth, "if I let a pack of piddling puppies interfere with my work!"

But of course it was going to interfere, if only by disturbing her helpers. Twice Maya had to raise her voice to be heard by her dressers over the boos, hisses, and catcalls coming down from above. Her hands started to shake, and she had to stop to steady herself as her impotent anger overwhelmed her own control.

"Now you see why females should never be surgeons!" Simon mocked. "Sentimental! She's going to kill her patient with sentiment over a fetus! By God, they shouldn't be allowed to practice medicine at all! They haven't the nerve for it! Just look at the puny little incision she's made! Is she afraid of a little blood?"

A burst of laughter followed.

"Not that it would make any difference, one Irish bitch more or less in the world to pour out litters of whelps every year," Simon continued with an air of casual glee. "They breed like flies anyway."

Maya actually heard O'Reilly's teeth grinding.

"Steady, Doctor," she told him.

But that last comment seemed to have gone a bit far, even for Parkening's friends. The catcalls died down, and there was an uneasy note to the muttering. "I say—" someone objected weakly. "Out of order, old man."

Maya had her hands full—literally. She was trying to locate the appendix by feel, through an incision too small for the pregnant uterus to bulge through. There were whispers of "What's she doing?" that she ignored completely, deciding at last to trust to instinct—and a little magic. She willed the thing to come into her fingers, concentrating a trickle of power into her hands, thinking of the diseased organ as an enemy that was trying to escape her. *It's there, somewhere . . . hot, diseased . . . like the polluted soil outside my house.*

She sensed it now, a swollen malevolence lurking beneath her fingers. Concentrating all her will on it, the hecklers and the theater receded to a mere whisper of annoyance in the background, inconsequential as the buzzing of a fly on a windowpane. She used her anger as power, poured it into her questing fingers. *Into my hands, damn you.*

Then, suddenly, she got a tip of her finger on it. It felt so hot it seemed to burn her hand, but she twisted her fingers after it, caught it, and slid it carefully into view in the center of the incision.

Triumph! At last she had the damned thing! And it *hadn't* burst, though its inflamed, swollen condition warned that it could, at any moment. She secured it with her left hand and held out her right.

"Clamp," she muttered; for a miracle, her dresser heard her, and the clamp slapped into her outstretched hand.

Within moments, the offending organ resided in the tray of sawdust at the foot of the table, and she was in the process of suturing the incision shut while O'Reilly madly sprayed the last of the carbolic over hands, incision, and anything else that happened to fall in his path.

Done! She stepped back from the table; her dressers swabbed up the last of the blood with sponges, and covered the incision with clean sticking plaster. A wave of exhaustion threatened; she drove it back and turned to gaze up at the theater full of now-silent on-lookers.

She was still so angry that her vision was blurred. She couldn't make out faces—but she sensed Simon Parkening to her left, and deliberately focused her attention slightly to the *right,* away from him, as if he was of no consequence to her.

"I direct the attention of you gentlemen to the plaques upon the wall, behind me there," she said, in a voice that dripped ice and scorn. "I assume, that since you who are medical students are all *learned* gentlemen, your Latin and Greek will extend to reading and understanding them. And in case your eyesight is faulty, I will tell you that the first reads, *Miseratione non Mercede* while the second is the Oath of Hippocrates. I suggest that you might benefit by taking them both to heart." She paused, while utter silence fell over the group. "And for those of you who were not capable of conning your Latin and Greek at University, I will translate the first, which means, *From compassion, not for gain.* I would take that to remind us that even those who cannot *pay* are to be treated here as equal to those whose deaths would make a stir in the world. As for the second—" Her gaze swept the room, blindly. "I think you will find an injunction both to *do no harm* and to respect the wishes of the patient. For the rest, I suggest you apply to someone who has made the effort to learn the language of our legendary forefather."

That said, she nodded to the dressers, who transferred the still-unconscious girl to the wheeled stretcher, and walked to the basin to wash her bloody hands and arms.

There's a couple in your eye, Parkening—and you can't claim I singled you out either.

There was not a single sound except for retreating footsteps echoing hollowly on the risers, as she washed, rinsed, and dried her hands, then took off the apron and dropped it on the floor to be collected and washed. Nor did she again turn to look at the retreating students. Her anger sustained and kept her head erect and her spine straight as she walked into the antechamber and shut the door.

Her patient was already gone, taken back to the ward. Hopefully, she would not start an infection. Hopefully, she would not have a miscarriage. Hopefully, the incision would be healed by the time she went into labor.

Hope, essentially, was all she had—but Maya had at least bought her that hope.

She sat down on the chair in the antechamber, drained, as one of the scrubwomen came in to fetch the soiled linen, take away the blood-soaked sawdust tray, and scrub down the table and floor—hopefully (there it was again!), in that order, and not the reverse. The old woman left the door open; there was no other sound now but her, shuffling about, picking up what had been dropped, cleaning, blithely ignoring the fact that it was human blood that soaked everything. Then again, the old woman probably cleaned this chamber many times a day, and had for years. By now, she probably never even noticed. Maya pulled off the band of toweling around her head, braced her elbows on her knees, and buried her face in her hands—not in despair, but in a white-hot rage.

Damn him! Damn him! Why and *how* had Simon Parkening got in? The last she heard, his uncle had banished him from the hospital! Maybe the heckling had been originally intended for Doctor O'Reilly, but most of it had been aimed at her.

I'll lodge a complaint with Doctor Clayton-Smythe! That was her initial thought, but what good would that do? As angry as she was, she still knew that she was only here on sufferance, and if she complained about something that Clayton-Smythe would regard as trivial—which he *would,* since a certain amount of criticism and heckling was expected of students to a very junior surgeon—that sufferance might well end. *Especially* since the target of her complaints was his nephew, who was evidently back in his uncle's good graces.

Yes, she had successfully completed a difficult and delicate operation. But it was not one which would have met with the Director's full approval; Clayton-Smythe would have been in agreement with those who would have wielded the scalpel ruthlessly and with a callous lack of compassion for the girl's own wishes.

Maya's rage built yet again, and her hands clenched on the band of toweling she held against her forehead, when the outer door swung open, and another pair of hands seized her wrists.

She looked up into Amelia's face; her friend dropped her wrists and stepped back a pace involuntarily.

"I just saw O'Reilly, and I came here at once to congratulate you. . . ." She faltered. "Good heavens, Maya, you look as if you wish to kill something!"

"I do," she replied, from between clenched teeth. And in a few terse sentences she related what had happened *off* the operating table.

Amelia's face went red, then white, and her own fists clenched. "So Simon Parkening, who *failed* every course he read for at Oxford, is now to be allowed to dictate what a competent physician and surgeon should do?" she hissed. "What next? Is he going to get his uncle to rescind your license to practice?"

"He can't do that," Maya began, but Amelia interrupted her, shaking her head.

"He *can,* and you have no recourse! Don't you know that if they wish to, these *men* can have laws passed to take away our very right to practice at all?" Her eyes were stormy, and her jaw set stubbornly.

Unfortunately, Maya knew very well that they could—which was one very good reason why she would not lodge a complaint against Parkening's behavior with his uncle. Her anger made her stomach roil.

"Listen," Amelia continued, seizing her hands again. "I also came to ask you if you would march in the suffrage parade today. Oh, I know you've always said no before, but don't you see why we need people like you, who are doctors and educated, to stand with us? Do you know *why* we're marching?"

"No—" Maya's anger ebbed a little, deflected momentarily by the quick change of subject.

Now it was Amelia's turn to look grim. "You know that some of us have been thrown in prison for our actions; you probably know that, following Mrs. Pankhurst's example, many of them have gone on hunger strikes. What you *don't* know is that they've started to force-feed the ones on strike. Today one of the girls being force-fed died."

"What?" She'd seen a lunatic being force-fed once; it had made her sick. To pry a person's mouth open with a metal instrument even at the cost of breaking teeth, to gag him so that he could not close his mouth again, to then feed a tube through the mouth or nose into the stomach and pour "nourishing liquid" down it from a funnel seemed more like a barbaric torture that should have vanished with the Mongols. To inflict that on a lunatic was bad enough, for this might be someone who was not able to recognize the difference between eating and not eating—but to do so on a sane, sober woman who was going on a hunger strike to prove the justice of her cause? And then to do so in such a way as to *kill* her? That was like inflicting a death-sentence on someone who had stolen a crust of bread!

"How? How did she die?" was all she could think to ask.

Amelia bit her lip. "They're claiming that it was an accident, that she choked later when she vomited," the young woman said grimly, "But one of the matrons admitted that she died while they were still pouring their foul mess into her. They probably put the tube into the lung instead of the stomach, the beasts! She was *only* a poor little Irish scullery maid, not a *lady,* not someone who would be missed. There are thousands like her, after all; she doesn't matter. Tomorrow her mistress can hire another just like her, from the hordes that live in the slums. *They breed like flies,* don't they?"

The words stung, just as Amelia had intended, and Maya shot to her feet. "When is the march?" she demanded. "And where?"

Maya had not expected to find herself at the front of the march, right behind the girls carrying banners—and the six who were carrying a vivid reminder of why they were all marching. Amelia had told her to wear her stethoscope about her neck and carry her Gladstone bag, the two items by which she would be identified as a doctor. "We *have* to show people that we are just as able to provide intelligent, professional workers as men do!" Amelia told her fiercely.

The only addition to her black suit was a white sash, reading "Votes for Women" that fitted from shoulder to hip. Her garb was peculiarly appropriate. She was in mourning for her father, but anyone looking at her wouldn't know that. It would appear, like many of the women in this march, that she was in mourning for the girl who had been murdered.

The force-feedings had not been discontinued after the death of one victim. As Amelia had bitterly pointed out, the authorities, assuming that the girl wasn't important enough to be noticed, had blithely continued in their brutality. But they were wrong.

The central banner, held aloft by two girls and hastily, but expertly, rendered by a suffragette who was an artist, depicted force-feeding in all its brutality; the victim tied down to a chair, four burly attendants restraining her, while a fifth, all but kneeling on her chest, poured something into the tube shoved down her throat. Behind the banner, six more girls carried a symbolic white coffin, draped with banners that read, "Mary O'Leary, Murdered By Police!"

The bulk of the marchers walked behind them. Unlike other marches that Maya had seen, this one was not characterized by chants of "Votes for Women!" and a brass band, but by silence broken only by the steady beating of muffled drums. Not a few faces bore the telltale signs of weeping—red eyes, or actual tears of mourning on pale cheeks—but there were no open sobs even though several of the younger women looked as if they might burst into tears on a slight provocation.

The silence was only on the part of the marchers, however. These marches were rarely accompanied by cheering, but in the silence, the shouting and jeering of the (predominantly male) onlookers was all the more shocking. Most of the hecklers were clearly of the laboring class, but by no means all of them, and Maya reflected that if the march had taken place on a Sunday or later in the day, there would have been *many* middle-class men adding their threats to those of the laborers. And there *were* threats, everything from declarations that the women should be taken home and locked up, to crude and graphic obscenities promising that the shouter would inflict a great deal more than a simple beating if he got his hands on one of the women.

Maya kept her eyes on the girls ahead of her, but she couldn't help but shiver internally. She considered herself to be brave, but it seemed to her that there was no doubt many of those men *would* do exactly as they threatened if they could catch a suffragette alone.

They were so *angry!* How could a demand by women that they have a right that these men had and didn't even value enough to exercise be so threatening to them? Why should they care?

Perhaps because if they "allow" us to vote, they will have to treat us as equals? Unbidden, memories arose with each step on the pavement, echoing in her mind in concert with the marching cadence behind her. So many women coming into the Fleet beaten within an inch of their lives—with broken bones or flesh not just bruised but pulped. So long as the woman didn't *die,* it was perfectly legal for a father or husband to treat her worse than a dog or a horse! He could starve her, beat her, torture her, abuse her in any way his mind could encompass. He could make her sleep on the dirt floor of a cellar dressed only in rags, force her to work until she dropped, then force her to turn over the fruits of her labor to him. She was his property, to do with as he willed, and the force of the law was behind him.

And then there were those who did die; all the man had to do was to claim he had caught "his" woman in adultery, and the law released him to the streets, to do the same to another woman, and another, and another.

Even among men who counted themselves as civilized and would not dream of physically hurting a female, there was the repeated and deliberate starvation of woman's intellect. Consider the refusal of male instructors to teach women subjects *they* considered improper—that was the reason the London School of Medicine for Women had been founded in the first place. For heaven's sake, Oxford hadn't even granted degrees to women in *anything* until the end of last century!

And the marriage laws! While a father lived, no matter how incompetent, a woman's property could be handled (or mishandled) by him. Once married, it belonged to her husband, again to be treated as *he* willed! Even when a woman earned money by her own work, it belonged to *him!* The only time a woman could be free from interference was when father and husband (if she had one) were both dead—and even *then,* any male relative who wished to have what she had earned could have her brought into court and declared incompetent! She had *seen* that happen, to women who were too intimidated to fight back, or those who lost in the court to a lawyer with a smoother tongue (or a readier hand with a bribe) than hers had been!

With every step, with every memory, her fear fled, and her anger rose. Last of all came the most recent memories, of Simon Parkening and his cronies heckling both her *and* her unconscious, helpless patient, afraid of her competence, and trying to overmaster her with brutal words because they could not beat her into submission.

And neither they, nor these other beasts will beat us down! she thought, her anger now bringing new energy to her steps, so that she raised her head and glared at the hecklers in the streets with white-hot rage in her eyes. *Go ahead!* she challenged silently. *Threaten me all you like! You only prove that you are worse than the brute animals!*

"Votes for Women" was only the battle cry, the hook upon which all else depended. It was *emancipation* of women that was the real issue—for until women could vote, they could never change the laws that oppressed them and made them slaves.

Maya was not the only one mustering anger as a weapon against the mob; she saw now that others were glaring at their tormentors with equal defiance as they marched. In the younger girls, the defiance was mixed partly with fear, but mostly with excitement. Perhaps they had not yet had enough experience with the worst that men could do for the fear to seem very real to them. But in the older women, it was clear that the anger had overmastered the fear, and their glares were intended to shame the instruments of that fear.

Sometimes it even worked, when they could actually catch and hold the eyes of those who shouted so angrily at the marchers. Now and again, a man stopped in mid-shout, his mouth gaping foolishly. His face flushed, he dropped his eyes, and he slunk into the crowd. But there was always another shoving forward to take his place.

At this moment, Maya almost hated Men, the entire brutal race of them.

Almost. For there were men among the marchers, and not the cowed, hen-pecked specimens depicted in the cartoons of the critical press either. Men who were *braver and stronger* than the ones shouting on the line of march, because they weren't afraid of women who were just as brave and strong as they were! For their sake, Maya could not take the easy route of condemning the whole sex—only those who were too cowardly, weak, and ignorant to bear the thought of losing their domination over those that should have been their partners.

At last their goal came within sight. Parliament, where the

marchers were going to lay their coffin, fill it with stones until it was too heavy to lift, and some of the women were going to chain themselves to it and to the railings of the stairs and the fences. These women would be arrested and dragged off to prison, of course, where they would also go on hunger strikes, and be force-fed—

And die, perhaps. Until shame overtakes those in authority and the murdering stops!

Amelia worked her way up through the marchers to Maya's side. "As soon as we gather and start to fill the coffin, you and I need to slip off," Amelia said quietly, under the muffled drumming and the shouts.

"I feel horrible to leave them," Maya said, looking about her at the determined faces of the women around her.

"You and I fight the fight where we are working, and we are needed there," Amelia told her, although she, too, looked guiltily at the others who marched past them and began to solemnly place the stones each one carried into the now-open coffin. "Who would take our place, guarding the Bridgets and the Alices of London from the Clayton-Smythes and Simon Parkenings who treat them like so many disposable experiments?"

Maya sighed and nodded, although it was hard to leave those others here to face whatever that fate and the police had in store for them. Hidden from the jeering onlookers by the other women around them, they removed their sashes and handed them to one of the others—nor were they the only ones who were taking off sashes and blending back into the crowd. The drummers formed a semicircle, continuing the death-march rhythm and distracting the eyes from those who were slipping away. Now that the marchers had reached Parliament, there were other people thronging the streets than merely those who had gathered to jeer, and it was much easier to move to the edge of the group and slip off to hide among them. Most of the women here would not be among those who courted arrest. Several, like Amelia and Maya, would not even remain here unchained to risk it.

But she still felt horribly guilty as she tucked her stethoscope into her bag and squeezed past a couple—a nursemaid and her beau—who were craning their necks to see what was going on to cause such an uproar.

Once past the crowd, she and Amelia walked briskly away, unmolested even by those who had been shouting at them a few moments before. Without that white sash branding them as suffragettes, men looked right past them as things of no threat, and hence, no importance.

And perhaps that spoke of their contempt and disregard for all women even more than the shouting. It certainly spoke eloquently of their blindness.

14

THE summons came just after sunset and found Peter Scott at his flat; a moment later, he was on a 'bus, figuring that the odds of finding a cab at that time of the evening in his neighborhood were pretty remote. He only had to change 'buses twice, when it all came down to cases, and the 'bus was just as fast as a cab would have been.

He swung himself off the back steps of the 'bus at the corner as it paused to make the turn, and trotted all the way to the club. He met another of the club members, young Reginald Fenyx, on the steps of the Exeter Club, as a third and fourth climbed grim-faced out of cabs behind him. The summons tonight had come in the person of a human messenger boy carrying an envelope with his name on it, not in some arcane fashion, and it had been marked "urgent." Only twice since he had been invited to join the White Lodge had he gotten such a summons, and both times the situation had, indeed, been urgent.

"Do you know what this is about?" he asked Reggie Fenyx, holding open the door for the younger man.

"Not a clue, I'm afraid," the latter replied, with a shake of his head. "I'd only just got to our town house, down from Oxford on the train, when the lad rang the bell. The card was for Pater as well, but he's down in Devon, and pretty well out of range for something that's urgent."

"Whatever it is, they've called in every member that's in London," put in one of the men who had just arrived by cab. "I'm not certain how the Old Man knew that *I* was back in town."

"I think he's just sending boys around with cards and a list of addresses," opined the fourth, as they all passed the guests' dining room, the Club Room, the public dining room, and headed for the stairs that would take them to the second-floor War Room.

The War Room took up half of the second floor, which shared the floor with the private rooms of Lord Alderscroft and Lord Owlswick. Both peers were already in the War Room, along with more members of the Council of the White Lodge than Peter had ever seen before together at once. There was a table here, at which about half of those assembled were seated, with the rest standing behind them. As yet, no one had donned the robes that hung on pegs along one wall, but every member wore whatever mystic jewels he deemed necessary in an emergency situation. In the case of Lord Alderscroft, that was nothing more than his signet ring; in the case of the weedy squire John Pagnell-Croyton, it was *two* rings, a massive gold necklace with a garnet pendant, and a pair of garnet cufflinks that might once have been earrings. The thin peer looked as if the weight of all that gold would crush him to the floor in a moment.

Peter had never bothered with focus stones or enchanted ornaments; he never felt comfortable wearing even a ring. As a ship's captain, he had not worn one because it was a hazard he did not need; all too often he had seen fingers torn off or hands mutilated because a ring got caught in machinery that could not be stopped in time. Now that he was a landlubber, he frankly could not afford the only gems that truly called to him—emeralds—and that, combined with his disinclination for anything ostentatious, meant he eschewed jewelry altogether.

That lack made him stand out yet again among the rest of the Elemental Masters. Even Almsley had a ring—though his was far simpler than most of the rest of the members of the Council. Almsley's ring was a cabochon emerald set in a wide silver band; it had belonged to his grandfather, and had been passed down to the first male who demonstrated Water Magery in each generation since the Roman-British times, for the Almsleys were a *very* old family. There were similar rings for Fire, Air, and Earth Masters, kept in a locked casket by Almsley's grandmother. What the female Elemental Masters of the Almsley line received was something Almsley had never disclosed to his "Twin," but since Grandmama was a Water Master in her own right, there were, presumably, provisions made for them as well. The Almsleys were not only an old family, they were perforce unusually egalitarian.

"Is this the last?" Alderscroft rumbled to Owlswick, who was ticking off names on a list as they all came in.

"Yes, my lord," Owlswick replied, setting pen and list down on the table before him. "The others are all too far away to be of any service for tonight, and I have seen to it that they shall be informed of the details of the current situation. God forbid—but it may creep beyond London."

"What situation, my lord?" asked Reggie Fenyx, somehow managing to combine a deferential manner with a bold and unshrinking gaze. Peter had the feeling that Reggie was destined, not for the role of a scholar, but for the military. *No matter what his father thinks, that one isn't going to stay at Oxford past attaining his degree.*

"Death!" replied a sepulchral voice, in tones of uttermost gloom, startling Peter, and many others as well. "Death Invisible stalks the streets of London!"

It was not Lord Alderscroft who answered, but Harold Fotheringay, who was, on occasion, given to overdramatization. Alderscroft shot him a look of annoyance, but he did not contradict the younger man. Instead, he merely added, "Something of the sort, at any rate. Please take your seats, gentlemen, and I will tell you all we know."

"I found the first one," Fotheringay moaned to no one in particular, as they took their seats. "My man of business. Horrible! Horrible!" Not to belittle Fotheringay's distress, he really *did* look deeply shaken; beneath the heavy mustache, his lips were pale, as was his complexion, there were dark circles under his eyes, and his hands trembled as he clasped them together on the table. *Whatever he's done in the past, he's not overdramatizing now. What he saw has him paralyzed with fear.*

"And it is to Lord Fotheringay's credit that he recognized at once the signs of a magical attack," Alderscroft rumbled. "If he had not, we would not yet be aware that there was anything amiss at all, for there has been no sign of movement among our enemies, and none of the victims are themselves mages."

What? Peter was as much taken by surprise as most of the rest of the Council. *Mages don't kill ordinary people by magic!*

The details came quickly. "Fotheringay went to pay a call on his man of business today, very early. The man was not yet down for breakfast, which was something of a surprise—" Alderscroft began.

"It was impossible," Fotheringay interrupted. "Man was always up at dawn." He shook his head, and Peter saw drops of perspiration on his forehead. "Sent the maid up. Knew there was something wrong. Man was *always* up at dawn." He grew paler as he continued the story. "Demned fool woman let out a shriek; I went running up. Demned fool useless woman—standing there screaming—ran off for the police before I could stop her."

He put his head down on the table, unable to go on for the moment.

"Fotheringay sent for me, of course," Lord Alderscroft continued. "I've managed the situation, which could have been very badly mishandled. What Fotheringay uncovered was the corpse of his man, with all the marks of asphyxiation on him. I think I need not go into details."

"Man looked like he'd been squeezed to death!" Fotheringay blurted, raising his head again, his blank eyes looking, not over the table, but into the recent past. "Never seen anything like it—demme if I have!" He shuddered violently. "Didn't have to check; the stink of power was all over him, but *nothing* like ours!" He squeezed his eyes shut again, much to Peter's relief. That blank stare was nothing less than unnerving.

"Indeed. And, might I add, nothing at all like that Hindu

woman you investigated for us, Scott, though it definitely *is* Indian," Alderscroft continued, unaware that his words had sent a chill down Peter's back. "This was my analysis, and it was confirmed by the one thing that linked all the other victims—and we have identified four, who all perished in the same way last night. All of the victims had served in India. The first victim we found had done so in a purely civilian capacity, two of the others in the Army, the last was born and raised to adulthood in the Raj and only recently returned home when his father died. Quite a young man, actually," Alderscroft added, meditatively. "It was that which confirmed to us that we were dealing with an extraordinary force. One old man, even three old men, could perish in the night of—say—magically induced apoplexy. That requires precision, but not a great deal of power. This, however—"

"*Squeezed* to death!" Fotheringay repeated, thoroughly unnerved. *He's going to be good for nothing for a while,* Peter decided.

Peter was just as unnerved as Fotheringay, though for different reasons than the others of the Council. Maya had not yet told him what it was she had been protecting herself *from* with those cobbled-together shields. Indeed, she had not even admitted to him that she *was* hiding herself.

This could not be coincidence. Whatever, or whoever, had killed those men was probably Maya's enemy, or at least, was the person (or persons) Maya was trying to hide from. And that only led to more questions, entirely different questions from the ones the rest of the Council now pondered.

She expected this power to follow her from India, or to be here already. Follow her, I think, or we'd have seen murders before this. But why is it killing Englishmen?

There must be a clue in the fact that it had taken only those who had *been* in India. Many spells required something of the target in order to be launched; had these men left articles behind that were now being used against them?

The only problem was that assumption implied that whoever had murdered them had brought those objects with him. That seemed unnecessarily complicated. Surely, *surely,* this thing was not operating from India itself?

"We must assume that it is possible this deadly force is operating from India itself," Alderscroft rumbled. "You all know how the natives have been foolishly agitating of late for the end to British guidance. The continent teems with their numbers, and they can easily fill temples to overflowing with worshipers lending their crude force to the focused power of an Adept. Why they have chosen to murder these men, I do not pretend to know. We must, however, assume that this is but the opening salvo to a war of the Unseen."

"Then we must seal the country!" someone blurted. "We must create a shield over England at once!"

"That is my conclusion," Alderscroft agreed, and a buzz of talk erupted, aimed at planning just how to create such a shield.

Peter could only watch and listen, helplessly. *That—I can't believe that,* he thought. *First of all, how would anyone, even an Eastern Adept, be able to focus power over that great a distance?* Oh, of course, there were legends of such things, but not ever in Peter's experience—and he had a great deal when it came to India and the East—had such a thing ever been accomplished. *And why would anyone bother with such small fry? To kill at such a distance would require* enormous *power. Why waste it on four nonentities? If these four had done anything* that *heinous, certainly they would not have been such—nobodies. And if this was meant as a strike against British rule, why strike at nobodies in the first place? Why not go after someone in a position of power in India—the Viceroy, or the Colonial Government?*

Alderscroft had jumped to his own conclusion, however, and from the look of things, he wasn't going to budge from it.

"Simple shields, made large enough, should disrupt power operating at such an extreme distance," Alderscroft said, loud enough for his voice to carry over the general babble, pulling Peter's attention back to the matter at hand. "I think we have enough Masters on hand to make such a shield, and as soon as we can gather all the members of the Exeter Club and White Lodge together at

Stonehenge, we will have enough to make such a shield impervious."

Stonehenge? We're all supposed to make an excursion out to Stonehenge? Peter thought incredulously. *This is insane!*

But what he said aloud was, "Lord Alderscroft—what if the menace isn't coming from outside England?"

He pitched his voice strongly enough to also carry over all the rest, and his words created a sudden silence. Alderscroft raised his eyes and stared at him. "What was that?" the Head of the Council demanded.

Peter cleared his throat nervously and repeated himself. "What if the menace *isn't* coming from outside England? What if it's right here? Won't we be sealing it in here *with* us? Essentially cutting *us* off from—oh—outside help?"

Some of the members snorted at that; the rest looked contemptuous. Only Almsley regarded him thoughtfully, as if giving his suggestions the full weight of being taken seriously.

"If there had been anyone with that sort of power among us in London, or even in England, Scott, we *would* have detected them before this," Alderscroft said, with a hint of warning in his tone. "The closest we came was that little doctor of yours, and she didn't have enough power *or* expertise to create a horror like the one we face."

Would you have detected it, can you be sure? What about those shields of Maya's, the ones that essentially made you look elsewhere? If those had been formed correctly, would you ever *have noticed her?* He wanted to ask those questions, but glanced first at Almsley, who shook his head very slightly and pursed his lips a little in warning. The Head of the Council was not going to listen to one of the most junior members of the White Lodge; he had already made up his mind. To force a confrontation at this point would accomplish nothing, and leave him unable to talk to Alderscroft later when events either proved or disproved the Head's conclusion.

Someone will die if that happens . . . but getting myself thrown out of the Club and the White Lodge won't do any good either.

Unsatisfied, he held his peace, as Alderscroft finished the design of the magic ritual they would all perform to create the initial shield.

"Don robes, and we will assemble in the second chamber," Alderscroft ordered, standing up and shoving his chair away from the table in a single decisive movement. Peter hung back a little, delaying the moment that he joined the others; there was a brief scramble for the robes, then those nearest the pegs began passing the common robes back to those behind them.

Some few of the members had special embroidered, personalized robes of various antique cuts and quaint designs. There was no uniformity to these robes; they ranged from something the most austere monk would feel comfortable wearing, to an elaborately embroidered creation that the Pope himself would have felt excessive for High Mass at Easter. Some were designed along the lines of those a Member of Parliament or a University don wore, others seemed to be recreations of a medieval burgher's festive attire. Alderscroft's hooded robe, of brilliant scarlet velvet, was somewhere between the two extremes.

The majority took one of the common robes passed to them, which were cut along the lines of the academic robes worn by the undergraduates of Oxford and Cambridge—but not constructed of sober scholastic black, but of burgundy red, sapphire blue, or emerald green. There *were* robes of the warm gold favored by Earth Masters on the hooks, but no one took any of them. Peter shrugged himself into a green robe, and joined the rest filing into the inner chamber of the War Room.

As each man entered the chamber, he took a plain wooden wand out of one of the four containers beside the door. Willow for the Water Masters, ash for the Fire, and birch for the Air; once again, there was a box of wands of oak for the Earth Masters, but there were none here tonight to take one.

Perhaps some will appear for Alderscroft's assemblage at Stonehenge, Peter thought, slipping the wand nervously through his fingers as he shuffled into a place in the circle. They really could not have fitted any more people into this room; they were all standing shoulder-to-shoulder as it was. There wasn't anything here but a series of concentric circles on the floor, the largest of which was flush to the walls. The walls, completely without windows, were painted a flat gray; the floor was of tan terrazzo with the circles inlaid in copper, so carefully that there wasn't the least crack or crevice to mar their perfect line. Gaslights high up on the walls gave perfect illumination to the room; someone, perhaps even the Head himself, had come in here earlier to light them.

By custom, Air Masters stood in the east, Fire in the south, and Water in the west. If there had been Earth Masters, they would have stood in the north; as it was, the Air and Water Masters spilled over into the northern quadrant, taking their place.

When they had all crowded into the room, Alderscroft nodded, and as one, they snapped their wands down to be held horizontally in front of them, each man's wand crossing the ends of the wands of the men to either side of him, rather like a giant Morris Dancers' figure. Peter supposed that they *could* have all held hands to maintain contact between them, but that would have been—well—rather embarrassing to most of them. Evidently at some time in the past, this method of linking all the members of the White Lodge had been decided on as being somehow more dignified than hand-holding like children in a circle dance.

The instant that full contact was made, the Lodge Shield sprang up behind them all. Peter felt it and Saw it; arcing over them all and glowing a violet-white, it hummed with the power of the three dozen Masters here tonight, along with all of the power invested in it by every Master who had ever stood in this room as a member of the White Lodge. If ever a thing made of magic was alive, it was this shield.

And it was this shield that they would use as the basis of the one meant to cover all of England.

However stupid an idea that is. . . .

Peter closed his eyes; it was not in anyone's best interest at the moment to argue with Alderscroft. He could do that later, if (when!) another death occurred, and became obvious that all they had done was to trap their enemy inside their own walls.

Now was the time to raise the Cone of Power that would make

it possible to expand the shield, and he was no less obliged to add his force to the rest, even though he privately considered the task to be absolutely futile.

He locked his knees, braced himself, and carefully detached his *self* from his body.

The ancient Egyptians had called this *self* the *ka,* and had portrayed it as a human-headed bird. Peter often wondered if, when an Egyptian mage had performed this same exercise, the ancient one had seen himself in that form. Peter never had; the form he took was of a younger, slimmer version of himself—basically, himself as he had been when he first achieved Mastery. Somehow that form never changed, though the outer one did. He knew that if he bothered to focus his attention on them, he would see the rest of his colleagues, in similar forms, detaching themselves from their corporal bodies—then vanishing, leaving behind the thin silver cords of power that tethered them to their bodies, trailing off into the void. These spirit forms were not limited to the dull plodding pace of their material hosts; they could be anywhere they chose in the blink of an eye. The Masters had gone to seek their natural allies, the creatures of magic and spirit that inhabited the particular Element of each mage.

And it was time that he did the same.

North, he thought.

In the speed of thought, he was *there,* in the place he felt most at home; hovering above the Great Deep, the ocean. Where he found himself, floating just above the moonlit waves, was somewhere off the coast of Scotland. It was an unusually calm night; a few clouds drifted across the sky, but there was only the usual breath of wind that blew from the sea to ruffle the surface of the waves.

Peter felt himself relax immediately. Let Almsley and the other Water Masters seek out the naiads and the other familiar creatures of river and spring; when it came down to cases, it was the Elementals of the deep ocean that he felt most akin to. There were fewer of them, but they were correspondingly more powerful—and *that* was wherein his value to the White Lodge lay.

But not Leviathan. Not today. He had already decided that he would not seek the Greatest Ones of the deeps. *I'll do my duty, but no more than that.*

Slowly, he moved himself landward over the waters under a brilliant moon, searching for the dark bobbing head of a seal, swimming a shadow amid shadows among the foam-flecked waves, and not finding one. The pull of power had led him here, though, so one or more of the Selkie should be about somewhere.

It was not until he reached the shore and alighted among the bushes just beyond the sands, that he saw one, and a passer-by would not have seen anything out of the ordinary about the fisherman who strolled beside the water's edge. True, there was something a little odd; as he walked above the waterline, the hems of his trousers were soaking wet, and although by the footprints he had been walking for some time, they never seemed to get any drier. Not only that, but the footprints themselves were full of water and bits of weed. But that was the only odd thing about him, and could be explained away readily enough.

Peter followed the faint tug of power until it brought him to a dark shape lying concealed within a gorse bush. It looked like—and in fact, it was—a sealskin. There he waited, until the fisherman came up the path and stopped beside it, eyeing him keenly, though he *should* have been invisible to mortal eyes.

" 'Tis you, is it, Peter Scott?" said the Selkie, bending over to pick up the sealskin and shake it out.

You've sharp eyes, my lad, Peter replied in thought, for of course his spirit form could not actually speak. *Courting the ladies, were you?*

"Visiting my good little wife Alice, and thanks to you," said the Selkie complacently, and by that, Peter knew which Selkie it was and blessed his good fortune in having come across one that he had directly aided.

The Selkie, uniquely among the magic creatures of England these days, retained their physical nature. They were human on land, but when they donned their magic cloaks, they lived as seals in the sea and Selkie spirits within the walls of their own magical homes. Yet every seven generations they had to seek human women to bear them children, (or, occasionally, a human male would take a Selkie bride) as their ties to land and physical form thinned and threatened to bind them into their seal- and spirit-forms for all time. In the old days, that had been of no great moment; it was understood that an occasional fisher girl or boy would have an "uncanny" spouse. It was considered lucky. A Selkie husband would bring back plenty of fish, and occasionally gold from the sea, and the relatives of a Selkie bride would drive fish into the nets of her husband (so long as he was kind to her and kept her safe and content). But in this age, that had all changed. A Selkie couldn't walk into a Registry Office and put down his name and address beside his would-be bride's. And a girl these days wanted something *material,* a lad with a boat, or a job in a shop, or a smart young clerk, or even a fellow with a steady place in a factory. More often than not, she wanted a young man that could take her away from these bleak and storm-racked shores into the city, where things were happening. Girls even in the wildest parts of Scotland didn't believe in Selkies, and as for the boys, they didn't believe in anything but God and shillings. If some strange man with melting brown eyes came 'round, talking sweet words, girls these days would tell him to be about his business, and that right sharp. And no boy would take up with a strange girl he found walking along the shore with her hems all wet. She might be a gypsy, intent on stealing everything he had that was portable.

So for the first time, the Selkies of Sul Skerry found themselves looking at the end of life as they had known it, and they were afraid.

Then came Peter Scott, drawn by their distress, and in a position to do something about it. In London there were plenty of young women who would have given their souls for a husband, *any* husband, with or without a Registry License or the posting of banns, any escape from the life of grinding poverty and endless humiliation that was the lot of a girl who no longer had "virtue" to protect. There were girls whose greatest ambition was to have three good meals, a roof, and a bed, with a man who wouldn't beat her or force her to do anything she didn't want to do. *How* he had found ten honest, clean-hearted ones among the gin-soaked floozies was a tale in itself, but he had, and brought them here, where the Selkies had built them a tiny enclave of stout stone cottages with magic and strong, brown hands on the site of a fishing village long abandoned.

With Selkie gold, Peter had bought glass windows, sturdy, well-built furnishings, and all the homely comforts these young women had dreamed of as they walked the filthy streets of Cheapside or Whitechapel. Alice and Annie, Mabel and Marie, Sara, Sophie, Delia, Maryanne, Stella, and Nan had moved into their cottages. They'd been properly courted and won, and married after the fashion of the Selkie, and it was enough and more than enough for them, who had dreamed only of a roof that didn't leak, a bed with more than a threadbare blanket, and not an entire cozy home of their very own and the means to keep it. There were no relatives or neighbors to ask awkward questions, and if the babies weren't in the parish register, that didn't much matter, since the fathers would be taking them off to sea as soon as they could swim.

Literally.

And in the meanwhile, they had sweet babies who never cried and never had tantrums, who suckled with the greatest of gusto and fell asleep like puppies when they were done with playing. A Selkie baby was a perfect baby in every respect, thanks to the magic that made them so. Unlike changelings, who made the lives of their "mothers" a misery until the poor things died, a Selkie babe made their lives a joy. The Selkie husbands took care not to bless their wives with new babies until after the current one was weaned and toddling, but that didn't mean that the gentle pleasures of the bedchamber were neglected until that time either.

And if the fathers had no job, they still brought income to their landward wives in the form of Selkie gold, the ancient gold pieces the Selkie had scavenged from wrecks since the time of the tin traders. It was Peter who took the gold away, converted it to proper shillings and sovereigns and good paper notes, and brought it back for the wives to spend to maintain their households. There was a donkey and cart that belonged to this tiny village of ten cottages, and the wives took it in turn to go to the village for a day of shopping—and once each year, each woman got a railroad ticket in the mail to take her into the nearest city, where she could satisfy whatever desires were left unfulfilled by the village shops and market stalls.

So, Ian, is your Alice still bonny in your eyes? Peter asked, with a grin.

"More bonny than ever, and another bairn coming," the Selkie replied happily. "That's the fourth, and never a scold from the lass for puttin' her in the family way!"

The Selkie were nothing if not plain-spoken, a trait which rather endeared them to Peter.

I'm glad you're in a good mood, Ian, Peter said, sobering. *I need the usual favor from you.*

Ian laughed. "After all you've done? You could ask the usual a thousand times over, and still not be repaid. Come on, then."

He shrugged the sealskin over his shoulders, just as an ordinary man would shrug on a coat—and then, there was no man standing there in the moonlight, but a great bull seal, strong-shouldered and in the prime of life. The seal cast a look over its back at Peter, barked once, and plunged down the slope into the water.

Peter followed; and once in the dark water, the seal began to shimmer as if coated with some phosphorescent chemical; as it swam, trickles of power ran along it like the trails of bubbles that followed ordinary seals. Ian was not just moving through the water with Peter following in his wake; he moved through the world of water and stone cottages and the rugged Scottish coastline into the world of Water and Ocean and Sul Skerry. The sea brightened and lightened; the seal glowed with an inner luminescence as it plunged down and down, never needing now to come to the surface for a breath. The medium that the seal knifed through became less liquid and more—something else—and the seal's sides heaved as it breathed in that substance, as easily as air. And then, ahead of them, in deeps that glowed pearl and silver, stood a shimmering city built of light and mother-of-pearl and shivering glass and things more strange and wonderful than any of these, and the seal did not so much swim anymore as fly. Peter could have come here on his own, but not easily, and not quickly. The way to Sul Skerry was perilous and sternly guarded. Humans came here sometimes, rarely—beloved husbands or wives, plucked from the shore or the sea, taken in the midst of terrible storms in such a fashion that those ashore would think them lost to the waves and mourn them as dead. They could come here, but they could never leave again, for to come to Sul Skerry in the flesh meant that the flesh was changed forever—and unless there was Selkie blood in one's veins, it could not be changed back again.

Peter moved alongside Ian, who blew a burst of radiant bubbles at him in seal fashion. They dove through the shadow gate of Sul Skerry side by side, flew upward to a landing platform of crystal and silver, and alighted like a pair of sea birds—and now the seal was a man of sorts again, as he was in Sul Skerry, a creature of light and shadow and only a little more substantial than Peter's spirit form.

Ian waved at him to follow, and raced up a set of stairs the exact shade of the inside of a conch shell but glowing and translucent, to a bell tower of something like spun glass, but full of liquid light. He rang the bell, which thrummed like a giant harpstring, sending its tones through Peter, and making the tower shiver.

Within moments, a host of creatures, male and female, surrounded them; like Ian, their forms shifted and changed from one moment to the next, flowing like water sculptures as their moods shifted. In some way that Peter had not yet fathomed, they had already learned *why* he had called them even before they arrived. Perhaps it was something in the bell that told them; perhaps Ian communicated it to them in some fashion more subtle than either speech or thought.

They flowed around Peter in a circling dance, making him the center of a whirlpool of light and movement. He heard their music as they danced, a music in which the sound of the sea in all its moods, the wash of wave on shore, the singing of the sands as the tide ebbed and flowed above them, and the slow, cold booming of the deeps was mingled with harp and flute and instruments for which he had no name. There was something in it of the familiar, but only enough to make it seem utterly alien and inhuman.

It called to him in a way that no land music ever had or ever could, and he gave himself up to it, allowing the dancers to spin him. And as they twisted him in their midst, he became the spindle upon which they spun the thread of their power.

Around and around he spun, faster and faster, as the dancing grew wilder and wilder and the music followed the dancers to some climax only they could foresee. It all became a blur, of light and sound and power, power, power that no one who was not a Master could ever conceive of, much less hold. Like a spring wound tighter and tighter, this could *not* continue, something was going to break, and yet he didn't want it to break, he wanted it to go on forever, this intoxication, this exhilaration like nothing on earth because it was not of this earth—

Crack!

Lightning struck in reverse! *He* flew up, catapulted out of Sul Skerry, out of the Water, into the world again, and into the sky and into his body, flung there with such force that he was flung back against the wall, arms spread to catch his fall.

His eyes flew open. He had not moved, nor had anyone else in the room. But in the center of the circle was the Cone of Power, a glowing smooth-sided construct that pulsed with the collective heartbeat of its creators that called, *demanded* that he pour into it that which he now held. As the others, each in his own measure and to his own ability, were doing now.

Obedient to its demand, he opened the vessel of his soul and let the Power of Water, green and fluorescing, join the electric blue of Air and the blazing scarlet of Fire in the dance of the Elements. Only the gold-brown of Earth was missing, and he felt that lack as an obscure ache in his soul.

The Power flowed from him, pouring in a stream that seemed endless, swirling into the Cone and building it, strengthening it, giving it a depth it had not possessed before. Alderscroft stood in the middle of the circle now, in the center of the Cone; Peter did not envy him his perilous place. If the Power got out of his control, it would destroy him with no warning whatsoever, as indifferently as a man would step on a microbe and destroy it.

Then, suddenly, Peter was empty.

Now he moved, sagging back against the wall, as no few of the others were doing. The White Lodge Circle was broken, but it didn't matter; the magic Circle, the shield that contained it held, Alderscroft had the reins of the Power in both hands, and it was all his show now.

The last trickle of Power flowed from the last member left standing. It was only Alderscroft and the Cone—

"Fiat!" the old man shouted, and flung up his arms.

The Cone expanded—so suddenly, and so swiftly, it felt like an explosion. The wall of Power rammed through Peter, taking his breath and thought with it for a moment. It felt *very* like being slammed into the rail by a Force Five gale-wind.

Damn!

Silence. A silence profound enough to be a thing, a presence in itself.

The room was empty again. The Old Man sagged against his staff. *When did he pick that up? I didn't see him get it—*

"Well," Alderscroft said, his voice hoarse with effort. "That's done it for now." He straightened with an effort, and looked around at the rest of the members of the Circle, who were, one by one, getting back to their feet and putting themselves to rights. He smiled, and Peter felt as if the Old Man had smiled at *him,* alone, although he knew very well that every other member of the White Lodge felt the same at that moment. It was part of Alderscroft's personal magic, his charisma, that had made him the Head of the Council for so very long and kept him there.

"Well done, old chaps," the Old Man said, in tones that made Peter glow and forget every grievance he had ever had for that moment. "Well done. Now, who's for a drink? I damned well think we've earned it."

Peter sighed, and followed the others out into the War Room, certain he *had* earned his drink, but equally certain that there was nothing to celebrate.

15

MAYA was hiding in the hospital linen closet, wishing that the day was over and she could go home to a cold supper and a colder bath.

It had been a long, exhausting day—first at the clinic, then here at the hospital. To begin with, London had been suffering from a heat wave for a week, and today had begun not just warm, but *hot,* even by her standards. After spending the morning sweating and panting in her black linen suit through one emergency after another, she came home drenched and ready to drop. She hadn't been able to face food, or even the thought of food, only glass after glass of tepid sweet tea. There was no ice; the ice man hadn't yet made his delivery. There was no breeze, and she had ordered Gupta to send a boy to the baker for precooked pies they could eat cold so that he could put out the fire in the kitchen stove.

The suit she had worn all morning was ready to stand by itself; she took it off, took everything off, and couldn't face putting all that hot black linen on again, nor the corsets, nor the layers of petticoats and camisoles. Retiring to the bathroom, she took a full cold bath, which finally made her feel less like a doll of melting wax, and wished that she could just *stay* there for the rest of the day.

But she had duty this afternoon at the hospital.

Finally, at the last possible moment, she pulled herself out of the bath and rummaged in the back of her closet for the garments she had brought from India, the clothing of coolest cotton gauze that she had worn when helping her father at the height of summer before the monsoons came. No corset, only a modesty vest and a lacy camisole to disguise the fact that she wasn't wearing a corset. *One* petticoat, and short drawers, with the lightest of silk stockings. Then a girlish, cotton "lingerie dress" of the kind worn to garden parties in the stifling heat—loosely-woven, reflective white, embellished with a froth of cotton lace, airy enough to be bearable. With this dress, she broke strict mourning. At the moment, it was either that, or die of heat stroke. If she looked more like a debutante at a garden party than a doctor, right now everyone else was so hot that no one seemed to have noticed what she was wearing. This dress was almost as comfortable and practical as her saris.

Almost as comfortable as a sari is not enough, not today. And she couldn't wait to get back home and put one of her saris on, for even the white dress seemed an unbearable burden.

The wards were full of cholera and typhoid patients; weather like this, with no rain for a week and none in sight, was ripe for an outbreak as water supplies grew stagnant and tainted. She made Gupta boil every drop of water they used, and tried to convince her patients to do the same, but it was a fruitless battle. Her people couldn't afford the fuel it took to boil water, even when it came from a pump that put out murky liquid that smelled like a cistern. That assumed they had something to boil it *on;* the poor often didn't even have much of a fireplace in their little rooms, just a tiny grate barely big enough for a single pot or kettle. When they cooked for themselves, they often they made up a dish and left it at the baker's, to be put in the oven for a fee. Mostly, they ate cheap fare from street vendors—who also weren't washing their hands or boiling their water.

The only reason they don't all die of cholera and typhoid is probably because they mostly don't drink water, they drink boiled tea or beer from a stall. Or gin.

The wards were like ovens. Only those with high fevers benefited, for to them, the air was cooler than they were. Poor things; there was ice here, but not for charity patients. People lay in their beds with a single sheet over them, sweating and in pain; the nurses couldn't bring water to them fast enough and boiling teakettles for clean, sterilized drinking water only added to the heat. Maya had put every visiting relative to work, fanning the invalids and sponging their faces, and even that didn't help much.

The only place she'd found that was even marginally cooler than the rest of the hospital was this small room for linen storage. Here, where the air smelled faintly of bleach and clean fabric, where the cries of those in the wards were muffled, and where she was, for the moment, alone, Maya rested her forehead on a shelf support and clung to it with both hands, hoping to find a little more energy to take her through the next two hours before she could go home. Tendrils of hair clung damply to her forehead and the back of her neck; her scalp was sweating, and the pompadour on the top of her head felt as if it weighed a hundred pounds.

I knew it would be like this. And I am *helping them. I'm helping them more than most of the other doctors here are.* Most—well, many, anyway—of the other doctors had made rounds early in the day before it became so terribly hot, and now were at home themselves, probably having iced gin and tonics. At least this once there was an advantage in being a woman. *She* could wear a cool dress here and a sari at home, but no gentleman would ever be seen, even in the comfort of his own parlor, without at least a linen suit coat, trousers, and fine shirt.

There were no surgeries scheduled in this heat, although, of course, if an emergency came in that needed immediate surgery, someone would have to be found to deal with it.

Pray God one doesn't come in. The operating theaters were worse than ovens, with the skylights letting in the direct sunlight. The Female Theater didn't bear thinking about, former attic as it was, and Maya swore to herself that if she had a woman come in needing an emergency operation, she was going to use the Men's Theater, and damn the consequences.

Wounds went septic horribly fast in this heat; limbs that could be salvaged in cooler weather almost always had to be amputated. *Please, no amputations today,* she thought, almost in despair. *I cannot deal with an amputation today, not on top of everything else—*

"Hiding, are we?" said a detested voice from behind her, in a tone probably intended to be suave, that only sounded slimy. "And just what are *you* doing here where you shouldn't be?"

Simon Parkening. Just *what I needed to put a cap on my day.* "I have every right to be here, *Mister* Parkening, since I work in this hospital," Maya replied crisply, turning to face the interloper, and emphasizing the man's lack of the honorific of "doctor." "I, however, would very much like to know why *you* are here. As far as I am aware, you have no need for hospital linens."

Parkening's eyes widened in momentary surprise, then a broad, smug grin spread over his face. "Well, well! If it isn't the little lady doctor. I didn't recognize you in such a very becoming gown. I thought you were some young wench on a larking visit, hiding from her beau."

"Well, now that you know better, you can go on about your business," Maya retorted, a queasy feeling rising in her stomach, her forehead starting to sweat with nervousness. She did *not* like the expression on Parkening's face, nor the speculative look in his eyes. "I have a great deal of work to do, and I need to get back to it, and if you came to see your uncle, you'll find him at his home."

"That's coming on a bit strong, don't you think?" Parkening replied, taking a step nearer. "You can't expect me to believe that you came here dressed like *that*—" he gestured at her gown, "—intending to work? Do you take me for a fool? You were waiting here to meet someone, weren't you?"

To Maya's horror, he moved closer.

"You're hiding in here to meet with your lover, aren't you?" he said, grinning nastily. "Who is it? That filthy Irishman? I suppose a little half-breed like you would take up with some mongrel like him—"

Suddenly his hands shot out, and he seized her by the upper arms before she could move.

"You ought to try a real white man, not a miserable dog of a Mick," he continued, then pulled her to him with a jerk, forcing his mouth down on hers. His teeth ground into her lips as he tried to force them open with his tongue. He crushed her against his chest in a cruelly hard grip with one hand clenched tight enough to bruise her biceps, while his free hand groped for her breast, pawing at her with lust. She couldn't open her mouth to scream without getting his filthy tongue down her throat.

But something in her reacted to the outrage with potent fury.

No!

Shock galvanized her and filled her with diamond-hard hate; they combined in a single moment of sheer outrage, and before she thought, she struck at him—but not with her fists, with her mind.

Earth-born power rose within her unbidden; lava-hot with rage, it welled up inside her and overflowed, all in an instant. She couldn't have controlled it if she'd wanted to, and she *didn't* want to. It rose up in a mountainous wave, paused, and avalanched down on Simon Parkening, smashing him with a crushing blow before she could take a smothered breath.

He choked, let her go; she staggered backward a pace, and he dropped like a stone, sprawling on the floor of the storage room as if a champion boxer had just laid him out.

Maya gasped, and stumbled back into the support of the shelves, one hand on the upright, the other at her bruised lips.

What have I done? Is he dead?

For one long moment she could hardly breathe for the panic that thought triggered. But then, when Parkening groaned and stirred a little, sense reasserted itself, and her outrage returned.

I defended myself, that's what I've done! And there's nothing *wrong with that!* As anger broke through the shock and allowed her to think again, Parkening brought up both hands, slowly, to his head, and curled into a fetal position. From the look of him, he wasn't going to wake up very soon, and when he did—he'd be hurting. She put out her hand, slowly, to get a sense of what she'd done to him.

Something—like a concussion. Serves you right, you—you cad!

she thought at him, hot anger choking her and making her flush. *If I didn't know that your uncle would blame* me *for this, I'd turn you in to him, I would!*

But Clayton-Smythe would take one look at her, and probably decide that *she* had tried to seduce his nephew, and not the other way around. No—this would have to do for punishment. She bent over and touched him on the shoulder—briefly—just long enough to determine exactly how much damage she'd done.

Not enough, she thought with scorn, her insides twisted with the wish that she had been able to do more than merely strike him. *He'll just have the devil of a headache when he wakes up. It probably won't be any worse than the hangovers he has all the time.* Wonder at her own strength broke through the anger then; she'd had no idea she could *hurt* someone as well as heal them! *I wonder what he'll think I did? Probably that I hit him with the nearest bedpan.*

Well, she had—it just wasn't what he'd *think* she'd hit him with.

Enough dithering. What do I look like? She spent a moment putting her dress back in order, and patted her hair into place. Above all, she had to make certain no one would suspect that she and Parkening had so much as exchanged a greeting, much less what he had actually attempted. Her reputation was at stake here, and she dared allow nothing to mar it. *There. Now—fix this situation—*

For the first time that day, she blessed the heat, blessed the fact that no one had actually seen her go into this room, and stepped over his body.

"Nurse!" she called shrilly, backing out of the door hastily, as if she had only just stepped in. "Nurse! Bring an orderly! There's a man on the floor of the linen room with heat stroke!"

The head ward nurse came running at her call, with an orderly following. She pursed her lips when she recognized Simon Parkening, but said nothing except, "Well! Master Parkening, is it? Now what business did *he* have here?"

Maya shrugged as if it was of no moment. "Is it Parkening, Nurse Haredy? I didn't recognize him. I don't know or care," she replied, supervising the orderly who hauled the unconscious man up and draped a limp arm over his shoulder. "But if we don't get him off the charity ward and into a private bed with all the little comforts, his uncle will blame *us*."

The head nurse frowned, then suddenly smiled. "Nurse Fortenbrase with all her airs can have the care of him, and I'll be washing my hands of him," she told the orderly, who hauled a groaning Parkening off to a wheeled stretcher for transport to a better class of care.

"I wish I could trade him weight-for-weight for a block of ice," Maya said sourly, startling a laugh out of the Nurse Haredy. "Well, let's get on with it. Just because a spoiled brat faints in our ward the work doesn't stop."

"True enough, Doctor," the nurse nodded, and the two of them went back to tending people who deserved better care than Simon Parkening, but unfortunately weren't likely to get it.

At last, at long last, Maya was finished; about eight o'clock, with two hours yet to full dark. She had done all she could for people who would either get better or die on their own. She had secretly imparted a breath of healing strength to each of the ones that seemed to be faltering, and it had taken everything she had left to finish the rounds of the wards afterwards. She was *so* tired, in fact, that she didn't even have the strength to catch a 'bus; fortunately there was an empty cab right at the foot of the steps, and despite the expense, she fell into it, giving her address to the driver.

"Take your time; don't force your horse," she told him through the hatch above, grateful that this was a hansom and not a motor cab. She didn't think she could bear the clattering and fumes of an engine so close to her right now.

The cabby's sweating, red face broke into a smile of gratitude. "Thenkee, Miss," he told her. "It's cruel hard on a beast today."

"It's cruel hard on a man," she replied, "Let's not make it any worse for both of you than it already is."

She wanted to lean back, but the horsehair upholstery was prickly and unbearable in this heat, so she put her bag at her feet and leaned forward instead. She watched the horse's swaying posterior in front of her as it ambled along at the same speed as the rest of the traffic, and had to fight to keep from falling into a dull, half-trance. The street was mostly in shadow, with hot, golden bars of sun streaked across the tops of the buildings or passing between them. The sky, an eye-watering blue overlaid with a golden haze of dust, promised nothing but more of the same for tomorrow.

This was death weather; heat and cold were equally punishing for the poor. Babies gasped in the heat and died; cholera and typhoid took off their elder siblings and their parents. If this heat kept on for much longer, there would be more bodies carried out of the hospital than there were patients coming in. The brassy-blue sky glared down on them with no pity and no help.

It has to break. Everyone says so. It has to break, it can't keep on like this. She took her handkerchief from her bag and wiped her face; it came away filthy with dust and sweat. *I'm one of the fortunate, and I don't know how much longer I can bear this.* She could afford ice, she had servants to do all the hard work of cleaning and cooking and looking after her. The poor had no ice, not a breath of breeze, their food spoiled before they could eat it, and they had to eat it anyway and sickened and died of food poisoning along with all the other forms of death that stalked them. They had no cooler clothes, it was wear what they had or strip half-naked and bear the consequences. She knew very well how much better her life was than that of her poorest patients, but it was hard to reflect on one's blessings when one *felt* so miserable.

The heat meant that there were fewer of her "ladies" about to add to the family coffers with their fees. Most of them weren't even here in London, for a good many of them were holidaying within reach of their wealthy clients, who were also on holiday—at the sea, in the country, even across the sea at resorts in Italy, France, anyplace cooler than here.

The rest, the actresses, the dancers, the music-hall singers—they were making do, just as she was, with iced drinks, walks in the dusk, open windows. The only difference between Maya's circumstances and those of the actresses was that they did most of their work at night—but the theaters were stifling, the limelights and gaslights hot, and the one advantage they had was that they *could* work half-naked.

Sometimes rather more than half, she thought wryly. She'd been called to theaters for girls who had collapsed in the heat during rehearsals at the beginning of this weather, but that hadn't happened in a couple of days. The dancers and actresses were good at following her advice, better than more respectable folk.

Traffic thinned as they neared her neighborhood, both because there were fewer people about this close to suppertime, and because there were fewer calls for wheeled vehicles around here. On the road itself, there was little but the occasional cart and handbarrow, and along the pavement, there were mostly children playing now that the heat of the day was over.

There it was—her own front door at last; she heaved a sigh of relief and mopped her brow once again, then tucked her handkerchief back in her bag and prepared to get out as the cab stopped in front of her door.

Gupta had been out scouring the steps again; they looked as if you could eat off them. She couldn't imagine how he'd done it.

She paid the driver, picked up her bag, and heaved it out of the cab. The horse ambled off immediately. There was not much prospect for a fare around here, and the cabby was anxious to get back to a spot with better prospects. It was almost too much effort to pull open her door, and she thanked God that there were no patients waiting for her in the dark, shadowed hallway as she stepped inside.

She left her bag just inside the door of her office, gathered up her skirts in both hands, and climbed the stairs, one slow, panting step at a time. But when she got to her room, she saw that her people had already anticipated her wishes; there was one of her saris laid out on the bed waiting for her, an everyday sari of cool blue silk with a darker blue border woven into the ends, and the short-sleeved top to match.

With a cry of joy, she flung off her English clothes, unwilling to bear the clinging weight a moment more.

Wrapping the intricate folds was a matter of habit; in less time than it took to put on one of her European gowns and all its accouterments, she was comfortable at last, barefoot, with her hair down and tied back in a single tail, the silk swishing softly around her bare legs and creating its own little breeze as she moved.

And when she came downstairs, there was another surprise.

Hanging in the ceiling of the conservatory was a *punkah*-fan, a huge slab of muslin stretched on a hinged frame so that it looked very like a door, meant to be swung back and forth by a rope attached to its bottom edge. In this case, the frame of the fan was tied to the decorative ironwork supporting the glass ceiling, and the rope ran to a pulley on the wall, and was attached to a wicker rocking chair. She could rock *and* fan herself with very little effort.

And Gupta was waiting with—at last!—a glorious pitcher of iced lemonade and a bowl of fresh fruit and cheese, and a broad smile on his face.

"You—are—a magician!" she exclaimed, embracing him as he put down the pitcher and plate on a little table beside the chair.

"Not I," he protested, a broad smile on his brown face. "How difficult is it to make a *punkah*-fan for one who has had such all his life? A little cloth, a bit of wood—nothing! I only wish I had known that this cold country could become so very warm three or four weeks ago, so that all would have been in place for you before this."

"Gupta, thank you; your protests don't fool me a bit. I have *no* idea how you got that thing up there." She waved at the fan overhead.

"You may thank little Charan for that. He managed to take the first ropes over the iron. After that, it was nothing, we merely hauled the *punkah* up and tied it in place. When it is cooler, if you like, we can bring it down again."

Charan tugged at her sari, chattering; she bent and he leaped into her arms to put his arms around her neck. Now she saw how the ropes that held the fan up were tied off to stanchions, one at either side of the conservatory. "You clever man!" she told the langur, who put his cheek against hers, and chuckled.

"The ice man has come, and I have obtained an extra block," Gupta told her. "Since it will melt so fast in this heat. And it seemed to me that it would be better to have cold, fresh things to eat than some pie from a strange baker with I know-not-what in it."

"Wise choice, and thank you." She settled into her rocking chair and looked up with delight as the fan moved, creating a stirring in the air. "Oh, Gupta, thank you so much!"

Gupta bowed, smiling, and left her alone to enjoy the first *cold* drink of the day.

As the chair moved, so did the fan, creating a delicious breeze. After the first glass of lemonade, her appetite returned and she was able to enjoy Gupta's selections.

Very clever of him not to have any meats, she thought. It wouldn't be wise to trust to *anything* like meat or fish to stay unspoiled in this weather, even stored in an ice box.

When the meal was gone, she remained where she was, rocking slowly to keep the air moving, as dusk descended and darkness filled the conservatory.

But as her discomfort eased and she was able to relax, emotions that she had purposely bottled up came flooding up unexpectedly, and she began to shiver with suppressed rage that had been pent up for too long.

I am going to burn that dress, she thought, her head throbbing in time with her pulse, and her face flooding with heat. *Or give it away.* She scrubbed at her lips with a napkin, as the memory of Parkening's mouth on hers made her feel nauseous. She shook with the desire to strike him all over again. *Oh, that* beast, *I would like to break his hands so he can never touch me again! I want to black both his eyes! I want—oh, I want—if only I could clip his manhood for him!*

That was the thing that made her want to run up to her room and never come out again. He would surely try to molest her again, and she was sickeningly sure he hadn't any intention of stopping at a kiss.

The animals must have sensed her disturbed emotions and wisely left her alone to deal with them herself. Right at the moment, she didn't want anything touching her; she couldn't be sure that she wouldn't strike at it.

She shook with conflicting emotions, wanting to kill him, wanting to run away, afraid of him, white-hot with anger at him. She heard the doorbell, but ignored it; if it was a patient, Gupta would come and get her. She hoped it wasn't a patient, that it was just some tradesman that Gupta could deal with or send away. Right now she didn't want to have to face a patient, not when she was so uncertain of her own control over herself. For at the moment, all of her emotions had given way before a terrible, black despair, and the certainty that she could never go back to the hospital again, nor out on the street, nor *anywhere* that Parkening might find her.

"Maya?" There had been no footsteps to warn her of Peter Scott's approach, but he was normally soft-footed. His voice startled her; she rose swiftly and turned to face him, the light from the hall lamp falling on her face, and her wide and dilated eyes.

His face was in shadow, but there was no mistaking the gasp he uttered. Nor the words he blurted out.

"Maya, my God—you are *beautiful*—"

His honest, clean reaction undid her. With a sob, she flung herself into his astonished arms.

". . . and the bitch *hit* me," Simon Parkening whined, for the tenth time. Shivani was heartily tired of his complaining. So far as she could make out, he had tried to seduce some hospital servant and been repulsed; why should she care? If he could not carry out a successful conquest on his own, how was she supposed to help him? He could use magic if he chose; he had the modicum of power needed to overcome a woman's reluctance, and the knowledge of how to apply it. If he failed to use what he had, what was she supposed to do about it?

Punkah-fans operated by ropes going through holes in the wall to two of her servants in the next room kept the air stirring, but the fact that there was no breeze outside meant that the room was stiflingly hot, the air heavy with the incense she burned to keep away the stench of the street outside. It was no worse than the stink of Delhi, but it was not a familiar stink, and therefore she hated it. She did not want Parkening here; he had come of his own, straight, it seemed, from the hospital and he stank of disease and despair. Why he had come *here* and not to his club where he might have a better reception for his complaints among his fellow sahibs, she was not certain.

Unless it was that he could not rail freely about what had made him so angry anywhere else. Perhaps his conduct was not acceptable even to similar arrogant English males, and he knew it.

She was far more interested in what he could tell her about the hospital, but from the moment he had walked in the door, all he had done was to whine about his problems. It was too hot. He couldn't leave London because his firm wouldn't allow him to take a holiday. He was tired of his current mistress, but the woman he wanted was the property of another and he didn't dare challenge the man for her. And the girl he had tried to seduce in the hospital that afternoon in his boredom and frustration had turned against him and struck him.

She yawned under the cover of her veil—and stopped with her mouth open, struck numb by his next words as his anger increased, as he uttered the first original thing he had said since he first began to whine.

"—that damned half-breed bitch, acting like a white woman, aping her betters, pretending to be a doctor—"

Shivani throttled her own impulse to interrupt his raving. She did *not* want him to know she was interested in what he had said. He would use it to try to manipulate her. He had done this before, and this time she was in no mood to fence with him, placate him, or give in to his demands. He was coming to the end of his usefulness, and was no longer worth the time it took to work with him. She would listen to him rant, and wait him out.

She had patience, more patience than he. And to make him more loquacious, she surreptitiously added a handful of drugs to the single block of charcoal in the incense brazier below her. Could it be? Could it possibly be that she had found her sister's child?

Carefully, surreptitiously, she opened her Third Eye, and practically shouted her contempt for *his* blindness aloud. How could he possibly have thought the girl had struck him physically, when he practically reeked of the power that had been used to render him unconscious? How could he have missed something so blindingly obvious? Perhaps only because he himself was so stubbornly blind. It would never have occurred to him that the girl could have as much or more power than he, therefore he had never looked for the signs of it. Stupid swine.

She couldn't tell much from the residue, but in a way, she felt a grudging admiration for the girl that had done this, even if it did prove to be the traitor she sought. The girl had, after all, managed to knock him unconscious without actually damaging him in any way.

But that might simply be a matter of accident rather than control. Admittedly, striking a man dead in the midst of a crowded building would leave one with a corpse that could prove very difficult to explain—but the man was a sahib, and arrogant sahibs were prone to do foolish things that caused them to die with great suddenness. There would be no marks on the body to explain, and heat did kill. And with every moment that passed, Shivani considered that if it had been her and not the unknown who had been molested, Parkening would be in his coffin at this very moment.

As the drugs filled the air, she armored herself against their effect, while waiting for them to loosen Parkening's tongue further.

She did not have long to wait.

Before long, Parkening embarked on a long, rambling condemnation of two of the doctors in the hospital, the one that Shivani was interested in, and a second, an Irishman, that Shivani could not have cared less about.

Unfortunately, this was the one that Parkening blamed for all his misfortune, so this was the one he expounded at length upon.

Great length. Shivani was getting ready to strike him down herself if he didn't get to the girl soon. How on earth could this fool be so obsessed with a man who probably didn't even think about *him* unless Parkening did something to interfere with him? If the Irish doctor was not his enemy yet, Parkening seemed determined to *make* an enemy of him. Was his life so very empty that he had to go out of his way to create enemies to enliven it?

Finally, he got around to the woman in the case.

"—O'Reilly's mistress," he growled. "She must be, I'm sure of it. Why no one but me has spotted it—she'd be thrown out of the hospital in a moment, if I could get the proof. Fornication; can't have that in my hospital. Very deep, that one. Must be her. Couldn't be O'Reilly, he hasn't the brains. But that half-breed—mongrel vigor, that's what it is. Cunning. Not brains, but cunning. Should have guessed it. Bloody wogs. Hindoos—can't trust 'em, too cunning by half."

He seemed to have forgotten that *Shivani,* upon whom he depended for his further magical instruction and before whom he sat, was Indian; she did snort with contempt at that faux pas, but the drugs had taken him far enough that he didn't even notice.

"Says her father was a doctor. Ha! Probably some ranker. Probably some Cockney Tommy. And *if* he married her mother I'd be surprised. Half-Hindoo wog bitch. *Hit* me! Me!" There was a fleck of foam on his mustache, and his eyes had begun to glaze. He would probably pass out shortly; she would have to have her servants revive him. Or—perhaps not. Perhaps she would simply have them bundle him into a cab and leave him to deal with cab and cabby when he arrived on his own doorstep. If he was lucky, the cabby would summon his servants. If he wasn't, he wouldn't wake up again, a body would be found in the Thames, and the cabby would be much, much richer. There was no telling which sort he'd get in this neighborhood.

It was of no great matter to Shivani; she had decided now that he was a risk and a nuisance, and she was going to be rid of him. She did not wish draw attention to herself and her dacoits and thugee by murdering him herself, but she would banish him from this place from now on.

"Witherspoon." He snorted. "A concocted name if ever I heard one! Doctor-my-ass Maya Witherspoon! Not bloody likely! Bastard bitch half-wog—b—b—b—"

He began to splutter, as if he no longer had any control over his tongue. He probably didn't; by now he had breathed in enough intoxicant to fell most men. His head wobbled loosely on his shoulders. He blinked, shook his head.

Then his eyes rolled up, and he dropped over onto the cushions in an untidy heap.

Shivani rang for the servants. Two of them came immediately, bowing to her with utmost servility.

"Take him away," she said languidly, waving a hand at him. "Put him in a cab, or drop him in the river, I care not which. Only take his stinking body from my sight, and do not admit him to my presence anymore. I am weary of him."

They bowed again, and hauled him off. They would probably put him in a cab, but only because it was too far to drag him to the river, and there was always at least one cab waiting outside the house of pleasure on the corner.

Shivani got up, and stretched, no longer languid. She had a great deal to do, for now she had a person, and a name. Revenge—and power—would be hers.

It was only a matter of time now.

Shivani flung back her veil, and smiled into the night.

16

I THINK I may be the happiest man in the world.

Peter had forgotten his original intention of warning Maya about the mysterious deaths the moment she flung herself, sobbing, into his arms. When he'd seen her in the light from the hallway, dressed in her exotic sari with her hair down and her eyes as wide as a frightened deer's, the last thing he would have said to her, had he had time to think about what he was saying, was how beautiful she was. But the exclamation had been startled out of him, and it had resulted in this—

He stroked her hair and said nothing as she wept and raged alternately, during which time he gathered the gist of what had happened to her at the hospital. He didn't know a great deal about women, but his instincts on this were that the best thing he could do for her right now was to listen. And meanwhile, he was beginning to have some glimmerings of what to do about this Simon Parkening.

What he *wanted* to do, of course, was to march over to the cad's flat and punch him in the nose. Maya's distress had awakened a number of very cavemanlike feelings that were not altogether unfamiliar to him—but he knew very well that what might pass for reasonable behavior on the deck of a ship would only lead to a great deal of trouble in this case. He hadn't worked his way up to captain by punching everyone who offended him.

Much as I would like to smash his face to a pulp, whoever this Simon Parkening is, I don't think that's the best tactic for getting him out of Maya's life.

No, satisfying as that would be for both of them, that was not the answer. Nor was showing up at the hospital and conspicuously carrying her off as soon as her duties were over every day. Given this canard's filthy mind, he would probably decide that Maya was Peter's mistress, and not rest until he had gotten her thrown out of the hospital on charges of immoral behavior. No, that would not work either, satisfying as it would be to demonstrate that Maya was *his* property.

First of all, she isn't my property. Secondly, she might punch me *in the nose for presuming. And third, in the long run, that will only make more trouble.*

No, no, no. Peter was fast building a much more involved and detailed plan in his mind.

Finally Maya pushed—reluctantly, he thought—away from him, and sat up straight, smoothing her hair away from her face with both hands. Her tear-stained cheeks and red eyes looked adorable to him at this moment. Her hair was loose on her shoulders, half-veiling her forehead; her eyes gazed at him in distress. "Oh, no—" she said, looking utterly appalled. "What you must think of me!"

He laughed, and caught her hands in his before she could push her hair back. "I think that if I had been in your position, this blackguard would be singing in a higher key," he replied. "And I understand exactly why you are in such distress. You're in an intolerable position, and if you were alone, you would have very few ways to escape. But I think that, between us, Almsley and I may be able to maneuver you out of it."

She started to protest. "I cannot involve you, you have done too much for me already—and as for your friend, he owes me nothing, in fact, it is I who am in his debt in the matter of that young man!"

"When was there ever a question between us of *debt* and *repay-*

ment?" he asked, not releasing her hands, and noting that she did not try to pull them away either, noting the flush in her cheeks. "I told you before; what I've done in the way of instructing you is the duty of a Master to someone who has the power to become another. And, in your turn, *you* will teach the ones you find—or who find you. There is no repayment, there is only duty to the future." He smiled at her; with her hair down, she looked so vulnerable. What a change from the controlled and subdued Doctor Witherspoon he had first seen! "I should think that you would be familiar with that as a doctor."

"I suppose—but—" She took a deep breath. "Parkening is a sneak. Worse than that, he is a *wealthy* sneak. He'll never forgive me, and if you get involved, he'll never forgive you; he'll do his best to ruin us both and he's rich enough to succeed."

"He may be rich, but I'll bet my last shilling that old Peter is richer," Peter replied. "Almsley may owe you nothing, but he owes me a very great deal. Or perhaps it would be safer to say that we've helped each other out so often that there's no point in reckoning favors owed." He pursed his lips in thought a moment. "Actually, he might well consider that he *does* owe you something of a favor. That young man you put in his path—Paul Jenner—is proving to be worth his weight in gold, according to my lord. You've no idea what a relief it is for someone with his fingers in as many pies as Almsley has to have a secretary he can trust with even the oddest of correspondence. And the fellow began working the moment he arrived at Heartwood House; he didn't even allow his invalid status to keep him from working. You don't think Almsley's likely to forget that, do you?"

"I . . . suppose not." Peter noted that the despair had left Maya's tear-reddened eyes, to be replaced by hope. "Do you really think he would be willing to—go so far out of his way as to—"

"Oh, my dear!" Peter laughed, squeezing both her hands. "All you have to do is look appealingly up into his eyes, and you shan't be able to stop him! There is a very great deal of the repressed knight-errant in Peter Almsley."

"And in another Peter as well," she retorted, squeezing his

hands back. "But I'm serious; Simon Parkening is a mean-spirited creature, and he *will* try to ruin you! I can't let you take that risk."

"Which is why I won't be on the scene—visibly," Peter told her. "Now listen; I've dealt with cads like this fellow before. I am much older than he, and old age and hard-won experience—and just a wee touch of treachery—will trump even the cleverest of callow young sneaks."

"You *aren't* old!" she interrupted.

It was his turn to flush, with pleasure. That had been a spontaneous protest. *If she thinks me something less than old enough to be her father—I think I just became happier.* "The point is, my dearest, that I am older than he is by a good many years, and I know how to handle him and use his weaknesses against him. Now, what do you think the first thing that he will expect out of *you* will be, come the morrow?"

Think, my love. I want you thinking. I refuse to take advantage of your fear to make you dependent on me.

She frowned. "I suppose—I don't know. I can't think—that I'll go to his uncle? No, he knows I won't, because I didn't when he made that scene in the operating theater. Besides, there is no question of whom Clayton-Smythe would believe in a choice between his word and mine. Then he must suppose that I'll run to *some* male for help." She flushed a painful-looking scarlet, and made a tentative attempt to remove her hands from his. "And now I have—"

"Oh, no, you haven't. I came to you, remember?" He let her hands go immediately, sensing that an impression that he was trying to keep "control" of her was the wrong one to give at this moment. "But do go on—that wasn't the whole thought. You're much wiser than he is. I suspect you can calculate exactly what he'll think and do long before he knows his own mind, so long as you distance yourself and look at it as an intellectual problem."

That's the ticket to restore her confidence; get her to think logically again.

Her brow furrowed deeply, but this time it was in thought. "Yes, he thinks any woman in trouble must run to a male, I'm sure, since he can't imagine a woman depending on herself—I don't have a father to run to—so I'll run to a lover!" She flushed again, but this time there was triumph mixed with the embarrassment. "And when I do that, he'll know who that lover is! He'll want revenge, and revenge not *just* on me!"

"My thought precisely." Peter nodded. "So what you need to do is to throw him off guard entirely. You *don't* want to avoid him. That will give him a taste of satisfaction, which will only make things worse for you. Now, you know him better than I, so what possible way could you act toward him that would confuse him, rather than angering him?"

"What do you mean?" she asked, wrinkling her nose in puzzlement.

"You aren't going to hide from him, so how will you act when you have to greet him?" he replied. "For instance—oh, you could treat him with the same kind of gentle condescension you would a naughty, but feeble-minded child."

"That would puzzle him then, but it would infuriate him later," she objected. "But I do see what you mean. Oh, I wish I knew more about him—I think the reason he's about the hospital so much is because he's up to *something,* but I don't know what it is."

Peter laughed. "Never mind, you don't have to! That's the jolly thing about having to outwit someone like him, with things to hide. All you have to do is throw out a vague hint and his own mind will fill it all in. He'll be certain you know what he's been up to! And that's our key, and the place where Almsley can help us out, because Almsley is welcome in every sort of social circle, and he knows exactly the kind of person we need to help us out. A high-ranking churchman."

"A what?" she asked, now completely lost.

"A high-ranking churchman. Someone important, as high as a bishop by preference." The plan all fell into place now, and Peter was as delighted with it as a child with a new toy, and just as eager to share it with his chosen playmate. "Firstly, we need to establish *you* in Doctor Clayton-Smythe's eyes as not only completely above reproach, but as someone to whom Clayton-Smythe is indebted. Now what does a hospital need above all else?"

"Money," she replied instantly. "Always money. And I think I can see where you are taking this; high-ranking churchmen are in charge of a great deal of charitable money and have access to people who can supply a great deal more if pressed. I already know that Clayton-Smythe wants money for a larger charity ward; it will make him look so *very* admirable and high-minded. Having a bigger hospital makes him look more important. He might even get that knighthood he's been hoping for."

"For that matter, being able to refer to a bishop familiarly will appeal to his vanity as well," Peter pointed out. "So Almsley will find us one of his tame churchmen who is currently feeling the need to feed the sheep. You'll have tea with the dear old gent, talk about your experiences in India with your father, charm him, then point out that the need right here in London is just as great, if not greater, than in India. *You* will be the one to take the gentleman around the hospital, then turn him over to Clayton-Smythe like a good little girl. *I* will arrange for Parkening to be there at the same time."

She shook her head a little, but only in puzzlement. "I don't know how you'll manage that."

"Well, I won't, Almsley will," Peter amended. "Don't worry, he'll do it. Your job will then be to stay with Clayton-Smythe and the padre until you run into him. Then you go to work on Parkening with your hints."

Puzzlement became understanding, then matured to what was definitely a variety of unholy glee. "Yes," she said simply. "I think I can do that."

The bishop was a much wiser and kinder man than Maya had expected; she had the feeling from the twinkling in his eyes that Peter Almsley had told him something of the truth about the situation, and also that he wouldn't have betrayed her for the world. And what was completely unexpected and delightful, he and her father had been at both the same public school and at Oxford. Not in the same college; that would have been too much to expect—but the bishop knew her father at a distance at least, and was able to tell her one or two anecdotes about Roger Witherspoon's misspent youth among Oxford's hearty gamesmen. By the time they went off to the hospital, he felt like an old family friend.

Clayton-Smythe had tried to be rid of her twice, but the bishop had managed to somehow dismiss the effort without Clayton-Smythe noticing—and now the Head was convinced that having her along on the tour was *his* idea.

"Doctor Witherspoon is an immense asset to the Poor Children's ward," he was saying, with a kind of too-hearty condescension that made her grit her teeth. "The woman's touch, don't you know. Little b— babies aren't afraid of a strange woman the way they are of a strange *man,* of course. And the young woman that's her protegée is a positive genius with 'em; she'll be a fine children's doctor in time."

"That would be my friend Miss Amelia Drew," Maya said helpfully. "She's studying at the London School of Medicine for Women. Her teachers all expect her to earn her medical degree within the coming year." She looked earnestly up at the bishop and the Head, clasping her hands together as if in entreaty as she noticed Simon Parkening approaching from behind his uncle. *Yes, I think now is the time.* "It would be so good for sick children if someone like Amelia was in charge of them; she could devote herself entirely to them and their ailments! If only this hospital had a new Poor Children's ward by then, there could be a place for her in it."

The bishop recognized his cue and came in on it like the seasoned professional he was. "Well, there are some Royal grants at my disposal—or perhaps I should say, my *direction,*" he said. "Their Majesties—Queen Alexandra in particular—are very keen on improving the lot of our poor children, and if you not only have the services of a fine physician like my young friend here, but the prospects of obtaining a second lady doctor like her, I cannot think of a better place in which to bestow the Queen's grant."

The Bishop beamed, Clayton-Smythe beamed, and Simon Parkening looked as if he'd been struck. At just that moment, his uncle noticed he was there.

"Ah, Simon!" Clayton-Smythe boomed expansively, prepared at this moment to be pleased with anyone who came within his purview, and feeling generous enough to share the reflected glory of his exalted new acquaintance. "Bishop Mannering, this is my sister's son, Simon Parkening. Not a doctor, I'm afraid, but we can't all be physicians, or there wouldn't be enough patients to go around!" He laughed at his own witticism, and Maya and the bishop joined in politely.

Simon did not. He was looking rather pale, in fact.

A little difficult to accuse someone of immorality who happens to be the "young friend" of a bishop isn't it, you filthy swine? she thought triumphantly. But she wasn't done with him yet, as he was about to discover.

"Oh, Mr. Parkening is in and out of the hospital quite as much as if he *was* a doctor," Maya said, with a light laugh and a penetrating glance at Parkening. "*Some* of the staff can't quite understand what he finds so fascinating, but I think there are one or two of us who've penetrated his secret!"

Parkening actually blanched; he went so white even his uncle noticed. "I say, nephew," the Head began.

But Maya was already offering a solicitous hand to help Parkening to a nearby chair. "Goodness, Mr. Parkening," she said, in tones of false sympathy. "Didn't your physician tell you that after a heat stroke like the one you suffered yesterday, you should never exert yourself? You really should not have come here today—the wards may not be as dreadful now that the heat has broken, but you should still be taking cooling drinks on a breezy veranda, not tottering about here! I'm sure your business here could bear your absence for a day or two!"

"Heat stroke?" Clayton-Smythe exclaimed in surprise. "Simon? You suffered a heat stroke here?"

Maya prevented Parkening from explaining by answering before he could. "Oh, my, yes, Doctor! I found him on the floor of the linen closet in the Women's Charity Ward and had him taken straight up to the Men's Private Ward where he could be properly cooled down with ice and alcohol rubs." She dropped her gaze modestly—so that Clayton-Smythe would not see the malicious glitter in them. Let the uncle make what he would of his nephew being found in one of the women's wards—and in a storage closet, no less!

Parkening looked positively green.

"What quick thinking, Doctor Witherspoon!" the bishop said cheerfully. "I must say, I should not worry a jot to find myself in competent hands like yours!"

"I am only one of many who are just as quick-thinking and competent, Bishop," Maya replied, raising her eyes again. "Doctor Clayton-Smythe attracts only the best, and I venture to say that those he allows to serve in his hospital are the cream of those. I am just glad he considered that I was good enough to practice in his hospital."

Clayton-Smythe positively swelled; any more compliments, and Maya was afraid he might burst. There was no doubt now that Maya was not only in his good books, but had risen so far in his eyes that Parkening would not dare molest her now, nor accuse her without absolute and irrevocable proof of misdeeds. And to a certain extent, Maya was not offering empty compliments. This hospital *was* one of the best; she would not have tried so hard to practice here if it hadn't been.

Parkening had evidently figured out that he was in a dilemma he could not get out of without giving up any hope of revenge on her—and that he would be fortunate if *she* chose not to play the cards in *her* hand. The bluff had worked. He could not possibly have looked any greener.

"Mr. Parkening, I really must insist on you seeing your physician," she chided. "Please, you simply must go up to the Men's Ward."

Feebly, he waved her away. "No, no, I'll be fine. I'll go home, just as you said. Send a messenger to the office—they can do without me, as you said—" He got up and staggered off, much to the surprise of his uncle and the bishop.

"My, my!" the bishop murmured. "Do you think it's wise to allow him to wander off in that state?"

"Probably not," Clayton-Smythe replied in irritation. He signaled to one of the orderlies, and murmured to the man, who hurried off after Parkening, as his uncle scowled after both of them.

Maya somehow managed to keep her face set in a mask of serenity, while inwardly she was convulsed with delighted laughter.

Peter had arranged to meet Maya near the boat house on the Serpentine in Hyde Park; he stood up from his bench and waved to her when he saw her walking briskly toward him in the distance. She picked up her pace, hurrying as well as her skirts would allow her. She had more sense than to wear one of the fashionable hobble skirts, at least, but Peter couldn't help but wish she was costumed as she had been last night. She had looked the very spirit of freedom in that sari.

She took the last few steps between them in a kind of running walk, and caught both his outstretched hands in hers, her teeth flashing whitely in an enormous smile.

"I take it the plan worked?" he asked archly.

"To perfection!" she crowed, hardly able to contain her glee. "Oh, if only you had seen him! I don't know what he really has been up to, but the thought that *I* knew had him white to the lips!"

She related the entire exchange so vividly that he had no difficulty in picturing it. It had not surprised him that Almsley had managed to dig up an actual bishop, but the fact that he had found one who either *had* known Maya's father or was willing to pretend he had was something of a corker.

It's the Oxford connection again. Old School ties and all that. The easy way that University men exchanged favors and backed each other up made him a little irritated and a bit jealous sometimes, but there was no doubt that *this* time the connections had served a higher purpose than usual.

"Well, since the enemy has retreated in disorder, that is at least one worry disposed of," he replied, then sobered. Drawing her over to the bench, he indicated she should be seated, and sat down beside her. "I would like to tempt you to a victory celebration, but before we even consider that, I need to tell you about something serious that has been happening. Four men have died of magical causes—"

Now it was his turn to explain, and he gave her every bit of information he had. And to his relief, although she listened attentively, there was no recognition in her face when he described the signs, and the way the men had been killed.

When he finished, she shook her head. "I know that your Lord Alderscroft is certain India is the source, but I've never seen or heard of any magic in India that could reach halfway around the world, Peter!" she exclaimed. "And if the Separatist movement *had* someone with powers like that at his disposal, don't you think they would do something more to the purpose? You know, all they would have to do would be to send a plague through all the barracks in India and there wouldn't be a single soldier or policeman able to counter a native uprising. With all of the government officials and their families held hostage, the King and the Prime Minister would have no choice but to give in to the Separatist demands."

"How would a magician do that?" Peter asked, his blood running a little cold. "How could one person send a plague to take the soldiers and not the natives?"

"Well, he couldn't; that's the point," she said with a shrug. "It would take too much power. But I can think of ways to do it if you *had* the power. You'd just send plague-carrying rats into the barracks full of fleas and bubonic plague, or you'd get at all the wells and poison them with cholera and typhoid, or you'd bring the rains early and use your power to make the mosquitoes that carry yellow fever breed faster. But I'm a doctor," she added. "I think of these things. It doesn't follow that the Separatists would. I suppose there are plenty of other ways to use magic to strike at the Colonial Government, if one wanted to. My point is that it doesn't make sense to use magic against little nuisances here when you could do much more damage on *big* nuisances in India."

"That was exactly what I thought," he sighed, relieved that she hadn't seen the four reported deaths as a sign that *she* was in danger from anything.

"There are *plenty* of people here from home, and some of them might very well have had grudges against these particular men," she added. "I think your gentleman is overreacting, to tell the truth. Well, perhaps not *that.* Four men did die—but I think he's seeing a menace to everyone that just isn't there." She shook her head and smiled again. "Now, didn't you say something about a victory celebration?"

"Indeed I did! Can your household spare you for the rest of the evening?" he asked, dismissing the matter from his mind for the moment.

"With no difficulty whatsoever," she replied, as he rose and offered her his hand. "What did you have in mind?"

"Better to ask, what did I have *planned?*" he smiled. "And it's a surprise, so come along and don't ask questions."

To his delight, she laughed, took his hand, and got to her feet. "Whatever it is, I hope it's cool," she told him. "It may not be quite as hot today as it has been, but it's still too hot for these ridiculous clothes you English insist on wearing."

"You know what they say. Mad dogs and Englishmen." She didn't reclaim her hand, so he tucked it into the corner of his elbow as they walked toward the street. "I can promise that it *will* be cool; whether you'll like it or not, I can't pledge."

They caught a 'bus for Southwark; he brought her carefully up the stairs to the exposed upper deck—dreadful in bad weather, but crowded now. He found two places on the benches and sat beside her, pointing out obscure landmarks and answering her questions with delight.

The docks and his warehouse were a short walk from the 'bus stop. She took in everything around her with great interest and no fear at all. Of course, she had been going into and out of a far worse neighborhood than this for months now, but it was still good to see. Most women would have protested at the smells, the condition of the street, and turned up their dainty noses at the rough characters at work here.

He pointed out the customs house, told her what each of the warehouses held and explained which firms imported what goods. If she wasn't interested, she was the best actress he'd ever seen—and cared enough about him to *pretend* she was interested.

"This is my warehouse," he said at last, with pardonable pride. "Would you like to see my imports?"

"Goodness, yes!" she exclaimed. "You know, you know all about what I do, but this is the first time you've ever talked about yourself and your everyday life. I had no idea you had a wonderful shop and brought in things all the way from Egypt!"

He laughed. "You make it sound far more glamorous than it is."

She wrinkled her nose at him. "Don't you realize that it is the highest ambition of hundreds of Indians who emigrate to London to one day own a shop or a restaurant of their very own and never work for anyone else again?"

He had to laugh as he opened the door for her. "We've been called a nation of shopkeepers before, but I don't think that was intended as a compliment."

He unpacked some of the crates, showing her the creations of his craftsmen, and in the end, insisted that she take an alabaster toiletry set she particularly admired. By then, he had heard the sounds of an engine followed by those of his men mooring a small boat up to his dock, and knew his surprise was ready.

"I hope you've an appetite," he said, as he took up the parcel he'd wrapped for her, and conducted her toward the door. "And I hope you don't suffer from seasickness."

"Why, no," she laughed. "But why—"

Then she saw the boat moored up to the dock, a handy little craft crewed by what was clearly a family: four rugged men with faces sculpted by storm and sea, one middle-aged, three of twenty, eighteen, and sixteen years.

"Hello, Captain!" shouted Andrew, as the other three men waved at him. "Ready for your jaunt?"

He waved back, escorted the delighted Maya to the dock, and helped her step across the plank into the little fishing boat crewed by Andrew and his three grown sons. Andrew had been another of his officers on his last ship, but had longed to go back to the life of fishing he'd known before he lost his boat in a storm. Peter had put him in the way of a few little money-making schemes, and when Peter had retired, Andrew had done the same, for he'd stuck on once he had enough for a new fishing boat only as long as Peter was his captain.

It wasn't pretty, but it was stout, and as Andrew and his sons put her out onto the Thames, heading for Thames mouth and the ocean, Peter saw that she was trim and steady, and answered neatly to the helm. She had sails, but also a motor for working in and out of the harbor, which chugged along with no hint of cough or hesitation. Once they were in a position where they had a good bit of breeze, Andrew, like the thrifty fellow he was, cut off the motor and went under full sail.

Maya's eyes were as wide as a child's and she looked around her avidly, drinking in everything with untrammeled delight. Peter, for whom all this was no novelty, caught fire from her enthusiasm, and when the engine was shut down, pointed out all the sights with as much pleasure in telling her about them as she took in hearing about them.

"I promised you that this would be cooler," he reminded her, as they passed Thames mouth and the breeze quickened to a wind that made the boat leap forward into the open ocean.

"You did, and it's *wonderful!*" she caroled. "It's like flying! Are we going to fish for our dinner?"

"Only if you want to eat it raw," he laughed. "This is no pleasure craft, and no cod fisher either. We've no way to cook on board. This little lady is an inshore fisher; she goes out before dawn and back by midday, and her catch is in the fishmarkets by teatime. Here." He reached under a tarp and brought out a stout basket. "Let's see what Andrew's good wife has put up for us."

Andrew's wife was a good plain cook, and though the victory feast was all victuals meant to be eaten cold, they were nonetheless appetizing for all that. Knowing her boys and her man, she'd packed enough food for a dozen in Peter's estimation. Maya paused halfway through her second sausage roll to exclaim over the youngest who had come back for his sixth.

They tacked along the shoreline, close enough to wave at the children who came down to the sea and the fishermen who were putting up their nets to dry overnight. Peter used the smallest bit of his magic to make sure that the sea stayed pleasantly calm—and then just a little more.

As Maya leaned out over the bow to see the bow wave pushing up, she suddenly exclaimed with surprise as a dolphin leaped out of the water just in front of her nose. The dolphin was swiftly joined by another, and another, until there was a school of twenty or more playing in the bow wave, leaping and gamboling in the water alongside. This, of course, was what Andrew and his boys saw, which to their minds would be enough to make a landlubber girl laugh and point. What Maya and Peter saw, however, was another matter.

Along with the dolphins had come the merfolk of the open ocean, the neriads, the tritons, the hippocampuses, all of whom (whatever they had been in the past) were now creatures of pure spirit to be seen only by those who had the special sight to do so. They were as clear and seemingly solid to Peter as the dolphins; they were probably less so to Maya, since they weren't of her Element, but she saw them well enough as they played among the very physical dolphins. She was enchanted, and the look on her face, her wide and shining eyes, the smile on her generous lips made his heart sing. The neriads winked and tossed their hair at him flirtatiously, but he only smiled at them briefly and returned his gaze to Maya—who laughed with delight at the swimming coquettes.

They finally came back into the harbor as sunset turned the sky to a blaze of crimson, and all of London was silhouetted against the fiery clouds, with the great dome of St Paul's looming over all. It was a sight perfect enough to make even Peter, seasoned sailor that he was, catch his breath. And Maya, completely enraptured, clasped her hands at her breast and drank it all in.

We'll do this again, he vowed to himself. *Often. And I'll take her out alone one day, perhaps up near Scotland, and introduce her to the Selkie—*

Too soon they nipped in to the dock; too soon Andrew threw the mooring rope to one of the hands on the wharf, and put out the plank. Maya said good-bye to all of them, shaking their hands and thanking each of them individually, and with such charm and warmth that even old Andrew blushed and allowed that it had been a pleasure.

Then they were safely on the dock again, and the boat moved out into the river, heading for its home dock nearer Thames mouth than this.

"Well?" he asked her. "I hope you weren't too disappointed."

"Disappointed!" She made a face at him. "If you think that, you must be the stupidest man who ever lived! It was wonderful!"

"Even when your hat blew off and we had to fish it out with a gaff?" he teased.

"Bother the old hat!" Her eyes shone and her cheeks glowed with pleasure. "This was worth a hundred hats! How can I ever thank you enough?"

He shrugged, and her eyes narrowed; she suddenly looked so impish that he wondered what she was thinking of.

Then, with no warning at all, she went on tiptoe and kissed him full on the mouth. And no little peck either—

"There!" she laughed. "Does that convince you?"

It took him a moment to catch his breath and his wits. "Ah—yes—" he managed.

"Good." She took his arm firmly, and linked hers into it. "Now, Captain Peter, will you be so kind as to escort your lady home?"

My lady? My *lady?* If the kiss had blown his wits to the four wits, her words blew them back. "I would consider it the highest honor in the world, lady mine," he replied to her manifest delight, and together they set off in search of a cab as the blue dusk enclosed them in their own little world.

17

MAYA drifted in through her front door in a kind of rosy fog, trailing her fingers along the wainscoting and humming to herself. The kiss with which she had thanked Peter—

Be honest, Miss Witherspoon. You ambushed him.

—all right, *ambushing* Peter had produced the result she had hoped for. He had held her arm all the way to the 'bus, held her hand *on* the 'bus (disregarding the arctic glares of two old ladies and the giggles of three nursemaids), and had kissed *her* right on her own doorstep! Not a little peck—and not, thank heavens, the kind of nasty, slobbering thing that Parkening had forced on her—

It was wonderful. She had never put any credence in silly romantic novels, but nothing in her life had prepared her for that experience. No wonder even the poorest, most wretched girl of the slums could cling to her man and forget her surroundings for a moment.

She had invited him inside for a last cup of tea in her conservatory, but he had smilingly declined. "I have an appointment at the Exeter Club that will keep me well past midnight," he had said, regret in his voice. "Much as I enjoy the peace of your haven." But he had accepted an invitation to dinner tomorrow, which would be the first time he had ever accepted an invitation to a meal in her home.

Surely this was significant!

Of course it is! You felt that kiss—you saw his eyes!

She laughed out loud, right there in the hallway, and twirled in place for the sheer pleasure of it. She couldn't possibly feel any more giddy than that kiss had made her!

But she stopped in mid-twirl; Gupta needed to know that she would have a guest for dinner, so that he had plenty of time to prepare. Never mind how many times he had been here before; tomorrow night she wanted to impress him!

She paused in the dusk-filled hall and listened carefully; there was definitely someone moving about in the kitchen. She followed the sounds, to discover Gupta himself puttering about in the kitchen, putting freshly-risen bread into the oven.

"Gupta!" she said as he straightened. He turned and saluted her, smiling slightly. "Master Scott will be taking dinner with us tomorrow night. Do you think you can accommodate a guest?"

Gupta met her eyes, and smiled broadly as she colored up.

"So, the Captain Sahib has at last begun courting you!" he said, as proudly as if he himself had been responsible for it. "Good! And after my meal, he will make the proposition!"

"Proposal!" she corrected, laughing and blushing at the same time. *Although a less honorable man might well have made a proposition before this!* "Really, Gupta, you can't expect the poor man to propose marriage just on the strength of a single dinner!"

"Hah!" Gupta replied, looking supremely confident. "He is a bachelor, yes? He eats in his club, or out of stalls, terrible English food, boiled to tasteless, fried in pools of grease, covered under gravy that is full of lumps and grease *and* tasteless! He will eat a fine dinner, he will have a fine whiskey as the *punkah*-fan makes a breeze, and he will think about going home to his little, little room, which is hot and smells of boiled cabbage, and he will make the proposal. Besides," Gupta added thoughtfully, "there are certain spices—"

"Which I very much doubt will be needed!" she said hastily.

"Just have Gopal make us a good dinner, please, Gupta. I'm sure you are right about that—"

"Of course, mem sahib," Gupta chuckled. "And there will be a dinner of the sort that Sahib Doctor your father gave to his important visitors. Besides, you would not care to think later that the proposal was due to spices."

Nor to anything else except how well the two of us are in accord, she reflected, as she thanked him smilingly and turned back to her office.

Although, as a whole, the girls of the street were not good at making and keeping appointments, they were anxious enough about the things that Maya could offer them that they were at least prepared to try.

As soon as the lamp in her office came on, she heard the bell ring. Gupta came from the kitchen to answer it, and her office door opened immediately.

"Well, Norrey!" she said in surprise as her "pet pickpocket" slipped in past Gupta and flopped wearily down into the chair. "What brings you here?"

Norrey was in a state of dress that most would likely consider to be "half naked." She wore nothing but a thin camisole or corset cover over nothing at all in the way of underthings, a dingy pink petticoat showing a pair of bare ankles and feet in stained green satin slippers, and incongruously enough, her treasured hat. Maya frankly envied her as Norrey's chosen wardrobe looked very much cooler than Maya's.

"Cough," Norrey said gloomily, and followed it by a demonstration, which unlike her performance when she had first come to Maya, sounded quite genuine. "Can't sleep, an' it's cruel 'ard on a gurl what needs t'be quiet in 'er work."

"Let's have a look at you, then," Maya said, making no comment on the "work." She brought Norrey into the surgery and gave her a thorough going over, but she feared the worst.

And her fears were justified. "Norrey, you have tuberculosis," she said flatly. "White lung."

"Oh Gawd." Norrey did not break out into tears, as Maya had

half feared she would. She only seemed resigned. Evidently she had already come to that conclusion on her own. "Wot's t'do, then? Nothin', I s'pose."

Maya hesitated. She had come to know Norrey over the past few months; she was better than her surroundings, and had a rude sense of honor. She had certainly been better than her word with Maya. Not only had she made it known on the street that anyone touching Maya, her servants or her house and office would be courting more trouble than *any* petty thief could withstand, she had brought Maya more than one little street waif for treatment who would otherwise not have come on his or her own.

"What would you do for a cure?" Maya asked cautiously. "Would you be willing to let me try something?"

Norrey looked at her with disbelief mixed with a little—just a little—hope. "Wotcha mean?" she asked. "There ain't no cure."

"What if there were?" Maya replied. "What would you do?"

Norrey laughed, bitterly. "Well, *if* there wuz t'be be some kinder mir'cle, an' *if* summun wuz t'give th' loiks'a'me a mir'cle, well, reckon I'd let y' do whatever."

"Remember that," Maya said, "because this may hurt a lot." And before Norrey could move, Maya caught up both her hands in an unbreakable grip.

This would be the first time she had ever tried to heal a disease. She had strengthened people who were failing, she had even encouraged surgical incisions to close faster, but she had never tried to drive out a disease before.

If I don't try, I'll never know if I can.

This was the safest possible place to try. There were no observers, no doctors to wonder at what had happened if she succeeded or what she was doing while she tried, and she was behind strong shields.

Norrey tried to pull her hands away, her eyes widening. Maya stared into Norrey's eyes and willed her to be still.

The girl froze, then relaxed, and stopped resisting; her mouth relaxed, and her eyelids drooped, although her eyes did not quite close. In fact, she seemed to have been hypnotized, though how could that be?

Never mind. If she could strike that cad Parkening down with her mind, perhaps she could hypnotize as well.

I feel like Svengali . . . if, when I am finished, she begins singing "Sweet Alice," I think I may scream.

She reached deeply into the earth beneath her for that magic which was hers alone in all of London, so far as she knew; the action was second nature to her now. The power flowed into her, sweet and golden as honey, stronger now than it had ever been before—as if the power itself wanted her to heal this child.

Very well, then; if that's the case, I am much obliged, I'm sure.

She poured out the power into Norrey, flooding the darkness in the girl's lungs with light. The disease was like a pernicious growth, a dark and creeping vine that choked out everything it encountered, stealing the breath and life for itself.

The darkness resisted, but she sensed its roots were not deep, and she pushed harder against it with the golden light, not burning it out, but uprooting and withering it before it could take root again. Little by little, it gave ground, retreating, shrinking in on itself. Relentlessly, she pursued it, and as it retreated, leaving raw and damaged flesh in its wake, she laid down a honey-glow balm that healed the lungs before they could scar.

Now it tried a different tactic; to wall itself off inside a stony cocoon, making her think she had defeated it. If she left now, it would emerge again later, the next time that conditions were favorable—and given the risky life that Norrey lived, conditions were almost always favorable. Maya knew this trick of old. This dormant state was the condition that sanitariums attempted to induce, since they could not cure—

But it always came back again.

Not this time. Ruthlessly she followed it into its hiding place, breaking the walls apart and continuing to uproot and wither. This *was* hurting Norrey. The girl gasped; her hands clenched tightly on Maya's, and tears streamed down her smudged cheeks. But it couldn't be helped. Better this than the slow and agonizing death by suffocation that awaited her.

Done!

With immense satisfaction, Maya inspected her work and found not a trace, not the least lingering taint of the disease. There was some damage, that was inevitable—but Norrey was cured, and having been cured, would not suffer from the White Plague again.

Maya drew a deep breath of her own, and dropped Norrey's hands.

Dazed, the girl slowly came back to herself, reaching up and scrubbing away her tears with the back of one hand. "Wotcher do?" she demanded hoarsely. " 'urt! Bloody 'ell! Tha' didn' 'alf 'urt! Felt loik y'lit a fire in me chest, it did!"

"Breathe," Maya ordered. "Take a deep breath."

Automatically, Norrey obeyed, pausing for an instant at the point where her coughing fits usually began, then continuing to fill her now-clean lungs. The more breath she took in, the wider her eyes grew, until they looked as big as a pair of prize bronze dahlias.

"It's—gawn!" she gasped. "Bloody 'ell! It's gawn! 'Ow the 'ell didjer do it?"

Maya decided to risk the truth. "If I told you it was magic, would you believe me?"

The admission didn't seem to trouble the girl in the least. "Blimey! Dunno 'ow it cud be ought else." She gave Maya a long hard stare. " 'Ow long y'bin doin' this?"

Now Maya laughed aloud, partly out of relief, partly out of elation. "I've never tried it before you," she admitted. "I knew it wouldn't hurt you, but I didn't know if it would help or not."

Norrey only shook her head. "Reckon I owes yer a bleedin' lot," she sighed. "Reckon I oughter gi' up th' ketchin' lay loik yer ast me."

"Reckon you ought to," Maya agreed, with just a touch of sternness. "I don't think it's too much to ask of you, considering. I don't ask you to give up anything else, or go into a sweatshop—just stop picking pockets and helping your friends cosh the swells for the swag."

"A'right. I will," Norrey said, with sudden determination. "Not a sparkler, not a wipe, not if th' King hisself came an' dangled 'is in front'a me. Ye got me word."

She held out her hand, and Maya shook it, sealing the bargain.

Maya let Norrey out into the night, and the girl frisked away out of sight like a young antelope. Maya wondered what she'd tell her friends about her new-won health.

Probably not that it was tuberculosis. Probably that it was something I made go away with a pill. This was a great secret, and one of immense value; Norrey would only let it go at a price, though given her good heart, for some the price would be very, very small.

Maya saw three more patients that evening before it grew too late to expect anything other than a terrible emergency. All three were women, and all the complaints were trifling in comparison with Norrey's, and dealt with by means of treatments any other doctor could give. That was just as well. Maya wasn't *tired* precisely, but she didn't think she'd be able to replicate anything like Norrey's cure for another day or so at least. A day? Well, probably more than a day.

Finally she locked up, turned out her lamp, and went to the conservatory for a little relaxation before she went to bed. As she had anticipated, Gupta had left a pitcher of iced lemonade there for her. The fountain sang in the corner, and as soon as she sat down in her chair, the *punkah* stirred up a delicious breeze. She could not imagine a more perfect evening—except that Peter was at the Exeter Club instead of being here.

She had—she freely admitted it now—been tempted to cast a little magic of attraction Peter's way. But she had resisted that temptation, and now she was glad. If she had given in, she would never know if what was happening between them was due to nature or the intervention of magic.

She allowed the memory of his face, out there on the boat, to linger in her thoughts; the far-seeing eyes that never hid what he was feeling from her anymore, the firm jaw, the way the sunlight touched his hair. When had she first realized what he meant to her? And *how* had she failed to notice it for so long?

Charan leaped into her lap, and offered her an apple gravely. She took it and thanked him; he should have been sleepy-eyed at this time of night, but he was unusually alert.

In fact, all of the pets were alert, even Mala, who was *always* asleep by now. Rhadi flew down to perch on the back of her chair, and Rajah paraded slowly back and forth in front of the fountain, his tail fanned. Sia and Singhe were nowhere to be seen, but that wasn't unusual. They were probably in the cellar, hunting mice.

Nisha was gone as well as the mongooses, but that only meant she was hunting early tonight. No one had to let her out in this weather; there was a platform just under the peaked roof of the conservatory that extended outside the glass. One pane had been left out and replaced with a hatch, which when open, gave Nisha and Mala a means to get outside to hunt. Just as Maya noticed that the eagle-owl was not in the conservatory, she heard a *thud* on the platform, and a moment later, the owl waddled ponderously into the light, then dropped down onto the dead tree and began to clean her talons meticulously.

Even in the dim light, Maya saw that the owl's talons were considerably bloodied; whatever she'd been hunting, it wasn't rats.

"Have you been eating the neighbor's cats?" she asked sternly.

Nisha looked down at her and gave a hoot that held so much derision it could not have been an accident, as if to say, "Surely you know that *I* wouldn't trouble myself with their scrawny moggies!"

Maya had to laugh at her tone. "I beg your pardon, dear. I *should* have known better."

Owls didn't snort, couldn't snort, but the sound Nisha produced was as close to a snort as a beak could manage, and she went back to the important task of talon sanitation.

Rhadi took that moment to lean forward and say distinctly into her ear, "*Good* Peter!"

"Very good Peter," she agreed. "Do you all like Peter?"

Rhadi chuckled, Charan made a contented little noise, and Rajah bowed his head. Neither Nisha nor Mala made any sounds, but both roused their feathers and fluffed up the tiny feathers around their beaks, a sign of supreme contentment. "Good Peter!"

Rhadi repeated, then leaned closer and whispered something in Urdu which was *highly* improper—if delightful to contemplate, in one's very private thoughts—and made Maya blush hotly even though there was no one about to hear the parrot except the other animals.

"Where did you learn *that?*" she demanded.

Rhadi only laughed and flew up to his favorite perch beside Mala. The two birds, who in any other circumstances than this would have been predator and prey, actually preened each others' heads before settling in for the night.

Rajah dropped his fan, and hopped up onto the rocks beside the fountain pool, also ready at last to sleep. They all seemed more relaxed; perhaps they had only been waiting for Nisha to return and all of the "family" to be within the bounds of the house. Even Nisha looked decidedly relaxed.

"Well, if you are all going sleep, I ought to as well," she said aloud. Charan looked up at her, and jumped down out of her lap onto the floor, walking toward the door a few paces, then looking back at her over his shoulder.

"All right, I'm coming!" she laughed, and followed him.

Deep in the heart of her sanctuary, Shivani frowned, though not at her wounded dacoit, who lay insensible on a blanket at her feet. *He* could not help his condition, inconvenient as it was. Her servants were trained, highly skilled, indeed, the pick of the warriors that her temple had to offer. But they could not guard against deadly force on silent wings coming down out of a night sky. Especially when such a formidable foe was completely unexpected.

The dacoit was a pitiful sight, if Shivani were inclined to pity. He had lost one eye to a gouging claw, and his scalp was furrowed from eyebrow to crown with great talon gashes. It was a wonder that he was not dead; he *should* have been dead, and would have been, had the talon that took his eye gotten all the way to his brain. At the moment, he was only semiconscious; Shivani had given him enough opium to drop a water buffalo to take away his pain. He moaned in delirium despite it, and might not survive the night. He had lost a great deal of blood, and she would not take him to an English hospital, nor would he wish her to. Her body servant had bandaged him as best she could, and that would have to do; he would rest here in the quiet of the warehouse on a clean pallet, and if the Goddess willed it, he would be gathered to her.

Meanwhile, she had lost his services and skills, which was a great inconvenience.

She had the name of Maya Witherspoon, she had the address at which the girl lived, and she had counted on being able to use the eyes and ears of her thugees and dacoits to spy out the details of her enemy's household. She had not counted on the vigilance of the girl's servants—one of whom was her sister's personal warrior of old—nor that the girl still had Surya's former "pets" with her.

Pets! What a trivial name for creatures with such preternatural intelligence! There was little doubt that the "pets" were nothing of the sort; how much Surya had altered them remained to be seen, but altered they certainly were—else some of them would be in decrepit old age, if not dead by now. One of them, the great eagle-owl, had made that attack on Shivani's man tonight, a move that no ordinary owl would even have contemplated, much less executed with such perfection.

Pets, indeed. Their presence rendered it unlikely that anyone could get near to the place, even over the rooftops, for there had been a falcon as well as an owl, and although it *might* be possible to avoid the falcon's attacks, it would not be possible to hide from its sharp eyes once it was in the sky.

She could not penetrate the girl's magical defenses herself either. She could not use ordinary means to spy on her. Under most circumstances, it would seem that there would be no way to see what the girl was up to. But it occurred to Shivani that there might be a third option, if the defenses were specifically keyed against Shivani herself, or against the magic of the homeland.

She left the dacoit in the hands of her body servant and retreated to her own quarters. There was still the mirror to try, and that was the third option; she had not troubled the servant of the glass for a few days now, and he should be cooperative after a rest in the darkness.

She smiled to herself. A "rest," indeed. With the mirror swathed in silk and muffled in spells that kept the servant from leaving the little, dark pocket of reality that enclosed him, he became very, very eager to please her. It was pleasantly easy to control this servant, at least.

She lit incense, picked up the box that held the mirror and settled into a pile of cushions, then removed the mirror from its container and unwrapped it.

The black surface was utterly blank, which was precisely as it should be, for the slave could no longer show himself until she summoned him. He had not yet found a way to break through her confining spells. There was a chance that one day he might, but that chance was remote, and grew more distant with every hour that passed. She sometimes wondered why she had never made a mirror-servant before this. They were so useful, and it grew easier to control them, not harder, with the passing of time.

"Mirror, mirror in my hand," she said softly, gazing at her own reflection in the black glass. "Come in haste to my command."

The wavering image of the mirror-slave appeared immediately, and his desperately coaxing tone left nothing to be desired in the way of obedience. *Oh, mistress, how may I please you?* he fawned.

He must have found this last bout of enforced inactivity very trying. No more did he vex her with wailing or protests, there was only instant obedience. He had broken at last, and it was high time, too.

"You know where my sister's child dwells; can you penetrate her defenses to show me her and her household?" she asked.

The image blanched; all color drained from it, and it became transparent with anxiety. *I beg of you, do not be angered with me,* the slave begged. *I cannot. Indeed, I have tried, but I might as well seek to penetrate a wall of steel with a knife of paper. But—* He brightened, and color came creeping delicately back into his visage. *But I can show her to you as she is when she walks* outside *those protections.*

"Show me!" Shivani demanded imperiously, eager for a sight of the girl she had sought for so very long.

The mirror clouded briefly, then brightened and cleared, revealing the interior of a very large room with many windows along one side. Shivani brought it closer to her eyes and studied the image moving therein.

There was a young woman, slender and not over-tall, dressed in English clothing of some white fabric, with her long, black hair bound up in some formal English style on her head. There was a great deal of Surya in the girl; the likeness showed in her eyes in particular, large and seeming-wise, dark with secrets. Her complexion was of a shade between that of her mother and her father, Shivani noted with disapproval; a mark of the tainted blood, dusky rather than dark.

She moved among low beds, each containing a single person covered with a clean, white sheet. The room was full of these beds, closely crowded together, sunlight streaming down upon them. This must be the hospital where Simon Parkening encountered her. She seemed most attentive to the occupants of those beds, also to Shivani's disapproval. Her expression was intent as she ministered to them; there was no sound, only a picture, but it was clear that she spoke to them with kind and gentle courtesy rather than issuing the orders that one of her exalted blood should have found natural.

There was little doubt that she had thrown her lot in completely with the English; it seemed that only her servants and her pets were left as reminders of her homeland, for in all else, she was Western to the core. *This* must be why Shivani could neither break nor subvert her magical protections. She had surely learned the magic of the West, which was completely alien to Shivani's own. This—was unexpected. And it could prove a major stumbling block.

Shivani ground her teeth in rage. How *dare* she? How *dare* she squander that precious gift of power in Western magery? How *dare* she reject the magic of the people who needed it?

She was just like her mother, turning her back on her own people to consort with, and to aid, these arrogant usurpers.

The image blurred again, and Shivani saw the girl in another place, one that she recognized from the descriptions of her servants as one of the great parks, the one with the large body of water in it. Overhead, a sky far less blue than that of the homeland; around her, trees and flowers that were the wrong shapes and colors. She was not alone.

There was a man. And from her scandalous behavior with him, permitting him to put her hand in the crook of his elbow, laughing up at him, she was not indifferent to him.

Worse upon worse! Now she would throw herself away on an English Sahib! Had she no *pride?* Was she to follow in her deceitful mother's footsteps?

Shivani kept herself from throwing the mirror against the wall with an effort.

Now there was an added urgency to her plans; she must take the girl and her power before she gave herself to this man, for there would be less of it if she were no longer virgin. . . .

Provided she had not already given herself to the man.

Shivani snatched up the mirror again and studied the image intently, looking for signs that the girl had done the unthinkable. Shortly she was able to assure herself that, although the prospect was imminent, it had not yet occurred. There was still the certain distance, the coy shyness, that spoke of passion as yet unconsummated, though acknowledged.

"That will be enough," she commanded, and the mirror went blank, then the slave's uncertain image reappeared in it.

Is there any other way in which I may serve you? the slave begged.

"No," Shivani replied. "You have done as well as you can. You may rest now."

She put the mirror down, but did not swathe it in silk again, nor invoke the barriers to the slave's coming and going. Leaving the box open as well, she set it all aside for the moment. The slave could, if he chose, see whatever transpired within the walls of her sanctuary, although he could not wander outside those bounds unless she gave him further freedoms she had no intention of granting unless it proved useful to do so on a temporary basis.

She tapped her lips with one finger, considering all her possible options, and wondering if the Serpent could take the girl if given enough power. There would be fog tonight; the Serpent would certainly hunt. She had already prepared the baits for it—but she had no bait for the girl, and it did not appear that she would be able to readily obtain one. The dacoit now resting in the cellar had been *supposed* to get something of the girl's. Well, obviously that was out of the question.

Still, she could try. The Serpent had ways and means of getting past protections that even Shivani did not entirely understand. The question was, how was she to get the Serpent the extra power it would need to make such an attempt? The victims she intended it to claim would not provide nearly enough to break through an alien magic. She had no ready sacrifices at hand, and it was not wise to risk exposure by merely taking one at random.

A voice shook her from her reverie. "Wise One?"

Her body servant hovered timorously in the doorway, her soft voice interrupting Shivani's thoughts.

"What?" she asked sharply, gazing on the body servant with disfavor.

"It is the English sahib, Wise One. He is at the door again, and most foully drunk. He demands entrance. There begins to be notice taken." The woman nervously twisted the scarf of her sari in her hands, torn between conflicting orders—that Shivani not be disturbed, and that nothing happen to cause attention to be drawn to this place.

"Drive him a—" she began. Then a sudden thought struck her, and she smiled. The woman shrank back involuntarily from that smile. As well she should; there was nothing of humor in it.

"Tell him that I will see him, if he will go away and come back in an hour, secretly," she said. "But he must come *secretly,* or I will not permit him within the door. Impress upon him the need for such secrecy, so that the police do not seek to interfere with us.

And when he comes—bring him within, and when the door has closed behind him, take him as an offering to the temple."

The servant bowed deeply, and scuttled away; with that order, there was no chance that Parkening would arrive in front of the statue of Kali Durga on his own two feet. Shivani laughed aloud at her own cleverness.

How perfect was this—that a suitable sacrifice, primed with crude magic power and full of the extra energies of unbridled emotions should present itself on her doorstep? Parkening had gone beyond being a mere nuisance, but until tonight, it had not occurred to Shivani that he had the potential to provide her with a last service before she rid herself of him.

He would be missed, of course, but by the time his body was found, her dacoits would have taken it far from this place. Even drunk, he was intelligent enough—barely—to lay a false trail before he returned. She decided, as she descended to the hidden temple, that she would have him taken to the Chinese quarter and dumped there. Let the foolish yellow men take the blame for his death; they were so busy with their quick profits in bodies and drugs that they paid little heed to what went on in their quarter until it was past mending.

Why had she not thought of this before? With every step she took, she wondered at her own obtuseness. At last she would be revenged on Parkening for every braying laugh, every whine, every complaint, and every petty annoyance. The Death of a Thousand Cuts would only be the *last* of the many experiences that awaited Parkening, and she had the shrewd notion that her loyal dacoits would enjoy helping her, for if Parkening had been annoying to her, he had delivered deadly insults to her underlings.

And she would start with his hands, and his lips—for he had dared to lay those hands and lips in a lustful manner upon one who, though outcaste and only half Indian, was still descended from the purest Brahmin blood.

Shivani paused only long enough on her way into the sanctum to select a very special set of sacrificial knives—for this would be a sacrifice she intended to make last a very long time.

18

THE only benefit that the Fleet had in this heat was that it was at the bottom of a building which in turn was overshadowed on all sides by taller tenements. If the sun seldom penetrated here and it was dank, dark, and chill by winter, at least now it was something less than ovenlike. "There's a perleesemun 'ere t'see ye, miss," said a timid voice at Maya's elbow as she collected her medical instruments and some of the drugs it wasn't safe to keep at the clinic. She was layering them carefully into her bag, preparing to go home now that the last patient at the Fleet had been dealt with.

She turned around and found one of the numerous offspring of a woman she had just treated for a broken arm hovering anxiously behind her. The poor thing had arrived with all of them in tow, like a wounded goose with anxious goslings paddling madly behind, her gander supporting her with anxious honks.

"A policeman?" she replied, wrinkling her brow in puzzlement. "Well, thank you dear. I'll come right along and see him."

The child's mother had *not,* for a wonder, been sent to the Fleet by a brutal husband; in fact, the husband was with her now, having held her while Maya set the broken limb, for a dose of opium could only do so much to keep her still during such an unpleasant operation. This time it was sheer bad luck and slippery steps that were to blame; seeing the poor man agonizing over his spouse's pain was a pleasant change from knowing that a similar injury was the result of one more in an endless series of beatings.

As if the same doesn't happen in "better" families—just not so publicly. But that was unfair. There was equal measure of good and evil at every level; *she* just saw more of the evil because of the consequences.

And I see good, too—little boys out sweeping crossings to bring precious pennies back to their mums, husbands giving up their 'baccy and beer to give the kids a Christmas, women working long into the night for the wherewithal to feed their families—

Maya put on her hat, skewered it in place with a hatpin the size of a stiletto, and went to see the "perleesmun" before he frightened three quarters of her patients. With her bag in hand, so that he would get the hint that she meant to be on her way home as soon as she'd done with him, she went out into the waiting room. The waiting room was full, of course, but thanks to Lord Peter's generosity, they'd been able to bring O'Reilly in on salary, and *he,* bless him, had arrived a half hour ago.

It wasn't difficult to pick the policeman out, although he was not in uniform; not too many men coming into the Fleet were so nattily attired, and those that were generally were ill at ease or even alarmed at the sight of so many members of the lowest class of society. Besides the neat brown suit, he was too well-groomed and prosperous to be from around here; his old-fashioned mutton-chop brown whiskers and mustache surrounded a well-shaved, firm chin—such a good, strong chin with no hint of middle-aged fat that Maya suspected he kept it bare out of vanity. The bowler hat had not a speck of dust to disfigure it. Maya went straight to him, her free hand held out. He took it, and shook it gravely.

"I am Doctor Witherspoon; I believe you are looking for me, Detective—?" she paused significantly, waiting for him to supply a name.

"Detective Crider," the man replied, taking her hand and shaking it firmly. She liked his handshake; strong without being overbearing, a warm, dry hand, neither too familiar nor too distant. "You're quick-witted to know me for a 'tec, if I do say so, miss."

"Well, a police officer, but out of uniform—what else could you be?" she said, smiling. "How can I help you?"

"I was just hoping you would tell me about the last time you saw a gentleman by the name of Simon Parkening," was the odd reply. "I'm told you have had a bit to do with him."

Maya frowned, puzzled. "Parkening? Goodness, the last time *I* saw him was at the hospital, when I was showing Bishop Mannering some of the charity wards I work in," she replied immediately. "I must say, he looked rather ill. He'd had what I thought might be a heatstroke the day before, I found him on the floor of one of the storage closets, you know. I sent him up to the regular Male Wards to have one of the other physicians look him over, since he wasn't my patient." She smiled deprecatingly. "I am a very junior surgeon and physician, you see. As a consequence, most of my patients are charity cases, and when they are not charity, they are uniformly female. I'm hardly the type of doctor that Simon Parkening would welcome as attending physician."

"You say he looked ill, miss?" the detective persisted.

She nodded. "Quite green, to be honest. If he had been my patient, I would have insisted that he stop at home for several days, and if he felt he needed further attention, I would have made a house call. I can't imagine what he was thinking, coming into the hospital like that after collapsing the day before. Even if it was because he urgently needed to see his uncle, surely Doctor Clayton-Smythe would have come to *him* if he'd sent a message."

"So—he wasn't thinking rational, you'd say?" The detective's mustache twitched, as if he were a bloodhound that had just sniffed something interesting.

Well, this is certainly an odd conversation. I wonder what Parkening has gotten himself into now? More than his uncle can hush up, if there's a police detective asking questions. "That would depend entirely on what you think of as 'rational,' " she temporized. "Do I think he still knew the difference between right and wrong? Definitely. Do I think he was capable of getting himself from his flat to the hospital and back without losing his way? Obviously, or *I* would have made sure someone went with him. But do I think he was prepared to treat himself as an invalid? Definitely not—but that was as likely to be from a reluctance to *accept* an infirmity, however temporary, as from a deficiency in judgment. A man like Simon Parkening," she added judiciously, "is unlikely to admit to any sort of weakness."

The detective nodded, but persisted. "Assumin' he *had* a heat-stroke, could he have, well, gone off his head after you saw him? Not in any violent way, you understand—just, go a bit barmy, so to speak, and wander off somewhere?"

Good heavens, don't tell me the man's gone missing! "It's less likely than that he'd simply fall down in a faint somewhere, but it could happen, I suppose," she replied. "The last I saw of him, his uncle had taken him in charge and was sending him back to his flat in a cab."

"And that would be where?" the policeman asked.

Curiouser and curiouser. "I'm not sure. We don't precisely move in the same social circles, you understand," she responded, and frowned. "Piccadilly? Or would that be—no, that's Doctor Greenway. I'm sure he must be in the West End somewhere. Doctor Clayton-Smythe is Sloane Square—well, Mister Parkening isn't a doctor; I know all of the other doctors' addresses of course, but I'm afraid I can't tell you where Mister Parkening lives."

Piccadilly probably wasn't where Parkening lived, but it was probably the right sort of area for him to be in. *If something's wrong, I don't want to immediately deny that I know where he lives. Oh, dear, this is so difficult! How to avoid looking suspicious when I don't know what I might be suspected of!*

"Belgravia," the policeman supplied absently. "He's got a flat in Belgravia." He seemed to find Maya's responses perfectly reasonable; she detected a relaxation that hadn't been there a moment before.

Oh, good. At least I'm not a suspect anymore!

"Oh—that makes sense—so handy to his uncle." Maya smiled cheerfully. "Although I would never have guessed it; Simon Parkening doesn't strike me as the sort of gentleman for such an *artistic* neighborhood. It just goes to show how little I know about him, I suppose. Perhaps he has secret yearnings to act, or writes unpublished poetry! I don't suppose you can tell me what all this is about, can you, detective?"

"Seein' as there's no connection with you and Mister Parkening—it seems he's gone missing, miss." The detective was very good at concealing his thoughts behind that walrus mustache, but Maya saw his eyes peering at her keenly, waiting for her reaction. Fortunately, since she had nothing whatsoever to hide, it was an honest one of surprise.

"Good heavens! Missing? But how? When? Oh, dear. Is Doctor Clayton-Smythe all right?"

"Happens he went out last night, and didn't come home at all, miss," the detective said with a certain subdued relish, but a very inquisitive and predatory gleam in his blue eyes. "His man alarmed the police this morning, thinking his master must have met with harm."

"Oh, no—how horrible!" she exclaimed. "And certainly if he'd met with an accident, he'd have been taken to his uncle's hospital immediately—oh, heavens!" Her tone took on annoyance as well as concern. "Oh, these young men *will* go out on their amusements, no matter what a doctor tells them! I swear to you, if it wasn't for young men behaving foolishly, I wouldn't have *half* the number of patients I see!"

Now the policeman chuckled, and there was sympathy in his voice. "I must agree with you, miss. If it wasn't for high-spirited young men, there wouldn't be no need for a quarter of the men on the Force."

She sighed. "I can't think what to suggest to you. I suppose there's no chance he could have come over ill and be safely in bed at a friend's flat?"

"We've checked that, miss," the detective replied, the keen look (which struck Maya as very like that of Mala with a pigeon in view) leaving his eyes. The corners of his mouth turned up a very little, and the hunting look was replaced by a marginally warmer expression. "None of his friends have seen him. We're going back over his movements, and—" He hesitated, and then had the grace to look embarrassed. "—well, there was some things said about you in his man's hearing. That's what brought me here, just on the chance that you might have had some—contact with him."

Maya sighed again, but now with unfeigned exasperation. "Mister Parkening does not approve of females being anything other than ornamental, I suspect," she said shortly. "I shall be charitable and diplomatic, you understand, but he has been something less than polite to me within the hospital. Although he is not a doctor and has no authority there, he seems to have the opinion that his relationship with Doctor Clayton-Smythe gives him the right to pass judgment on everything and everyone in the hospital. I believe that *his* view is that the only reason for a female to *intrude* upon a place normally occupied by gentlemen, such as a hospital, is so that she could draw masculine attention to herself. It is an attitude I, of course, have no sympathy for." She shrugged. "He never can believe that a woman could be as dedicated to medicine as any man."

The detective unbent just the slightest. "I believe you're correct, miss. Which is to say that the things as was said about you by Mister Parkening follow that line of reasoning, and may I say are not in keeping with the opinions of most other people. Mister Parkening seems to have had a what-you-call—a *prejudice* where you were concerned. Didn't seem likely that anything he spouted was true, but we have to check everything out, if you take my meaning, most especially since it was you that found him after his fit, and not some other doctor."

"Of course." She nodded graciously. "That—well, frankly, I wish it *had* been some other doctor; it was quite a shock to find a man lying on the floor of the linen closet! If I can be of any service to you in a further way, I hope you will let me know. You have my address at my own surgery?"

The detective patted his pocket, in which she discerned the shape of a notebook he had not removed during the interview. "I don't think we'll need to speak any more with you, miss, and thank you."

"Thank *you,*" she replied, and saw him out, much to the relief of the patients on the benches.

He took the cab that had been waiting for him; she walked as far as a 'bus stop, where she caught a horse-drawn conveyance and ascended to the open top where she stood a chance of getting some moving air. The sun was setting; the sky overhead brassy and unrelenting.

So Simon Parkening is missing! How very strange. If he'd come to some misadventure in the slums, he should have turned up by morning. It was unlikely that any of the myriad woes that could befall a poor man would strike someone dressed the way Parkening dressed.

No one would "shanghai" a gentleman to crew some tramp ship; for one thing, what was the point? A gentleman would be absolutely useless on board a ship as a common seaman, he wouldn't be half strong enough, nor would he have even a rudimentary grasp of how to perform manual labor. For another, there'd be sure to be a row when he went missing. By the same token, a footpad might rob gentlemen, but seldom killed them. There was sure to be a row, and rows brought police in force to hunt for the murderer. So what could have happened to him?

Oh, I'm uncharitable enough to hope he was beaten up by some poor little whore's protector, she thought, just a bit maliciously. *And I hope he's been stripped of everything and as a consequence is just now waking up in an alley or a Salvation Army clinic or a shilling doss house.* Not that he'd learn any lessons from his experience, but it would be nice to think of him finding himself at the mercy of others for a change.

Bah. He's not my *problem. Let the police find him.*

Her feet had been hurting her all day; it was such a relief to finally be off them that she closed her eyes for a moment, flexing her toes inside her boots to relieve the cramp in her arches.

If only it would rain! The heat wave had eased, but not yet

broken; it was almost as if there was an invisible bowl over England, keeping the heat in.

But just as that thought came to her, she felt the touch of a cool zephyr on her cheek. She opened her eyes, wondering if it had been her imagination, but—oh, joy!—it wasn't! Dusk had come a half-hour early, for clouds boiled up in the west and rolled slowly across the sky above her, moving ponderously toward the east.

By heaven—a thunderstorm at last! She was so happy to see it that she didn't care if she got within doors before the rain descended.

It was a near thing, as it turned out. Only by scampering to her door from the corner where the 'bus left her did she manage to beat the first fat droplets that splatted down into the dusty street behind her.

Thunder shook the house as she shut the door behind her, and she went straight into her surgery office. With a rain like this coming down, the girls of the street would know that there was no use looking for men until it passed, and some of them would finally come to see their doctor. It would, without a doubt, be a very busy evening.

The rain let up around suppertime. By bedtime, just after eleven, it had gone off altogether. Maya looked down onto the street once she had turned her light off, so her eyes could adjust to the relative darkness outside. From her bedroom window, Maya noted mist rising from the cobblestones, eddying around the gaslight in thin, snakelike coils. It looked positively uncanny, especially in light of how hot and dry it had been just this afternoon.

Of course. One downpour won't have cooled all of the heat stored in those stones, or in the ground beneath them. By midnight the fog is going to be too thick to see in. She shivered a little. The poor girls would be out on the street by now, trying to make up for lost custom, and in a fog this thick, they were easy targets for men who wanted their fun without having to pay for it. On such nights the notorious Jack the Ripper had done his foul work—and "working girls" still faced the prospect of being murdered by their customers, even though the "Ripper" was no longer in evidence.

There were other perils, too. Accidents of all sorts could take place in a thick fog. The one great advantage that a horse-drawn cab had in this weather was that the horse's senses were keener than the driver's. You didn't get hansoms going into the Thames, and collisions between horse-drawn vehicles going at a reasonable pace were rare. There were more and more motorcars and motor-buses on the London streets, however, and the drivers seemed to Maya to be more than reckless when it came to taking a reasonable pace in bad weather. There was always at least one bad collision in a fog, and when one came up as suddenly as this one, there were usually more. Far more frequent were the instances of people being run over by drivers going too fast for the conditions. By the time she got to the hospital in the morning, the wards would be buzzing with tales of the latest horrific accidents. It wasn't just motorcars either. There were terrible bicycle accidents in bad fogs, for the riders were just as heedless of conditions as the drivers of motor vehicles, and it was as easy to break one's neck on the cobbles in a tumble from a fast-moving bicycle as it was to break one's neck by being thrown from a motor.

She turned away from the window and saw to her amusement that Charan, Sia, and Singhe were all waiting for her on her bed, wearing expectant—and slightly impatient—expressions.

So—it's going to be cooler tonight, and apparently I am supposed to function as a warming pan! she thought with great amusement as she got into bed. *At least that means that it* will *be cooler tonight; they're fairly good judges when it comes to weather.*

As she lay in bed with the mongooses pressed firmly, one along-side each leg, and Charan curled up in the crook of her arm, her thoughts drifted back to that odd interview at the Fleet with the police detective. Of all of the things that could have happened, she would never have expected something of that nature.

I wonder if Parkening ever turned up again? She might have felt a slight twinge of concern about him if his malady had really been heatstroke. As it was, she wasn't the least sympathetic. If she hadn't been able to give him a good thrashing for his beggarly behavior, it seemed that Fate had stepped in to give her a hand. It was a good thing that the policeman hadn't expected a show of "womanly concern" from her, because she didn't think she'd have been able to produce a convincing expression for him.

And just how would I have explained that, anyway? "Well, officer, the fact is he's not actually suffering from heatstroke. The man tried to force his attentions on me in that closet, and I used magic to knock him to the ground. So you don't need to worry that he's wandering about half-delirious somewhere. The worst he got from it was a well-deserved headache." Oh, that would have sounded rational! If the fellow didn't bustle me down to the police station on suspicion, he'd have hauled me into a lunatic asylum!

She wondered if Parkening was the sort to contrive his own disappearance in order to get attention. If he hadn't turned up by now, he'd certainly be in all the papers, if only because of his connection to his uncle.

If he has engineered this, he'll likely materialize in a police station or hospital without coat or hat, and with some wild tale of abduction. By Chinese, of course—or perhaps by evil Hindu dacoits! The latter idea made her smother a cross between a snort and a chuckle. *They will, of course, have lured him into their clutches with the promise of an Asian beauty—no, wait, that's not heroic enough. I know! He'll have* seen *the blackguards dragging some poor white girl away, meaning, no doubt, to sell her into White Slavery. It would have to be a beautiful and pure, honest serving girl—as if he'd pay such a scene a moment of his attention!—and he rushed to her rescue. They overpowered him, drugged him, and left him bound and gagged in some dank warehouse while they made off with the maiden! And of course, by the time he woke up and freed himself, they were gone without a trace.* That would certainly be enough to make Parkening a nine-days' wonder in the newspapers—and to make life misery for the Chinese or Indian population of London until people forgot about his story.

I hope he is in trouble of his own making, and hasn't the wit to make up a tale, she thought, sobered. *I'll have to speak to Gupta about this in the morning, just in case. The wretch is mean enough and vindictive enough to make up just such a fantasy so that he can revenge himself on me through my household, and the only doubt I have is whether he's intelligent enough to think of doing so.*

It occurred to her that if Parkening continued to plague her, it might not be a bad thing to gradually turn over most of her hospital work to O'Reilly. The Irishman was her full partner at the Fleet now and, thanks to her, a full surgeon as well. When the "ladies of leisure" returned from their holidays and the theaters opened in full force, she would have plenty of paying patients to occupy her time without taking on the additional work in the charity wards, and besides, less time spent at the hospital would mean more time for the Fleet. Granted, she wouldn't get as much practice in surgery . . . and that was definitely a drawback. But she *was* doing surgery in the clinic, after all. If one of the patients from the Fleet were to be sent to the hospital, O'Reilly could take him in charge—unless, of course, the patient specifically wanted Maya.

But that would be running away.

The admonition stopped her spinning thoughts for a moment. *The suffragettes don't run away. They let themselves be jailed, they even go on hunger strikes knowing that they'll be force-fed and might even die of it.*

True, but sometimes it was a great deal wiser to run from a problem than to confront it. Parkening's behavior was not something she had any control over, and if he decided to enlarge his circle of potential victims to all those around her, wouldn't it be better just to take herself out of his purview and hope he would forget about her?

So long as he did *forget.* Some people continued to pursue even when the object of pursuit was well out of reach.

It seemed such a coward's portion. And when he stopped pursuing Maya, who could, after all, defend herself and had powerful friends like Lord Almsley, who would he choose to pursue next? With a man like Parkening, there would *always* be a "next" victim.

I'll worry about it after he resurfaces, she decided. With any luck at all, Parkening would be made much of, and the attention would distract him from making the lives of others miserable.

And if I'm really, truly lucky, came the nasty little thought, just as she drifted off to sleep, *something terrible* has *happened to him and I'll never have to worry about him again.*

She paid for that nasty little thought with dreams of being pursued through the fog by some nameless, faceless menace. She woke just after dawn with an aching head and a strong disinclination to go out until the sun had burned that fog away. It lay in thick swaths all around the block, and it seemed that Maya's reluctance was shared by everyone else in the neighborhood, for there was nothing stirring out on the streets.

With the first touch of the rays of the sun, however, the stuff vanished like her dreams, and she packed up her bag as usual to see to her patients at the Fleet. A boy was selling papers on the corner, crying headlines that had something to do with politics in Europe. She bought one for the ride to the clinic. The omnibus was usually empty and she took full advantage of the fact to put her bag on the bench beside her and open the paper.

The headlines on the front page might have been about Balkan unrest, but the first "screamer" inside struck her with the news that social lion Simon Parkening was still missing, and foul play was no longer suspected, but a certainty.

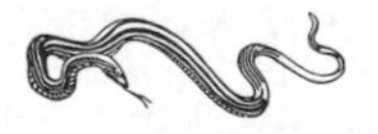

Lord Alderscroft contemplated the saddle of mutton before him with gloom, while Peter Scott waited for the apology he already knew was forthcoming. Finally the peer raised his eyes and looked straight into Peter's face.

"I asked you here for luncheon so that I could apologize to you, Scott," Alderscroft said manfully. "I've taken down the Great Shield; it's utterly useless, and the power wasted on it can be put to more productive efforts. You were right about this India business, and I was wrong. There were more deaths last night, and all the signs point to that missing man being mixed in with it somehow. *He's* probably dead, too," Alderscroft added glumly, as an afterthought.

"If it's any consolation to you, I know something about the fellow, myself," Peter replied. "He is—or was—more than a bit of a rotter. I doubt he'll be mourned or missed by anyone but his own family, and possibly not even by them much."

"Personal information, Scott?" Alderscroft looked at him keenly from under his shaggy brows. "From that little Hindu doctor of yours?"

Peter coughed. "Well, yes, actually. The man had a habit of making a nuisance of himself around her hospital."

Alderscroft helped himself to mutton, chewed thoughtfully, then replied, "I don't suppose the doctor-gel could be mixed up in this. . . ." But then to Peter's relief, he shook his head, and answered his own question. "No, not likely. We *know* her, we've had our eyes on her, and not only has she no connection whatsoever to the men who were murdered—well, bar the rotter—but there's been nothing from *her* quarter but the shields and defenses and a trifling bit of healing magic."

"I am a bit concerned that she might be a target of this—" he ventured. "My lord, I really do think we ought to invite her into the White Lodge, not only because she is becoming a formidable Earth Master, but for her protection. As long as she must function alone, she will be in danger, if not from this menace, than from others who will wish to gather her into their fold."

Alderscroft's brows contracted together in a frown, and he stabbed at an inoffensive piece of mutton savagely. "A woman? And a foreigner to boot? Out of the question! East is East and West is West, my boy—*we* don't mix our magic with Eastern magic, that only brings trouble. Well, look at the messes that Blavatsky woman got herself into, and the Besant girl is no better *nor* saner!"

"Yes, but—" Peter began just as stubbornly.

"But me no buts. There never has been a woman in the Exeter Club, nor a foreigner, and there never will be." Alderscroft stared at Peter as though daring him to attempt a contradiction, but Peter was not about to fight a battle against a windmill, and changed the subject.

"How many victims were there last night?" he asked.

"Eh?" Alderscroft said, surprised. Clearly he'd expected an argument, and when Peter had declined to give him one, was taken a little aback. "Ah—seven, I believe. At least that's the count this morning. All of 'em, bar the missing one, retired Army. None mages. All smothered, the breath squeezed out of 'em." He shook his head. "Can't link the missing man in with that set, but Owlswick swears he's getting the same sort of taint on the fellow when he tries to scry out what's happened to him, and I suppose he *could* be linked into Hindus in some other way—" his gaze sharpened, "—if he offered some insult to that Hindu doctor of yours. Did he?"

"I gather that he made some improper advances, yes," Peter said reluctantly. When Alderscroft pinned a person with that direct gaze, it was damnably hard not to give him what he wanted out of you.

"Huh. So that would be where your information came from. No reason for the girl to lie, I suppose. No, of course not, she's a doctor, she'd have more reason to cover it up to preserve her reputation. What happened, exactly?" Alderscroft's glacial gaze pried every last detail out of Peter, including the little plot that he and Almsley had made up to free Maya from the unwanted attentions.

"Ha!" the old man barked, amused, when Peter was finished. "Clever enough, all of you! Good trick of hers, callin' what she did to the fellow 'heatstroke.' Ha!" He pondered the tale, stabbing bites of his luncheon and chewing them with deliberation while he did so.

At least I've managed to restore his appetite.

"Well-played," he said at last. "Nothing to connect us, or magic in general, with what went on. Managing to hush the fellow up. Perfectly allowable use of magic in self-defense, especially considering the situation. Though—someone should have *noticed* when she struck him."

"It was a very transitory phenomenon, my lord," Peter said cautiously. "It didn't take place at night, nor in one of the venues we've been watching. Under such circumstances, I can see how it would not be caught by a watcher."

"True, true. But still." Alderscroft frowned. "Someone should have noticed, use of power like that, and unshielded. I'll have a word with Owlswick. *He's* supposed to be watching by daylight, whether or not anyone else is, and he's supposed to report things like that to me."

Aha—so that's *why Lord Owlswick never leaves the club!* "She is a doctor, my lord. It might not have been as great a use of power as you are assuming. A doctor would know better than anyone else how and where to strike to incapacitate someone." Peter had more in mind than merely helping Lord Owlswick out of a reprimand by pointing that out. He hoped that—after later consideration at least—giving evidence of Maya's multiple talents might yet pave the way for her entry into the Club and Lodge, if only Lord Alderscroft could be made to see past his Old School Tie prejudices.

"Hmm. A point. Well, there's the link from the missing man to the killer—the cad laid hands on a Hindu wench, and with intentions, to boot." Alderscroft nodded. "Don't matter if she never told anyone but you and her servants, or even if she *didn't* tell the servants. Servants overhear everything, and they gossip. Wouldn't be long before it was all over, at least with the Hindu population." He brooded over his potatoes. "Wish we had some sort of hook into the ranks of Hindu servants in London. If anyone knows anything that might lead us to the killer, it'll be with them."

"You surely don't suspect them of helping the killer?" Peter exclaimed, appalled. He hadn't thought Alderscroft to be *that* insular!

But Alderscroft shook his head. "No, no, not a bit of it. For one thing, there wasn't a victim that still *had* Indian servants. No, I'm just thinking that there may be rumors in the bazaar, so to speak, rumors that would be damned useful to *us,* and of no use to the police, and I wish we were in a position to hear 'em."

Peter thought of Gupta and Gopal, and wondered just how open they would be with him. Well, what could it hurt to ask? And that might be yet one more reason for Club and Lodge to feel obligated to Maya. The more obligations that piled up, the less resistance there would be to bringing her into the fold.

After all, that was one reason why they brought me in.

"Doctor Witherspoon's servants might be willing to talk to me," he said cautiously. "Especially if she asked them to. She treats them less as servants and more as family, from what I've seen."

Alderscroft cleared his throat, and looked a little embarrassed. "It's not my place to criticize how a woman runs her own household," he said, "But in most cases, that's a mistake—"

"But not in all—and anyway, this just means they're more likely to talk to me to oblige her," Peter said firmly. "I take it you'd like me to have a word, then?"

Alderscroft nodded. "I'd be obliged to the doctor," he responded, much to Peter's pleasure. "Especially if they can tell us anything interesting."

"Then I'll see to it immediately," Peter promised. "I'll be happy to."

And if ever there was an understatement, that was surely a mammoth.

19

IN the end, Peter decided to approach Gupta privately, rather than going through Maya first. If Maya's chief servant and oldest friend *did* know something regarding Maya's safety, he might be more willing, rather than less, to talk to Peter about it without Maya present. If this ploy didn't work, he could always backtrack and go through Maya anyway.

As a consequence, he shut up his shop during the early afternoon when he knew that Maya would be at the Fleet clinic, and took a 'bus to her home. There had been a dramatic change in the weather at long last, with much lower temperatures and frequent rains. It was now a normal, ordinary English summer in all respects but one. The heat wave had broken, but now thanks to the rains and coolness, fogs marched through the streets at night, and with the fog, came more of the mysterious deaths. Simon Parkening was still missing, and although Peter would have been perfectly pleased if he never appeared again, his continued absence boded little good. And at any rate, although the man was a bounder and a cad, even Peter wouldn't wish him dead.

The narrow little street in which Maya lived, heavily overshadowed by the buildings on either side with the dome of St. Paul's looming over all in the distance, was remarkably quiet today. The only vehicle on the pavement was a milk float returning empty to the dairy. There were some small children, toddlers, playing together on a doorstep, but other than that, no other people were about. There was traffic and the sounds of people two or three streets away, but not here. Peter rang Maya's bell and it seemed unnaturally loud in such quietude; after a moment, he heard Gupta's footsteps within, and the door opened.

Maya's chief servitor appeared within, his white tunic and bloused trousers spotlessly correct, even though he must have been working in the kitchen all morning. "The doctor will be—" Gupta began, and stopped, a look of surprise on his weathered face, when he saw who it was, for Peter should have known (as in fact, he did) that Maya was not in this afternoon.

"I didn't come to see Doctor Maya, Gupta," Peter said, before Gupta could gather his wits. "I came to see you. May I come in and speak with you?"

"Of course, sahib," Gupta said politely, a mask of calculated indifference dropping over his features. Peter wasn't worried. This was only Gupta's public face. He thought it was likely that once Gupta was in a place where he felt comfortable and in control, the mask would come off again.

So when Gupta hesitated between going in the direction of Maya's office and her conservatory, Peter smiled disarmingly, and said, "Why don't we go to the kitchen?"

The mask flickered for a moment. Then Gupta bowed his head and turned to lead the way to *his* sanctum.

With the break in the weather, the kitchen was now cozy rather than stifling, and Gupta acknowledged Peter's appreciative sniff at the scent of baking bread with a slight smile. The mask was beginning to crack.

Gupta nodded at a stool, and Peter sat himself down beside the kitchen table, scoured spotless, scored with the knife cuts and marks of the preparation of many, many meals. Gupta poured two cups of tea from the kettle he always had ready, and offered Peter the milk and sugar, though he himself took neither.

Peter waited until Gupta took a second stool before he spoke;

he put his tea down on the table and looked straight into the old man's eyes, and asked, "What enemy is it that has followed Maya from India?"

Gupta started; the mask shattered. "What is it you know?" the old man demanded harshly—and now Peter saw, thinly veiled, the warrior that hid within the butler and servant—the bodyguard that Peter had always suspected he truly was.

Peter took a sip of tea, as if he had not seen so much when the mask came off. "I know that when she came here—and I discovered her—she had done her best to create defenses against something. I know that *you* were certain she needed those defenses. And I know—" he hesitated, then plunged in further. "—I know that there is something in this city now, that kills by night, crushing the breath from men. These are all *pukka sahibs,* Englishmen, many officers of the Army who once dwelt in your homeland and, I presume, did harm to your people there. Or at least, whoever sent this thing to kill them, thought that they had done harm."

Gupta's eyes widened at this last intelligence, and he sucked in his breath in a hiss. "And it comes—when?" he asked urgently. "In the hot night?"

Peter shook his head. "In the fog," he said. "Always with the fog. The fog creeps in, and men die alone, suffocated, as if something had crushed the life from them."

And that opened the floodgates.

Within the next hour, Peter got all of Maya's life history, as well as that of her mother and of as much of her father's that Gupta knew. He also got the history of the woman he supposed must be regarded as Maya's aunt—the devotee of Kali Durga, the sorceress Shivani, who had sworn eternal enmity with her own sister when she married an Englishman, and presumably was still the enemy of Surya's daughter.

All of this poured forth in a torrent of mixed English and Urdu that taxed Peter's knowledge of the latter to the limit. Sometimes he had to make Gupta stop and explain himself. But in the end, he knew as much as Gupta did—and had just as much reason to be alarmed.

And yet— "Do you think our defenses have stopped her?" he asked doubtfully. "I've taught her all I know about shields, and there are some things that *she* knows that are as good or better than anything I showed her."

"That—and the little ones—the pets," Gupta added, when Peter looked puzzled. "I think—" He hesitated, then plunged boldly on. "I think that they are more than pets."

Peter waited, keeping his expression quietly expectant. At this point, he wasn't about to discount anything the old man said. There were long traditions of 'familiars' among the families in whom the talent for magic ran deeply, even in this island nation.

Gupta paused for another moment, then continued. "I do not know what they are. They were Surya's; they were grown when *she* first obtained them, and I do not know from where they came. So. She was fourteen years then; Maya was born when she was twenty. That is six years. Maya is now more than twenty. So how is it that none, *none* of these 'pets' look more than three or four years at most?"

"Uh—I don't know." He wasn't sure how old Hanuman langurs lived, or parrots—but falcons certainly didn't live to be more than twenty, nor, he thought, did peacocks. Nor did mongooses. Certainly *all* of the animals should be showing the signs of great maturity by now, if not of old age! So they were not "familiars" as he knew them. What *were* they?

"Right. They are not pets, but at the moment, it doesn't matter what they are, since they are *our* creatures. *But what is killing those men?*" That was the important question.

"It must be some thing of Shivani's," Gupta replied. "And I think it must take the form of a snake. One of the great, crushing snakes, perhaps?"

Peter nodded. "A constrictor—a python—and that makes sense."

"The cobra is holy," Gupta agreed. "I do not think she would risk invoking the form of a cobra by magic, just to slay a few sahibs. But even a python would not dare to cross paths with Singhe and Sia—for surely *they* are as magical as it is. If Shivani could have attacked Maya in this way, it would have happened some time ago. So Maya is safe from it."

"Even if Maya is safe in *here,*" he asked, urgently, "What about when she's out *there?*"

Gupta could only shake his head.

Shivani ground her teeth in anger, and paced back and forth in her room, her bangles and anklets chinking softly with each step, her sari swishing around her feet. She was so enraged she could not have spoken if she had tried. It hadn't worked! All that effort, all the preparation, all the hours spent in extracting the tiniest atom of power from that wretched man Parkening, and it *still* hadn't allowed her Shadow to penetrate the girl's defenses! Now the Shadow was spent, unable to go forth even to replenish itself from other sources, and still the girl's very existence mocked her! All her carefully laid plans were stalled, because of this one miserable girl!

She could not get near the girl, either directly or indirectly by means of her dacoits, without alerting her to the peril she lay in and probably causing her to bolt for yet another far country. That would spell the end to *all* of Shivani's plans; she could hide herself and her men in London, but *not* in barbaric New York! Who had ever heard of Hindus in New York? No, above all else, the girl *must not* know how close Shivani was to taking her!

So close—so agonizingly close, and yet no *closer* than before. The traitor was protected physically and magically within her dwelling, and she never ventured out of it alone—by day she was in the protection of crowds, and on the rare times when she traveled by night, she was with cab drivers, other doctors, or that man. *That* man, mostly. And he, *he* was fully protected by magic she did not understand, and was wary of. It would be one thing, were she to deal with him on *her* terms; quite another to attempt to take him on his.

No native could get within striking distance of the girl without her noting and probably reacting before a strike could be made, for she avoided the presence of her own countrymen—other than her personal servants—as if she *knew* that those of the homeland could be dangerous to her. Oh, perhaps one could simply *kill* her with an English gun, at a distance—but that was not the point! The point was for Shivani to recover the *power* this girl had, and to add it to her own, so that she could continue to wreak vengeance on the Sahibs! Even more to the point would be to enslave her spirit so that Shivani could force *her* to help in Shivani's crusade! To merely *slay* her would be sheer futility and criminal waste!

She stood up, and paced the floor. *If* she could get a drop of the girl's blood—or *if* she could somehow get one of several special potions into her—the girl could die however she died, and it would still be possible to steal her spirit and power. But how could that be accomplished? Her dacoits had tried, and failed to invade her home. She guarded every hair that fell from her head with obsessive care, and she never ate or drank anything that was not from the hands of her servants or prepared in English kitchens by English cooks.

Perhaps—perhaps she was not studying her enemy thoroughly enough.

She stopped pacing, and strode instead to the table on which her mirror rested. The mirror-slave was so much more tractable now that Shivani kept the mirror completely unshrouded. As tenuous as his grip on sanity was, she deemed it prudent not to push him any nearer to the brink.

She picked it up and retired with it to her favorite corner. Curled up among her cushions, with insect netting shielding her from flying pests that came in the open windows and a cool breeze to calm her and set the wind chimes singing softly, she spoke to the eager face, changing with the swirling darkness in the glass, that looked up into hers.

"Show me more of the girl," she commanded. "What has she done today and yesterday, outside of her house?"

She didn't have to be any more specific than that. The slave knew very well who *she* was, and immediately showed her the girl walking out of her own doorway, perhaps to get a cab or find a 'bus.

But this time, Shivani paid no attention to the girl herself; now she concentrated on her surroundings. She ordered the slave to show her the street where the girl lived.

Not a wealthy place, though not quite as impoverished as this slum where Shivani had hidden her people. Narrow buildings of brick and stone, gray and brown, crammed together, three and four and even six stories tall—the girl's little white-stone house seemed shrunken by comparison. The men here wore rough, workingman's clothing, dungarees and flannel shirts and heavy, laced boots. The women, with their aprons and shabby little straw hats, their checked shirtwaists and skirts worn shiny in places, were well enough off to show no visible patches or mends, but clearly did not often see a new garment. Working poor; hoping for better, but not likely to ever see it, and far too foolish-proud to turn to charity or crime to save themselves.

So, so, so. This situation had some promise. She wasn't protected *all* the time. "Show me the next portion of her day," she directed. The slave showed the girl catching the 'bus which took her deeper into the slums, to the place where her clinic lay. Shivani shook her head when the path led there. There was no hope of getting at her in that place. She had already tried to send her dacoits to the neighborhood of the clinic, hoping that among the thieves and bandits, they would be, if not invisible, at least inconspicuous. A vain hope; the thieves and bandits were fiercely territorial, the beggars acting as their eyes and ears, and the dacoits were swiftly driven out of hiding places and sent off with a pack of brats in full cry at their heels. In the teeming warrens where the girl had gone in her foolish quest to help the poor, there *were* no unclaimed hiding places, and any interloper was assumed to be another bandit trying to cut out a territory for himself. Shivani had not appreciated until that moment how lucky she had been to find this habitation in the quarter where the immigrant Jews had collected; there were few outright thieves here, and one set of foreigners was invisible in the midst of the hordes of villagers uprooted from places like Russia and Belarus, Slovakia and Serbia. Most here were Jews, who were incurious about any other race. Her people were no darker in complexion than some of these, nor were their accents and customs any stranger. So long as they kept to themselves, the neighbors did the same.

But in the realm of that clinic, not only did the bandits drive out anyone perceived as an interloper, they watched over the people who worked at this clinic. Even as Shivani watched, several apparent loafers moved in at the sound of a raised voice, and threw a troublemaker out into the street. No, there was no hope of coming at the girl in her own place. The people there were as fiercely loyal as her own servitors. The very footpads saw to it that she was left unmolested, curse her.

Shivani followed the girl's progress throughout her day, paying careful attention to her surroundings and the people she came into contact with. The hospital? Hopeless; there were far too many English, and not even the lowliest scrubwoman was of any other color than white. Going to and from the hospital, the girl took public conveyances. The dacoits were skilled, but not at driving English cabs, and Shivani's kind were not welcome on English 'buses. She was *not* going to make even the ghost of an attempt in the presence of the Man.

But the street just outside the girl's own door—now *that* had promise. . . .

Once more she called upon the mirror-slave. "I wish to see the girl's street—*just* the street, as it is now, and continue to show it to me as the day moves on."

It was not the most fascinating of studies. People came and went, greeting each other, and parting. No hope of blending in among these, for they all knew each other. Children looked up with recognition at their neighbors, or with suspicion at strangers, and if the latter appeared to pause for a moment, ran into their own doors to bring out a mother or an older sister. Sellers of various items called at houses—milk floats, men with blocks of ice, vendors of vegetables and fruit, men with the bits and scraps of meat sold for feeding cats. Women with baskets of bits and pieces; lace and ribbons, needleworking tools, trinkets, apples, strawberries, cherries or pears—

Shivani felt a surge of interest. The men with the pushcarts were all young and vigorous, like her dacoits, and also like her dacoits, they were not native English. Some were Jews like those in *her* neighborhood, some were Irish, there was even a single Chinaman. And the women with their baskets—

Even more interesting; these were not young, and they also were not all native English—but it was difficult to tell just *what* nationality they were. Old women, wrinkled of face, weather-beaten, gray or white-haired, looked very much alike. Bundled in multiple skirts and petticoats as they were, bent with age, they were shapeless, unidentifiable. And their baskets could hold anything, anything at all. A plan began to form in her mind.

But first, she would need something from the hospital after all. Or—wait. Perhaps not the hospital.

Putting the mirror down, she summoned a dacoit with a sharp double clap of her hands. One arrived within moments, abased himself at the doorway, and crawled on hands and knees to her feet.

"You have been among the English as they disport themselves in the places of pleasure?" she asked, intending to have him summon another, if he had not.

"I have, Holy One," he replied from the floor without looking up. "As you ordered, seeking there the items you required to make the trace for the Shadow to follow."

"Good." She leaned forward. "Then, have you seen the thorn of steel and glass that the English use to put drugs into their veins? Not opium, but the other, that makes them excited?"

"I have, Holy One." Now the dacoit raised his dark head, cautiously; she recognized him now. Not one of her chief men, but one of intense devotion and ambition. "Do you wish one of these instruments?"

"Yes, clever one!" she applauded, greatly pleased with him. "I do. Can you obtain one?"

The dacoit did not snort, but he made his contempt for their enemies plain with a twitch of his lips. "Nothing could be easier.

When darkness falls, one will be in your hands, Holy One. Do you wish the drug also?"

She shook her head. "No, the instrument only, my faithful and cunning one. Go, and bring me this thing, and you may take yourself out of my presence on your feet."

He put his forehead briefly to the carpet. "I go," he said, then rose and backed out, making little bows with every other step.

Shivani watched him go with intense pleasure. This was a good omen, that what she needed would fall so quickly to her hand. There was no doubt; Kali Durga must favor this plan. All would be well—

All would be well for Shivani, at least. As for the girl—

Well, she would serve her purpose at last.

Maya looked up in triumph, holding up the results of the last test that Peter had given her, a glowing sphere resting in the curl of her upturned palm. This had been very much in the way of a test—a little, steadily-burning blue "witchlight," set inside a shield, which in turn was inside a bubble that would protect it physically from anything trying to interfere with it. The whole was tapped into the power Maya herself controlled, energy supplying bubble, shields, and the light itself. It had been a neat little problem, and Peter had hoped it would give her at least a moment's trouble.

It hadn't; she'd frowned over his description for a moment, then conjured the thing up with a deft touch he envied.

"Well, there isn't a great deal more that I can teach you," Peter said regretfully. "You've just proved that. I'm going to have to find you a real Earth Master to teach you now. You don't need *me* anymore."

And that will mean one excuse fewer to see you, he thought glumly. *One less reason to come here of a night.*

"I suppose that's true so far as it goes, but that doesn't mean I don't need you!" she retorted, her eyes going wide with surprise. "Peter, one never stops needing one's friends just because some minor connection with them ends, or turns to some other course!

Why, outside of my household, I can count the real friends I have in this place on the fingers of one hand! Of course I still need you!"

He felt his spirits rising a little. "I should think you'd have gotten weary of seeing me so often," he replied, fixing his gaze on her face and searching her expression for some hint as to her feelings. "I should think you'd welcome a bit of a rest from my presence. Oh, don't think I won't leap to help you, if you ran into some difficulty! But I thought maybe you wanted some time to yourself, or to see other people."

She laughed, but he thought there was a strained quality to it, as if she was afraid of something.

Perhaps afraid that I am tired of her? Oh, I hope so!

"If anything, I would like to have you here more often," she said softly. "Truly. And it would be very pleasant to simply sit and talk with you, or go to a music hall or a concert, or just do the other things that ordinary people do, instead of always worrying about magic and power and all the rest of it. I sometimes wish that I was one of *them,* out there—" she waved in the direction of the world beyond the walls of the conservatory. "—and that I could go about my business in blissful ignorance. Life would be so very much easier."

"It would, but you and I would be able to do less good," he pointed out. "Would you wish your ability to heal your patients to be gone?"

"No. But then I run right up against *my* limitations," she sighed. "I see so many things that I wish I could cure, and I can do nothing about them."

"This magic is a tool, and nothing more, Maya," he said, putting his hand atop hers for a moment. "Like a stethoscope or a scalpel. You can't use a scalpel to listen to a heartbeat." He smiled into her eyes. "Some people can't use magic, and some can't use medical instruments either. Everything has its limitations. The real answer is to use what you have right to the edge of its limitations."

He thought that he detected a kind of flinch, and took his hand from hers. *Too soon, too soon, and never mind that kiss—* That was his thought, but as soon as he removed his hand, she seized it in both hers.

"I want you to keep coming here of an evening, Peter," she told him intently. "I *do*. I would miss you very, very much if you skipped so much as a single evening."

He almost said something then—almost asked her, *Will you marry me?*

But he didn't dare; he couldn't face the possibility that she might say no. So he simply smiled back into her eyes, promised that he would not skip so much as a single evening, and turned the conversation to something else, he didn't even recall what, later.

And later, on his way home, he cursed himself for a fool and a coward, and vowed that the next time the opportunity showed itself, he would seize it, and let come what may.

"Mem sahib," Gupta said, in a tone of great seriousness, as he set Maya's breakfast before her the next morning, "Sahib Scott has spoken with me, yesterday."

She looked up, a bit startled at both the words and the tone, and wondered, for one wild moment, *Spoken about what?* Had he a complaint? Did he disapprove of the way that Maya made these faithful friends more than servants and more like family? Surely not—he seemed to approve very much of just that—

Good heavens, he didn't ask Gupta *for my hand, did he?* He had come close to declaring his feelings last night—he was so cursed reserved! There was no mistaking the way he looked at her, the reasons he concocted to be in her presence. Oh, the English, the English, why were they so frightened of their feelings?

"Sahib Scott told me about the deaths of other English sahibs," Gupta continued somberly, "And how the one who brought you distress has also vanished. It is your enemy's work, mem sahib. It is the work of Shivani, sister of your mother."

She felt keenly disappointed. Only that? The threat of Shivani seemed a distant thing, compared to the intensity of her affection for Peter Scott. "Is it? I suppose it must be—" Her attention sharpened again. Peter would not have approached Gupta unless he was worried. "There is reason to be concerned?"

"While you are within these walls, we think not," Gupta replied, wrinkling his brow. "But once you are without—yes, there is danger. His people will not help; he has asked, and they will not, other than a friend or so."

Maya fancied she knew who that "friend" was, and in spite of Gupta's worried expression, she smiled a little. It was no bad thing to have Lord Peter Almsley on your side. Still, if Gupta and Peter were both worried, it didn't bode well.

"I will be careful," she promised. "I won't go anywhere other than the hospital or the clinic alone, and I'll make a point of renewing and strengthening the house defenses every night. And I pledge you, I won't go *anywhere* after dark." She paused for a moment, then added, "I do not think that Shivani will be able to pass the protections I have put on the house, even in person, but I believe that I can make certain of that."

Because I believe, if I petition him, Charan will speak for Hanuman and the others, and they will help me in this. She had done some long thinking on the subject, and it seemed to her that she had a basic grasp of what was possible and what was not. The others would not wage a direct conflict with Kali Durga; gods evidently no longer warred with gods, no matter what was in the legends and sacred texts. But they *would* help her with passive defenses.

That would have to be enough.

"I think that is all we can do," Gupta admitted. "Perhaps she will give up—"

"And if she does not—we will leave," Maya said firmly. "We will go to America, and live among the Red Indians if need be. Surely she will not follow us where she is in danger of being scalped."

Gupta smiled weakly at that. "You will be wise, I know," he replied, and stood up. "And you have your duties. What would our lives be worth, if we allowed fear to keep us pinned within our own dwelling?"

Gupta's words were on Maya's mind as she finished her breakfast, and the more she thought about it, the angrier she became.

What have I ever done to this woman that I deserve to be so persecuted? she thought hotly, stabbing at her eggs with her fork. *What have I done to* anyone? *Father and I treated hundreds of my people without ever asking to be paid—and if I had ever done anything to offend any priest or temple, why is it that I have the help of seven gods? What is wrong with me, that this is happening?*

She lost her appetite, poked at the cooling remains of breakfast for a moment, then gave up. *I have done nothing,* she decided. *It has nothing to do with me, and everything to do with her. And I doubt that after all this time anything is going to make a difference in what she thinks.* She took up her tea and drank it down, forcing it past the angry knot in her throat. She felt curiously adrift as well as angry; she didn't even know what this woman looked like! She wanted to hate her, but how did one hate someone who was faceless?

Oh, to the devil with it, and with her! she decided, all but slamming her cup down on the saucer—in fact, she "put it down" so hard that it cracked. *Curse it all! She has killed—what?—a dozen people thus far? Maybe more? She wants to kill me, and maybe all my people into the bargain! She's a vicious animal and I will* not *let her drive me into a hole to cower like a rabbit!*

She got up abruptly, shook her skirt out, and headed for her office. She packed her medical bag, putting everything else out of her mind. She owed it to her patients not to be distracted by this.

Or at least, she had to try.

She put on her hat, took her bag in hand, and went out into the street, pausing to close the door of the house behind her. It was a slightly overcast morning. Blue sky showed between the slatey clouds, and there was a hint of damp in the air. She took a deep breath of cool air to steady herself.

Somehow nothing had changed, not here. Not in this calm and peaceful street, narrow and shabby, but now become home through some strange alchemy of time and circumstance. And the ordinary, homely sights of men on their way to work, women sweeping their steps before going on to their own tasks either here or elsewhere, and all the other bits of everyday life somehow steadied her as nothing else had. She even smiled at an old apple seller who approached her with a matching smile on her wrinkled face.

The woman looked like a withered old apple herself; shrunk and bent beneath her layers of skirts, smocks, and shawls. Maya had seen her sort a thousand times in this street—and hundreds of times in the Fleet, poor things. But this one looked in good health, moving spryly enough. She wouldn't be showing up in the Fleet any time soon.

With hair as silver as a new-minted coin under her shabby little black hat, the woman was obviously old. Maya wondered what it was that made her so healthy that her stride had the bounce of a much younger woman. Perhaps she wasn't really a Londoner. Perhaps she came in from the country just outside the city. Maya had heard it claimed that people of country stock were hardier.

And perhaps it is just that she is the best customer for her own apples. They do say that "an apple a day keeps the doctor away," she thought, with better humor than she had felt since Gupta approached her this morning.

The old woman continued smiling at her as they neared one another. Maya smiled back, and felt in her skirt pocket for some change. No doubt the dear old thing expected her to buy an apple or two—and why not? They'd make a nice little present for Nurse Sarah.

But just as the old woman came even with her, the poor thing suddenly seemed to lose her balance. She stumbled, the apples tumbling out of her tray, and she fell heavily into Maya.

The woman was much heavier than she looked. She clutched desperately at Maya, clung to her, and pulled her off her own feet. And as she did so, Maya felt a sudden sharp pain in her side.

"Ah!" she exclaimed, in surprise as much as in pain, and her legs gave way under her. She landed heavily on her knees and hands. But the impact of landing hurt quite as much as that odd pain, and drove it right out of her mind. A scattering of street ur-

chins appeared from out of nowhere and began snatching up the rolling fruit, shouting with glee and greed.

"*Curse* it!" she swore, and looked up. Somehow the old lady had managed to remain—or struggle—upright, probably because it was Maya who had taken the brunt of the collision.

The old woman shook her head, looking remorseful, and made a helpless gesture with both hands.

"Oh, dear—are you mute?" Maya asked, mouthing the words carefully so that the old woman might be able to make out what she was saying if she was also deaf. The old woman nodded sadly.

"I'm sorry. It's all right, dear, it wasn't your fault. Here, let me help you—" She groaned a little for her bruises as she levered herself up off the street, then stooped to help the old lady gather up the scattered fruit and replace it in her tray. They weren't able to gather anywhere near as much as had fallen—the little brats had stolen half of them and carried them off.

"Here you are—and here, dear, this is for the apples that were run off with—" Maya said, giving her a handful of random coins. The old lady nodded, and patted her hand, then turned to go back the way she had come.

Sudden dizziness overcame her, and she put one hand against the wall to steady herself. A second wave, more powerful than the first, struck her, and she had to cling to the wall with both hands.

What—

The old woman turned around and looked back at her—and smiled—and held up a syringe filled with red, filling her sight, red, filling her mind with red—-

Then black, black, black came up and filled mind and eyes and everything, and she slid down the wall and knew nothing more.

20

IT was a dull day; no one had come in at all this morning, and Peter moved restlessly about the shop, dusting off his curios even though they didn't need dusting, moving them fractions of an inch to display them better. He couldn't feel settled, somehow. He was ill-at-ease and fretful.

For one thing, he couldn't stop worrying about Maya. He hadn't slept much last night, thinking about her, worrying over the increased danger she might be in. Unfortunately, the future was as opaque to him as a block of stone. Prescience was not a gift often given to Masters of any sort. Perhaps the Greater Powers felt that Masters had gifts enough without being able to see into the future as well. He could easily be worrying about nothing, and that was the problem, he just didn't *know.*

If only he could find a way to persuade the White Lodge to help protect her! He'd bearded old Alderscroft again in his den last night, to no avail. "Let the foreigners contend among themselves," the Old Man had rumbled. "We have no reason to embroil ourselves in *their* quarrels."

No matter how much Peter tried to persuade him, to the Old Man, Maya was an Outsider, and never mind that half of her was as English as the Old Man. The White Lodge had enough on its plate, he said, trying to defeat this mysterious killer-by-night—which might, or might not, be Shivani, according to the Old Man—and now Alderscroft was not *entirely* certain they should even do that, not without investigating the past lives of all those who had been killed! The Old Man had actually voiced the thought that if these men *had* committed a crime against Indians worthy of the punishment, it would be better to let the vengeful entity sate itself, for the victims had brought their punishment on themselves!

Sophistry—and an excuse for doing nothing—if ever he had heard one! Perhaps his distaste had shown itself in his expression, for the Old Man had quickly retracted the doubtful argument, and gone back to insisting that the White Lodge had all it could do to try and stop the killer in its tracks.

But he did hint that Maya *herself* wouldn't be in danger if she had simply reconciled with her sister. Peter had been hard-put to hold down his anger. *If she was my wife, he wouldn't have a choice,* Peter reflected sourly. *He'd* have *to help protect her—or risk alienating three quarters of the Lodge—for if he wouldn't move to protect* my *wife, how could he be depended upon to order the protection of the wives and children of anyone else?*

Then it hit him, with the sudden impact of a thunderbolt. *Dear God, if You put that into my head, thank You!* he thought, mood turning abruptly from anxiety to elation. *I'll marry her! By heaven, I'll shut up the shop right now and get hold of Almsley; he can get a Special License in two hours with his connections. If I put it to her that it's for her protection, surely, surely—* Oh, of course she'd consent! And put so sensibly, she would not think the proposal amiss, or too sudden, or too forward, or too *anything!*

And as an excuse to get past his own cowardice over proposing to her—

Damn it, I love her, and she loves me, I know it. Make it only the excuse to marry now, *the excuse to Almsley to get us a Special License, you fool!* Yes, he'd go to Almsley, get the license, then go right to Maya and throw himself at her feet—

He turned, tossing the duster aside—

And a burst of light before his face nearly blinded him.

An aureole of brilliance, rainbowed at the edges, but electric white at the center, blossomed no more than three feet from him. It screamed *magic* to all his senses, overwhelming all other impressions; he threw his arm up instinctively, sheltering his face against the glare.

Out of the center of the light flew a small green parrot, screaming like a terrified banshee. It shrieked in Urdu—he could only make out a few things in his confusion. *Murder. Serpent. Help.*

Maya's name.

It was only there a moment, then it turned and flew back into the light, which collapsed and vanished behind it, leaving his eyes dazzled and ears buzzing in the silence.

But he didn't need an interpreter to know that something terrible had happened to Maya.

He didn't stop to think, didn't pause for anything, not for a hat, not even to lock up the shop. He ran out into the street, waving wildly at a hansom cab just up the block. The driver looked vaguely familiar—was it the one that often brought Maya home at night? At any rate, he knew a desperate man when he saw one; he pulled up his horse long enough for Peter to fling himself inside, waited only to hear the address before shouting at his beast and giving the reins a mighty shake to send it into a headlong gallop, cracking his whip over its head to urge it on. The cab lurched as the horse surged forward into the traces so eagerly it might have been a racehorse or a cavalry mount that had only been waiting for the opportunity to launch into a full-out charge. Peter clung to the inside of the cab like grim death; either the driver had guessed at the level of emergency from his face, or he was hoping for a handsome tip—which he *would* get—or both.

Probably both.

Hansoms were two-wheeled vehicles; this one not only bounced over the cobbles but occasionally went airborne for a moment as it hit a particularly large bump. People flung themselves out of their path as they careened headlong down the street, but they needn't have bothered; the driver *and* his horse showed a level of skill at judging the traffic ahead and the places that they could squeeze through that was positively supernatural. The horse was soon drenched in sweat, drops of foam and sweat flying from its mouth and neck as it pounded around a corner, yet it showed no sign of wanting to slacken its pace, and the driver never again touched his whip, which remained in its socket up beside him.

The torture of each hard bump and landing was nothing compared to the torture of his heart. His gut clenched; his heart was a cold lump of icy terror. The cab swayed wildly from side to side as the driver swerved around slower-moving vehicles. Mindful that he might need the man's services immediately after he got to Maya's home, Peter let go of one side of the cab and pulled out his notecase, extracting a tenner which he stuck in his breast pocket. He stuffed the pocketbook back in his coat, grabbing the side of the cab again as they cut around a corner on one wheel. A tenner was more than double the proper fare; the man and his horse weren't going to suffer for this.

At last the cab clattered down Maya's street, and pulled up to the door, the horse actually going down on its haunches and skidding to a halt. Peter thrust the money up at the cabby as he leaped out, then had a second thought, and called "Wait a moment!"

He pulled out his notecase again, and scribbled a note to Almsley. At this hour, his Twin would still be sleeping the sleep of the idle rich in his Piccadilly apartment. He extracted another note and thrust it and the note with Peter's address on it at the cabby.

"Give this to Lord Almsley's man," he said, already turning away. "Tell him it's an emergency."

"Roight yew are, guv'nor!" the cabby said, and before Peter had even touched the door, was off, his horse again at the gallop, drawing on reserves of strength and stamina that Peter would never have expected.

The door flew open as he turned back around; it was Gupta, who uttered an inarticulate groan, and gestured him inside. Peter pushed past him.

He didn't have to ask "where"—there was a small crowd crammed into Maya's office and spilling out into the corridor. It was all of Maya's own household, neighbors—

The sight of one of them, a girl in shabby satins, triggered another brainstorm. He knew her only from Maya's description, but he had no doubt who she was, and he grabbed her by the elbow. She rounded on him, fist pulled back and clenched to strike, eyes red, hair disheveled, and face streaked with dirt and tears.

He grabbed her wrist before she could hit him. The wiry strength in it didn't surprise him. "Norrey!" he hissed, and she started back, eyes going wide, at the sight of a strange man dressed like a "toff" who knew her name. "Listen to me—you *have* to do something for us. Maya needs your help, and she needs it *now.*"

"But she's—" the girl burst into tears, and Peter let go of her wrist, seized her shoulders and shook them until her teeth rattled and she pushed him away, angry again.

"No, she's not!" He was certain, as he was certain of nothing else, that whatever had happened to Maya, she was not dead *yet,* no matter what this girl might think. Her shields were all still in place, and her magic was still a *presence* that would not have been there if she was dead. But overlying it was another magic, an inimical force that might well kill her unless he could somehow find its source. "I know who did this to her, but I don't know *where* they are, and if we're going to help her, I have to find that out!"

Norrey's tears stopped as if they had been shut off, and her expression warred between doubt and hope. "But—"

"You get your friends, and you get the word out, girl!" he said fiercely. "The people that did this are Hindu, Indians like Maya and Gupta. They'll have taken a place somewhere that they think they won't be noticed. There'll be a lot of them—mostly men. You might think they're thieves; they aren't, but that's what they'll move and act like."

Norrey's eyes narrowed in concentration as he described the look and habits of dacoits as he recalled them from India. "Now, do you think you can pass that on? We need to know where they are quickly, Norrey, the quicker the better." He took a risk, and lowered his voice still further. "This is magic, Norrey, black, evil magic; we have to find the people who are doing it and stop them, or they *will* kill her by midnight!"

" 'f they be in th' city, Oi'll winkle 'em out!" Norrey said, with the fervency of a vow. She wriggled out of his grip and shot out the door. Now he could push and shove his way through to the examining room, his heart plummeting with dread at what he would find there.

They had laid her out on her own examination table, and at first sight, with her face so white and still, and not so much as a flutter of her eyelids, she *did* look dead. All of her pets had crowded into the room, and surrounded the table; the moment that they sighted *him,* they burst into a clamor or made for him. Charan leaped up into his arms, and the three birds waved their wings frantically at him. Then the green parrot launched itself across the gap to land on his shoulder.

Peter put Charan on his other shoulder, and went to Maya's side, heart in mouth. There were no outward signs of life, not even the rise and fall of Maya's chest to show that she breathed. But when he took up her hand and felt her wrist, there was a faint pulse—and over her hung an invisible pall that only he could see, a nasty, clinging yellow-gray fog that made him sick when it brushed against him.

Gupta made his way back into the room. "Get these people out!" he snapped. "No one here but household, Lord Almsley when he arrives, and Norrey when she returns. Have you sent for a doctor?"

Gupta cast him a reproachful look. "From the Fleet, sahib," was all he said, then set about clearing the office, then the hall, of people who, however well-meaning they were, at this point were nothing but a nuisance.

When he had closed the door on the last of them, Gupta returned. "What *is* this, sahib? Magic—surely—"

"Magic and something else, I don't know what—" Peter was half into a trance. He might not be a doctor—he wasn't any kind of a healer—but he *was* a Water Master—

And the body is—what? Three-fourths water?

Well, in this case, it was water with something horribly wrong about it. It wasn't only the sickening fog that hung over it, there was something foul in her very blood—coursing all through her veins, some poison or drug or both—

"Move yer bloomin' arse, ye wretched donkey!" said an Irish-accented voice, and he came abruptly out of trance as a rough hand shoved him to one side.

"Doctor O'Reilly—" Gupta protested, while Peter coughed and shook his head to clear it.

The newcomer had a beard and head of fiery red curls, and a temper to match—but had the air of authority and the slender hands of a surgeon. He pulled off his coat in such haste that the sleeve tore. "Quiet!" O'Reilly snapped, as the man snatched up a scalpel from a tray of instruments and began cutting Maya's clothing off of her, with a fine disregard for propriety. And as he moved, Peter saw with his inner eye a very familiar flicker of power around him. "But—you're a Fire Master!" he gasped. "How—where—"

"In Eire, of course, ye gurt fool!" O'Reilly growled. "An' as to *why* I'd no joined yer precious club, ye can ask that bigger fool Aldershot or whate'er it is he calls hisself when he's at home!" He threw the remains of Maya's shirtwaist on the floor and started on her camisole and corset cover. "Didn't guess *she* was a young mage till after ye came along." More rags joined the shirtwaist. "Saw no rhyme nor reason t' interfere then when *you* had her in hand, and her takin' a likin' to ye, so kept meself to meself. If I'd known she was with troubles, though— Hah! *There!*"

He'd gotten the corset cut off and tossed it aside, much to Peter's acute embarrassment; the doctor didn't seem to care, but Peter couldn't help flushing painfully at Maya's nude torso laid bare for all of them to see—

But his flush faded as O'Reilly pointed at a nasty round bruise on her side, just above her hip.

"That's a syringe mark, or I'll eat me own shoes," O'Reilly said in angry triumph. "And that 'counts for how they got their divil brew into her! Happen they got summat *from* her, too, or I miss my guess, filthy heathen."

He flung the scalpel down on the floor and seized the stethoscope, hauling it on over his ears and putting the listening end to her chest, then jerking it from his ears again.

"There's two sorts uv diviltry here, drugs *and* magic. An' the one that'll kill her first is the drugs." O'Reilly's accent got thicker as time flew past and tension grew. "You—" He glanced up at Peter. "You, Water Master! You can be givin' me a hand here—I'll be wantin' ye to drive what's *in* her back out toward th' wound, here. That's not somethin' *I* can do; I can't work inside uv her wit'out burnin' her up. Can ye do that?"

"I—" he was going to say he would try, but *trying* was not good enough, not here, not now. He nodded, dumbly, placed his hands gently on the cool skin of her abdomen, and fought his way down past that sickening fog mantling her body again. It was harder the second time; the magic was stronger. How *much* stronger would it get?

The *wrongness* was everywhere; where to start? It was only going to continue to get pumped around in her veins as he worked! He couldn't count on keeping any place "clean" for longer than a heartbeat or two.

It didn't matter. What mattered was that he started. Indecision and hesitation were the enemy's allies. *Work like a seine net; strain out the stuff and shove it in front of me, then go back again and again—*

Herding phantoms, chasing mist; that was what it felt like, and all on a miniature scale. He pushed the poisons ahead of a thread of power; they flooded in behind his sweep, and he had to force himself to ignore them, concentrating on the evil he had captured, and all the time that malevolent magical miasma he worked in thickened and grew stronger. It wasn't until the sphere of his awareness reached the area of the puncture that he understood what O'Reilly was up to.

With a needle of Fire as finely regulated and controlled as any master embroiderer ever wielded, O'Reilly vaporized every tiny atom of poison oozing from the puncture, without ever cauterizing the wound itself. In fact, he created a kind of suction as he evaporated the vile stuff, a suction that hastened the process of drawing out the poison. It was a brilliant display, but Peter had no time to admire it. Maya sank further with every passing moment, physically and magically.

Peter completely lost track of time and his surroundings. His focus, his life, now centered on herding the poisons, and taking note and hope from the slow but steady improvement in Maya's heartbeat and breathing as he cleared her system of them. At some point, he felt the presence of another joining him in this task, the familiar deft touch of Peter Almsley; with his Twin came a little more strength, and a little less fear, and the knowledge that he wasn't fighting evil magic and poisons all alone.

The stuff was getting thinner, less a sludge in the blood and more a color—then less a color than a stain—then it had thinned to the point where he could barely find any of it at all—

And that was when Almsley shook his elbow, and he fought his way back *out* through that horrid fog, which had by this point thickened to the point that *it* was a sludge, or a kind of quicksand. It left a taint in the back of the mind in the same way that a mouthful of foul liquid left a taint in the back of the throat. He came back to himself, retching in reaction to it.

Gopal was at his elbow, steadying him, as he opened his eyes on the surgery.

Almsley looked like hell, dark circles under his eyes and strain in every feature; he knew he didn't look much better. It was hard to make out O'Reilly's face under all that hair, but his complexion was certainly pale enough.

And we aren't even close to finished yet—

His hand sought Maya's, and he felt her wrist for a pulse. Strong and steady, thank God! And her chest, now decently covered with a sheet, rose and fell normally. She looked asleep to all outer appearance, except that her eyes, too, were sunken, her cheeks hollowed, and her skin as pale as porcelain, every vestige of color drained from it.

"We're holdin' our own," O'Reilly said, as Peter looked up at him. "That was good work ye done." He glanced past Peter at the other man. "Almsley, I had no notion from that silly-ass manner uv yours that ye had that level uv skill."

"Well, that's rather the point of the manner, old man. I *want* people to underestimate me," Almsley said wearily, then turned to Peter. "What are we going to do about that spell that's on her?"

No beating around the bush with Almsley, thank God. "I have someone out trying to find out where these dacoits are; where *they* are, that's where we'll find the source of all this." His own gaze moved past Peter Almsley to Gupta, who shook his head slightly. He stifled a groan. "Well, she's not back yet—frankly, Twin, she's a member of a gang of thieves and footpads, and if *they* can't find what we're looking for, no one will."

"Seeing as we already know your Hindu sorceress has managed to cloak herself handily from everything the Lodge has tried, even that idiot Owlswick couldn't manage," Almsley agreed, and grimaced. "Damn the Old Man for a fool! There are half a dozen other things he could have done when you first asked him for help that would *not* leave us at such an impasse!"

O'Reilly growled in his throat. And he might have said something himself on the subject, but just at that moment, the doorbell rang, and Norrey burst into the surgery.

"We found 'em!" she shouted in near-hysterical triumph. "We got 'em pinned i' their 'ole!"

It took time to get organized; Peter fretted more with every passing second, his nerves at such a pitch that he thought the top of his head would split. He ordered Gopal to stay behind, for he didn't want to leave the house physically undefended. *Magically,* O'Reilly, who would also stay behind because of his medical skills, was more than a match for most direct attacks. Of all the Masters, the Fire Masters were the most adept at combat, as well as having the power best suited to fighting. And while it would have been ideal to have that combative ability with them, O'Reilly was their only physician, and he *had* to stay with Maya.

Peter wanted to leave Gupta behind as well, but the old man

wouldn't hear of it. He vanished briefly and came back armed to the teeth with a brace of ancient Army pistols, knives in his belt, and even a sword slung over his back. "I have slain men ere this," the old man insisted. "I can slay dacoits now, with little more harm to my karma."

Almsley insisted on going as well, nor was *he* unarmed; he'd brought his own revolver and a second one for Peter, and a pocketful of ammunition.

And they quickly found, as they looked for a second cab—their remarkable first driver and his fantastic horse having been hired by Almsley for the day, with immense forethought on Almsley's part—that the animals were not going to be left behind either.

All but Rajah the peacock, that is; *he* placed himself at O'Reilly's side, somewhat to the bemusement of the doctor, and would not stir. But Charan and Rhadi could not be separated from Peter, Sia and Singhe fastened themselves to Norrey, and Mala and Nisha set up such a clamor of falcon screams and hoots that it was clear they *were* going along with someone. So once their redoubtable cabby had summoned another of his brotherhood, Norrey and Peter crammed themselves into the first cab, and Gupta and Almsley into the second—Almsley bearing Mala on a leather driving glove like a knight of old, and Gupta with Nisha on the improvised protection of multiple layers of rags wrapped over his left arm and wrist, held in place by an additional wrapping of harness leather.

By now it was dark; none of them had eaten, so Gupta made them all wait long enough to drink a concoction of eggs, cream, and sweet sherry to sustain them. Only then did they take to their chariots for another wild ride through the streets of London.

The langur and the parrot were silent—unnaturally so—during the careening drive. Charan gave little more than a chitter or a grunt of protest when he was squeezed by one of the cab's more violent movements, Rhadi uttered no sounds at all from his perch on Peter's shoulder. The streets were a little clearer—most people were at their suppers—and the horse pounded almost unimpeded into the depths of the East End.

"I want to stop a block or so away from this place!" Peter

shouted into Norrey's ear over the thunder of hooves and the rattle of wheels on the pavement, the creaks and groans of the cab as it shuddered with every bump and lurch. "I don't want to alert them—"

"Already thunk o' that, guv!" Norrey shouted back. "An' Oi got some mates waitin', too!"

No sooner had she said that, than they pulled up at the mouth of a dark and noisome little street—more of an alley—and once they were all out of the cabs, Norrey led them down it at a trot, one mongoose on her shoulder, the other cradled in her arms.

This was all happening much too fast for proper thought, much less planning. Part of Peter wanted to bring everything to a complete halt, to return to the house and map things out properly, but the rest of him screamed in growing panic that it wasn't going fast enough, that they had to hurry, hurry, *hurry!* If it hadn't been that the animals were so supremely calm and confident at this point, Peter would never have ventured down this street at all, for he'd have been certain Norrey was going to betray them—

Especially when a scurvy lot of ne'er-do-wells materialized around them as Norrey stopped halfway down, just outside a little hole in the wall that might be what passed for a pub in these parts. Certainly there was some sort of light passing through the greasy, cracked windowpanes, and the sound of shrieks and laughter coming from inside.

"These are m' mates," Norrey said, gesturing with her free hand to the dozen or so cutthroats and footpads around her. "These are the blokes for Miss Maya, lads."

"Don't unnerstan' more'n 'alf whut Norrey sez," spoke up the tallest and nastiest-looking of the lot. "But she 'ad th' White Cough, an' she ain't got it naow, so—" He shrugged. "Reckon Miss Maya fixed 'er, an' since there ain't no cure, 'adda bin—magic, I guess. So I guess there cood be magic as 'as 'urt 'er."

Peter was at a loss, but Almsley wasn't. "We've got work for you, whether you believe in magic or not—and if *we* don't get to these people and stop what they're doing, Doctor Maya *will* die," he said, stepping forward, with Mala mantling on his wrist.

Norrey hissed at the leader and tugged at his sleeve; he made as if to cuff her, until one of the mongooses ran up on her shoulder and showed its teeth at him. He laughed uneasily, then turned back to Almsley. "Aye, some on us owes Miss Maya—but some on us *don't,*" he replied aggressively. "So whut's in it fer all on us?"

Almsley leaned forward, his eyes glittering in the dim light from the single street lamp at the corner and the fitful illumination from the pub. "I'll not spin you any Banbury tales," he said, "but think about this. Those people must have *bought* that building they're in—a whole building—or they couldn't be doing what they are without a landlord nosing around! Where did that money come from? They don't work and don't steal—but they have to eat, so where's their living coming from? There's more money in that place; there *has* to be."

"Eh," the leader replied thoughtfully, stroking the sparse whiskers on his scruffy young chin.

"Hindu women have all their wealth in gold jewelry," Peter spoke up suddenly, out of his own memory. "Oh, surely *you've* seen that, seen one or two of them walking around! Well, the woman who bosses all of those men is from a high-caste family—*and* she's a powerfully important person in her own right, too! Doctor Maya came to England with all her people, bought her house, rebuilt it, and started her surgery with what she got from *her* own jewelry, and she wasn't nearly so high-caste or important. What do you think *that* woman's fortune looks like?"

"Ah!" said the leader, as some inarticulate mumbles from the rest of the group indicated their growing interest.

"And besides all that, there's a temple in there somewhere," Almsley concluded triumphantly. "*You* know what's in temples!"

That got them muttering. Perhaps one or two of them had gone into the British Museum out of curiosity. The rest would have heard the stories from returning soldiers or even seen a moving picture.

Almsley went on persuasively. "Even if there's no gold and gems, there'll be silks and statues and lots of things you can sell, and not to some pawnbrokers either! *Whatever* is in there is yours. All we want is the woman herself."

"Done!" said the leader, holding out his hand to Almsley, who shook it with the full solemnity the pact deserved. "Let's get 'em!"

Maya woke.

Between the time that she fell into blackness and the time that she woke, her mind had not been idle. There were conclusions ready for her the moment that she was conscious—that the old apple seller *must* have been her aunt Shivani, or in Shivani's pay, that this had been a trap. She knew when she woke that she would awaken in Shivani's power, and that Shivani expected her to be frightened, disoriented, and helpless.

Shivani was wrong. She woke angry, and prepared to fight.

So when she found herself floating—in midair—unable to move or make a sound, it was the "floating" part that momentarily confused her, and not her surroundings.

How can I—wait—of course. She had learned enough from Peter, had traveled in the realms of Earth Magic often enough, to recognize after a moment that Shivani had somehow managed to magically dissociate her spirit from her body, and now held the spirit captive. When she looked for it, she could still find the frail "silver cord" that attached her to her physical body, but Shivani had done something that made it impossible for her to follow it back home.

Stop. Look. Where am I?

If she couldn't move or speak, she could still see and hear, and what she observed did not bode well for her.

She hovered, as it were, just above something that could only be an altar. Behind her was a many-armed, brightly-painted statue of a woman bedecked in necklaces of flowers and skulls. Each hand held a different weapon, or a severed head. She had no difficulty in recognizing Kali Durga, and that was no great surprise—though it was odd that the statue's eyes were closed.

Didn't I hear something about that, somewhere, in a street tale?

That someone in Ganesh's temple once offended him, and the statue of Ganesh closed its eyes to show that Ganesh would no longer answer his prayers?

She was immediately distracted by the sight of her aunt, however, who now bore no resemblance to the old apple woman at all. Shivani, the Priestess of Kali Durga, was, in fact, remarkably young-looking; except for a very few fine lines at the corners of her eyes and mouth, she looked just as young as Maya. Her hair was black and glossy, plaited into a thick braid along with thin gold chains. She might have been considered a handsome woman except for those lines, which gave a cast of cruelty to her features, and except for her eyes, which were hard and cold. Anyone seeing her would have known at once that she and Surya had been sisters—and would have known at once that they were nothing at all alike.

The woman knelt at a brazier just in front of the altar, casting bits of this and that into it so that smoke rose in thin curls from the charcoal. Beside the brazier was a tube of red—Maya's own blood, still in the syringe. Involuntarily, Maya strained toward it.

"You are awake," the woman said, in a calm, and silky voice. "Do not trouble to speak; you cannot."

Do not trouble to boast, I am not impressed, Maya retorted, forming the words and *thinking* them fiercely at her captor, as she had learned to do when her spirit went deep into the realm of Earth Magic.

Startled, the woman looked up from her task in spite of herself. Their "eyes" met, and Maya strove to put nothing in her own gaze but defiance as she held her thoughts behind a tightly-woven shield.

"I *will* have you," Shivani said quietly.

You will not. You cannot overcome me. You may kill me, but you will never *have me.* With that challenge, and before Shivani could react to it, Maya gathered her strength, and drove her *self* down into the earth below, searching for a link into Earth Magic.

It was tainted, stinking with blood; she drove down further, sensing that behind her Shivani had leaped to her feet and was belatedly trying to prevent her from going in this unanticipated direction. She felt her progress slowing, as Shivani "pulled" against her flight, using whatever hold she'd put on Maya's spirit to drag her back.

She strained against the pull, striving to inch herself clear of the polluted soil, trying to get even a fraction of her "self" into a place where she, and not Shivani, had the advantage. It was like trying to swim to the bank of a stagnant cesspool with a rope around her waist and someone pulling her deeper into the pool with it.

She would *not* submit! Never!

Her progress slowed—stopped altogether—

Slowly, Shivani began to pull her back.

In one final effort, Maya hurled herself forward—not *all* of her self, but just a tiny thread connected to a miniature javelin, a little anchor, the most invisible of grapples to connect her to a source of additional, clean strength. And the thread caught, held, fused—

She gave up the fight, and let Shivani bring her back like a dog on a leash, or a fish on a line. But behind her that thinnest, barely perceptible thread unreeled, and the magic of the Earth pulsed up it, giving her renewed strength and hope.

Shivani, however, gloated in triumph as she brought Maya back to her place above the altar. "You stupid, stubborn brat!" Shivani crowed. "I am older, stronger, and far cleverer than you! And very, very soon you will know just how little you can do against me. Look there—"

She gestured to the side of the altar, where there was a small mirror of black glass lying on a square of red silk. Maya looked closer at what seemed to be an entirely innocuous object, and to her horror, she realized that there was—something *in* it.

No, not some*thing*. Some*one*. A tortured spirit, more than half mad, imprisoned within the circle of ensorceled glass. A movement of Shivani's hands caught Maya's attention, and she saw that Shivani held up a similar mirror for her inspection.

"This one will shortly be *your* home, English witch," Shivani said sweetly. "Examine it as much as you please for the next hour or so. It will be the last time you see it again from the outside."

With her own laughter ringing through the temple, the priestess of Kali Durga went back to her magics, leaving her victim to contemplate the fate her captor had designed for her with a sinking, terror-filled heart.

21

ALMSLEY passed the falcon Mala to Gupta, glove and all, and peered around the corner of the building from the place where their party huddled in the alley. Peter was already burdened with Charan and Rhadi, Norrey with Sia and Singhe. Almsley would lead the initial assault force of Norrey's "mates," breaking into the building and distracting the dacoits, while Norrey, Gupta, and Peter tried to find the temple and the priestess. It would, of course, be hidden—but the moment that Gupta had pointed that out, Rhadi had leaned down and whispered into Peter's ear a single clear word.

"Guide."

From that moment, Peter had no doubt that they would be able to find the temple.

Footpad stealth and Almsley's magic had gotten them here from the place where they left the cabs without being detected, so far as they knew. Nisha the owl had made several flights to ensure that they were not observed from above, and Peter had never been so thankful for an owl's silent flight. The owl had found nothing—or at least, if she had found anyone, she had taken care of the problem without anything being heard where they waited below. Now, though, there was nothing for it. They would have to make a dash into the open, across the narrow street, to rush the door. There was no other way to break into the building.

"Ready?" Almsley whispered. His motley army nodded, and clutched their weapons.

Peter had expected them to charge across the street shouting; they didn't. They poured across the street in deadly silence that was somehow more menacing than war cries. The only sound came when their leader kicked the door open and they rushed inside.

After that, though, came a pistol shot, and the sounds of fighting: blows of fist, foot, or lead-pipe on flesh; grunts and yelps; scuffling feet; bodies hitting walls.

Peter's group waited in cover, Peter's heart racing and his body tense with strain, to see how the initial attack went. Almsley's men were to clear the dacoits from the door, and if they could, carry the fight far enough into the building that Peter and his crew could get inside undetected.

The door remained open, now sagging by one hinge. The sounds of fighting grew more distant and muffled.

Gupta nodded, and the remaining three dashed across the street, the owl flying in close formation behind Norrey. They darted inside the shattered door and found themselves in an antechamber that had probably once served as an office for this warehouse, lit by a pair of gas fixtures above the fireplace. Now, it was clearly serving as a guard room. Two of the guards still remained on the floor, two dacoits in dark cotton tunics and bloused pants, with the characteristic scarlet strangling cords at the belts and scarlet scarves around their heads. One was unconscious, the other dead. Beyond them was an open door. There were no furnishings besides a couple of chairs that would serve only for kindling at this point.

The owl waddled up behind them from the outer doorway, and Gupta took her up on his fist. Norrey put Sia and Singhe down on the floor and accepted Mala and his glove from Gupta. The mongooses nosed the bodies sprawled amid the broken chairs, then looked up at Peter.

"Forward," Rhadi whispered. Peter nodded at the open door,

through which the ongoing sounds of struggle still came, but distantly.

"Through there," he said, as Rhadi bobbed agreement. Gupta drew his broad, curved sword and went through first.

They entered a huge and mostly empty room. A faint glow of light came from the room behind them and the ceiling far above; just enough to give them the sense of the size of the room, but not the shape nor the contents. The ceiling light was more like a smear of foxfire than an actual light, and Peter thought that he recalled the thugee cult using foxfire or something like it in lieu of other illumination to strengthen their night vision. A faint, darker rectangle opposite them marked what might be a door on the other side of the cavernous warehouse.

"I don't like this place," he muttered. He couldn't put his finger on it, but there was something *wrong* here, as if this warehouse was something more—

And that was when two enormous cobras, shining with a sickly yellow light of their own, suddenly reared up between them and the next doorway.

The door behind them slammed shut.

"Hell!" he shouted, frantically scrambling backward, heart pounding and every nerve thrilling with atavistic fear. Norrey screamed; Gupta shouted something in Urdu. Both of them stood frozen against the unholy glare surrounding the cobras.

Peter had *never* seen snakes this size. Rearing up on their coils with hoods spread, hissing, they were easily as tall as he. They were black, *completely* black, without the characteristic "eyes" on the backs of their hoods, each scale outlined in yellow phosphorescence. He fumbled for the revolver Almsley had given him as they swayed, hissing, their malevolent little eyes glittering like tiny rubies.

But Sia and Singhe were faster than their human companions.

Backs humped, fur bristling, teeth bared, they advanced on the cobras stiffly. The serpents, in their turn, were alerted by the movement, and fixed their attention on the mongooses.

"Right," Rhadi whispered into Peter's ear.

Moving slowly—for although the cobras had fixated on their hereditary enemy, the humans were all still in reach of those deadly fangs—Peter inched forward to touch Norrey's sleeve. She shook off her paralysis to look out of the corner of her eye at him; the hell-glare surrounding the snakes at least gave them some illumination to see each other by. He jerked his head to the right; she managed to ease herself backward until she had her back against the wall, then edged crabwise along it. Her movement took Gupta's attention from the cobras. He saw what she was doing, and did the same. And finally Peter backed up, to discover by touch that the door that *had* been there was there no longer.

If they were still in the warehouse—and the wall behind him *felt* like the rough wood of the warehouse wall—something had significantly changed. As they stood there, watching cobras and mongooses challenge each other, the place began to fill with mist that glowed with the same, faint yellow-green as the phosphorescent smear above them. The brightest light surrounded the two cobras as they swayed back and forth, eyes fixed on the mongooses bobbing and dancing in front of them, never stopping for a single moment. Then Sia and Singhe froze for one moment—

The cobras struck, twin lances of death hurtling through the thickening mist at the mongooses. Who weren't there.

The mongooses leaped straight up, the instant that the snakes struck, and came down with all four sets of claws ready to grab, landing right behind the cobra's hoods. They latched on and each sunk a set of sharp little teeth into the neck at the base of the snake's skull where the head met the hood. And they held on for dear life.

The cobras went into a frenzy of thrashing, trying to throw them off, trying to batter them against the wall and floor. And as they thrashed, traveling inexorably away from Peter, they began to grow—

But before the mist thickened and then swirled between Peter and the terrible combat, he caught a glimpse of something else. It might have been hallucination; it might have been illusion. But he *thought* he caught sight of faces and bodies overlaying the forms of enormous cobras and mongooses. Wrestling against a pair of blue-faced demons were a pair of beings he thought he recognized. Could one of them have been the god Rama—and the other, the goddess Sita?

It was only a moment that he saw them, or thought he did.

But then the mist came up and carried the combat away—or it moved away from him—and even the sounds of hissing and thrashing faded and were gone.

"Right," Rhadi insisted in his ear, and Peter started, then felt his way along the wall and resumed his journey.

What next? he wondered, as he caught up with the other two. There *would* be something next. He knew it by the thickening, suffocating mist, by the oppressive sense of being watched, by the increasing taint of inimical magic. He recognized this mist now; it was close kin to the fog that had smothered Maya's body, but tangible and 'real' to the ordinary senses.

He put Charan up on the shoulder opposite Rhadi. The langur buried both his hands in Peter's hair and clenched his prehensile toes in the fabric of his shirt. The parrot clung on like a tick with his little claws. *Nothing* was going to dislodge either of them short of a hurricane.

Now it was not only heat, but humidity creeping into the fog and unpleasant scent, the dankness of the swamp, fetid and clinging. If Peter hadn't known he was in a warehouse in the heart of London, he would have been certain he was groping his way through the jungle, up to his knees in swamp water. The warehouse wall was slick with damp, and his hand occasionally brushed a patch of something slimy.

His foot splashed into a puddle. He looked down, and barely made out standing water along the wall. A few steps and it was ankle-deep, with swirls of something greenish and unpleasant floating on it.

"Ew," Norrey complained ahead of him.

"Sahib," Gupta whispered in Urdu, "I do not wish to frighten the child, but this is not natural. This building has taken us to some—other place. Or else it contains that place. Or else this is all an illusion."

"I think you're right," Peter whispered back.

The question was, how to behave? If it was illusion, would it be best to try to disbelieve in it and break it? What if it wasn't? He wasn't certain that he wanted to contemplate how *much* power it would take to bring the priestess' world to London—or London to India.

But there was a third option, that this was neither wholly real, nor wholly illusion; that the priestess had brought them to *her* version of the Elemental Worlds. That would require far less power—though it was still considerable.

The mongooses were certainly acting as if they *believed the cobras were real. We'll do the same.*

"Keep going," Peter urged both of his companions. "Still right. Follow the wall."

"I 'ear something—'issing—" Norrey began.

And a trident buried itself in the wood of the wall between Peter and Norrey.

They *both* leaped apart with curses, and a dark-skinned woman with a mouth full of pointed teeth reared up out of the mist, hissed at them and yanked the trident free. Another lunged up beside her, both of them aiming their trident weapons at the men, and grinning fiendishly, both glowing with the same hell-light as the great cobras.

Peter fumbled and dropped the revolver in the water; something lashed at his feet and sent it flying off into the darkness. It was then he realized that these women were not exactly human.

In fact, from the waist down, they were enormous snakes.

The second moved sinuously toward him through the mist—and both attacked the men with their tridents, ignoring Norrey, making sharp jabs to separate them. Gupta held his attacker off with his sword. It tried to catch the blade in the tines of the trident and twist it away, but he parried its attempts, cursing freely. Peter dodged and ducked the lightning jabs, circling toward Gupta and getting Norrey behind them both, until Gupta managed to pass him one of the long knives in his belt.

Steel clanked on steel; Rhadi and Charan plastered themselves against his neck as he fended off the blows of the wicked weapon. *Fortunately,* neither of these creatures seemed to be particularly good fighters, but that didn't make their peril any less, for besides having to fend off the tridents, Gupta and Peter had to beware the lashing tails that threatened to knock them off their feet.

"Duck!" cried Norrey behind them; he and Gupta dropped to their knees without question, splashing down into the swampy water—

Nisha and Mala arrowed over their bent heads, screaming their war-cries, heading straight for the heads of their demonic opponents. The women slithered backward, hissing in alarm; both birds were growing larger—enormously larger—with every wingbeat. Nisha had turned to a snowy-white, and glowed so brightly it made Peter's eyes water; Mala had become something else altogether, an enormous multicolored bird with a raptor's beak and tearing talons, fully large enough to ride on—

As they closed with the monsters, the mist came up and swirled them away before Peter had a chance to see more than that. But that glimpse was all Gupta needed.

"Vishnu—" the old man breathed prayerfully. "Laksmi. The Gods are with us—"

"Well, there's at least one that's still *against* us," Peter snapped. "Keep going, before that witch we're after comes up with some other surprise for us!"

A few steps back in the direction of the wall, and the water was gone, the floor dry once more. The mist thinned a little, and they made their way back to the wall while they could still see it. Was that a good sign, or a bad one? As the mist dissipated, it took the light with it, leaving them in darkness again. They reached the wall in the nick of time before it vanished altogether, leaving Peter blinking and feeling uncomfortably helpless. Without the revolver, his only weapon was Gupta's knife, and he wasn't a particularly good knife fighter. He groped for the support of the rough wood behind him.

Was Almsley coming up against any of this?

Probably not. With her *physical* guards busied elsewhere, and no way to divide her forces once they were engaged, the priestess must have called up her supernatural protections to deal with the second invasion. With any luck, she didn't even know where they were exactly, or how many of them there were—only that there was another enemy to be driven out or killed.

"Right," Rhadi said, loud enough for all of them to hear; Gupta grunted agreement.

"Got a door!" Norrey exclaimed a moment later. "Cor—this hain't the door we was lookin' at before. 'Ang on a mo—"

There was a scratch, and ordinary, yellow light flared up from the match that Norrey held in her hand. Beside her was a perfectly normal door, past it was a storage closet. Peter swallowed disappointment.

"In!" said Rhadi, before Peter could speak. He suited his action to his words, flew across the closet to the far wall, and landed on a broom. And there was a *click.* The broom moved, and the wall pivoted in its center, showing a set of spiral stairs that led down into what looked like a storage cellar. That was all they saw before the match burned down to Norrey's fingers and she dropped it with a curse.

"Down!" said Rhadi insistently from his perch on the broom.

"I will stay here to guard your back, sahib," Gupta said after a moment. "I do not know what you may encounter there, but we *know* this place here holds evil things."

" 'Old still, old 'eathen," Norrey told him. There was the sound of a blade being drawn. "There. Oi'm a dab 'and wit' a sticker. Oi'll bide 'ere with ye. Naow, if't gets loight agin, yew gimme one o' them popguns, eh?"

"I shall, little mem'sab," Gupta promised. "Go, sahib! Time flies!"

Peter didn't need any further encouragement; he groped his way into the closet and put his hand under Rhadi. The parrot pulled himself up to Peter's shoulder again. Peter felt his way past the hidden door, then worked his way carefully, a step at a time, down the staircase in utter blackness. As the stairs took another turn, he saw a thin, faint line of light somewhere at the bottom. If there had been *any* other light, even the glow of fox fire or Norrey's match, he'd never have seen it.

"Door," Rhadi agreed.

He groped his way down the stairs toward that beckoning thread of palest yellow, that suggestion of illumination. The stairs ended; floor began. The strip of light was just higher than his head, suggesting the top of a door. *"Careful!"* Rhadi warned, and instead of rushing toward it, he felt ahead with his foot, encountering something—a bucket, a box—immediately.

The hero trips over a bucket and breaks his neck. He went to his hands and knees and groped his way through the litter to the wall, only to find junk piled up against it.

But Rhadi ran down onto his arm and hand, and tapped his beak lightly on the wall. *"Hand,"* he said. *"Up!"*

There's another secret catch. Peter moved his hand up a trifle.

"More!" Rhadi insisted. Then, *"Right! More!"* He felt the bird lean forward; there was a loud *click.*

The wall, junk and all, swung outward.

He threw up his hand to ward off the flood of light and the billow of harsh incense smoke that came at him. Squinting through the glare of many lanterns, he made out the figure of a woman in a red sari, an altar with something golden flickering above it that trailed a faint silver cord out through the wall beyond, and the poisonously beautiful statue of Kali Durga, glittering with enough gold to make every pickpocket in London wealthy.

The woman had not been expecting an intruder—or at least, she had not expected anyone other than her own people—for she had not yet turned to see who had triggered the secret door.

Peter cursed his clumsiness in losing the revolver. As inexperienced a shot as he was, one bullet would have finished it all.

Peter!

The sound of his own name rang in his head in familiar and beloved tones, and without thinking, he answered.

"Maya!"

Unfortunately, he answered aloud.

Now the woman whirled, scarlet skirts swirling around her bare ankles, and she hissed in shocked surprise when she saw him.

I'm getting very tired of things that hiss—

He stood up, and attempted to look like the brave hero in a thrilling story. "My men have taken your dacoits, priestess," he said in Urdu, hoping he could end all this without further conflict. "You are defeated. Break your magics and go, and I will allow you to flee my country."

She drew herself up, and smiled at him. Despite the fact that she was a handsome woman (and looked far too young to be Maya's aunt), he did not in the least care for that smile. There was so much hate in it that he had to force himself not to flinch. "I think not, English," she said in buttery tones. "I have something that you and I both want, but *I* will keep it, and *you* will die."

Rhadi screeched and fluttered away and Charan leaped from his shoulder, as something shadowy and huge oozed out of the darkness of the closet behind him. Charan and the parrot both screamed as the shadow of a python at least a hundred feet long flung enormous coils about him before he could move, and began to squeeze.

Peter! The golden shape flickered and fluttered above the altar like a bird trapped in a cage. Peter fought for breath as the cold muscles closed in on him. The priestess laughed.

"The traitor has succeeded in keeping me at bay for much longer than I thought, and I was angry," she mocked, dark eyes flashing with glee. The shadow snake crushing Peter loosed its hold a little, just enough for him to catch a strangled breath, but nowhere near enough to escape. "But now I see that Kali Durga has rewarded me! I shall have *your* death and *hers*—and she will see you die, and you will know that *she* is to die, and your mutual agonies will be such—blissssss—"

"Then why does Kali Durga close her eyes to you, false one?" said

an entirely new voice—and the coils about Peter loosened a little more.

Peter couldn't turn his head, but the speaker leaped forward over the serpent holding him.

It was—a monkey. A man-sized monkey. A man-sized *langur,* dressed in elaborately embroidered Indian festival garments, with a sacred crown upon its—His—head, garlands about His neck, and a spear in His hands.

Good God—

"Thank you," Hanuman said, bowing a little to Peter. Then, as the huge and shadowy constrictor holding Peter started to raise its head in alarm, He struck.

The serpent dodged the first blow of the spear, but in trying to escape, it loosed its coils completely and allowed Peter to tumble free. Peter, however, had no thought for the combat.

The priestess had seized a knife from the altar beside her, a blade that glittered with magic. She stared at Peter as he sprinted desperately for her, then raised her arm.

"*You* will not have her, English!" she shouted, and slashed the knife down through the air beside Maya—severing the silver cord that bound Maya to her own physical body.

Peter! she wailed, and Peter fell to his knees and screamed her name, feeling his own heart torn from his body and ripped into pieces before his eyes.

And—

Hanuman plunged His Spear into the head of the Serpent—

As Rhadi sped toward the fading golden light above the altar—

The Serpent gave one, final, agonized lash of its enormous tail. The tail whipped over Peter's head, and impacted the priestess, knocking her past the altar—

Allowing Rhadi to reach it just before the last of the golden light faded away.

There was a soundless explosion of light—exactly the light that had burst out the moment that Rhadi had appeared in the shop. Except that *this* time, for a single moment, Peter thought he saw, not a bird, but a handsome, smiling young Hindu man.

The light vanished.

There was no Shadow Serpent. And Rhadi, who was aglow with golden light, flitted to Peter's shoulder.

"Kiss," he said, and touched his beak to Peter's lips.

The glow flowed into him, drying his tears of loss and anguish in a heartbeat, filling him with a loving and familiar presence, and a strange, slow, power that made him feel as if he was swimming in honey.

Maya? he thought, in disbelief.

Peter, she said, from within his heart. *Oh, Peter!*

"Take her home, for you do not have much time to restore her before Kama's power fades," said Hanuman. *"It is over. The evil one has gotten her reward from her own Goddess and will trouble you no more on this turn of the Wheel."* Peter turned to see that Shivani, the priestess of Kali Durga, was, indeed, nestled among the many arms of Kali Durga, her head lolling sideways in a way that could only mean a broken neck—and if that wasn't enough to ensure that she was dead, two of the dagger-bearing arms had closed on Kali Durga's votary, driving the blades they held deep into her body.

The eyes of the statue were open again.

Peter turned again—but there was no Hanuman. Only Charan, who chittered and ran toward him, scampering up his leg to his arms, and from there to his shoulder.

"Home," said Rhadi. *"Quick!"*

Peter took one of the lanterns from the wall, and headed for the stairs in a kind of shock or daze. It felt as if he was floating, not walking; his head buzzed with confined power that was not his own, and he could hardly manage to put one thought after another. He went right past Gupta and Norrey as if he were sleepwalking. They stared at him and tried to stop him, but *now* he knew what he had to do, and he began to run. Strengthened and sustained beyond his own abilities by Earth magic that poured into him *directly* instead of through an intermediary, he felt he could run forever—

But there were faster feet than his, and he made for them. He leapt into the hansom of their faithful cab driver, then under silent urging from within, spread his arms and allowed the Earth Magic to engulf cab and horse and all. Without whip or orders, the horse surged forward into the traces and in moments was at the gallop again, but *this* time, the more the gallant beast strove, the more energy poured into him. He ran as he had never run in all of his life as a racehorse, ran as if he raced in freedom across the sweet, soft meadows of his colthood and not the hard pavements of the city. Charan clung to one shoulder, Rhadi to the other, and the cab scarcely seemed to touch the street as they flew onward.

When they stopped, Peter burst from the cab; Maya's door flew open at his touch. He sprinted into the surgery, shoved O'Reilly away with an absent push, and bent to place his lips on Maya's.

"Kiss!" said Rhadi, joyfully, and the warm, golden presence left him in that kiss, flowed out of him and into *her,* leaving him. But not empty; never empty. And never alone again.

Her lips warmed beneath his. He opened his eyes and reluctantly ended the kiss, and as he did so, *she* opened her eyes, and smiled.

This time, she reached for him, and the kiss lasted as long as either of them could have wanted.

Epilogue

From: Nurse Sarah Pleine
Fleet Clinic
Cheapside

To: Jane Millicent Lambert
5 Carnock Road
Manadon

Dear Jane;
Well, my dear, we had our wedding! Our *double* wedding, I should say, since it was Miss Amelia and her beau, that sweet young man we had at the clinic that I told you about, and Miss Maya and her Captain! I was matron of honor to both of them, and I was *that* nervous when I saw the native dress that Miss Maya intended to wear, but it was all right, for they gave me a *handsome* suit and didn't expect me to get all tangled up in one of those "sorry" things, which is *just* as well, for you know, I haven't the figure to wear anything that looks like yards and yards of bedsheet! Doctor O'Reilly and Lord Peter Almsley were best man—men?—and oh, I never saw a handsomer set of fellows, and O'Reilly's wife the match for him, a regular Lady of Shallots. Six of the girls and teachers from the London School were maids of honor and half of them

wore those "sorrys"—well, I didn't envy them a bit, no matter that it's twelve full yards of silk and you could make it up into a very nice frock later—and each of them carried one of Miss Maya's pets instead of a bouquet! And the peacock was up at the altar behind the bishop, with his tail spread the whole time and so quiet and good you'd have thought he knew *exactly* what was going on. . . .

From:
Helene, Duchess of Almsley

To: Her Grace Katherine, Dowager Duchess of Almsley
Heartwood Hall
Newport Pagnell

Your Grace,

Well, my *dear* son—your grandson—has done it again with this "little wedding" he organized for his friends. I shan't be able to show my face in London for months. A circus, a positive *circus,* not a wedding—women in native dress, animals, creatures *straight* from a suffragette meeting and criminals and only the Good Lord knows *what* else in attendance, and as if that wasn't bad enough, for he could have kept it *quiet* if he had confined his mischief to just those, he has had Bishop Mannering to officiate and *everyone from his Club* to attend! The humiliation! I can't keep him in order, but he listens to *you,* surely *you.* . . .

To: Her Grace, the Dowager Duchess of Almsley
Heartwood Hall
Newport Pagnell

Dear Grandmama;

Well, we've done the deed, and it came out splendidly, like the first act of *Aida,* only the animals were guaranteed not to disgrace themselves on the church carpet. Thank you for denuding your garden and hothouse for us; Maya was nearly in tears of joy over the flowers.

Alderscroft has done the handsome thing; he's admitted he was wrong, which may be the first time in history, and he's not only brought in O'Reilly and *his* wife (she's Fire, too—I wouldn't care to be a fly on the wall in that house during a marital squabble!) to the Lodge, and brought in Maya as a full Club Member in her own right, but he's issuing invitations to every Master we know of to join the Club and Lodge. Some will decline, of course, but they will still be official Auxiliaries. I, by the by, am to convey his humble respects and invitation to you, etc. etc. There have been words and even some (few) resignations over this; there are still some old mummies who can't stomach the notion of a tradesman or a good yeoman farmer in "the company of Gentlemen," much less (oh, horrors!) a mere Female Creature as a member of the Exeter Club, but they were fair useless to begin with.

Now the part of the letter I know you want—the wedding. Grandmama, it was a picture. Maya and half the ladies in wedding saris embroidered in gold, she said to tell you that the color is traditional for wedding saris and she'll be sending you a bolt of the silk to thank you. The other half matched Miss Amelia's gown, which I know you've seen since you were the one who organized the making of it. They all carried one of the "pets" instead of bouquets—a quite brave pair had matching hawking gloves for the owl and the falcon. The pets were good as gold—the peacock stood like a statue in front of the altar, behind the bishop, with his tail fanned during the whole ceremony. Every member of the Exeter Club still speaking to us that could toddle helped to fill in the pews, which were liberally larded with some of Amelia's suffragette friends (who thankfully did not wear their banners and badges). Any empty spaces were taken by Norrey and her "mates"—who, to their credit, now that they have the pelf from our raid on the temple in their pockets, do seem to be *trying* to "go straight." Twin is helping them there, getting them set up in little businesses that are bound to do well if they are properly managed. Miss Norrey has found an entirely new calling; she's training to be a cook under Gopal, if you can credit it!

Ceremony modern—no "obeying" allowed, thank you, in the

presence of so many suffragettes. Bishop beaming, grooms and brides beaming, general company beaming, everyone retired to the Club itself for wedding supper, and pets as good as gold. Much spoiled, too; half expected the little monkey to be sick, he was fed so many sugarplums. Much more admiration of the floral decorations.

We've got them all off on a train an hour ago, for honeymoons all around. Only a fortnight though; *Mrs.* Amelia still has classes and the clinic will be shorthanded without *Mrs.* Maya.

Cousin Reuben's eldest son Bertie will make the perfect Earth Master to complete Maya's training; they got along like two old friends at the wedding, and bless you for suggesting him. I'm putting him up at my flat in Piccadilly for the nonce; he can decide later if he wants to make an extended stay and join my bachelor shambles or find some digs of his own. He's going to help Twin out with the shop and import business, as you suggested; I would never have guessed that an offspring of Cousin Reuben would turn out to have such a good head for it.

I consulted with Maya's Peter about the wedding present you suggested, and he agreed that it is the perfect answer, and I really do think I can find everything within a fortnight so we can surprise Maya when the bride and groom return home. Old Gupta is positively ebullient over the idea, which means that there are *no* objections. So, once I fan my fevered brow and recover from all this, I will be out hunting: one female Hanuman langur, one female saker falcon, one male Eurasian eagle-owl. I know you can persuade old Lord Nettleton to part with one of the female Indian Ringnecks from his aviaries, and would you sort through our livestock at the manor for a particularly nice peahen?

All my love
Your grandson, Lord Peter Almsley